D0296113

Havana Sleeping

Also by Martin Davies

The Conjuror's Bird
The Unicorn Road
The Year After

Martin Davies

Havana Sleeping

HODDER &
STOUGHTON

First published in Great Britain in 2014 by Hodder & Stoughton
An Hachette UK company

1

Copyright © Martin Davies 2014

The right of Martin Davies to be identified as the Author of the Work has been
asserted by him in accordance with the Copyright, Designs and Patents Act 1988.

All rights reserved. No part of this publication may be reproduced, stored
in a retrieval system, or transmitted, in any form or by any means without
the prior written permission of the publisher, nor be otherwise circulated
in any form of binding or cover other than that in which it is published and
without a similar condition being imposed on the subsequent purchaser.

All characters in this publication are fictitious, or are historical
figures whose words and actions are fictitious. Any resemblance
to real persons, living or dead, is purely coincidental.

A CIP catalogue record for this title is available from the British Library

Hardback ISBN 978 0 340 98045 3
Trade Paperback ISBN 978 0 340 98046 0

Typeset by Hewer Text UK Ltd, Edinburgh
Printed and bound by CPI Group (UK) Ltd, Croydon, CR0 4YY

Hodder & Stoughton policy is to use papers that are natural, renewable
and recyclable products and made from wood grown in sustainable
forests. The logging and manufacturing processes are expected to
conform to the environmental regulations of the country of origin.

Hodder & Stoughton Ltd
338 Euston Road
London NW1 3BH

www.hodder.co.uk

There is a Spirit sits by us in sleep
Nearer than those who walk with us in the bright day.

Charlotte Mew, *The Forest Road*

EDITOR'S NOTE

Havana Sleeping is based on a real-life unsolved murder in Cuba in the 1850s and for readers interested in learning more about the novel's historical background the author's historical notes have been included at the end of the novel. However, it is only right that I should warn anyone tempted to skip straight there that the notes do contain spoilers. Much better to leave them till the end . . .

You come to me earlier than I expect. It is that moment of the day when the hasty Havana dusk appears to promise every pleasure. As I look out, I see lamps everywhere, at every window, above every door, all of them softly beautiful, telling us that this is a city of magical loveliness; lying to us with their blinking, amber eyes. Tonight is the last time we shall meet.

My shutters are open to the night, but my rooms are dark. The scent is musk rose, the light four dozen tiny candles in domes of coloured glass. Nowhere in the world could you look more out of place. And yet you are here.

When your stay in this city is over you will return to your orderly, wintry country, to forget this other life. Soon Havana will be no more to you than a feverish dream.

So let us make the most of this last hour. Let us look out together across the exquisite, perfidious lights and imagine different lives in different places, and the world as it might have been had we been different people.

PART ONE

I

The captain of police pointed to where the dark boards of the consul's office met the faded cream panels of the veranda.

'And this, señora, is where the murdered man fell.'

He accompanied the words with a dramatic gesture, but he was not entirely at ease. He was a man of twenty-three, not long of out of Spain, and he had been taken by surprise. He had expected an older woman.

The letter he'd received had been written in rather formal Castilian, and the name at the bottom was surely English. It was the sort of letter he received regularly, and in reading it he had imagined the fleshy wife of a British merchant, middle-aged and fussy and uncomfortable in the Havana heat, the sort who kept a portrait of the young English queen above her mantelpiece and a black boy in livery on the box of her carriage. He had expected too a party of her friends, chattering like sparrows, all hoping to be pleasantly shocked by a tale of bloodshed and gore. And from each generously proportioned English lady, he had anticipated a similarly generous tip.

But the woman waiting for him in the garden of the consul's house was unaccompanied, and she was not of middle years. His own age, perhaps; perhaps not even that. When he first saw her she was standing in full sunlight, her back turned to him, her head and shoulders shaded by one of those short-handled parasols that were so fashionable that season. He had been struck at once, even from a distance, by the pleasing shape and symmetry of her form. And then she had turned and he had seen her face. Her dress and her gloves were white, but her skin was dark.

So he had taken her for a servant, and had looked beyond for the stout Englishwoman of his imagination. It had not been a promising start.

'There was a great deal of blood, señora. The blow had laid open the crown of the unfortunate fellow as he rushed to the defence of his master's property. Imagine the horror of the scene the following morning as it presented itself to the young maid, Floretta, stumbling across the bloodied corpse, here, just where we stand . . .'

He paused. At this point in the recital he had come to expect well-bred shudders and a conspicuous fluttering of fans. But on this occasion his audience appeared unmoved. Her head was turned to the open doors and to the veranda beyond as though her thoughts had drifted from the consul's office to the bright world that lay outside. He could see clearly now what he should have noticed instantly: the fineness of her clothes, the elegance of their cut, the exquisite delicacy of the lace at her neck; lace that seemed to the captain of police to rest so lightly against her skin that the merest sigh might stir it, as the wind ruffles water.

'The honest fellow had fallen here, across the door, and his lifeblood spread around him in a pool, flooding the doorway, the righteous blood of a worthy servant.'

The script was not his own, but generally it had proved popular. In the weeks following the incident, as was the custom, the polite circles of Havana society had found a visit to the scene of the murder pleasantly diverting. Such visits were lucrative; every officer in the district relied upon them to some degree. Of course, murders were commonplace in the streets of Havana, but a murder in a European house was a rarity, and good for business, especially if a suitably stirring commentary could be found to accompany it. Sadly, visitors requesting a view of the British consul's office were no longer frequent – time had passed, and there had been other, better murders since – but if the tale could be made exciting, the rewards should be no less handsome.

The captain of police had not himself seen the body of the murdered man – in truth he had not visited the scene of the crime until every trace of it had been expunged – but at this point in the narrative, looking down at the wooden boards of the consul's office, he found it strangely easy to imagine the fallen man, the thick blood spreading around him.

'The villains – there were three of them, you understand – had been interrupted at the very climax of their nefarious venture. To them the life of an honest man counted for nothing. The mortal blow was struck from here, señora, from behind the door, a cowardly stroke by one concealed in darkness.' And he demonstrated, stepping forward and chopping down sharply with the side of his hand.

At this the visitor raised her eyes to his.

'And these men, Captain . . .' Her voice was low and rather deep, and in it he could recognise the unmistakable accents of a *habanera*, one raised from childhood in the city's tangled streets 'These *villains* . . .' A trace of amusement, he thought. 'All three were arrested?'

'That's right, señora. Ruffians of the worst sort. The lowest of the low. Two Negroes and . . .' For the first time when delivering this part of the speech, the captain hesitated. He had been little more than a year in Havana. There were niceties in Cuban life, delicacies of wording and minute indicators of status, which were not yet instinctive to him. He found himself acutely aware of that smooth brown skin, so striking beneath the lace. He had no idea what precise combination of slave and Spanish blood ran beneath it; and even though he felt that by conducting this tour at all he was most certainly compromising his own dignity, he had no desire to offend.

'Two Negroes and a mulatto,' he continued, faltering. 'Afterwards, señora, they were heard boasting of their crimes, although of course when arrested they denied everything, on pain of their mortal souls. It is unfortunate that there was not enough formal evidence with which to charge them. But that's often the way in this lawless city. The thief and assassin can simply slip away into the darkness.'

That line was his own, and he was proud of it.

'We should take comfort, señora, that one of them at least did not go free, being taken by the cholera – or by God's justice, if you will – while still in custody.'

The visitor nodded. Her eyes were moving around the room, taking in the English furniture, the cabinets, the neat books.

'I understand completely, Captain. Please go on.'

So he described, in suitably dramatic terms, the ransacking of the consul's office, the wanton damage, the smashed chairs, the bureau forced open from which the jewellery had been stolen. Jewels of enormous value, the captain emphasised, items unsurpassed by any seen in Cuba before or since; they had been the property of a wealthy young English lady who had entrusted them to her consul for safe-keeping. They had never been recovered.

'Pity the poor maid, Floretta, when she discovered the results of these brutal depredations. The night-watchman dead, the bureau smashed open, and between the two, made visible by the morning light, the bloody boot prints of the culprits, left behind like callous and sinister calling cards to bear witness to their crimes.'

But the señora's eyes had returned to the veranda and to the white sunshine of the early afternoon, as if weary of his narrative and wishing to be gone from that shadowy room with its dark boards and heavy, unforgiving furniture.

'Did those tracks lead you far, Captain?'

'Alas, no. My colleagues who were here before me found that the trail led them no further than the garden. The footprints had petered out even before they reached the street.'

He could see that she was preparing for departure and he was embarrassed. The tips of the fat Englishwomen were undeniably useful to him, and he had gone to some expense to bribe the servants of the British consul so that he might conduct the tour without interruptions. But a mulatta, and his own age? To accept anything at all would be degrading. It was out of the question.

He followed her out into the sunshine, her figure silhouetted against the light. Were she an *old* mulatta it would be different perhaps. Perhaps then he could see his way. But not one whose gaze unsettled him as hers did . . .

"Tell me, Captain . . .' They had reached the gate in the garden wall that led to the street. Her hand, he noticed, hovered close to her purse. 'Tell me, those three you arrested. Low fellows from the slums, ruffians, I think you said. Can you recall at all, at the time they were arrested – I know it is a long time ago – but can you recall, perhaps, how many of the three were wearing boots?'

II

He hardly noticed the rain. It swept up the Thames in angry gusts, carried on a cold and spiteful wind. Beneath a sky smeared with smoke, the afternoon was blurring into dusk. On pavements rendered greasy by the downpour pedestrians made their way cautiously, eyes down, umbrellas up. December in Westminster, and the city could hardly have been greyer.

But Backhouse barely noticed. All the hansoms were taken so he walked, threading his way through the crowds at a jaunty pace, edging sideways past obstacles, sometimes stepping out on to the cobbles in his haste.

It was the most extraordinary thing. His salary trebled, plus allowances, and a generous pension. A promotion, whichever way you looked at it, and out of nowhere. Who would have thought it? All those applications, all those rejections . . . He had thought his career destined to stagnate. Even his closest friends had stopped enquiring about his prospects. Who would have thought that old Addington of all people would find something for him?

And proper work, too. Not some moribund sinecure with a title and no duties; a position to be relished, a chance to make a difference. He was to take up arms in a fine cause. Grace would be so proud! Finally she would have something to boast about to her family, to her friends. And Addington had spoken favourably of the climate. It would surely suit her, in a way that British winters did not. Havana! The two of them would promenade in the evenings and marvel at the blue waters. And Grace would no longer be the wife of an insignificant Foreign Office drudge. She would be the British judge's wife, and able to hold her head high as she walked.

More than any other, this was the thought that warmed him as he crossed Great George Street, dodging between carriages, oblivious of the mud splashing his trousers well above the knee. This was his opportunity. He would make a difference. He would make her proud.

III

Barefoot and in rags, she had become invisible.

It was not yet midnight and crowds still thronged the streets. In the Plaza de Armas, a troupe of acrobats were forming pyramids and turning cartwheels for a noisy and appreciative crowd, and in the street outside La Dominica carriages had gathered in such great numbers that they almost blocked the thoroughfare. The performance at the Teatro Tacón was not long finished and at pavement cafés all over the city theatre-goers were marvelling at the talents of di Salerno, the unsurpassed beauty of La Luna. Even the smaller avenues were still busy, with groups of *habaneros* drifting one way or the other, some heading into town to join the throng, others retreating homewards, defeated by the heat, or by the crowds, or by the ruinous prices. But whatever their direction, they did not see Leonarda.

She had hated it once, the contempt of that cramped city. Every lamplit doorway, every bright window, had emphasised her exclusion; had offered her a glimpse of a world from which she was barred.

But now the loneliness of the streets felt like freedom. The dirt beneath her feet, the slipperiness of the cobbles; and beneath her ragged garments, the night playing like a warm breath against her skin. These were familiar, forgotten things – sweet now because not permanent, but powerful and intoxicating all the same. To the people who brushed against her in the street she was nobody. They made no demands, had no expectations; they saw nothing, sought nothing, asked nothing. It was a kind of weightlessness.

And the scent of the night! How had she forgotten it? She'd come to think that every place smelled much the same, but now, back where she'd begun, free from the distraction of perfumes or nosegays, the long-remembered scents drifted back to her: the stench of unwashed bodies; human waste; the smoke from the fires of the street vendors, fish blackening on the grills; spices and seasonings and the handfuls of mountain sage thrown into the flames to make bad meat taste sweeter. Clouds of hot fat wafted from the back windows of teeming kitchens. And above all, never entirely vanquished, waiting for its moment, the fragrance of orange blossom and musk vine and the wistful scent of that twisting plant known across the island as thief-in-the-night.

It was all as it had always been. As a child she had known every one of those dark streets, every hidden courtyard, every concealed archway where a dark-skinned youth could merge into the gloom. She had haunted every café, every cheap eating-house, and every greasy alley where kitchens emptied their scraps. She had been deft at slipping between tables in the very shadows of the waiters, begging from the diners, one eye always open for a fallen coin or a negligently placed wallet. She had been good at it, she knew, daring and disarming and fleet of foot. And always she had been watching the people – their manners and their moods, how they spoke, how they held themselves, what made them smile. She had become expert in their habits, and in the many different ways they could be fooled or soothed or flattered.

Keeping to the darker side of the street, she followed the general drift of the crowds towards the Plaza de Armas and then cut away towards the docks, down a series of smaller streets, until she reached the place she had visited earlier that day.

The British consul had his place of business in a smart building three storeys high, given over entirely to offices. It was a good address, not far from the waterfront, in a commercial area that grew quiet when the sun set. Even so, she was not alone. For those *habaneros* tiring of the crowds in the main plaza and opting instead for the seedier attractions of the docks, the street made a good route to the water. Had any of those revellers looked closely at the urchin lurking in an archway, they would have seen it was not a boy; the loose trousers and blouson, the ragged sleeves, the broad-brimmed hat – the ubiquitous uniform of Havana's poor – could not completely hide the truth. But no one had any reason to look closely. They made their way laughing and arguing towards the docks, oblivious of her existence. Curled up in the shadows, her knees pulled up under her chin, she sat unnoticed. She was, she estimated, no more than thirty paces from the spot where the murdered man had fallen.

She had come prepared to wait. The building opposite her was dark, its windows shuttered, but a lamp burned above the main entrance and the guichet – the little window in the front door – was open, allowing a breath of evening air into the interior. Behind it, she knew, on a small stool in the hallway, the night-watchman would be seated.

The garden lay, not behind the building, but to its side, screened from the street by a very high stone wall. It could be reached from the road through a heavy iron gate, left open for her that morning by the captain of police, but otherwise, he had assured her, rarely used and secured at all times by a substantial lock. A second lamp burned above that gate, and from her position in the shadows Leonarda could see that the light it gave was strong enough to illuminate the whole length of the garden wall.

A high, well-lit wall. Not impossible, she thought, but risky and daring. A thief in Havana would not want for easier targets.

And as she had seen for herself that morning, on its other three sides the garden was bounded by blind walls, each three storeys high, the creeper-clad ends of neighbouring buildings. By ensuring its privacy, they gave the little garden its charm. Other than the street gate, the only access to the garden was through the consul's study: those double doors, the narrow veranda, three steps down to the lawn . . .

Leonarda settled deeper into the shadow and waited.

At midnight, prompted by the chorus of the city's clocks, the night-watchman began his rounds. Leonarda watched the progress of his lantern from room to room, visible only as a low glow between the shutters. First she glimpsed it in the consul's study, then back in the hallway, then in the other ground-floor room. After that the light disappeared for a few moments, before reappearing on the first floor. She counted under her breath until the round was complete. Eleven minutes.

Half an hour after midnight, the number of pedestrians passing the building was greatly reduced. For five minutes at a time the street might be deserted.

When the clock struck one, the watchman's rounds were repeated in the same order.

At half past one, the street was empty. Elsewhere the city was still awake, still dancing and eating and flirting. But where Leonarda kept watch, there was silence.

At twenty minutes to two, a small mulatto boy appeared, sidling uneasily down the brighter side of the street, his eyes turned towards the shadows opposite him as if searching for something in their depths. On reaching the iron gate he paused and, as if seized by a sudden and unconvincing bout of weariness, lolled casually against it. He remained in that position, yawning theatrically, until reassured by the silence of the street. Then he turned and knelt, and Leonarda watched him working at the iron lock with something that looked like a narrow blade. Twice he stopped to listen but no one came. A minute passed, perhaps two, before he straightened and shook his head. Turning again to the shadows where Leonarda sat, unsure where to direct his signal, he shrugged, then rattled the gate against its hinges to show that it still held firm.

With a final shrug in Leonarda's direction, the boy slipped away. Whoever had ransacked the consul's study, they had surely not reached it through the garden.

At two o'clock, the night-watchman's round was completed in the same order as before. Leonarda stayed to watch it but it told her nothing new. She could have left before then, returned to the silken comfort of her bedroom overlooking the Calle Chacón. But she wanted to witness the ritual once more. As she watched this time she was not counting the seconds, nor memorising the order in which the rooms were visited. She was imagining the same lantern in a different hand, and the weary, pre-dawn footsteps of the old man who had loved her.

IV

Backhouse knew almost nothing of Cuba, and even less of the post to which he had so suddenly been appointed. Until that morning he would have struggled to place Havana correctly on a map of the wider Caribbean. He knew only that Cuba was a Spanish island, the last remaining fingerhold of an empire that had once spanned the Americas. Backhouse dimly remembered there had been trouble there a few months earlier. What had it been? An invasion by Americans? The invaders, he recalled, had been swiftly defeated and the leaders publicly garrotted by order of the Spanish governor; but it had not been the first such attempt upon the island, and Backhouse wondered if it would be the last.

That night, however, was one for celebration. Already the new opportunities opening to him seemed boundless in their promise, and his elation proved contagious. Grace had received his news with great excitement, any misgivings she might have felt about a foreign posting quickly put to rest by his reassurances. Their daughter, Alice, then six months old, would thrive in the warmer climate, he felt sure of it; leaving the filthy air of London would be beneficial for them all; and Alice would grow up in much finer surroundings in Havana than if they were to remain in London.

Hans Place was, of course, a respectable address, but the Backhouse family did not live on the best side of it. When Backhouse looked out across the leaf-scattered grass, the houses facing him were very similar to his own, different only in the light they received, in the degree to which they faced the morning sun; and yet, as he knew, the inhabitants of those houses were a little bit wealthier, a fraction better connected, the wines in their cellars of very slightly better vintage.

In his duties at the Foreign Office Backhouse was always pains-taking, and he took pride in the fact that his diligence was never questioned, his work never sent back. There had been men promoted above him who could not have said the same. But the helpful connections, the beneficent patronage, the moments of sheer good luck – all the things that led to advancement – had never quite materialised for Backhouse in the way he'd hoped. And Grace, he knew, felt this situation more acutely than he did.

She had understood the state of his prospects when she accepted his proposal of marriage, and she had never complained, not for one moment. But her friends had married more advantageously, and the difference showed itself in countless small ways – in the invitations received, the guests welcomed; an extra servant here, the latest carriage there – quiet, unspoken differences that pained him more than he could say.

But not for much longer. In London, a Foreign Office clerk, second class, with only limited private means, did not entertain expansively. In Havana, things would be very different. They would have a gracious home, generous rooms, and would be able to offer their guests every luxury. Grace would, at last, have the prominence she deserved.

So it had been an afternoon of rejoicing followed by an evening of quiet satisfaction and an excellent dinner. His unsuccessful applications for consular posts were forgotten. This was a better position than any of those. *Her Majesty's Judge in the Havana Mixed Commission for the Suppression of the Slave Trade.* Why, after the consul, that made him the highest ranking British official on the island! The thought was certainly gratifying, and after dinner he allowed himself a glass of the very special brandy.

Grace had already retired for the night when a servant announced the arrival of Thomas Staveley, Backhouse's superior at the Foreign Office. He and Staveley were on amiable terms, but such a late visit was unusual and Backhouse immediately feared the worst.

'Nothing to do with our conversation earlier today, is it, Staveley? Nothing's changed?'

His visitor was a fleshy individual and rather pale, who gave the impression that he himself might perhaps have benefited from a posting in the sun. But he allayed Backhouse's fears with a serene wave of the hand.

'No, nothing has changed. Don't worry, old man, the post is still very much yours if you want it. I just wanted to call by to offer my congratulations in a private capacity. The appointment is thoroughly deserved.'

Over more brandy (Backhouse's second glass, an unprecedented event) the two men talked: about Havana, about Cuba, about Backhouse's new posting. Staveley, it seemed, was something of an expert on these subjects.

'The Mixed Commission is a strange beast,' he explained, settling back comfortably into Backhouse's best armchair. 'The Spanish don't much like it, but they're stuck with it. We rather twisted their arms into outlawing the slave trade, you see, then made them agree that the Royal Navy could patrol Cuban waters to enforce the ban. Frankly, I think the Spanish would be selling slaves all around the Caribbean if they thought they could get away with it, but they need our support in Europe so they sit on their hands and pretend to be very virtuous. Meanwhile, any vessels we capture are taken into Havana, and that's where the Mixed Commission comes in. You and a Spanish judge will hear all the evidence, George, and it's up to you to make sure the right verdict is returned.'

Backhouse enjoyed himself. To sit and discuss such issues with Staveley, frankly and as equals, confirmed his sense that his life had changed utterly in the course of just a few hours. No more dreary copying at the FO. No more anxious scanning of bills. No more drudgery and pettiness. He would be arbitrating on issues of the greatest significance, not just to the welfare of countless unfortunates, but to the very crusade against slavery itself. It was an honour of which he had never dreamed.

'Of course,' Staveley confided, 'the diplomatic situation is a touch delicate just at the moment. The government in Madrid may be opposed to the slave trade, nominally at least, but the Cuban aristocracy makes no such pretence. They rely on slaves to keep their sugar plantations going, and because they treat the poor brutes so badly they're in constant need of new ones. So the Cuban landowners distrust the politicians in Spain and are always plotting against them. And both sides hate us, of course. The Spanish resent us, and the Cubans are convinced we want to free their slaves and put the black man over them.'

'But don't we?' Backhouse asked. 'Want to free their slaves, I mean?'

'Well . . .' Staveley pursed his lips. 'Officially, of course, we are opposed to slavery as an institution. But we have to tread carefully. If you're a Cuban grandee desperate to keep your slaves, where do you turn for help? To a nation that shares your own passion for slavery, of course.'

'To America, you mean?' Backhouse hazarded a guess.

'Precisely. A big, confident neighbour whose government is dominated by the slaving interest. There're a lot of Americans made very nervous about the prospect of abolition in Cuba. A nation of free blacks, just a few miles across the water? They'd go to any lengths to prevent that. Hence these various private armies and their ill-fated invasions. It's tinderbox stuff over there, George.'

Staveley pursed his lips again.

'As for us, well, we can tolerate the Spanish in Cuba because frankly they don't pose any threat to us. But let our Yankee cousins replace them and things could get damnably awkward. Great Britain is the dominant power in the Caribbean, and we want it to stay that way. So we mustn't push the Cubans into the arms of the Americans. In fact, we have to do everything we can to make sure America and Spain don't come to blows.'

'You think there could be a war?' Backhouse tried to sound as casual as possible.

'Oh, there are certainly some Americans itching for a fight. But not too many of them. Make no mistake, it would be a bloody business.' He paused, as if weighing up the various possibilities. 'Of course if America and Spain *did* come to blows, we'd have no choice but to come in on the Spanish side. And I don't need to tell you that the last thing we need is another war. We've got trouble enough brewing with Russia. You've heard there's a fleet being prepared to sail to the Crimea?'

Backhouse nodded. He had heard some such rumour.

'But I know you'll do us proud, George. Go and show the Spaniard how an honest Englishman goes about his business.'

It was not until he was about to take his leave that Staveley broached a slightly different subject.

'There is another piece of business I need to talk to you about before you go,' he confided. 'Something confidential that we can't put in the official correspondence. Would this be a good time?'

'Of course.' Staveley's change of tone was intriguing and George was curious.

'It's just that we have one or two concerns about the work our sailors are doing out there. As I said, the navy is putting on any number of patrols to try to stem the flow of slaves into the island. Everywhere else they do rather well, but in Cuba ... Well, the number of slaving vessels intercepted is frankly minimal. It's almost as if ...'

Staveley paused as if searching for appropriate words.

'At first we just put it down to bad luck, of course. But as month follows month follows month, well, pure chance doesn't seem to explain it.' He swallowed. 'Frankly, old man, the suspicion is that somehow the sailing plans of our patrols are finding their way into the wrong hands. Now, those plans are filed in Kingston, so we're looking into the Jamaica end of things, but we're pretty certain that the slavers operating out of Cuba are getting wind of them from somewhere closer to hand. Without going into too much detail, old man, our investigations suggest that the slave captains are getting their information in Havana.'

'But surely you're not implying . . .?' George found himself floundering slightly.

'That the information is being supplied by anyone in Havana's British community?' Staveley pursed his lips. 'One would certainly hope not. But of course we would like to reassure ourselves that is not the case. And from this distance that sort of thing can be tricky. There's no denying that we'd greatly appreciate the first-hand opinion of someone we trust. Quite unofficially, of course.'

'Of course.' George was flattered, though in truth he wasn't entirely clear what his visitor was asking of him. Staveley seemed to sense his confusion.

'Don't worry too much about it now, old man. We'll talk more before you go. At my club, perhaps. The burgundy there is superb. But if you were to ask a few questions on our behalf and perhaps drop us a line every now and then in a private capacity telling us how you see things – your own particular observations – we'd be enormously grateful.' Staveley waved his hand airily. 'Obviously, if you *were* to write it's better not to use the official post bag for that sort of thing. Not until we know exactly how the land lies. But there's a man living above the English book-shop there who handles certain matters on our behalf. Name of Lavender. Go and see him when you get there. I'm sure he'll be a helpful chap to know.'

George nodded confidently, but perhaps his expression betrayed him because his visitor smiled.

'I know, I know. All very irregular. But it's a regrettable truth that sometimes vital communications are better not shared around Whitehall.'

'Yes. Yes, of course.' In all his years at the Foreign Office, George had never been abroad. The realities of foreign postings were new to him, and evidently more complicated than he had anticipated.

'Excellent, excellent.' Staveley was finally ready to depart. 'I hardly need to warn you to be careful with your personal papers too. Diaries, private correspondence, personal memoranda . . . Nothing indiscreet, eh?'

Backhouse assured him that discretion was his forte, and Staveley gripped his hand firmly, with great warmth.

'It's been good talking to you, George. I knew you were the man for us. And I think Havana will suit you very nicely.'

Left alone in the drawing room, Backhouse became aware of the rain rattling against his windows and the rise and fall of the wind. He thought how different they sounded, now that he was to leave them behind.

V

Leonarda lay that night in her old rooms near the water. On the Cortina de Valdés the crowds had finally exhausted themselves. She could still hear strains of music from the main square but beneath her window the street was silent, disturbed only by the occasional footsteps of late revellers hurrying home. Sometimes she thought she could hear, faint and almost soothing, the distant sound of the sea.

But she could not settle. Her thoughts returned over and over again to those dark floorboards where the old watchman had died. What wood was it that aged to such a deep, intense hue? She did not know. But she had seen for herself how dark it was. As dark as blood. By moonlight, probably darker.

Was he aware of that hard wood as he lay there, dying? Was that the last caress he felt, the last thing to press against his cheek? So much blood. How long does it take to bleed so much? It must have begun as a few drops, a trickle only, feeling its way, growing faster; until, like a dark spring, it began to froth and bubble, to flood out across the doorway and into the room.

They must have stepped over him to make their escape. But they did not step in his blood: there had been no marks of bare feet. They had stepped clear of it. By moonlight.

Murders were common in Havana, investigations cursory. And this was an old black man. Not even a slave, so of no value to anyone.

The man with boots had *not* seen the blood. He must have arrived before dawn, before there was light to show him what his boots were treading in. He had not known to step clear of that dark, drying pool. The moonlight had not been enough.

So before that, there must have been light. Lamps. Enough to show up the blood so that the bare feet might avoid it. That fatal blow had not fallen out of darkness.

But if there were lamps, there was no ambush. No assailant in the shadows. And common thieves do not work by lamplight.

A watchman is cautious by nature. And this watchman? She had known him all her life. She had been away three years but she had never feared for him. He had a nose for danger, an instinct. She'd thought he would live for ever. No concealed attacker would ever have surprised him by lamplight: he was an old man, but not a fool.

And she had loved him. For years she had been too restless, too angry to own it. And when she finally understood, she had never told him, just as she had never said goodbye. She had left the island without a word to him, confident that later – always later – there would be time.

But while she travelled, he had died all alone on those hard, bare boards.

Why? She had visited the consul's room as a way of saying goodbye, but had found only questions. No burglary by force, no stealthy entry through the garden, no common thieves working in darkness. Only a death unexplained. And now sleep would not come. She would say goodbye, yes. But first she would understand why.

VI

The December night was turning wintry by the time Thomas Staveley left Hans Place. His interview with George Backhouse had taken longer than he'd intended, and by the time he reached his next destination the clock of St Edwin's had already struck one, and the wind that had been showing its temper throughout the afternoon had finally started to rage. The rain driving against the windows of his hansom was bitterly cold.

Lowther Street, although respectable, was not a fashionable address, and at such an hour the street was still but for the confused eddies of leaves that lifted and fell, and swept in waves across the cobbles. And yet Staveley was not surprised, on reaching the house he sought, to find a lamp burning above the front door and the ground-floor windows still bright behind the shutters. The door was opened swiftly, almost at the moment of his knocking, by a manservant who appeared to expect late callers and who explained that Mr Jerusalems was currently occupied. But if Mr Staveley would care to wait in the library . . .? He managed to convey through his manner rather than his words that he didn't think the wait would be a long one.

Again Staveley was not surprised. The house on Lowther Street was frequently busy with visitors regardless of the hour, and he had encountered all sorts there: various peers, for instance, once even a duke. Rubbing shoulders with them – metaphorically if not physically – there had always been any number of dubious-looking characters, many of them foreigners, of the sort who made Staveley's hands instinctively move to his pockets.

A dozen years had passed since Staveley's predecessor at the Foreign Office first brought him to Lowther Street, and the reason for the introduction had then been unclear. 'Don't worry,' his companion had assured him. 'It will all make sense shortly. The Old Man is going to have a word with you about it. Think of it as unofficial extra duties. And there's really nothing to it. You just call here once a month, and keep the fellow informed about what's going on, answer any questions, that sort of thing. Easy money. Have they told you much about him?'

They hadn't. It was the first time Staveley had ever heard of John Jerusalems.

'Well, he's a strange fellow, and no mistake. Scarcely exists in society. His name's never in the court circulars, and he's never mentioned at Whitehall. But he certainly has friends. They say Wellesley tried to give him a title. He swims with some pretty big fish.'

As the pike swims with the perch, Staveley thought later, when he had come to know Jerusalems better. An entertaining companion, certainly, likeable even, but always one to be handled with caution.

It was fully twenty minutes past one o'clock when Staveley was finally ushered into the drawing room of John Jerusalems' house – or the room that had clearly once been a drawing room and which had now become a chaotic mixture of study, library and receiving room. Where at one time perhaps there had been pictures, the walls were now lined with maps, some of them broad in range – Europe, India, Afghanistan – and others much smaller in scale. Among them Staveley could make out town plans, at least a dozen hand-drawn sketches, even one or two nautical charts.

Elsewhere the room was dominated by books, but few of them were on shelves. They stood in piles, on small tables, on the floor, on the backs of armchairs. Gazetteers, encyclopedias, army lists, volumes in various languages, including one or two Staveley didn't even recognise. Among these unsteady ziggurats stood a writing desk covered in loose papers and a small dining table cluttered with three different tea trays and any number of stained, discarded cups. A fire burned brightly in the grate – Staveley had never known it otherwise, not even in the height of summer.

The creator of this extraordinary scene was seated at the dining table when Staveley entered, and rose eagerly to greet him. John Jerusalems was a surprising figure – a tiny sparrow of a man, no higher than Staveley's shoulder and as slim as a child. His hair and beard were grey and cropped short. He was, Staveley estimated, around fifty years old, but his build and stature gave the impression of someone a good deal younger.

This impression of youthfulness, Staveley knew, also owed a great deal to his host's constant, bustling energy. He was rarely still, even when sitting, and was more often than not on his feet. While listening to others he paced; while speaking he would spring around the room gesticulating. It was said that even during formal dinners he would leap up between mouthfuls when a subject excited him, but Staveley had no way of verifying the rumour as no one he knew had ever dined formally with John Jerusalems. Staveley himself had extended an invitation, but to no avail. The little man appeared to decline all such approaches.

And yet there could be no doubt that the fellow had an appetite. Staveley had witnessed platters of cold meats and bowls of fruit arriving in that room at all hours, and there was seldom a time when their remains were not in evidence, scattered over the table or curling forgotten on one of the piles of books. That night, as his host hurried forward to welcome him, Staveley observed a half-eaten apple still clutched in one hand.

'Thomas, Thomas, so good of you to come. Tea? There is no doubt whisky somewhere if you ring for it . . .'

He waved his guest towards an empty dining chair then turned to the writing desk and began to sort through the papers.

'I understand the current ministry has finally fallen? Is that correct?' He asked the question without turning round.

'That is correct. Derby goes to the palace tomorrow.' Staveley checked the clock on the mantelpiece. 'Or, rather, later today.' In the carriage on the way to Lowther Street, he had been feeling immensely weary but in the presence of Jerusalems it was difficult to feel lethargic. 'That's why I came. To warn you.'

'Warn me?' His host turned and eyed him with mild amusement. He had the habit on such occasions of lowering his head and peering, as if over the frame of a pince-nez – although he never did have a pince-nez on his nose, and Staveley had never seen him use one.

'Don't you worry at all that a change of ministry might affect your position, John?'

'Why should it?' Jerusalems was raising himself up and down on the balls of his feet, as if to stretch his calves. 'Officially I don't exist, so they can hardly replace me. I assume the change of ministry will not affect your position either?'

'No, I shall continue to be Her Majesty's Ambassador to Lowther Street.' He said it with a sigh, but in truth he rather enjoyed his dealings with Jerusalems.

'Anyway,' the little man went on, 'what we do here is far more important than politics, as you well know. Who could object to it? Victories without fighting.'

'Though not,' Staveley pointed out, 'always without cost.'

'Alas, no.' His host was still for a moment, and in that moment Staveley recognised the other Jerusalems, the one he had glimpsed only occasionally – sombre, contemplative, plunged so deeply into thought that he seemed unaware of day turning into night.

'Alas, no,' he repeated. 'The collision of great nations is rarely without casualties. But if we can frustrate the machinations of our rivals without resorting to armies on the battlefield, I think the many lives we save justify the losses. Even the old goats who think that what I do is underhand and dishonourable acknowledge that it comes at a very reasonable price.'

He gave a little chuckle and turned back to his papers.

'Ah! Here we are. *The sailing plans of naval squadrons off the coast of Cuba.* The Admiralty has written to the minister giving its absolute assurance that these are secret and that the low rate of successful interventions is down to reduced slaving traffic in that region.'

He chuckled again and tossed the paper towards Staveley, then began to pace in the small open space in front of the fire.

'And do you believe that?' Staveley asked him.

'Of course not. There are probably more slaves arriving in Cuba today than there were when the trade was still legal. They are the blood that keeps the island's heart pumping.' He paused. 'If Britain ever were to succeed in cutting off the supply, what then, Thomas?'

But before Staveley could reply, Jerusalems had jumped back to the original subject.

'No, you can take it from me that those sailing plans are reaching the slave traders, and reaching them via Havana. Our new man is aware?'

'Backhouse? Yes, I spoke to him this evening. As you suggested, I've asked him to investigate.'

'And you put him in touch with Lavender?' Jerusalems had stopped pacing and had begun to rearrange the objects on the mantelpiece.

'I did. Though I still don't understand why we don't just ask Lavender to look into it. He knows the place better than anyone. Backhouse doesn't even speak Spanish.'

'Oh, he'll learn, he'll learn. And you do trust him, don't you, Thomas? A man to do things methodically?' Jerusalems' back was still turned.

'Yes, of course. He's a thoroughly decent fellow. He'll stick to the rules and won't make waves.'

'Well, there you are. Now, tell me, what's all this about the Americans and their battleships?'

Staveley was not surprised Jerusalems had heard the rumours.

'It seems the American navy has doubled the watches on all its ships in the Gulf of Mexico and surrounding waters. They seem to be expecting some sort of Spanish attack.' Staveley, spotting a box of cigars within his reach wondered if he should help himself.

'Sabotage of some sort, I suppose. I can't see it myself though. It's clearly not in Spain's interests to provoke a war. In fact it would be utter lunacy. And the Spanish deny everything, of course.'

'Well, yes.' Jerusalems edged his carriage clock a few inches along the mantelpiece. 'They would.' Then he turned and pursed his lips. 'Meanwhile, Thomas, I gather the new expeditionary force being raised in America is growing by the day, with Havana firmly in its sights. It would appear another invasion is imminent.'

But Staveley shook his head.

'Surely not, John. I can't see Washington allowing yet another private army to land in Cuba. Not after the shambles of the last one. Besides, we've made it abundantly clear we won't tolerate it.'

'And you think that will stop them, Thomas?'

Jerusalems gestured towards a large map of the North American continent that hung near the fireplace. Sections of it had been shaded in different colours, as if by hand.

'It's easy to sit in Westminster and sneer at Americans for their bad manners and their dirty fingernails, but it would be a mistake to underestimate their hunger. They've already prised Texas off the Mexicans, and they won't stop there. They'll be halted by the Pacific in the west and by Canada in the north, perhaps, if we're sufficiently resolute. By Mexico in the south eventually, but not until they've stripped it of everything they want.'

As he spoke, his hands swept to and fro across the map, pushing westward, north, south . . .

'By then we'll no longer be facing a nation, Thomas, but an entire continent. A new empire. And after that?'

Jerusalems jabbed his finger with a little thump into the sea off Florida.

'The Caribbean. That's where the logic takes them. Cuba is not the backwater people think. Just look. Havana's closer to America than Bristol is to London. And mark my words, if we allow the Americans into Cuba, it will only be the beginning. They are a very new nation, and foolish enough to imagine that some great destiny beckons them. And they genuinely believe that the Americas should be free of all European interference.' The little man shook his head. 'Unfortunately, in terms of geography, they are rather well placed to back up these beliefs with action. It will not be overnight, Thomas, but in time, if we are not watchful, the entire Caribbean will be lost to us.'

The strength of Jerusalems' feelings was very clear, and Staveley rather admired him for his passion. But surely, in this matter at least, the little man was overreacting. The Americans were difficult, it was true. But in guns, in ships, in factories and finance, in every possible arena, Great Britain had their measure. Staveley was not unduly alarmed.

'But of course we won't let that happen, will we, Thomas?' His host's voice was calm again, quite possibly even amused, and he turned away from the charts as abruptly as he had turned to face them. Once again he was smiling brightly.

'I feel Backhouse is an excellent choice, my friend.'

His tone was, in the nicest way, a dismissal, and Staveley rose to his feet. It was almost two o'clock in the morning and many hours since he had seen his bed.

'Yes, an excellent choice,' Jerusalems continued, offering him his hand. 'I'm quite sure he'll do everything we need of him in the matter of these stolen sailing plans.'

Staveley departed yawning, already beginning to ache a little with tiredness. As the door closed behind him, John Jerusalems was returning to his maps, and to the quiet contemplation of the waters around Havana.

VII

For a few seconds after waking, she thought nothing had changed.

Pale daylight rippled between the shutters and traced patterns across her ceiling, touching the heavy drapes with traces of gold. From the street outside came the sound of Havana waking: shopfronts opening, goods being laid out, traders whistling carelessly as they swept their steps. For those few minutes, while the sun was still low over the sea, the city felt clean and new, all the noise and the reckless passions of the night sponged away by the gentle dawn light. It was an hour of fresh hopes and clear thoughts; an hour when the world could seem strangely simple.

So, for the briefest of moments, she felt again the pleasure she had always felt on waking in that room. Her own place, sanctuary. But before her head had even stirred on the pillow, the grief returned, undiminished, stabbing at her again with that raw, unforgiving edge. Every morning the same.

Lying motionless, she let the moment pass. From the room next door came the rattle of china. Rosa was making coffee. Leonarda knew that if she waited, thinking of nothing but the patterns of the light upon the ceiling, then that first, sharp pain would pale. By the time Rosa came in, she would be sitting up, making her plans for the day, nursing her wound as best she could. And Rosa would smile and be pleased and would think her mistress's grief not as bad as it had been.

The rituals of dressing at the apartment on the Calle Chacón had a gentle rhythm to them that Leonarda found soothing. First Rosa would position her at the mirror and, with firm fingertips, would rub her temples, then her neck, then her cheeks just below the eyes. Then came the brushing of her hair, long slow strokes repeated over and over, languorous and soothing.

Rosa was nearly fifty years of age, a small, lean woman with a deformed lip which made her repulsive to many *habaneros*, who equated deformity with contagious misfortune. Like many domestic servants in Havana, she was a slave, leased by her owner for domestic service. But she had been with Leonarda since her first days in the Calle Chacón, and she considered it her home; and in her years there, the joy she took in brushing her mistress's hair had never diminished. Spanish hair, she called it, as it did not curl like her own, but cascaded down Leonarda's back in great unruly waves. With care it could be pinned or twisted into any style, could for a time sit as neatly and as primly as any white woman's, but Rosa loved it most as it was in the mornings, loose and tousled and magnificent, awaiting her careful, taming touch.

That morning, however, Rosa could sense that Leonarda was not at peace. The night before they had picked out a dress of exquisite blue silk bought on one of the English islands and as fine as anything in Havana; a dress to put to shame the island's society ladies with their year-old Madrid fashions, most of them outmoded before they had even begun their long sea journey westwards.

When Leonarda came to dress, however, she hesitated and changed her mind, choosing instead a plain dress in navy, something so unremarkable and demure it might have been worn by a governess or a *duenna* or any superior lady's servant. Ever since they'd returned to Havana, Rosa knew, her mistress had been dreading going back to St Simeon.

The dwelling was little more than a shack, a lopsided construction of scavenged timber and mud bricks, squeezed into a tiny gap between other, larger dwellings, reliant upon its neighbours for support. Slum, shanty town, the armpit of Havana – whatever you called it, this was St Simeon. From the shack a mud track meandered between other haphazard constructions down to a filthy pond. That track, its route littered with the debris and detritus of its inhabitants, was where Hector had found her, and the ramshackle hut was where he had taken her, where Leonarda had remained, off and on, for the rest of her childhood. Her home. Its two rooms – two simple, dirt-floored rectangles – were scarcely larger, combined, than her silk-draped bed in the rooms on the Calle Chacón.

It was five years since she had last been there, but, from outside, the place was unchanged, altered only by a clothes line strung above the doorway to a corner of the opposite dwelling. From it were hanging various items of female clothing: all of them large and brash, in bright, clashing colours. She had promised herself that morning that nothing would shake her composure, but something about them irritated her, as if they were an affront to the memory of the quiet man who had once lived there. Five years on, and it seemed the sour tang of her resentment had not lost its edge.

The door was open but she could tell no one was at home; there was a stillness about the place that spoke of emptiness. Leonarda had to stoop to enter.

She had known what to expect, and she had prepared herself for it. Even before Hector died, there must have been many changes. With a wife to accommodate, his simple, sparse space must necessarily have altered. And enough time had passed since his death for his widow to press her own stamp upon the place.

But the reality shook her even more than she'd anticipated. Of the memories Leonarda carried inside her head, almost nothing was left.

The first room had been for cooking and eating and talking, and had been furnished with a simple mat, a couple of iron pots and some shelves for cups and cutlery. It was where Leonarda had slept, and she thought of it as hers. Now it was changed utterly. The sides of the room were hung with shelves wherever the walls were strong enough to support them, and each shelf was crammed with objects – cheap ornaments, statues of the Madonna, empty bottles and jars, chipped cups of the brightest imaginable designs. The floor had been raised on boards hidden beneath blankets, making the room seem low to her and cramped as it had never been before. Nowhere could she find any trace of the man who had once lived there.

The second room, separated from the first by a curtain, was worse still. It had been his room for sleeping and reading; now every inch of the walls was draped with clothes, few of them clean or fresh. Nails had been driven in wherever possible and it seemed that garments had been flung at them carelessly until the walls were lost behind them. The floor was a litter of fallen fabrics.

'If it's Hector you're looking for, you're too late, girl. He's cold in the ground by now.'

Leonarda had not heard any footsteps, but when she turned she saw a large figure filling the doorway.

'Course, you could have come any time these last five years, girl, but I guess you didn't care for the smell.'

Marguerite was twice Leonarda's age and a formidable physical presence. She had been born on one of the French islands and she spoke with a distinctive lilt, as if every sentence was a performance. She was making no effort to hide the dislike in her voice.

But if she hoped to intimidate, she was disappointed. Leonarda simply nodded, and turned back to the room.

'We buried him at the Santa Maria,' Marguerite went on. 'But there's no stone, if that's what you want to know. He's in the common plot, along with his neighbours. We're simple, honest people here.'

Still Leonarda said nothing. It was a full seven years since that place had last been where she slept, but she had never turned her back on it. For two years she had visited often. Only when Marguerite began to appear there, busy and loud and claiming precedence, had Leonarda's visits become less frequent. Marguerite had sensed the younger woman's resentment from the first, and had steered her course around it. There had been no defiant act of occupation, no moment of invasion. She had infiltrated the place by stealth, occupying it in tiny increments until the day came when she was its mistress.

'If it's his things you're after, they're gone too. Sold, some of them, or given away. His books too. What use were they to me? Or to anyone round here? And you were off plying your trade overseas. What else was I to do? I didn't know if you were ever coming back.'

Leonarda found her eyes moving to the place where the books had once stood. There had been only a dozen of them. Hector had known each one by heart.

'Marguerite,' she said, turning to meet the challenge in the other woman's eye. 'I need to know what happened.'

'What happened? What happened to Hector, you mean? Bless me, girl, everyone knows that. Hit on the head by a gang of thieves and never woke up. Too stupid to let them get on with it like any other watchman would have done. Has no one even told you that?'

Leonarda stepped from the sleeping area back into the other room, and as she did so she noticed that Marguerite moved back, away from her. The movement surprised her. She had expected aggression, to be challenged at every step. But at that moment, looking up at Marguerite's face, she understood. *She is afraid*, she thought. *Afraid that I will try to take all this from her.* It was a startling revelation. Marguerite the schemer, the she-devil, the usurper. Behind her anger, cowering.

'I didn't come for his things,' she said quietly, although in truth she had longed for them. 'And I'm sorry I didn't come here for so many years. I used to meet him by the harbour instead, you know, after his shifts. It was more convenient.'

'You and he were both working through the night, girl. That's what you mean.'

The jibe was old and stale and deliberate and once it would have provoked her. But this time Leonarda felt able to let it pass. When she offered no response, the older woman carried on.

'Well, I can't tell you any more about Hector than the whole world knows. It happened, that's all.'

'I was hoping ...' That morning, the thought of throwing herself upon Marguerite's mercy would have been unthinkable. For five years, the two had fought a silent war. And over what? Over the kindness of a simple man. In the end neither of them had really won. 'Marguerite, I was hoping you'd tell me a little about his last few days. How was he? Was he well? Happy? I promise afterwards I'll leave you alone. I know he'd want you to be comfortable here.'

Marguerite seemed about to speak, her eyes still sharp with suspicion, but in the end she simply shrugged, and stepped back, out of the doorway, allowing Leonarda to follow her into the sunlight.

The two women walked as they talked, Leonarda with her gaze cast down. Marguerite, less at ease, moved with awkward, rolling steps, casting frequent glances at her companion as though trying to work out what to make of the unexpected peace she'd been offered. Perhaps what she saw reassured her. Leonarda, in the plain blue dress, could not have looked less threatening. Gradually Marguerite's shoulders began to relax.

'He was tired that month, girl. Not sleeping well, and Hector *always* slept well. I said to him, Hector, you get old Menendez to stand in for a night or two, you get some sleep. But he never trusted any other body to do his work for him, you know that. In the end I persuaded him to let Moses Le Castre do a week for him, just so he could get some rest. But Moses got ill, only did two nights. When they told me what had happened to Hector, may the Lord forgive me, my first thought was, This shouldn't be him, it should be Moses.'

Leonarda listened in silence. From the moment she'd heard of Hector's death, she'd known this interview was inevitable, but she still wasn't sure what she wanted from it. Perhaps just to be reassured he had gone to his death cheerful and untroubled, or to be told that he had been thinking of her before he died. Or perhaps she simply wanted to hear his name spoken again by someone who, whatever her faults, had also loved him.

'Why wasn't he sleeping, Marguerite? Was he ill?' He'd always been a good sleeper, even on those bright, breathless mornings when he came from work so late that the heat was already gathering.

'He was getting old, and that's the truth. A couple of times he'd found himself dozing on the job, and that worried him. Thought he'd be caught and lose his place. He even started taking a book in with him, although it was against the rules, to help him stay awake. But when a soul gets worried about not sleeping, that's when the Devil sings his songs. You know how it is. Just keeps on getting worse and worse.'

They had come to the point where the road ended, where a small boy was throwing stones into the greasy waters of the pond. With nowhere else to go, they turned around and retraced their steps. Their progress was observed, without curiosity, by three children who were foraging in the piles of refuse between two dwellings.

When Leonarda asked Marguerite about the place Hector was paid to guard, the older woman simply shook her head.

'No idea, girl. Hector didn't say a word about it. It was just a job. He just went in and sat on his stool and did his rounds in the dark whenever the clocks struck. He never said there were jewels there. I don't think he knew. It was only papers. I thought, well, that's a safe place for him. Who wants to steal papers?'

They had arrived back where they'd begun. The sun was higher; soon the strange peace that prevailed there would be gone. Men would be drifting back to eat, women to cook; there would be a time of noise and shouting and smoke, of scolding and jocularity, before the quiet of the afternoon settled upon the untidy streets of St Simeon.

The two women had never before spent so long alone together without their mutual dislike sparking into flames. For what? Looking again at the line of Marguerite's clothes, Leonarda found them less irritating than before. They were just clothes. Hector wouldn't have minded. And the rooms were just rooms, where a woman lived alone, filling the emptiness with yards of fabric.

'His books . . .' She hesitated, afraid of re-igniting Marguerite's hostility. But the other was busying herself with the canvas flap that hung over the doorway.

'Moses took them. To sell.' Marguerite's voice was neutral, but then she turned and met Leonarda's eye. 'I thought you were gone for good, girl. Why would you come back here?' She turned to the doorway again. 'You know why I always hated those books? He'd sit down with them, and he'd be gone for hours to some place I couldn't follow. But you could go there with him, couldn't you, girl? You and he had been to all them places together. No one else round here. No one else in the whole of St Simeon can read more than their names. Only you two.'

Before Leonarda could reply, one final spark of anger.

'And you could do no wrong for him, you know that? The little girl he'd gathered up off the street, grown into a white man's whore. But he didn't care. Just said you'd find your own way to where you were going.'

Marguerite straightened then, and brushed her hands against her hips.

'I'm sorry about the books, girl. I dare say you'll find Moses down by the water most evenings. Mother Alençon's place, probably. He may be able to help you find them.'

Sometimes she thought she could remember the day Hector found her: the dust, the glare, the white lane in St Simeon where the rubbish stood in piles. But she couldn't be sure. It could have been any day. That scene rarely changed, and no day in St Simeon was much better or much worse than any other.

Yet she even thought she could remember the moment itself – a shouting crowd, an angry woman cursing, then Hector's black face, kind, resolute, slightly stern. But she knew Hector recalled it differently. He told her that she fought him like a cat. Fought him when he swept her up and carried her home; fought for the food she saw on his plate, not understanding that he intended it for her.

No one could say where she had come from, nor how long she had wandered that street alone. Abandoned children were commonplace in that part of Havana. Those that survived ran with the narrow-ribbed dogs on the piles of waste behind the lines of shacks. They were the minority.

Even so, she had not taken easily to the comfort of safety. She had battled Hector from the beginning, at first unable to believe in his kindness, then unable to forgive him for it. It was as if something of the wild had lingered in her soul. By day she was fretful; by night, while Hector was working his weary shifts, she found sleep impossible. As soon as she was old enough to find her own way through the streets, she would rise by moonlight and dress herself, then wander freely. The more certain she became of Hector, the further she would venture.

Those nights in the old city belonged to her and her alone: slipping invisibly through the crowds, foraging with the ferocity of an eel for the scraps that fell her way, curling up to sleep in the shadows of doorways; waking exultant in the quiet of the night with an open window or an unlocked door beckoning. She had no need to fight or beg or steal. She had food waiting for her, a place to sleep; in fact, a home. She went because she wanted to.

She knew that Hector knew. His neighbours had complained from the first of the unruly child fostered upon them. She was a foundling, of mixed blood, not even a proper Negro. Sin ran in her veins, they said, you could tell from the look of her. So there must have been witnesses aplenty to testify to her nocturnal departures, her dawn homecomings. Sometimes, in defiance of their sneers, she stayed away – for three nights, four, sometimes longer. Hector never condemned. He never showed any anger or disappointment. He knew she would come back; she knew he would be waiting.

That night in the Calle Chacón, she couldn't rest. Something Marguerite had said repeated itself in the night-time sounds of the city, nagging at the edges of her sleep.

He said you'd find your own way . . . your own way to where you're going . . .

Was it true? She was far from certain. But that could wait. First she must answer the other questions that gathered around her in the darkness. His body still warm on the boards, an assassin stepping over him, and later a man in boots . . .

She was still thinking of Hector as the dawn's first breath stirred the darkness. Such gentle, uncomplaining kindness. Such patience. Such love.

Surely she had never deserved such love.

The captain of police was surprised the following day to receive a further letter from the mysterious *habanera* with the English surname. He had tried to put her visit to the consul's offices out of his mind. Agreeing to act as her guide had been a mistake, one that would cost him his reputation were it known to his colleagues. He had, of course, refused all payment when the tour was over, but he had blushed with embarrassment, his dignity in tatters. So he had said nothing to anyone and had tried to forget all about it.

Nevertheless, he did not discard this second letter as perhaps he should have done. It remained in his desk for a day or two, and in that time, without really intending to, he found himself asking certain questions of his fellow officers. On the third day, he took the letter from his drawer and took up his pen. The note he began to write was terse, written he hoped in the tone of one bestowing an exceptional favour.

Señora,
  The names you were seeking are these. I must repeat that these are rough and dangerous men.
  Antonio Canaria, once of the Anchor
  Felipe Martinez, known also as Tartuffo
  The Negro known as Pedro the Salt-Eater, who died of the cholera

It is rumoured that Martinez died in a brawl last December, but I cannot say for certain.

In addition, madam, I have thought further of the incident at the British consulate and it occurs to me . . .

Here the captain of police paused. He could think of no wording that was discreet and suitably formal, yet not ridiculous. So the unfinished letter rested upon his desk for a further day before he returned to it and tore it to shreds. He would write, yes, but listing the names only, shorn of all niceties. His further thoughts on the matter he would not include.

For the sake of discretion, he told himself, it would be better to communicate those in person.

VIII

In the office of his elegant home, well away from the stench of the old city, the American consul was drafting a letter.

Consulate of The United States
Havana, February 21st 1853

Most Excellent Sir,
    Information has reached me . . .

Although the clock above his mantelpiece was not yet indicating ten, the heat was already oppressive. Even there, in the city's lush outskirts, there was no escaping it – a damp, breathless humidity that made his neck chafe at the collar. The white-fronted European houses had high ceilings and shaded verandas, but the sticky heat crept through every defence. However it was not the heat that was most irritating the American consul that morning.

Most Excellent Sir,
    Information has reached me that on the 19th & 20th Inst <u>the mailbags intended for the United States mail steamers Empire City and Crescent City were seized by the Public Authorities</u> after they had been closed and sealed, as they were being carried from the home of the consigners and agents of those ships (Messrs Drake & Co) to the wharfs; the seals broken and the contents of the bags examined.
    It is not my province to discuss this question as one of national concern, it will be referred to the Government in Washington, where, I doubt not, it will be duly considered. But I must

nevertheless avail myself of the occasion to express my deep regret at the occurrence, and respectfully, <u>but decidedly</u>, to remonstrate - against it as discourteous towards my Government . . .

A knock at the door interrupted his flow and he cursed under his breath.

'Mr Dale has arrived, sir, with your visitor.'

The butler, a man of advancing years, wore full uniform and gloves. The consul did not rely upon local staff but had brought all his domestic servants with him from Virginia.

'Very good, Bartholomew. Tell Mr Dale to wait in the hall. You'd better bring Mr . . .'

'Mr Jepson, sir.'

'You'd better bring Mr Jepson up straight away. I suppose he must be seen.'

The formalities of his post were frequently wearisome to him, and looking after new arrivals sent over by Washington was invariably a thankless task. They would arrive knowing nothing of the island and would expect it to work as smoothly as the cotton states back home – a sort of Spanish-speaking Georgia, comfortable and stable, serene in the certainties of confident authority. The complexities of Cuba, where nothing worked quite as it should and no one was certain of anything, were almost always beyond them. It was painful trying to convince them that Washington methods were of limited value in a place where even identifying the best person to bribe was a slow and costly business.

But the man who was ushered in to his study on that clammy, breathless morning looked nothing like the usual bureaucrats wished upon the consul for short spells by his government. The visitor's suit of clothes was impeccable, for one thing – every bit as good as his own, the consul conceded – but it looked absurdly out of place on its wearer. Mr Jepson was a big man of no more than forty, not particularly tall but broad-shouldered and powerful, with a face tanned as if by over-exposure to the elements; and fair hair, close cropped, perhaps bleached by the sun. His eyes seemed very close together. A striking figure, certainly, but the consul was frankly appalled. The man looked like a brawler, a prize-fighter, a great hunk of muscle and bone squeezed ridiculously into an excellent linen suit. What on earth, he wondered, was going on back home?

'Mr Jepson,' he began, shuffling the papers on his desk in an attempt to mask his confusion. 'You must excuse me. The letter from Mr Shawcross . . . Ah, here it is! Please come on in.'

He rose and offered the visitor his hand, fully expecting it to be crushed between those big, brutish fingers. But the hand that took his was cool, its pressure delicate, the contact oddly fleeting.

'Let me see . . .' The consul sank back into his chair and consulted one of the documents in front of him. It did not occur to him to offer the newcomer a seat. 'According to Mr Shawcross you are here as a special agent to look into this tiresome issue of the mails. In that, your timing is excellent. You'll be sorry to hear that there was another incident yesterday. I was just writing about it to the Captain-General – that is the title they give the island's Spanish governor. I am complaining in the strongest terms.'

To the consul's annoyance, Jepson appeared to show little interest in this piece of news. He merely nodded and looked around the room, as if more interested in the décor than he was in the consul. Really, the consul decided, it would be impossible to invite him out socially in the usual way. By the look of things, the inside of a drawing room was foreign territory to him; he could hardly be imposed on the neighbours.

'A pleasant room, this.' The newcomer's accent struck the consul as strangely muted. 'It faces the right way. No sun in the morning, when you want to work.' New England, perhaps? It was hard to tell.

'Tell me, sir,' Jepson went on, 'is there someone here you would like me to deal with on a day-to-day basis? If I were to have any questions?'

The consul was relieved. The fellow seemed to understand his place.

'I have asked Mr Dale to show you around the city. He acts as my general manager here and knows Havana as well as anyone. I know he'll be delighted to help in any way he can. For instance, he may be able to assist you with accommodation. Havana's hotels are not to be borne by even the hardiest soul for more than a couple of nights.'

'Thank you, sir, but that's completely unnecessary.' The visitor seemed to be studying a bust of George Washington that stood near the window. 'I have already made suitable arrangements. But I'm sure Mr Dale will be of great assistance in other ways.'

With that he removed his eyes from the bust and nodded to the consul as if he felt the interview had reached its natural conclusion.

Without knowing quite why, the consul was feeling a little uncomfortable. It should have been the oaf in the suit who felt awkward in such a situation, but Jepson seemed utterly at his ease while the consul found himself painfully aware that the Washington bust was a cheap object and not even a very good likeness. He had rescued it from a bankruptcy sale down on the dockside and after placing it by the window had scarcely thought of it again. Now he wished he had not given it such prominence. It was out of place in such an elegant room. It let him down. It was a little tasteless and a little tawdry.

'Of course, Mr Jepson, you will no doubt wish me to brief you in person about the details with regard to the mails. Perhaps we can agree a time when you have settled in . . .'

'Thank you again, sir, but I won't need to trouble you.' The visitor was looking away once more, this time at a portrait of the consul's wife. 'I have read all the correspondence, and of course I have done some research of my own.'

'Research, Mr Jepson?'

Jepson finally returned the consul's gaze.

'Perhaps Mr Shawcross's letter was unclear, sir. He should have explained that I have been working on this for some months. I didn't need to be in Havana to do that. My job is to make sure that we have the right people in the right places, looking and listening on our behalf. Some people in Washington are beginning to understand that knowledge wins wars, sir, diplomatic ones as well as the other sort. In that sense Havana is no different from anywhere else.'

The consul barely attempted to hide his annoyance. 'On the contrary, Mr Jepson, I'd hazard a guess that you will find Havana very different to any place you've visited before. Here more than anywhere there's no substitute for personal experience.'

'Well, let's see, sir . . .' Jepson was smiling – a rather patronising smile, the consul thought. 'The mailbags that were opened last night. They were opened at four minutes past eleven, on the express orders of Colonel Ferdinand Aguero, who although nominally an adviser to the Spanish Crown is actually running the island's secret police. He gave the order because the authorities suspect, rightly, that certain individuals on the island are acting to assist the invasion and annexation of Cuba by the private army currently gathering in Louisiana. The contents of the mailbags were examined by three senior officials, overseen by Aguero himself. No relevant information was discovered.' Jepson grinned. 'And that's about all I know of the matter, sir.'

At a loss, the consul resorted to bluster. 'Why wasn't I informed of all this, Mr Jepson?'

'Please consider that my first report, sir.'

'Pah! It all sounds highly suspect to me, Jepson. You can't possibly be sure of it. It's bar-room talk, that's all. Tittle-tattle.'

His visitor shrugged. 'If we have the right people in the right places, sir . . .'

'You mean *spies*?'

'Yes, sir. That's what I do for the government. I create spies, pay spies, position spies.' He paused for a moment. 'And if necessary I remove other people's.'

The consul was not sorry when Mr Jepson took his leave. The room seemed airier. And all that business about looking and listening was a lot of dirty nonsense. Games played by guttersnipes. It was frightful that such a person should be at large on the island.

Returning to his papers, he remembered that he had not, as was customary, invited the new arrival to dinner. The thought came as something of a relief to him; he must remember to tell his wife not to order an extra place. After all, he reflected, no one enjoyed a dinner party where one of the guests was unfamiliar with proper cutlery.

Henry Dale, who assisted the consul in various ways, had formed a rather more positive impression of the newcomer. Special envoys were invariably a nuisance to him too – getting lost, complaining about the heat and the food, demanding long lists of unobtainable facts and figures about the island's consumption of grain, or its rates of mineral extraction, or its readiness for democracy. This one, however, struck him as refreshingly different, and when Jepson emerged from the consul's study there was no standing on ceremony.

'There, that's over. Now we can get down to work. You offered to show me the city, Mr Dale. Where do we start?'

They drove back towards the old town in Dale's two-seat buggy. The showers of early morning had passed, leaving the avenues in the outlying districts pockmarked with puddles and surfaced with a thin, clinging layer of mud. Around them as they drove, traces of mist rose like steam from the deep vegetation that crowded in between the villas and pressed down upon the road. The traffic – mule carts, packhorses, labourers, sometimes slave women with great bundles upon their heads – was mostly bound in the same direction, so progress was slow.

But Dale was in no hurry and he handled the reins with careful competence. Out there, where Havana was still new, where the forest had only recently been driven back and the undergrowth had not yet entirely released its grip, sounds fell softly. The mornings were heavy with a slow, lazy sense of calm, and Dale enjoyed the peace he found there. His visitor, however, seemed inclined to talk.

'You've observed a few different consuls out here, Dale. How would you rate this one?'

Dale pulled a face, his eyes fixed on the road ahead.

'The answer to that, of course, is that it is hardly my place to rate one consul against another, especially not one who is currently paying me a salary.'

'Oh, come on! Don't tell me you don't have a view.'

But Dale wasn't to be drawn. 'To be honest, Mr Jepson, there isn't very much to rate them on. They sign the paperwork, issue the licences, take their cut. Havana is a lucrative posting. But it doesn't take a genius to do the work.'

Rather to Dale's embarrassment, Jepson spat into the road. 'Political appointees. They make me puke. A new President comes in, brings in his friends, none of them knows anything, and by the time they've learned enough to wipe their own arses, someone new comes in who knows even less.'

Dale smiled. They weren't the words he'd have employed himself, but the analysis was not one he could entirely disagree with.

'But isn't that democracy?' he asked.

'I couldn't say. But it's certainly a way of screwing up our national interests.'

'You sound very passionate, Mr Jepson. You are clearly a patriot.'

'I believe in getting things right. If I wanted to work with gentlemen half-wits, I'd join the British.'

Dale smiled again. He was not yet forty – old enough to be cynical, young enough to believe in change. He found himself quite liking Jepson.

'Well, the consul behaves extremely properly in all things,' he commented. 'He likes propriety. That's why he gets so cross about the mails.'

'Fuck the mails. The Spanish have been opening our post for decades and will go on opening it for as long as we remember how to write. The last Spaniard to leave this island will probably take one of our mailbags with him for reading on the journey.'

'But if it's not the post, what brings you here?'

It was the newcomer's turn to smile.

'I'm here to prevent a war, Mr Dale. To prevent a war and to catch a rat.'

It was a tour unlike any Dale had ever conducted. Over the years he had developed a system for entertaining visitors to the island, a simple route taking in the city's most famous tourist attractions alongside other, less obvious locations, the sort of places new arrivals would in time be glad to know about – one or two good restaurants, an adequate tailor, the English bookshop, the best cafés. Jepson tore up that plan and replaced it with his own, a street by street tramp along the city's gridlines intended to flesh with reality the bones of the map he carried in his head. And the questions he asked were startling too.

'If I was a Negro with ten dollars to my name, where would I go to drink?'

'If you wanted to bribe a Spanish post office official, where would you start?'

'If you were overseas, in Europe say, and you wanted to move a lot of money to someone in Havana without anyone noticing, how would you go about it?'

They ended the day at a bar on the waterfront, Jepson ordering the drinks in excellent Spanish. He seemed instantly at home and still full of energy, while Dale felt utterly weary. However, he could not deny that the view, facing out across the water, was a pleasant one. Out in the bay, a Spanish warship lay at anchor. Jepson appeared to be studying it.

'Tell me, Mr Dale, have you heard any rumours about an attack on one of our battleships?'

Dale pursed his lips. 'Only rumours of rumours. I'd heard that extra watches were being posted just in case. But the rumours can't be true, can they? The Spanish don't want to start a war.'

Jepson turned and looked at him.

'The Spanish government doesn't, that's for sure. But someone does, I'm convinced of it. My business is information, and all the information I have suggests that plans are being laid for a spectacular attack on one of our ships.' He looked away again. 'American firebrands, disaffected Cubans, fanatics, dreamers, maniacs of every kind. There are all sorts of people who might want to do it. But it's not them I'm worried about. You remember I mentioned a rat? That's why I'm here. I don't know who he is or who's behind him, but I know he's clever. And I know he's up to something. Something big and nasty. Something that isn't going to happen, because I'm going to catch him first, before any of our shipping feels his bite. Before his nasty little teeth start a war.'

IX

Leonarda was barely sixteen when she first saw Arturo Gustavo Rodriguez, seated at an indoor table in a café on the Calle Obispo. She had stolen his purse so deftly that he hadn't even seen it go. Perhaps it was surprise at the ease of her success that made her pause, for when she reached the doorway, when she was as good as safe, she turned, intrigued to see her victim's reaction when he realised his loss.

But even then the young gentleman did not look up. He was reading a book, and was so engrossed that he hadn't noticed a fat Havana horse-fly drowning itself noisily in the wine glass at his elbow. He had, she thought, a gentle face. His fingers, fanned across his cheek as he read, were long and pale and delicate. A peninsular Spaniard. She could tell by his dress. Besides, there was something about him as he sat there, an indefinable *softness*, that one did not encounter in the men of Havana. He was perhaps twenty five or thirty; at her age the two seemed much the same. She waited, watching, while those unsullied fingers left his cheek and hovered over the book, awaiting their moment to turn the page.

'Señor, I believe you dropped this.'

She hadn't intended to go back. She was never able to explain it, not even to herself.

He had looked startled at the sound of her voice, blinking slightly as he looked up. Even when he recognised the purse she held, it took him a moment or two to understand.

'You were lost in La Mancha, I think, señor.'

He looked down at the volume in front of him, then back at her.

'You can read?' he asked, astonished. 'You know Cervantes?'

'Of course, señor. Parts of it by heart.'

And it was true. Of the dozen books Hector owned, that was the one to which he most frequently returned. It was the volume from which she had learned to read. She had never met anyone in the whole of St Simeon who knew enough to read even one printed page, but she and Hector could. It was their special secret. Perhaps it was the book that had attracted her to Rodriguez.

The pale Spaniard took the purse and thanked her, then seemed to hesitate. Later she wondered what he must have been thinking in those first few moments as she stood there all dark eyes and dark hair, in bare feet and a dirty smock. She was already tall, already what in Havana passed for a woman. Innocence was a short-lived blossom in the backstreets of that city, and she was no stranger to men and their ways. She knew well enough the way they liked to watch her; she heard the comments they passed. But she had never before courted those looks deliberately as she did that day, standing by his table.

'Could I perhaps . . .? Perhaps some sort of reward?' He stammered slightly, unsure of what was expected of him.

She had already surprised herself, and now she went further. She was certain, were she to leave that place with a bow and a muttered goodbye, that she would never see him again.

'Have you many books with you here in Havana, señor?'

'Why, yes, a great many.' The question clearly puzzled him. 'In my rooms on the Calle Empedrado.'

'Perhaps, señor, if your chapter is nearly finished, you might show them to me?'

She had stayed with him that afternoon, that night, the following day. For eight months, she never really left. Afraid of Hector's reproaches, she told him almost nothing – not that she was leaving, nor where she was going, nor why. He would, she knew, gather for himself enough information to understand her situation, the choices she had made. She returned to St Simeon only to collect the one or two possessions she most treasured, and she timed her visits to coincide with his hours of work.

Only when the passage of time had confirmed the alteration in her circumstances did she feel able to see Hector again, and then he made it easy for her. No reproaches, no questions, no references to any difference between them. That first time they cooked together as they had always done, and he told her the news from St Simeon. When she left him, he had held her hand a fraction longer than was usual but that was all. He let her go as he had always done. And although nothing had been said, she left knowing that, should she need it, there was still a welcome for her in St Simeon.

But when the time came for her lover to return to Spain, she did not go back to her former home. Those last weeks in the Spaniard's rooms were painful in a way she had never before imagined. She had loved Rodriguez with a passion he scarcely deserved, one that had sunk its roots deep inside her. When apart from him, she longed for his touch, longed to be pressed against his pale nakedness. When near him, she longed to protect him from the world. Yet she had never been blind to his weaknesses. As his departure grew nearer, he would weep, would declare that he loved her, would promise to fabricate an excuse that would enable him to stay. Were he not married, he vowed, he would take her with him, would marry her in the church where for generations his family had been wed. He would die if they were to be parted. And she listened, dry-eyed, the pain sharp as briars, loving him regardless, knowing that not one word of it was true.

But if Rodriguez was selfish and sentimental, he was not ungenerous. He obtained for her the lease on a highly desirable apartment in the Calle Chacón, and provided her with all the clothes and linens and jewellery she could possibly need for life as another man's mistress. He spent far more than he could afford, yet she scarcely thanked him. By then a debilitating numbness had settled upon her. She watched, but barely even understood.

They said their farewells at a place near the waterfront out of sight of his ship. He wept again. She kissed him for a last time, hungrily, trying to recapture the dizzying sensations that had once almost overwhelmed her. But the numbness remained. She could not kiss it away. After that day she never heard from him again.

Still dazed by his departure, she allowed herself to be comforted by one of his friends, a dashing and amoral Catalan she had previously scarcely noticed. It was the one episode of her life she truly regretted. But by the time the numbness had begun to pass, the Catalan was also gone. By then the rooms in the Calle Chacón had become her home; her course was set. It was shortly after the Catalan's departure that Marty first noticed her.

X

There were no black faces at La Dominica. Not unless you counted the waiters, and James Dalrymple, clerk to the Mixed Commission, had no intention of doing that. This was the only hour of his week in which he was treated as an English gentleman should be treated; and an English gentleman never noticed his waiter. Besides, there was no need. The service was always flaw-less at La Dominica.

Not that Dalrymple had any great belief in the superiority of his race. He disliked and distrusted most of the Europeans on the island. The Spanish, he felt, were venal and dirty, the Americans aggressive and annoyingly naïve, and the English . . . He barely knew where to start on his fellow countrymen, but he blamed them for nearly all his slights and the majority of his hardships. He was painfully aware that on Cuba a white skin alone was not enough to preserve an unfortunate man from poverty; he was, he felt bitterly, more wretched and more wronged than any of the black men of his acquaintance, and a good deal poorer than many of them. Excepting the slaves, of course, but he didn't count them.

In the meantime, an ice at La Dominica on a hot afternoon was one of the few privileges of birth that remained to him. Only once a week, and paid for by someone else, yet it confirmed him as a gentleman, and filled him with a sort of wistful contentment, a sense of his true but neglected worth.

If there were no black faces around the marble-topped tables of La Dominica, nor were there any female ones, and this exclusion was one that pleased Dalrymple rather less. In Havana, white women did not venture out unless accompanied by a husband or a male relative; and even accompanied, they did not frequent cafés, not even ones as superior as La Dominica. It was a sensibility that Dalrymple found rather irritating.

His fellow lounger seemed less exercised by the subject. Lavender was a long-limbed, rather languorous individual in his late forties, marked out as an Englishman by his dress as well as by his speech. He had rooms above the English bookshop on the Calle Obispo, from where he ran some sort of shipping business.

'Really, my friend, you may see young ladies aplenty come dusk,' he pointed out when Dalrymple expressed his frustration.

'Oh, I know.' Dalrymple sounded peevish. 'Promenading in their carriages under the strictest guard. There's no getting near 'em. Thank God for their duskier sisters, that's what I say.' As he spoke he was wondering if Lavender might be persuaded to order brandies when the ices were finished. A brandy would not only be highly satisfactory in itself, but would also extend his precious time at La Dominica. 'Speaking of which, Lavender my friend, I witnessed something rather peculiar at the Opera House yesterday morning . . .'

The Teatro Tacón was an enormous building just outside the walls of the old city. During the season, operatic performances there were lavish and frequent.

'I was there to enquire about the next performance by Mariani,' Dalrymple lied glibly. In fact he had been there in pursuit of the slim-waisted daughter of one of the clerks who worked in the Box Office, an individual who had, Dalrymple felt almost sure, a suggestive gleam in her dark, downcast eyes.

'I was just coming away,' he continued, 'when I noticed a young woman in conversation with the manager. A rather attractive young woman, as it happens, and dressed like a lady, though brown as a boot-strap beneath all the finery. I had a vague feeling I'd seen her somewhere before, but I may be wrong . . .'

Lavender was finishing his ice. Dalrymple knew that his next action, if he were not distracted, would be to call for the bill.

'Anyway, old fellow,' he hurried on, 'it appears this young Venus had done something rather impertinent. She'd had the temerity to write to the management to reserve a box at the opera for next season. You know, one of the ones on the top tier, the ones reserved for unaccompanied ladies. I don't know what name she'd used, but apparently they'd accepted her application without anyone thinking to check the colour of her skin. Of course the manager was desperately trying to wriggle out of it, but it was what happened next that was surprising.'

He watched Lavender lay down his spoon. The hottest part of the day had passed, but Dalrymple knew that beyond La Dominica's elaborate doors the heat was still stifling. His craving for a brandy was growing with every moment. At La Dominica they poured the brandy in the cellar so that it arrived at the table still cool, with a light sheen of moisture misting the glass.

'I knew she was wasting her time, of course, and I was just wondering if I should go over and tell her not to waste her money too, by attempting a bribe, when I realised the whole exchange was being watched by old Marty himself. Must have come in off the street as I had. And I'll be damned if she didn't get her box after all. He just sauntered over, said a few words to the manager, bowed to the beauty as though the two were old friends, then turned on his heel and walked off. Astonishing, eh? I know Marty's one for the ladies, but mulatto girls in private boxes? It will cause an enormous scandal if it goes ahead.'

Dalrymple noticed with some satisfaction that his companion was sinking back in his chair with the air of someone in no hurry to leave.

'So Marty's back on the island, is he?' Lavender asked. The fact seemed to interest him. 'I'd heard he was over in Florida doing something for the Captain-General.'

'He's back all right,' Dalrymple confirmed, pleased at the way things were going. 'Is it true he's in the Captain-General's pocket then?'

Lavender shrugged. 'I should think Marty is his own man. You don't become as rich as he is through excessive loyalty to anyone.'

'The word on the street,' Dalrymple put in, 'is that Marty knows more about what goes on on this island than the Captain-General's secret police.'

'So they say.' Lavender's eyebrow twitched slightly. 'Now, James, how about a brandy to finish off?'

Dalrymple didn't much like Lavender, who asked too many questions and never got drunk. And he had dry, sore-looking lips that Dalrymple found rather repulsive. Dalrymple was certain that someone was paying Lavender to ask all those questions, but that neither surprised nor bothered him. In Havana, everyone was being paid by someone for something. But Dalrymple rather wished that the unknown individual who was ultimately funding his brandy had thought to approach him directly. After all, he knew a great deal more about Havana than Lavender, and a middleman was always bound to garble things.

Even so, he was prepared to enjoy his afternoons at La Dominica while they lasted. He would make sure that he held his cards close to his chest, that was all.

Lavender waited until the brandies had arrived, until Dalrymple had taken his first rapturous sip, before asking anything further.

'So, James, it's said the plantation owners are stockpiling guns out at St Isidoro. If the Americans invade, they plan to pull down the Spanish flag and try to claim the island for themselves. What have you heard?'

Dalrymple liked the way the question was framed. It allowed him to feel authoritative and well-connected, even though both men knew that Dalrymple's unique insights relied entirely upon the fact that he shared a bed with a black woman in a part of town generally unvisited by Europeans.

'There'll be no support from the blacks in Havana, if that's what you mean. They've no interest in any landowner rebellion.

They don't like the plantation owners, they don't like the Spanish, and those who know what goes on over the water dislike the Americans more than either. In fact, the slums here are the only part of Havana where being British might make you popular. Tell me, is it true that the private army gathered outside New Orleans is now ten thousand strong?'

Lavender shook his head.

'Rather fewer than that, from what I hear. But growing.' He smiled, then licked those dry lips of his. 'It would appear the Foreign Office is getting anxious.'

Mention of the Foreign Office reminded Dalrymple of another grievance. 'Look here, Lavender, I'm told they've finally appointed a new judge for the Mixed Commission. Someone from London. Already on his way. What do you know about it?'

Dalrymple, as assistant to the Mixed Commission, was an employee of the Foreign Office. Lavender had no official standing at all. Yet both men knew that Lavender's contacts were the better when it came to events back in Whitehall.

This time however he shook his head.

'I know very little, I'm afraid. It's not an appointment anyone expected. Rather a hurried decision, I understand. The consul is livid, as you can imagine.'

That thought seemed to mollify Dalrymple somewhat.

'Crawford? Yes, I suppose he must be. Been angling for the post for years, hasn't he?'

'And who can blame him, my friend? A very acceptable additional salary, and I don't imagine Mr Crawford would feel obliged to do very much for the money.' He smiled a dry, teasing smile. 'Meanwhile, it occurs to me that the arrival of a new judge at the Mixed Commission is likely to make life a little uncomfortable for you, James. Had you considered that? A new man from London is hardly likely to put his feet up straight away. He may expect you to do some work for your salary.'

The same thought had occurred to Dalrymple.

'Who is this man Backhouse, then?' he asked irritably, already disliking him. 'What do you know about him?'

'He's nobody, James. Nobody.' Lavender said it dispassionately, not as a judgement but as fact. 'And do you know what? I rather think that's the point.'

XI

For several days after the arrival on the island of Washington's latest special envoy, Henry Dale saw nothing of him. He had expected the newcomer to cause quite a stir, but instead Jepson simply disappeared. For a day or two, Dale heard rumours – that his new acquaintance had been seen in a very seedy tavern at the southern end of the old town, that an unknown American had been spotted up the coast, drinking in an obscure fishing village with the Spanish grandee who owned the place – but after that nothing was heard of him until he appeared at Dale's office one morning, immaculately clad and proposing a drive in the country.

The fact that Dale accepted the offer was testament to the impression the new envoy had made on him, and as they headed out of the city on the rough road that hugged the coast, Dale wondered how his visitor had managed to keep such a low profile. Havana was a busy city, but Jepson was clearly not the retiring type, and well-dressed Americans of his physique and physiognomy were undoubtedly a rarity.

Since their previous meeting Jepson had evidently acquired the use of a carriage, a modern and rather impressive two-wheeler which he drove with great confidence and no little skill. It struck Dale that he was also being rather more open than on their first acquaintance.

'The truth is, Mr Dale, I've brought you out here for a reason. First, I want to share a couple of things with you, and to do it somewhere where we won't be disturbed. Second, I have a small favour to ask you. Do you have access to a good safe, a proper American one?

If so, I was hoping to give you something to put in it for safekeeping.'

Dale confirmed that he did indeed have access to such a piece of equipment, and without really expecting an answer asked what Jepson wanted to keep in it.

'Money,' his companion replied without hesitation. 'Notes and coins. About four thousand dollars.'

Dale did his best not to register surprise.

'A not inconsiderable sum,' he observed.

'To cover expenses,' Jepson replied. 'Fresh in from Washington by special courier. No receipts required. Mine is a cash business, you understand. You can't bribe an official with a promissory note, not even in Havana.'

'And is that what you've been busy doing? Bribing officials?'

'Some of that.' The big man showed no trace of embarrassment. 'A bit of blackmail too. Trickier, but much more reliable in its outcome.' He gave the reins a carefree shake. 'Do I shock you, Mr Dale?'

'Utterly. I have lived a sheltered existence. But do go on.'

As the road edged away from the sea, Jepson talked quite freely. Dale listened and said very little. A lot of what he was hearing seemed as outrageous and as unlikely as the speaker himself.

'Let's be clear about one thing, Mr Dale. The Spanish opening our mail is the least of our worries. In fact, it interests me. I'd say the Spanish authorities may well be after the same thing as me.'

'And what is that?'

'They might be wondering about my rat.' He chuckled to himself at Dale's mystification.

'A spy, you mean?'

'More dangerous than that. Spies are mice. Simple creatures. Easy to catch. Predictable. A rat is a much more troublesome rodent. I wouldn't even know this one existed, except that wherever there's trouble I keep finding his droppings.'

They had branched away from the sea, and now they were putting on height. Jepson drove as though the road were already familiar to him.

'Let's talk about Cuba, Mr Dale. Nice place?'

'It has its points.'

'Oh, come on, my friend!' Jepson was smiling as if at a particularly amusing joke. 'It's a heap of shit, and you know it. The Spanish have spent three hundred years fouling it and now it's a dung heap. Too much greed, too many whores, too many sweaty, ignorant officials, and all of it wallowing in the froth of its own corruption. If the fever doesn't get you, the pox probably will. Our government would be much better off if the whole island sank into the sea.'

Dale was tempted to point out that this was quite a decided opinion to hold after little more than a week in a place, but his companion was rattling on.

'But unfortunately it does exist, and we can't ignore it. Cuba is a gun pointing straight at our heads. Luckily it's a gun in the hands of the Spaniards, who don't have any ammunition, and, even if they did, wouldn't know how to fire it. But imagine if the British got hold of it, Mr Dale!'

Jepson shook his head as if in horror.

'The British will happily stick a flag on any pile of shit, my friend – they don't care if it's still steaming. But *this* pile of shit would suit them particularly well. From here, a half-competent admiral – and the British do have one or two – could command the whole of the Gulf of Florida. Let the British in and we'd be conducting foreign affairs with a knife between our shoulder blades. We might as well start practising "God Save the Queen" right now so that we can all hum it nicely as we kiss the royal arse.'

Dale, who was beginning to get use to Jepson's language, was still a little mystified.

'So we're happier with the Spanish in Havana than the British. Fair enough. But if the next invasion works out, we won't have either, will we?'

63

They were pushing on through lush vegetation which in places erupted into lavish tangles of pink and purple flowers. Dale hadn't much liked Cuba himself at first, but with time its careless beauty, its lush, insistent fecundity, had seduced him. In the company of his countrymen, his feelings for the place could feel a little shameful.

'Please, Mr Dale! Don't talk to me about the invasion. There are idiots back home who talk about liberating Cuba from the yoke of imperial Spain. But the plantation owners here don't want to be liberated. They just want to be allowed to carry on eating and drinking and screwing their servants, and making a great deal of money without anyone interfering. And what do they need to do that? Slaves, Mr Dale. Slaves. That's what this is all about.'

Dale was not a political creature. He came from an old New England family and knew very little about slaves. If he had any opinion at all it was probably that slavery was an unfortunate economic necessity.

'Whatever anyone tells you, Mr Dale, the next invasion – if it happens – will not be about freedom for the Cubans, it will be about slavery for Africans. A lot of our countrymen are very eager to add a new slave state to the Union. It's a question of numbers. If we start adding new states in the west, states where there are no slaves, states that *oppose* slavery . . . Well, some people think that adding all those Cuban slave-owners to the Union would be a nice counter-balance.'

'So if the next invasion succeeds—'

'Oh, come *on*, Mr Dale,' Jepson interrupted. 'You think the British will allow that? Next time the boot of an American soldier sets foot on Cuban soil, Her Majesty's navy will start blasting the rest of the invasion army out of the water. They're Spain's allies, remember, and they like to think of the Caribbean as their own private boating lake.'

'War with Britain . . .' Dale mused. 'Would that really be so bad? We've beaten them before.'

'Not in this sort of war. This won't be about witless redcoats blundering around in forests. This will be a naval war, in and out of the islands. And any land fighting we do will be on foreign soil, surrounded by water we don't control, where the local people don't trust us and don't speak our language.'

Jepson shook the reins hard.

'This time we'd be the ones blundering around in the jungle, Mr Dale, while the British go behind the backs of the Spanish and start to mobilise the entire slave population against us. Imagine that! A slave army fighting for its freedom right on our doorstep. Where might that lead? No, sir, I'm telling you right now, I don't much fancy it.'

Ahead the path lay through trees, shady but airless. They had already lost sight of the sea.

'So you want to make sure there's no war. And all this stuff about battleships . . .?'

'Worries me, Mr Dale. That's why I've got to catch this rat of mine, before he sets the whole Caribbean ablaze.'

'And who is he working for exactly?' Dale asked, but Jepson only shrugged.

'Not clear. Not important. He wants to start a war, that's all I know for certain. Havana is his lair, but now he's causing a lot of trouble on our patch. Wherever there's pro-slavery against free soil. He's doing it by proxy, of course. Societies are springing up like weeds back home. Pro-slavery, anti-slavery, pro-annexation of the moon for all I know. Most of them are genuine enough, but others seem to exist purely to put money into the pockets of the worst firebrands and troublemakers. And when I investigate the worst of these so-called committees, what do I find? They're fake. And they're funded by money from over here.'

'From the Spanish?'

'Even in my wildest dreams I can't imagine the Spanish authorities being organised enough or clever enough to attempt anything of the sort. But *someone* is causing mischief. And if he blows up an American ship, we can expect things to get very nasty indeed.'

Dale raised an eyebrow.

'You really believe that's possible?'

'I've staked my reputation on it. On doubling the watches. I can't tell you how difficult to achieve that was. Some of our navy men need to have an enemy fart in their faces before they'll believe they're under attack.'

Jepson gave a little laugh. A rather hard little laugh, Dale thought.

'But I promise you one thing, Mr Dale. When I've worked out who my rat is, I'm going to make damned sure he never troubles us again.'

XII

Dusk in Havana wore many different faces. It was the hour when the city shrugged off its work-a-day clothes and pulled on its finery, when people of every colour and class quit the suburbs and the shanties and converged on the heart of the city. It was an hour to drink or to dance, to seek love or oblivion. An hour to prey upon your fellows.

In the Paseo de Isabel II, dusk brought with it the strictly regulated parade of carriages, with the young ladies of Havana's first families perched prominently on display for the inspection of their suitors. On the Cortina de Valdés, the meeting place of those respectable citizens who could not afford to keep a carriage, the broad avenue became bright with the colours of the swirling crowds, all gathered to promenade on foot where the grand buildings and the pavement cafés looked out over the sweep of the bay.

Even at the other end of the waterfront, near the wharves and the warehouses, dusk touched the grubby drinking houses with a fleeting shard of magic. Lamps peeped out from every tavern and lodging house, and the streets began to fill with music so that, viewed from across the water in the thickening light, the dockside beckoned to the unwary with soft hands and a sweet voice. There, behind those shimmering lights, the city promised every illicit pleasure.

But dusk fades quickly in the tropics, and by nightfall the neat boundaries of convention had begun to dissolve. In the Plaza de Armas a band played and *habaneros* of very different classes rubbed shoulders. When the white señoritas had been safely returned to their homes, their immaculate suitors were free to pursue different quarry. A gentleman might marry late in life; he could not be expected to delay his pleasures for ever.

And in the busy streets around the main square there were many who came to seek out those same young men; not least the pretty flower girls who appeared only in the evenings and who sold few flowers.

Three days after Leonarda's visit to the house in St Simeon, a well-dressed man of around sixty, corpulent but undoubtedly well-groomed, was accosted by one such young woman near the edge of the plaza, just as the clocks were striking eleven. She had chosen him because she liked his face. He had a benign look, she thought, and was not too young, the sort who demanded little, finished quickly and tipped well. Not until he turned her down – firmly, but not unkindly – did she recognise him. If she felt any pang of disappointment as she turned away, she did not show it. Such big fish were not for her. She had heard that this particular gentleman was not averse to paying for his pleasures, but his money would be spent in the elegant apartments of the Calle Chacón where the services offered were more elaborate and took place – if rumour were to be believed – upon sheets of real silk.

As it happened, Francisco Marty y Torrens was indeed heading towards the Calle Chacón but he did not make his way there directly. Instead he strolled away from the plaza towards the old city walls, where the streets, though still busy, allowed more comfortable progress. When he could – and his many business interests allowed him too little time – he liked to meander through the old city at his leisure. As he walked he took in the details around him: a business closed here or re-opened there, lights burning late above shuttered shops, the positions of the posters that advertised his theatre and his operas. Small things mattered, he knew; perhaps they mattered more than anything else.

When he finally arrived at his destination, the porter by the front door was new, but everything else was pleasingly familiar: the stairs hung in red paper, the boards hollowed slightly by years of footfalls, the low-burning lamp above. The effect of all this familiarity took him a little by surprise, and as he climbed the staircase he felt rather moved. Three or four years had passed since he had last come that way and his life had moved on, his arrangements had altered. It surprised him to feel those old stirrings.

The door he sought was at the top of the house – a broad, double doorway, grander than the rest, for in these old buildings the best apartments were frequently higher up, where the air was fresher and there was the faint possibility of a breeze off the sea. He paused for a moment to recover from the stairs, but before he had even knocked the door was opened to him by a female servant, and he was met by the drowsy scent of lilies. He'd forgotten the lilies, forgotten that sense of falling . . .

'Hello, Marty.' The room into which he was ushered was familiar too, but as Leonarda rose from her day-bed to greet him, he was struck by how different she looked. She wore a simple gown in a delicate shade of blue which cleverly set off the colour of her skin and drew attention to the line of her neck, to the curve of her breasts above her corsage. It was, he knew, cut in the very latest fashion and its effect was dramatic, but it was not the dress of a courtesan. Any rich young *habanera* would have been proud to step out in it, though none, he suspected, could have worn it quite so well. And where they would have over-elaborated with pearls or amethysts, here there was nothing but a crescent moon in silver on a simple silver chain.

'Leonarda . . .'

The maid had withdrawn and they were alone. Marty watched her move to the cheap decanters that stood, just as they always had, in one corner of the room. She was smiling as she did so, as if something in the familiarity of the ritual amused her. That dress and those decanters, Marty thought, should surely have belonged in different worlds.

He took a small piece of paper from his pocket. Her letter to the theatre.

'My apologies. I believe I am in fact addressing *Mrs Leonarda Leigh*.'

She smiled again and handed him his drink.

'Do sit down, Marty. You're looking very distinguished. Are the fish selling well?'

It was the old jibe, but one that few dared deliver to his face. Among his many lucrative interests was the monopoly on Havana's fish market, and the island's finest families – finding themselves neither as rich nor as powerful as Marty – would refer to him among themselves as *the fishmonger*.

On this occasion, he simply laughed.

'The fish are always selling well. They are the only one of God's creatures that never disappoints.'

He seated himself in the chair she indicated, and watched as she moved back to the tray to mix a drink for herself. Her movements were languid, calming.

'So you married that fool, did you? Am I allowed to enquire where you left him?'

'In Jamaica.' She spoke without looking up.

'And what did he have to say about that? Did he beg you to stay? Or was he too drunk to notice?'

'He's dead, Marty.' She looked at him. 'I'm a widow.'

She stated it simply, but there was something in her tone that made him bite back any frivolous reply.

'Forgive me. I was indelicate. Are commiserations required?'

'Are they being offered?'

'Of course.' Marty remembered the Englishman as a drunkard who had drifted to Havana from Jamaica for the usual reasons – because in Havana an Englishman was free to behave in any bestial fashion he wished, with none of his stern, joyless country-men on hand to condemn him. Marty had known many such men. But by marrying Leonarda this one had defied his expecta-tions. 'Was it sudden?'

'He knew he was dying, if that's what you mean. When I married him, he already knew. That's partly why he came to Havana. To drown the fear, I think. But he found the courage to go back. I don't expect you to believe this, but he died with great dignity.'

Marty raised an eyebrow, remembering the tearful, shambolic creature who had haunted the taverns and whorehouses of Havana.

'And the cause of this transformation?'

But Leonarda had turned her back and was measuring brandy carefully into a glass.

'He was a good man. A better man than you know.'

'And a rich one.' Marty blinked as a thought struck him. 'My God, he *was* rich, wasn't he? That estate in Jamaica. You're not telling me . . .? No. Surely it isn't possible that under English law all those plantations and the like passed to his widow?'

She arranged herself carefully on the chaise longue beneath the window, her legs folded neatly, discreetly beneath her. It was a position he recognised: Leonarda at ease. Hers had always been a serene, unhurried beauty.

'His will was very clear, Marty. There were no objections, no other family. And he wanted me to have everything. That's why he married me.'

'But that would mean . . .' Marty's brain was racing, doing the sums. 'That would be a very substantial annual income. It would make you a very wealthy woman. You got it *all*?'

'He had no one else.' She watched him for a moment. 'Does it shock you, Marty? All that wealth in the hands of someone with skin the colour of mine?'

But Marty brushed away the question with contempt.

'Ah, Leonarda, you know me better than that. Spanish, Negro, mulatto, Chinese – they're all the same to me. I would cheat all of them equally, without prejudice, if there was a profit in it for me.'

And Leonarda knew that was true. Marty was many things – a cheat, a rogue, a philanderer – and she knew that beneath his bluff charm lay a relentless, calculating ruthlessness. But in a city where different creeds and castes and races jostled so closely against one another, Marty had never shown any respect for the strict boundaries drawn by others. Marty divided the world into his own categories: the helpful, the dangerous, the desirable.

'No, my dear,' he went on, 'what shocks me is not that you should inherit. It is the thought that someone other than myself should pull off such a sensational coup. May I offer my heartiest congratulations?'

But she merely shook her head as if in disappointment, and Marty, who had few regrets, wished he had been more tactful.

'So, my dear, may I ask how your affairs currently stand? Are Leigh's estates actually in your hands, or are there still formalities to be finalised?'

'No further formalities, Marty. It really is all mine.'

'It is just that . . .' Marty paused. 'Well, if you will forgive my coarseness, one wouldn't usually expect to find a well-to-do English widow living in the rooms of a courtesan on the Calle Chacón.'

If he had hoped to provoke a reaction, he was disappointed. Leonarda merely shrugged.

'I don't suppose a visitor to the island would expect to find the richest man in Havana living above his own fish market. But it happens.' She paused to allow him to acknowledge the hit. 'We all have a place we call home, Marty. Would you have had me stay on in Jamaica in a plantation house with twenty bedrooms?'

'Then you have sold Leigh's properties? For a good price, I hope?'

'On the contrary. There is a lawyer there who manages them on my behalf. He is what the English call a reformer. He endeavours to run the estate as a model of fair practice.'

Marty sighed and shook his head.

'Then he will certainly bankrupt you.'

'Perhaps.' Leonarda still lounged calmly, her empty glass balanced between her fingertips. 'But not quickly. And with the best of intentions. In the meantime there are matters here that I wish to settle.'

'Indeed?' Marty had finished his own drink and rose to make himself another. Leonarda noticed that this time – for the first time – he also prepared a glass for her. 'If I can be of any assistance, my dear . . .'

'I think you can. First there is Rosa.'

He looked at her blankly so she went on.

'Rosa, my servant. She is a slave. Your slave, as it happens.'

'Really? One of mine?' Marty showed no great surprise. 'I hadn't realised. You will appreciate that I do not oversee these matters personally.'

'I want her freed.'

'Consider her yours. A homecoming gift. Then you may do with her as you wish. I will have my man draw up the necessary documents.' A thought struck him and he smiled. 'Although, if she was with you in Jamaica, she was free already. English soil and all that. By dragging her back you are guilty of enslaving her again. There are laws against that, you know.'

Again, if he hoped to provoke her, she refused to rise to his bait. She knew that fish were only one of Marty's sources of income, and not even the most lucrative. Cuba's coastline was a long one, and everyone in Havana knew that the British navy which patrolled its waters looking for slave ships intercepted only a fraction of the total.

'Did you say there was another matter with which I might help you, my dear?'

He realised that he very much wanted her to say yes. Marty had always enjoyed his evenings with Leonarda, and not for the obvious reasons. Sexual gratification was surprisingly unimportant to him. If anything, he found that more often than not it rather bored him; it had become a ritual he performed out of belief in its necessity rather than from any great expectation of personal delight.

But on meeting Leonarda he found someone who intrigued him. She saw beyond the obvious and, perhaps alone among all his Havana acquaintances, she did not appear afraid of him. She was certainly never afraid to puncture him if he became too pompous. And she would do it dispassionately – with neither cruelty nor affection – as though to her he was simply an interesting object of observation.

She was not even particularly impressed by his wealth. He had kept mistresses before and it had always been a simple business arrangement. With Leonarda things were less clear. He had been forced to court her for a great many weeks before she had yielded to his entreaties, and then she did so only occasionally, as one who gives way out of curiosity, despite herself. Marty liked to be generous, but she resolutely refused his generosity, although he knew she spent her mornings repairing clothes and mending sheets. As a result, when he sent up his card he was never quite certain whether or not he would be given permission to follow it up the stairs.

Now he hoped very much that she would ask some service of him for which she would feel obliged to give him thanks.

But her question was not a demanding one.

'What do you know of the people at the British consulate?' she asked.

'Ah, the English . . .' Marty shook his head sadly, as if reluctant to begin on a subject so mystifying. 'I do not mix with them.'

'I don't want you to ask them to dine, Marty. Just tell me what you know. And don't pretend you don't make it your business to know at least a little.'

The hint of flattery worked, as she had known it would.

'Well, of course, I do make it my business to know a little of everything. So let me see. There's the consul, Crawford. Does well for himself out here. Not stupid. To use an English phrase, he plays a clever game. His staff are local people, but there's a private secretary who works for him from time to time. I can't remember his name. And there's a man called Dalrymple, a very low sort who consorts with Negroes and borrows money from them.'

Leonarda waited, as if allowing the names to sink in.

'And are they honest?' she asked.

'Ah! The English are always honest. Even when they rob you, they do it with such utter decency that it is a pleasure to be robbed. Tell me, my beautiful one, what do you wish to know? I will make it my mission to find out. Some matter relating to your late husband's affairs?'

'Something like that.'

A lie, but Leonarda was still not quite sure of herself. Marty's assistance would undoubtedly be useful, but it needed to be employed with caution.

Sensing that she was not yet ready to elaborate, Marty rose and moved to the window. Opening one of the shutters a little, he peered out. The lamps of the city touched the night sky with a glow that paled the stars.

'So it is your intention to stay in Havana? I can honestly say that I am delighted. It would give me great pleasure to be allowed to call from time to time. I understand, of course, that your new circumstances change a great deal, but I trust we can continue our friendship on a different footing.'

'Of course, Marty.' She was watching him closely but when his eyes met hers he could see in them nothing but the lamplight.

'Excellent. It is said nostalgia for former pleasures can prove a powerful force. Needless to say, were you ever to feel so inclined . . .'

Was that a smile on her lips? Or was that too simply a trick of the light?

He clicked his heels.

'You can, of course, find me in all the usual places, my dear. And it will always be my pleasure to attend you here should you wish it.'

Through the open shutter, she watched him go: a portly figure of no particular distinction. And she remembered the piece of wisdom repeated by the divers from the oyster beds: that it was not always the fiercest-looking fish that took off your hand.

XIII

It was not until some weeks later that Thomas Staveley next called on John Jerusalems in Lowther Street. It was not unusual for the little man to disappear from view from time to time, and Staveley had heard a rumour he'd been spotted on the Continent. It was not one he was inclined to dismiss. Discreet enquiries many years previously had suggested that Jerusalems' family could be traced back to crusading times, and yet there was nothing of the typical Englishman about John Jerusalems, and from the books in his library Staveley had deduced that he spoke – or at least read – a startling range of languages. He could as easily imagine Jerusalems at home in Rome or Vienna or Constantinople as in a grey and wintry London.

Staveley was again received in the anarchic drawing room at the front of the house but this time his was a morning visit – it was not yet nine o'clock – and the room felt different. It was no less cluttered than previously, and as before dirty cups littered the table, but with pale light filtering between half-opened shutters it felt somehow less vital than before, as though the hand of the weary London dawn had touched it with fatigue. Jerusalems stood, unshaven, still clad in the remains of evening dress, near the blazing fire, a pile of that morning's newspapers at his feet. Staveley had sometimes wondered when and for how long Jerusalems slept; he suspected the little man rarely retired before sunrise.

'Thomas, Thomas.' He looked up, apparently unsurprised, as though it were commonplace for Staveley to call on him at precisely that hour. 'Nothing at all in the newspapers about anything that matters, which is how I like it. The usual misinformation about the Russian situation, of course. The movement of

Hapsburg troops in the Balkans is mentioned here and there but is universally described as *manoeuvres*. Tchah! There is nothing even remotely manoeuvrable about the Hapsburg army. Once any part of it is in motion, it defies the ability of mankind to alter its course. Fortunately, however, its own inertia will always bring it to a halt before any actual damage is done.'

But Staveley had not called to discuss the shortcomings of the newspapers, nor of the Hapsburg army, however diverting Jerusalems' views might be.

'I have some news from my friend in the Spanish embassy,' he began. 'About the situation in the Caribbean. He says his government is getting very jumpy. They think this business of the Americans putting extra guards on their boats is some sort of provocation. There's a war party at court apparently, which is calling for some sort of response.'

'A war party at the Spanish court? Well, well.' The little man had taken up a newspaper and appeared to be scanning its columns with great interest. 'I suppose they want to re-conquer Peru too. The idiocy of some people never ceases to amaze me.'

'It's not really something to laugh about.' Staveley was aware how pompous he sounded. 'There are orders going out to the Spanish navy to be on a heightened state of alert. One view is that the whole thing is a plot by the Americans, that they're blaming the Spanish in advance. That way, if the unofficial invasion force runs into any trouble, they'll scuttle some minor vessel of their own and use it as an excuse to declare war on Spain.'

'How fiendishly Machiavellian of them.' Jerusalems discarded his newspaper casually on to a pile by the grate, took up another one in its place, then peered over the top of it at his visitor. 'In that case, those who want peace to prevail in the Caribbean had better pray that no American ship gets sunk. Do you think such an event likely?'

'Surely not. Neither side wants a war. It would be disastrous for them both – and for us too, of course. But the *threat* of war might be all it takes.'

Jerusalems peered down at his pile of discarded newspapers, fanning them out with his foot as if better to find one he wanted to retrieve. He appeared completely unconcerned about the growing tensions over Cuba.

'The Spanish don't want a war. The Americans don't want a war. Our government doesn't want a war. Such an appetite for peace! It would seem there's nothing to worry about, wouldn't it, Thomas? Now, tell me, have you breakfasted?'

Although curious to discover what breakfast at the house in Lowther Street might consist of, Staveley made his excuses. He had another appointment, and besides he was a little disappointed in Jerusalems. Having been lectured by him previously on the crucial strategic importance of Cuba, he'd expected the little man to appreciate the latest information from the Spanish court and to be brimming over with plans and schemes for how to exploit the situation. Instead Jerusalems had seemed oddly accepting of things, almost as if the precariousness of the peace was not something that concerned him. He had never known his friend so passive.

Even so, Staveley left with the feeling, not uncommon after his visits, that none of the news he'd come to impart had been entirely new to its recipient.

XIV

Mother Alençon's place was little more than a fisherman's shack on the edge of the bay, some two or three miles south of the old city. In those days, before the growth of Havana swamped it, the setting still retained some of its rural charm, and the men who drank there, most of them from the very poor fringes of the city, were able to imagine themselves in a cleaner, better place – even if the smoke of burning rubbish from St Simeon would sometimes drift across and fleck the water's edge with soot.

With the exception of the proprietor, it was not a place for women, but Leonarda went anyway, in search of Moses Le Castre.

Moses had been one of Hector's oldest friends, and Leonarda had known him from childhood, a slightly irresponsible, unpredictable figure who was rarely employed on a regular basis, preferring instead to pick up shifts from other night-watchmen when they needed someone to stand in for them. Often he would drop out of sight for weeks at a time in pursuit of some scheme or other by which he hoped to make his fortune. Hector had recognised Moses' flaws but took pleasure in his company regardless of them. Moses was to be enjoyed rather than admired.

Leonarda had expected her old friend to seek her out on her return to the island, if only to offer his condolences. It surprised her that, so many weeks after her return, she had still heard nothing from him; but her meeting with Marguerite suggested an explanation for his reticence. Moses had known how dear Hector's books were to her, and if he had been involved in their sale it was possible he felt awkward about seeing her again.

Moses could be jovial, funny, sly even, but courage was not his strong suit.

Mother Alençon's place could be approached by carriage, along one of the many tracks that ran near the shore of the bay, but the last forty yards or so across the sand had to be completed on foot. It was mid-morning, and the heat was already blurring the coastline. As Leonarda approached, she was aware of the silence that gathered by the water. No hawkers, no shouting, none of the city's restless drawl; only birdsong and crickets, and nearer the shack itself the ragged buzzing of flies. She knew before she pushed open the door that Moses wasn't there.

But the elderly man behind the counter knew him well enough. Mostly, he told her, Moses spent his mornings running errands for some white man. But he would surely be there before eleven. He always was.

Leonarda decided to wait in her carriage. Pulled into the shade of the trees with its hood up, it was a great deal cooler than the shack by the water.

He came, as predicted, a little before eleven o'clock. Whistling to himself, he didn't notice her carriage until she called his name and then he turned sharply, instantly on edge, startled by her voice amid the silence.

She had imagined their meeting would be a cordial one, affectionate even, and she was taken aback by the extent of his suspicion. It was with great reluctance that he even agreed to join her in the carriage, and as he did so he was looking down, mumbling excuses for not having called upon her previously. He had been busy, he said, he had been away in the east of the island for a time. And she was grown so grand now he had been afraid to seek her out.

'The books, Moses.' Her attempts at pleasantries having been blocked by monosyllables, she hoped that a clear, simple reason for her visit might put him at his ease. 'Marguerite says you sold Hector's books for her. If I could, I'd like to buy them back.'

Again he mumbled something. He was a man of slight build who had always seemed to her rather youthful. But he had altered since she'd seen him last, and she was taken aback by the extent of his grey hair, by the way his movement as he climbed into the carriage was no longer supple. Try as she might, she could not get him to meet her eye.

'I'm not angry about the books, Moses,' she persisted. 'They were Marguerite's to sell, and you couldn't have known I was coming back. But if I knew where they'd gone, I'd try to find them. Do you think you can help me?'

The question appeared to reassure him a little.

'Well, I suppose . . .' He was looking down at his fingers. 'A man on the Calle Luz took them all. He gave me almost nothing.'

The Calle Luz was not the most obvious place to sell old books. Moses, it seemed, had been too intimidated to approach the regular booksellers on the Calle Obispo, with their dignified shopfronts and their displays of leather bindings. Instead he had gone to a less reputable individual, the sort of man who offered loans against valuables and who dealt in anything, however shabby, from which a profit might be extracted.

Nevertheless, the news cheered Leonarda. A specialist bookseller would certainly have priced each book individually. They might be all over the island by now. The man on the Calle Luz on the other hand was more likely to have kept them together, to be sold as a lot to the first person who expressed an interest. And if they were still together, there was hope.

But she had not finished with Moses.

'Now tell me about Hector.' She knew he didn't want to. She could feel him drawing away. 'You haven't even mentioned him. Marguerite says you saw him in the days before he died.'

Moses nodded and looked down at his fingers.

'He was himself, you know.' His voice was thin, even a little shrill. 'Nothing different. Nothing unusual. Still reading.' It was said with something approaching a sneer. 'Unlucky, that's all. It's something that happens. Hector knew that. Someone sees a loose window and takes a chance. I guess it was just Hector's turn.'

But Leonarda shook her head.

'I don't think so,' she told him. 'I don't think there was any loose window. I don't think there was even a break-in. I think Hector must have opened the door for the men who killed him.'

Moses rolled his eyes, but whether in irritation or disbelief she couldn't be sure.

'That's foolish talk. It makes no sense. No, you take it from me, he was killed by those men, the ones they arrested. They were known killers. Always ready with a knife.'

'You knew them?' Leonarda looked at him steadily. 'I want to speak to them, Moses. Can you help me find them?'

But Moses smiled at the idea. 'I didn't know them. And they are not the sort of men you'd want to find.' He rose from his seat and lowered himself from the carriage. 'You take it from me.'

She leaned forward, closer to where he was standing.

'But you know where they are?' she persisted.

'Girl, I don't even remember their names.' He shrugged and began to turn away.

'Oh, I know their names,' she replied. 'And I already have an idea where to look.'

But his back was turned to her, and as he walked away he did not look back.

'The Anchor, Moses,' she called after him. 'That's where I'll start.'

But he didn't react, just carried on walking, muttering to himself, shaking his head.

She watched him as far as Mother Alençon's shack. His refusal to help, his refusal even to listen, had made her angry. She'd hoped for better from him. But the morning had not been entirely wasted. Putting her feelings about Moses to one side, she asked to be driven directly to the Calle Luz, to the shop where Hector's books had last been seen.

It was not an easy journey, back into the old town at an hour when the streets were still thronged with traders and hawkers and hurried shoppers, all impatient to be home before the afternoon heat pressed itself upon the streets. But the place she was looking for did not prove hard to find, and it appeared to be open. From the outside it looked ordinary enough – not smart, but not particularly disreputable either, with a single sign above the door declaring boldly 'La Probidad'. Inside it proved dark and rather poky, and hotter than the street. Behind a bare wooden counter, lines of shelves displayed a bewildering miscellany of goods, none of them new or even very clean. Still unsorted on the counter lay a broken ink-stand, a box of collar studs and some roughly folded shirts. Behind them, a glass cabinet contained cheap jewellery.

The only person on duty there was a young boy, dark-skinned and rather beautiful, conspicuously out of place in his surroundings. When asked about books he looked first alarmed and then perplexed, as though her request were something utterly beyond his experience.

But when Leonarda explained carefully that the books she was looking for had been brought in some years before, all of them together in one box, and that she hoped his employer might recall their purchase, a glimmer of comprehension appeared in the boy's face. Yes, there *was* a box, he thought. He had seen it somewhere once, perhaps in one of the attics. If it had been sold since then he would surely have heard of it. Such a transaction would have been a surprising event. If the señorita would return another day, Señor Melendez would know where to find it. Señor Melendez could lay his hands on anything in only an instant. Tomorrow? Alas, no. Señor Melendez was away. Perhaps for a week, perhaps longer. If the señorita would try again later in the month . . .

Leonarda had to be content with that tantalising promise. But she left the shop in high spirits. In such a place, books were not a frequently traded commodity. It was not impossible that a collection acquired for a pittance might have lingered somewhere, ignored and out of sight, for all this time.

Yet by nightfall, her elation had been replaced by a stubborn melancholy that she found impossible to shift. She and Moses Le Castre had been friends. Theirs had been a jocular, irreverent friendship, it was true, but real nonetheless. Yet that morning he had avoided her gaze so stubbornly, had been so anxious to be away, it was as if she had become a stranger to him. Worse than a stranger. Someone he deeply mistrusted.

It was, in its own small way, another bereavement.

On the evening of that same day, not far from the Calle Luz, the Englishman Lavender was sitting up late, reading a letter from London. The letter was from Henry Addington, permanent under-secretary at the Foreign Office, and it was addressed in a private capacity to Joseph Crawford, the British consul in Havana. Lavender's version was not the original but a copy, and not an official copy either. Neither sender nor receiver would have been aware of its existence. The version intended for Crawford, having been dispatched through official channels, had almost certainly not yet arrived in Havana, and that thought made Lavender smile.

'So, old Addington thinks there's something up, does he?'

He scanned the letter again.

> *Evidence of a plot against American shipping ... An individual or small group plotting to destabilise the international situation ... Imperative that any such individual be identified and made known to the Spanish authorities at once ... Appreciate if the consul would consult widely and communicate his findings, unofficially, directly to the office of the Captain-General in Havana ...*

Also interesting to Lavender, although a little less so, was mention of the new judge to the Mixed Commission. In a postscript, Addington's tone was apologetic.

A political appointment ... Rather forced upon us by advisers ...A very average sort of candidate, unlikely to upset the status quo ...

As he held the letter to the flame of his candle, Lavender smiled.

XV

The Backhouse family arrived in Havana in excellent spirits. The crossing had been calm and the sea journey had suited them. Grace in particular had flourished, enjoying the courtesies extended to her as the wife of an important official by the *Medea*'s officers and captain.

But without the sea breezes that had sustained them for the latter part of their journey, the heat of Havana Bay proved almost impossible to bear. Unprepared and inappropriately dressed, they were made to wait for over an hour, swinging at anchor in full sun, while the Spanish health authorities performed their leisurely rituals.

Then, when the inspection was complete and they were finally allowed ashore, they were confined for a further two hours in the appalling airlessness of the Customs House while searches were made and papers were checked. Throughout it all, Alice – still only nine months old – whimpered and fretted, and Grace, whose spirits had been so high at sea, grew silent and anxious.

Few Englishmen who spent an extended period of time in Havana returned unchanged by the experience. Later it seemed to Backhouse that for him the change began that very day, there in the airless purgatory of the Customs House. He had expected his diplomatic status to smooth their path. By the end of that day he knew it had made things worse. Official after official smiled and bowed and showed exemplary respect, but spoke only Spanish and seemed delighted to contribute to the delay. When, during the customs inspection, the glass on his portrait of Queen Victoria was broken in two, it felt to Backhouse less like clumsiness, more like an act of deliberate and calculated defiance. He recognised that he was being toyed with, and his cheeks flushed with anger.

It was six o'clock and already growing dark when they were finally given permission to leave the Customs House. Backhouse had intended to report to Mr Crawford, the British consul, directly on arrival; but, misinformed that the consul's residence was a great distance from the old town, and unnerved by the gathering darkness, he decided a wiser course was to seek out a good hotel, somewhere respectable but not too far from the docks.

'A chance to wash and get something to eat,' he explained to Grace. 'I'm told that Miss Gilbert's house is the place to go.'

But things did not get better. Seen for the first time with the light fading, Havana struck them as a strange and frightening city. The streets teemed with people who jostled their carriage and called to them in voices they didn't understand. There was noise, and a cacophony of music, and there were black faces everywhere, more in one glance than Backhouse had seen in his whole previous existence. On the docks some of the slaves employed to move their belongings had worked stripped to the waist, unashamed of their nakedness, their torsos glistening with sweat. The sight was doubly troubling to Backhouse. He was acutely aware that Grace, for all that she averted her gaze, could not help but witness it; and he felt far from comfortable, given his position, that he should be benefiting so soon and so visibly from the assistance of slave labour.

And above everything, worse than the noise and the crowds and the stench of the streets, was the heat. Even after dark it did not relent. Backhouse could feel himself perspiring freely, and was uncomfortably aware that the fabric of his shirt adhered to his back. When Grace, still unusually quiet, seated herself very close to him in the carriage, the heat of his thigh against hers, unmistakable despite so many layers of fabric, embarrassed him. The baby, held tightly to her body, seemed to have fallen into an exhausted sleep.

Things got no better at the conclusion of their journey. No sooner had the wheels stopped turning than the driver changed his price, demanding twenty times the sum Backhouse thought they had agreed. An argument ensued, fruitless and exhausting and conducted mainly in gestures, until Miss Gilbert herself emerged to settle the matter in Backhouse's favour. But their brief sense of relief dissipated almost instantly upon viewing their rooms, which were airless and shabby, the paint flaking and the bedding grey.

Even with the windows open, a good night's sleep proved impossible. The noise from the streets gave no sign of abating as the hour advanced, and their little room seemed to grow hotter. Not having been provided with nets against insects, and not thinking to ask for them, they were tormented by mosquitoes throughout the night and when the morning light allowed them to inspect the damage, they found little Alice's face and arms disfigured by countless angry red bites. When Backhouse looked across at Grace in that pale light, he saw an expression on her face he had never seen before. Later he wondered if, on that very first morning, he had witnessed the first small step of a slow and inexorable retreat.

At the time, however, Backhouse felt confident that all their difficulties would quickly be resolved. After all, he assured Grace, some degree of confusion and discomfort was inevitable in such a posting, but with the assistance of the consul and his people, they would quickly find their feet. Backhouse had written to Crawford from London, requesting that some suitable accommodation might be found for them in advance of their arrival, and never had the need for a roof of his own seemed more pressing than it did that morning at Miss Gilbert's hotel. As soon as he was dressed, he set out in search of the consul, leaving Grace busy at the dressing table, writing all the necessary letters to tell of their safe arrival.

But his interview with Crawford proved disappointing. Backhouse had expected to be welcomed cordially. Instead he found in the consul's demeanour only a rather pained impatience, as if the arrival of the new appointee was both troublesome and unnecessary.

Joseph Crawford was a man of late middle years, balding and troubled by perspiration so that every minute or so, regardless of the state of his brow, he would mop at his pate with a pale blue silk handkerchief. But his other movements were careful and unhurried, and beneath the fluttering handkerchief his gaze was steady. No fool, Backhouse quickly realised, and apparently no great friend either. Backhouse had been told in London that Crawford's business interests in the region were extensive; he also knew that, prior to his own appointment, the consul had been filling the role of judge to the Mixed Commission on a temporary basis. Back at home, Backhouse had imagined this an imposition on a busy man: surely such an important post would weigh heavily alongside his consular duties and the demands of his commercial affairs?

But here, with Crawford lounging back in his chair, studying him so carefully, Backhouse understood that another interpretation was possible. Perhaps there was a type of individual who would see the temporary post as a welcome sinecure, a generous additional salary in return for duties that could perhaps be skimped or skipped or deputed to others. That would certainly explain the coolness of his welcome.

Not that Crawford was anything but impeccable in his manners. Backhouse and his wife must come to dinner. It would be delightful to get to know them better. Over dinner he would explain a few of the diplomatic complexities that Backhouse would encounter. It was important that consul and judge were pulling in the same direction . . .

But there was no great warmth beneath the words, rather traces of a carefully worded condescension intended to convey to Backhouse his relative insignificance. And there was no talk of accommodation. Crawford seemed surprised and a little pained when Backhouse raised the subject. A letter? Arrangements on Backhouse's behalf? He could only offer apologies. A misunderstanding, clearly. But there were many agents on the island who could assist Backhouse in his search, and some hotels marginally superior to Miss Gilbert's where the family could stay in the meantime. He would ask his son to store the Backhouses' baggage until permanent arrangements were made, and if he could offer any other assistance then Backhouse had only to ask . . .

Backhouse returned to Miss Gilbert's hotel that morning aware that the object he'd set out to grasp had somehow slipped between his fingers. It was a feeling that was to become more familiar the longer he remained in Havana.

Later, when he understood the ways of the island a little better, it seemed remarkable to Backhouse how heavily he had relied upon James Dalrymple in those very early days.

First impressions had not been favourable. Dalrymple had called at Miss Gilbert's while Backhouse was still with the consul. Grace had been a little shocked by the encounter. The thin-faced Englishman who purported to be Backhouse's new assistant had seemed to her unkempt in his dress and over-familiar in his manners. It was inconceivable that any such individual could have been employed by the Foreign Office back in London, where the highest standards of dress and manners were expected. Her husband, she knew, was punctilious about such things, and Grace more so. A person of Dalrymple's stamp, she felt certain, was unlikely to remain in her husband's service for very long.

And yet, that day and that week, he proved their saviour. Hotels? Accommodation? A doctor for Alice? All these things were easy, he could arrange them in an instant. He knew the island better than anyone, he assured Backhouse, and they could leave all such matters to him. A good tailor, a respectable dressmaker, insect nets, a pleasant place for ices, a good restaurant, honest carriage hire, a reputable laundry . . .? For all his shortcomings, Backhouse couldn't deny that Dalrymple seemed indefatigable on their behalf.

Better lodgings were found, their luggage stored, all manner of small personal comforts were addressed. Prices were high – far,

far higher than Backhouse had anticipated – but the improvement in their situation could not be overstated.

Two days after their arrival, with James Dalrymple for company, Backhouse set about the task of finding a place to live. Perhaps, after all, Havana would soon feel like home.

XVI

The fashion in Havana that year was for tiny French biscuits to be taken with iced coffee in the middle of the morning. The best examples were to be found *extramuros*, in the cafés on the broad avenues that fanned out from the walls of the old city; but the café frequented by any particular *habanero* was dictated by a great deal more than the quality of its pastries.

At the top end of the scale, the island's Creoles – the white Cubans of pure Spanish descent – thronged to those smart establishments on the new boulevards, where they could sit in the shade of orange trees and talk business, lamenting the shortage of slaves, the low price of sugar, the villainy of the English who wanted to rob them of their livelihoods. These were male gatherings. Their wives and daughters, if permitted to venture out at that hour, were confined by custom to their carriages, the little three-seat *volantas* that were all the rage. These could be pulled up outside respectable establishments where waiters would rush to bring refreshments, to be consumed beneath the shade of the *volantas'* large hoods. From these discreet vantage points, the young ladies of Havana were able to peep out at their friends and rivals, all in similar carriages, similarly engaged.

They were not joined by Havana's expatriate communities. Peninsular Spaniards tended to cling together, slightly suspicious of their island cousins, and the Americans kept aloof from Spanish speakers of every sort, preferring the cafés on the Calle Obrapía in the heart of the old city. The British, shunning the Americans, gravitated towards the cathedral area, or to the area near the waterfront close to the British consulate. Only La Dominica provided common ground for all nationalities.

Other establishments, scattered across the old town, catered for the island's black and mixed race populations, where those who had elevated themselves above the poverty of their neighbours, those who could afford European dress and European habits, would repair in the middle of the morning for their own French biscuits and their own elegant glasses of spiced iced coffee. One such establishment was Eduardo's towards the southern end of the old city, not far from the docks, and it was there that the captain of police had arranged to meet Leonarda.

She had chosen a table inside, in a discreet corner, screened from the rest of the room by a stand of potted lemon trees. From there she saw him approach across the little square, past stalls selling butter fruit and dusty, half-sized oranges. She saw him hesitate before entering. Behind him, between the tall buildings, she could glimpse a turquoise smudge of sea.

He was handsome, she thought, in that soft, Spanish way that was so admired by the daughters of the island's plantation owners. But young. How old exactly? She couldn't tell. Perhaps no younger than she was. But young in experience. Young enough still to be honest on an island that scorned honesty. And not yet comfortable under the monstrous dignity required of an imperial Spaniard.

His hesitation didn't surprise her at all. For a young Spaniard to be seen stepping out after dark in Havana with a woman of mixed blood would not have provoked comment, would most likely have been met with the ribald admiration of his fellows. But to consort in a mulatto café with a mulatto woman in the early part of the day – a woman wealthier than he was – these were things that even someone new to Cuban society understood to be highly irregular. Eventually, taking pity on him, she sent a waiter to bring him to her table.

Before that day he had seen her twice: the first time in the garden of the British consul, and then, a day or two later, riding in a *volanta* with her servant, the hood pushed back leaving them exposed to the elements. It had been one of those dark moments just before a storm, when the sky turns leaden and the wind, having died to nothing, whips suddenly into a fury that brings with it the downpour. Then, for an instant, the temperature drops and the wind seems to freshen all it touches. He had seen the way she leaned forward, smiling, to face the coming gale, laughing as it tugged at her lace and ruffled her hair. She had waited until the first savage moments of rain before helping her servant to raise the carriage hood.

Back in Spain the captain of police had heard all about the allure of Cuba's hot-blooded sirens, the dusky mulattas who would beg for the touch of a pure-blood Spaniard and who, in return, would teach him things unknown to any man foolish enough to remain at home in Castile. There had been jokes and warnings aplenty on the subject, but he had largely ignored them. The attractions of such women seemed obscure to him, and he disliked that sort of coarse tavern banter. Besides, he was all but engaged to the delicate daughter of his father's oldest friend. It was impossible that the temptations of the tropics could distract him from such a high and honourable purpose.

But there she was, waiting for him behind a screen of green leaves, more lovely than he remembered. She had loosened her hair into a half-knot, a style strictly forbidden to the island's Spanish women, and it hinted at an ease and informality that made him flush. His eyes rested for a moment on the disturbing nakedness of her throat.

'Señora,' he began, bowing from the neck, but she interrupted his formalities.

'Please, Captain, take a seat. This one, out of the sun.' She indicated the chair next to her own. 'Will you take any refreshment?'

But he could not. To have her order on his behalf was unthinkable, and yet to raise his hand, to summon the waiter and give orders – in this place where he felt himself so clearly an intruder – was beyond him. Nevertheless, although he declined with great awkwardness, she smiled at him, and he was not altogether sorry that he'd come.

'Your message intrigued me,' she went on. 'It was good of you to find out those names for me. But you hinted that there was more?'

She had before her on the table the note he'd sent her, and now her eyes returned to it. He tried very hard not to watch her as she read.

'Indeed, señora.' He flushed as she looked up and met his eye. 'That last question you asked when we met, the one about the boots – I thought of it a great deal after we parted. For it is obvious, is it not, that the sort of men accused of the crime – the men whose names are on that list – had never worn boots in their lives? So the boot prints found at the scene of the crime, what is their significance?'

He went on to explain, very earnestly, as if to one who might not share his icy command of logic, that he had sought the recollections of his colleagues and that it had been generally agreed that the men arrested had been unshod, that the boot prints had been very clear, that probably they had been made by one of the first to discover the crime.

'And yet it is interesting, is it not, señora, that those boot prints led away into the garden. You would expect one who discovered such horror to turn at once to the main hallway, the main door, to call for assistance. Perhaps, yes, they would step outside for a moment, to check that the assailants were gone. But it would not be necessary to continue down the steps and so far across the grass. I think it would be strange. And besides, it was the maid, Floretta, who raised the alarm. None of my colleagues could recall any male, servant or otherwise, in attendance that morning.'

He tried to avoid her gaze as he spoke. Those dark eyes engaging so fully with his were too difficult, too troubling. Instead he studied the glass of coffee that stood on the table in front of her, or allowed his eyes to wander to the white-gloved fingertips that rested beside it.

'So what is your explanation, Captain?'

'I have two possible explanations. The first . . . Well, señora, I have not yet spoken to the officer who was first to the scene. He has been promoted to a better position in Santiago. His recollections may be very important. The boot prints, for instance . . . It is just possible they did not lead into the garden as I told you. It is possible that this particular detail might have been added retrospectively, an embellishment for visitors, something to add excitement to the story.'

He blushed again, embarrassed to confess openly the nature of the performance enacted for her in the consul's study.

'And the other explanation?'

He made an effort to meet her eye and saw she was smiling.

'It seems to me unlikely, señora, that the men who were arrested had an accomplice so very different from themselves. Is it not more probable that the man in boots arrived later, after the initial robbery?'

'And did not raise the alarm?'

'Apparently not.'

Rather than hold her gaze, he turned away again, as if his attention had been caught by movements in the square.

'So this new arrival must have occupied himself in some other way, Captain?'

He nodded. Around them the room had emptied a little and he felt her attention was fully his. They might have been anywhere, alone together. He was pleased now to have suggested such a meeting.

'The three men were arrested very quickly after the murder was discovered and various items that belonged to the British consul were found in a bag dumped near one of their drinking haunts. But not the jewels. The jewels were never recovered. One might almost think they had been magicked away by someone else. By a man in boots, perhaps.'

'Thank you, Captain.' The softness of her voice was reassuring. 'And this . . . this possibility, is it one that might be investigated further, do you think?'

The young man had no choice but to shake his head.

'Alas, I'm afraid the matter is closed. It would be impossible for anyone to investigate officially unless a request were received from the Captain-General's office, or unless the English themselves requested it.'

She nodded. 'Yes, of course. Now, Captain, Eduardo is famous for his coffee. Are you sure you will not reconsider?'

He had imagined a longer conversation. He had imagined his observations would have the force of a great revelation, that there would be many questions. But even as he was speaking, his theory had begun to appear less and less astonishing, and now he knew that she had reached the same conclusions for herself, long before he laid them before her. And so the meeting had been pointless for her, a waste of her time. And patronising too. He felt himself begin to flush furiously at his own stupidity.

'Or, if not coffee, perhaps you would prefer something stronger at this hour?'

He had wanted to ask questions of his own, to understand who she was, and why the affair was of interest to her. But now it was impossible to stay. His wounded dignity would not allow it. So instead he took his leave, awkwardly and in haste, and departed without answers. He left Leonarda sitting coolly in the shade.

She waited until he was out of sight behind the lemon trees before she removed the long white gloves which had felt so hot and restricting throughout the interview. When the captain of police turned at the door, he glimpsed the lace rolled down, her smooth, bare arms emerging. And as he walked away, slightly dazzled by the sudden brightness of the square, he cursed himself as both a fool and a coward.

XVII

Noon the following day found the American, Dale, in the dusty plaza by the San Francisco depository. He had gone there in response to a handwritten note from his new friend Jepson, a note that had reached him rather late the night before. In it the special envoy had suggested that, if Dale wished to observe a busy man at work, he should find his way to a certain Café Santa Anna at midday.

It was not a salubrious address, one of the small, down-at-heel establishments that sheltered under the square's narrow colonnade. At first he looked for Jepson at one of the pavement tables where foreigners were wont to sit, but he found him instead in the shadowy interior, at a table near the window where he could watch the world go by with a certain degree of discretion. Such cafés were the notorious haunts of the pickpockets and confidence tricksters who preyed upon visitors to Havana, but it was noticeable that none of them seemed to be troubling Jepson. Havana's criminals were quick learners, Dale thought. As the shoal separates around the shark, so the café's usual habitués were allowing the big American a considerable amount of space.

'Good afternoon, Mr Dale.' Jepson checked his pocket watch as he spoke, as if to confirm the other's timekeeping. 'One minute after noon. Excellent. It won't be long now.'

Dale seated himself next to his compatriot and called to the waiter for crème de menthe and iced water. Their table looked out across the square and afforded a clear view of La Rectitud, an establishment that was part pharmacy and part purveyor of stationery, and which also served as the city's leading – and unofficial – *poste restante*.

'You are familiar with that store, Mr Dale?'

Coming from someone who had been on the island for barely a fortnight, Dale considered the question rather impertinent.

'Of course. We've all used it for post from time to time. It's probably safer than the official mail and a good deal more convenient.'

And it was true that the *poste restante* service at La Rectitud had over many years maintained a good reputation. Sailors and travellers bound for Havana would be entrusted with letters or packages to deposit there, and, on payment of a small charge, recipients could collect them at their leisure. Many places in the city offered such services, but no one delivered them with the same professionalism. The proprietor, Señor Costa, had gone to great lengths to ensure that his system was both trustworthy and convenient. His was a rare thing in Havana – a business as reliable as its name suggested.

Jepson checked his watch again.

'They receive hundreds of items there each day, Mr Dale, so if you wanted to hide a letter somewhere in Havana, this would be the place to do it. Just watch what happens now. That Negro there, leaving the shop. See him? The one with the red kerchief. If I'm not mistaken, he has just picked up a letter that arrived yesterday evening from New Orleans addressed to a Mr Robertson, care of La Rectitud.'

Dale saw at once the man Jepson meant – an ordinary enough fellow typical of the dozens who loitered near the docks waiting for casual work. Mostly they were *emancipados* – freed slaves forced to work out punitive labour contracts before they were allowed to enjoy their freedom.

'How do you know? About the letter, I mean.'

'I know because I wrote it, and because one of my men is following the fellow who's just picked it up. That coffee-coloured fellow in the white hat.'

Dale watched as the two men crossed the square, one a little behind the other, the two of them equally inconspicuous among the milling crowds.

'Robertson, you say? Is that your rat?'

'It's a name he sometimes employs.'

'But you think his mail might lead you to him?'

Jepson replied with a shrug, as though the question was so obvious it barely warranted an answer.

The letter carrier had reached the far side of the square and disappeared down one of the streets that led north, towards the cathedral. Dale half expected Jepson to leap up in pursuit himself, but the big man was calmly sipping what looked like a brandy and water.

'What now?' Dale asked him.

'The beauty of this particular exercise, Mr Dale, is that we don't have to move a muscle. We just sit here and admire.'

He stretched his arms above his head.

'I used to have a man working for me over here, you know, Mr Dale. He was a Cuban-born Spaniard called Alvarez, a clever fellow who travelled around the plantations mending machinery. I signed him up years ago, when I needed someone to provide various bits of information, and it soon turned out that he had a natural gift for my sort of work. He enjoyed being cleverer than the authorities, which to be honest wasn't particularly difficult. But in all the time I knew him, Alvarez never put a foot wrong.'

The big man paused, and took another sip of his drink. He still appeared supremely relaxed, but his voice had turned cold.

'So when I first realised there was someone over here working against us, I thought Alvarez would sniff him out in no time. We underestimated our rat, you see.' The confession clearly pained him. 'Back then we thought he must be new here. It didn't occur to us that he'd been in place longer than we had, working so quietly we'd never noticed.'

Jepson frowned at the bottom of his glass.

'But Alvarez nearly got him anyway. He heard from one of his informers about a man who'd stolen some papers, stuff that promised to nail my rat to the floor. The fellow had stolen them with an idea of blackmail, then got scared and hid them away. Alvarez had to promise him a great deal of money.'

The big man's eyes were scanning the square outside, but Dale could tell his thoughts were elsewhere.

'Needless to say, it went wrong. The fellow with the papers wouldn't name names until he'd got his reward, and he hid himself away in the country while Alvarez raised the money. But someone got to him first and left him dead in a ditch. Of course by then I reckon Alvarez had a pretty good idea whose name was on that paper, but before he could share it with me, he was dead too.'

Jepson ran a hand down one cheek.

'It happened very quickly. One morning he woke up to find the police at his door and a pile of incriminating paperwork under his bed. It was planted, obviously, but what did that matter? He was executed that same afternoon.'

Jepson fell silent, his eyes returning to the square. Dale didn't know what to say.

'And you think this rat of yours planted the evidence?' he ventured.

'Not in person, if that's what you mean. But, yes, someone in Havana arranged all the details. Of course, he could simply have had Alvarez knifed in an alley one night, but it was much neater to let the authorities do the work. That way it wasn't only Alvarez they got, it was his family and friends and all his associates too.' He paused, took another sip from his glass, then paused again. 'So that, Mr Dale, if for no other reason, is why we're going to get our man.'

Several minutes had passed since the man in the red kerchief left the square, but now he was back. He was still moving at an unhurried pace, slouching along with the satisfied air of one who has completed an awkward task. A line of slightly scruffy workers lounged along one wall of the depository, waiting without urgency for any casual work that might come their way, and it was to this line that the man in the kerchief headed, taking his place at the end of the queue. From the familiar nods that greeted him, Dale gathered that his presence there was nothing new.

'So what do you make of that, Mr Dale?' Jepson looked amused.

'I'm not sure I entirely understand it. Has he already delivered the letter?'

'He has. In a manner of speaking.'

At that moment the man who'd been following reappeared in the square and shook his head ruefully in the direction of the Café Santa Anna. Jepson grinned then turned back to Dale.

'We've been doing this every day for nearly a month. I've got half a dozen men out there. And they fool us every time.'

'You mean your men lose him?'

'They lose the *letter*, Mr Dale. That's a very different thing.'

He sat up a little straighter.

'Imagine you're my rat. You lord it here in the sewers of Havana and you feel pretty safe. But you have your tail in all sorts of other sewers too – in some murky American sewers, for instance – so you need to have a way for people over there to contact you. You don't worry about your letters being intercepted. They'll be in cipher anyway. No, what worries you is how those letters reach you without leaving a trail of dirt straight to your door. What we've just been looking at is our rat's solution to the problem. It's so neat I almost want to shake his hand.'

To Dale's surprise, the admiration seemed genuine. Yet Jepson was not the sort of man to enjoy being bested. At least not for very long.

'Pickpockets,' the big American went on. 'That's his answer, you see. This city must boast the best pickpockets in the world. So a man like red kerchief over there is picked from one of the labour queues. He's approached by a stranger and given money to collect any letters under a certain name. He must put them in the pocket of his smock, then take them to the steps of the cathedral where someone will collect them from him. If no one comes, after five minutes he should destroy the letters, and then he is free to go about his business.

'Of course, no one ever does come. Think of the crowds in that square, Mr Dale! As he pushes his way through, dozens of people brush against him. Our men cannot possibly follow all of them. By the time he reaches the cathedral steps, his pockets are empty. He probably doesn't even realise the post is missing until the time comes to throw it away.'

Dale looked out across the square. It looked a very ordinary scene, Havana at its least exotic, and it made all Jepson's talk of subterfuge seem outlandish and rather hard to believe. Not for the first time he wondered if his companion's theories were altogether to be trusted.

'So does today's performance tell us anything at all?' he asked.

'It tells us that this man is good, Mr Dale. There's a serious game being played here. But don't worry, my friend, I give you my solemn word that before very long we'll be shining some light into my rat's nasty little hole.'

And watching his compatriot drain his glass at a gulp, Dale was aware of a pulse of patriotic pride. Somewhere in Havana someone was conspiring against the best interests of the United States of America, and he was pretty sure they had an unpleasant surprise coming their way.

XVIII

When Leonarda next called at the premises of the pawnbroker and general merchant on the Calle Luz, it was evident that news of her first visit had already reached the proprietor. Señor Melendez was a rather rough-looking individual with no collar, and his eyes brightened when he saw her.

'That box of books, señora? Some fine volumes there. I've pulled it out for you.' He lifted an old wooden orange box on to the counter. 'I should warn you now that I've had to put a high price on it.'

She recognised them instantly. They were the friends she had grown up with, each of them exactly as she remembered. She knew them by the patterns of fading on their bindings, by their thumbed decrepitude, by the familiar rips and tatters on their spines. When, after a pause, she reached down and opened one, every page was familiar: a smear of grease across a famous love scene; her own thumb print, very small and repeated more than once, from a day aged nine when she had settled to read with sooty hands; a disastrous spillage (her fault) over an entire page. Memories so strong she felt the stirring of tears.

However, respecting the conventions of such occasions, Leonarda's features remained impassive as she made a show of studying each volume with great care. Finally she shrugged, with the traditional, bored indifference that was the correct starting point for every negotiation in Havana.

'How much?' she asked, and Melendez named a price ten times the amount he'd paid for them, a fraction of the amount she'd have been prepared to pay. She was tempted to accept at once, immediately and without demur, knowing that such a display of eagerness would have left the seller aghast at his evident under-pricing. But out of pity for him she played the game, offering next to nothing and eventually agreeing a figure somewhere between his starting point and her own. Honour satisfied, Melendez allowed himself a rather smug smile, and insisted that his young assistant should help her to her carriage.

It was only as she was about to leave the shop that she realised one volume was missing – and of all Hector's books, the one she held most dear. She had passed more hours than she could count sitting with his volume of Cervantes, and Hector had always said it was Don Quixote himself who'd taught her to read. It had been his favourite too, and he had referred to it constantly, so that it seemed to her less a book, more a little piece of his soul captured on paper.

She broached the subject with care.

'I notice, señor, there is one volume missing from this collection. It was a more valuable item than any of these. A fat book, a bit worn to be sure, but the binding was of the very best. Red calf skin, I think. I would pay the same price again for that one book if you still have it.'

The shopkeeper's eyebrows twitched at that, and he called the boy back to the counter so he could examine the crate for himself. But after a moment or two he shook his head.

'Alas, that was all, señora. Look, they fit exactly in the box. If any had been removed it would be obvious, and I would remember selling it. Perhaps the man who brought these in might be able to help you? If it was a more valuable volume, he might have taken it to one of the booksellers by the cathedral.'

Her instincts were to beg him to look again, to ransack his attics and storerooms until it was found. But there was something impressive about his certainty. Had there been the slightest doubt in his mind about the volume, the prospect of such significant reward would have sent him scurrying to seek it.

And so she passed that afternoon in a hot, slow search for Moses Le Castre. The long journey out to Mother Alençon's proved fruitless, yielding only the suggestion of another tavern he sometimes frequented. There she was directed to a third, and from there to another. As the day grew hotter, Leonarda grew only more determined.

She found him in the late afternoon, back in the old city, sorting rags in a filthy yard behind a shop. Her sudden appearance there clearly startled him, and again she was aware of his suspicion. But when pressed, he was adamant. There had been no other book. He had packed them all into one box with his own hands. If there'd been too many, he'd have used a bigger box. Could he have missed one? Could he have left one at Marguerite's? He didn't think so. She had laid out all Hector's things while she decided what to do with them. There hadn't been many. And she'd been keen to be rid of the books. In such a small place they could hardly have missed one.

For all his wariness, Leonarda believed him. Marguerite would have been thorough in her purge; and it would never have occurred to Moses to seek a different buyer for one particular volume. Even if it had, he was unlikely to have done so. It was Moses' nature to seek out the easiest solution to any difficulty.

And yet the book *was* missing. Hector would never willingly have parted with it. And if it hadn't been among his belongings in St Simeon at the time of his death, it was hard to imagine where it might be.

Arriving back at the Calle Chacón as the day dwindled into shadow, she already knew what she must do. That evening, as soon as she was washed and changed, she wrote again to the young captain of police.

XIX

Nothing was as Backhouse had imagined it.

Not the climate, which stifled them with its thick, heavy heat; not the city, which bewildered them with its noise and its horrors of dirt and poverty; not the prices, which were astronomical; not the populace, who were shameless; nor his compatriots, who seemed to have forgotten all the simple strengths that made them British.

And most certainly not the respect he commanded, nor the deference due to him. Backhouse had thought his position a solemn and significant one. In London, his appointment had been greeted with uniform congratulations. But in Havana, both outside the English community and within it, the Mixed Commission was spoken of with mockery; and it was assumed that the new judge, like his predecessors, would quickly settle down to enjoy the perks of his position while taking as little trouble as possible over the fruitless duties assigned to him.

Worst of all was the isolation. Every meeting with Crawford, the British consul, emphasised the gulf between them. To Backhouse, Crawford began to seem one of the worst kinds of Englishmen, standing for nothing, accommodating everything, putting his own interests before any matter of principle. And he felt certain Crawford despised him equally, an ignorant and naïve newcomer, perhaps even something of a joke. It was a discomforting and unsettling thought.

For other than Crawford, who was there? There were many British merchants who drifted in and out of Havana, of course, but few had put down roots there. So when Backhouse looked around for allies, he found only Dalrymple – who for all his help-fulness, Backhouse could not warm to – and Lavender, the man recommended to him by Thomas Staveley.

At first Backhouse thought Lavender might be the friend he so badly needed. They met by arrangement in a café on the Calle Mercaderes, a couple of weeks after Backhouse's arrival. Lavender was serious and polite, respectably dressed, interested in the news from home. Better still, he was generous with his offers of assis-tance and seemed genuinely interested in learning as much as possible about the new British judge. When Backhouse explained to him London's concerns about the navy's sailing plans, his eyebrow arched to a point.

'So they believe there's dirty work going on, do they? Very interesting. And you say it was Thomas Staveley who asked you to look into the matter?'

Backhouse nodded. 'Unofficially, of course. I'm to report informally. I understand you can help me with that side of things?'

'Of course, old man. Not a problem. You can drop off your post at the shop under a plain cover. Mark it for me, and I'll see it gets to its destination safely enough. Rather quicker than the diplo-matic mail, I suspect.'

He looked at Backhouse appraisingly, a look of genuine curiosity.

'Do you have any thoughts yet about how you may prosecute your investigations?'

'None at all.' Backhouse felt a little wary, alert to any mockery in the other's tone. Lavender, however, appeared sincere. 'I was rather hoping you might be able to suggest something.'

But Lavender shook his head.

'I've never heard any whisper of such a thing from the British community here. It's generally assumed that the lack of arrests by the naval patrols is to be laid at the door of your department.'

'Mine?' Backhouse was confused. 'You mean the Mixed Commission?'

'Precisely.' Lavender smiled and Backhouse noticed the dryness of his lips. 'You can hardly blame the British navy for wondering if there's any point chasing slave ships. Even if they do bring one in, it makes no difference. Oh, I know you'll bring in an honest verdict, old man, and I'm sure your predecessors always did the same. But your Spanish counterpart will always find a reason to acquit. It wouldn't matter if there were Africans hanging out of the portholes in manacles, he'd contrive to find an innocent explanation. And with the two judges divided, it's invariably the Spanish administrator who gets the casting vote. So the ship is released, the owner complains and our government is presented with a bill for compensation. And they pay it too. Money that is then put towards the next raid on the African coast.'

He smiled again. Not a particularly attractive smile, Backhouse thought. To someone who believed passionately in British justice, who felt an instinctive sympathy with the abolitionist cause, Lavender's was not a cheering analysis. Backhouse chose to put it to one side.

'So how *do* I follow up this business about the sailing plans?' he asked. 'Is there anyone I could talk to?'

Lavender considered.

'Certainly not Crawford. He'd get in a great huff if he thought London was asking questions behind his back. There's always Dalrymple, of course. He knows a lot, but a good deal of it is unreliable, and he'd make a terrible witness. I'd say your best plan was simply to sit back, keep your ears open and see if anything crops up. Needless to say, if I can be of any help in the meantime, you've only to let me know.'

For all Lavender's reassuring tones, the meeting left Backhouse strangely deflated. Lavender's comments about the Mixed Commission chimed only too well with his initial conclusions, formed after diligent study of the files: the repeated failure to prosecute slave traders, the persistent and blatant perversity of the Spanish judges, the laughable precedent of compensation for owners of impounded ships, even when the evidence against them was, to any honest eyes, overwhelming.

In London, Backhouse had viewed the continuation of the trade in human beings with abhorrence; he had travelled to Cuba eager to strike a blow against it. But in Havana, where the brutal realities of the trade were so much more apparent, it seemed he was destined to spend his time in endless petty skirmishes with Spanish bureaucracy. It was even possible, he was forced to concede, that the Spanish officials were worse than simply awkward. There arose from the Commission's papers, stronger with every page he turned, the unmistakable stench of corruption.

As for the matter of the navy's sailing plans, it was not, he realised, something he could hope to investigate fully until he knew a good deal more about the island. Until his Spanish was better. Until his family was properly settled. Until he knew who to trust.

So, as Lavender had suggested, he would wait and see. His first posting overseas was not proving anywhere near as straightforward as he had anticipated.

XX

The captain of police had no business in the cellars of the main police building, just as he had no right to interfere with the records of cases that had long been closed. His only hope, should he be discovered, was that his behaviour would appear so aberrant it would automatically be put down to eccentricity rather than insubordination. In the imperial police force, initiative in junior officers was not encouraged. So clearly was this understood that few of his superiors had ever actually encountered any.

Obtaining the key had not been difficult. It hung very obviously by the door to the cellar steps. From there a narrow staircase led down to two cavernous cellar rooms where the forgotten paperwork of many years was left to moulder gently, prey to ants and damp and neglect. The police force in Havana was not particularly efficacious, but it had a great talent for keeping records of its own deficiencies. Somewhere in the gloom, the captain knew, the box he sought would be lurking.

And it had not been hard to find an opportunity to look. He'd simply waited until mid-afternoon, when his fellow officers and all the other staff left the building for the day and he was certain of being alone. Only when he held up his lamp to reveal the chaos of boxes through which he must sort did he pause to consider the wisdom of his actions.

After their meeting at Eduardo's he had felt certain he would not see Leonarda again. He had made a fool of himself, and he had scurried off like an embarrassed schoolboy. His colleagues would have said it was his own fault for socialising with mulattos.

But he hated to be thought a fool. And Señora Leonarda Leigh was not an easy woman to put out of mind.

Her subsequent letter had been polite but not too formal, and gave him hope that his awkwardness at Eduardo's had been less obvious than he'd thought. Of course, there had been no suggestion in her note that she wished him to take any action on her behalf. She simply sought advice as to how she might discover certain information held in the files of the Havana police.

Technically, of course, there was an official process for her to follow, one that he knew instinctively would require a great many letters of application, would take a great deal of time and which, after many months, would lead nowhere. The information she sought was in a box in the room below him. What could be simpler than for him to step downstairs and retrieve it?

The truth, of course, was very different, and became obvious to him as soon as he had descended the cellar steps. The boxes were stacked against walls or tottered in columns, with no apparent system to their placing and with very few proper labels. A fool's errand, he realised. And yet he did not retrace his steps immediately. He would give it half an hour, he decided. The cellars were cool compared to the rooms upstairs, and although the air smelled musty, and thick ropes of cobwebs bound some containers to the walls, it was not too bad a place. The captain of police, once he had set out on a course of action, did not like to abandon it.

A grille high up in one wall let in enough light for him to navigate by, and he used it to decide upon a plan of attack. If the boxes had simply been thrust in as they became full, then those nearest the door must be the most recent, while those at the back – the most cobwebbed and the most decrepit – might have been there for fifty years or more. A series of exploratory sorties enabled him to narrow his area of search remarkably quickly, but even when he had begun to unearth records from the year he was looking for, checking the contents of an entire box was still a slow process. The papers themselves were often in a poor state, even after such a relatively short time in storage. Some were marked with damp; some had begun to dissolve into a grey, messy pulp.

In the end it took him nearly two hours to find what he was looking for but, given the obstacles, finding them so quickly felt like a triumph. After checking discreetly that the rooms above were still unoccupied, he repaired to his desk with the relevant file to examine the contents more carefully.

The first document he wanted was a standard one, the inventory of items found on the murdered man and returned to his next of kin. It was, he felt, pathetic in its brevity: a cotton rag, some small change, a pocket knife, a small ball of twine. At the bottom of this list, smudged and uncertain, was the mark of whoever had received them.

The next document he sought was also a list: the inventory of objects reported stolen from the British consulate on that fateful night. It was, once you discounted the missing jewellery, short and mostly rather mundane. Next to it, secured by a pin, was the list of objects subsequently recovered by the police, items that had been found abandoned in an alleyway very close to the tavern where the arrested men were known to drink. This list corresponded almost exactly with the register of stolen objects. Neither contained any mention of a book. Conscientiously, the captain of police took up his pen and began to make copies of both.

With the exception of the jewellery, he noted, only two items were reported missing that had not subsequently been recovered: the consul's watch, inscribed as a gift from his wife, and which the consul had described rather pompously as 'beyond value'; and a wooden paperknife marked with the consul's initials, valued – somewhat optimistically, the captain thought – at three English shillings.

His copying finished, he looked at the two lists again. The afternoon light sloped through the half-closed shutters and touched the papers with harsh white light. Odd, he thought, that everything had been abandoned by the thieves but for those two items. In their haste they had mostly stolen objects of little value, and he was not surprised those things had been swiftly discarded. And a watch, even an inscribed watch, was both valuable and portable, so it was equally unsurprising that they had retained it.

But the paperknife was different. It was not something easy to turn into cash. Was it pure chance that the two items that remained missing were the only ones with inscriptions, the only things that were clearly and undeniably the possessions of the British consul?

The captain of police shrugged and folded the two lists together. There was no mention of a book, at any rate. Should he deliver the disappointing news to Señora Leigh in person? Rather reluctantly, he concluded he should not. A letter would be more appropriate. But something else had suggested itself to him, something he might investigate a little further. Perhaps then, if he no longer appeared an utter fool, he might venture to propose another meeting.

XXI

In the house on Lowther Street, Staveley often felt that time was standing still. In London's parks and gardens, the first vestiges of spring were making themselves known with timid persistence: the early crocuses, the blackbirds still singing at five o'clock, the very first leaves. But in John Jerusalems' lair, the shutters were clamped shut and the fire had been banked up against the evening chill, as if determined to resist the advance of the seasons.

Jerusalems was not alone when Staveley called. Asked to wait in the library, and peering idly through the window, Staveley watched as his host escorted a well-dressed woman of striking good looks down the steps to the street. There they paused to exchange a few further words. Watching their lips, Staveley concluded that their farewells were not said in English. Jerusalems really was an intriguing fellow.

When Staveley had first been asked by his mentor at the Foreign Office – at his club, over a glass of Madeira – to take on certain unofficial liaison duties, it had been made clear to him that communications with Lowther Street were to be strictly in one direction. Staveley was to call there once a month – more frequently if circumstances demanded it – to answer any questions the gentleman there might have about goings-on at the Foreign Office. However, he was not on any account to report back. He was not to mention Jerusalems to either his colleagues or his superiors. These visits were his own affair, and he was to keep them to himself.

The instructions had been clear and had never been repeated. Other than the small additional payment that appeared each month in his salary, Staveley received no indication that his visits to Lowther Street were supposed to continue. Indeed, were it not for the money, he might have thought his original instructions had been utterly forgotten.

His visitor safely loaded into a cab, Jerusalems bounded up the steps and bustled into the library.

'Thomas, Thomas! To what do I owe the pleasure? Come through! Come through!'

'I have another bit of news for you, John.' Staveley looked around him to work out the safest route through the chaos of Jerusalems' drawing room to the chair he was being offered. 'A piece of gossip really. You may already have heard it. But one of Wyville's sons is very friendly with the Spanish ambassador.'

'Indeed?'

Staveley recognised the interest in Jerusalems' voice, although he was apparently intent on moving a heavy pile of books from one armchair to the floor.

'It appears they executed a man for spying in Havana a little while back. A Cuban of Spanish extraction called Alvarez, some sort of engineer who travelled around to maintain the sugar presses. He was denounced by anonymous letter and when the Spanish police searched his things they found correspondence from an Englishman called Hugh Pennington Manners who appeared to be working for the Foreign Office.'

'Go on, Thomas. I think I remember the case you mention.'

'The letters from Manners all came from New York and they requested information about Spanish troop deployments, the strengths of garrisons, that sort of thing. They also mentioned details of payments made by Manners to Alvarez through a New York bank.'

Jerusalems, having cleared the chair, flopped down into it, then immediately bobbed forward again so that he was perched on its very edge.

'How strange, Thomas, that Alvarez had not destroyed the correspondence, given that his life depended upon it.'

'He'd had precious little opportunity,' Staveley explained. 'Two letters had apparently arrived on the very eve of his arrest. The next couple, which confirmed the man's guilt, arrived subsequently. It's assumed that all earlier correspondence had been disposed of.'

'I see. Unfortunate. And embarrassing for the Foreign Office. What did they tell the Spanish?'

'Oh, the usual.' Staveley shrugged. 'Denied all knowledge of Manners and suggested he was probably working for the Americans. Assured them of our honourable intentions. The unusual thing is that for once they meant it. They really hadn't heard of Manners. In fact, no one had. When one of our people in New York investigated, it became clear that Hugh Pennington Manners didn't exist.'

'Hardly surprising, Thomas. Whoever he was working for, he would hardly be using his own name. Was this the gossip from Spain you came to tell me? I was expecting something rather more sensational.'

'Well, there's been something of a development. A chest has been discovered, quite by chance, under the floorboards of Alvarez's workshop. They'd never have found it but for a small fire. It was full of code books, account books, all sorts. Most of it was in cipher, of course, but the Spanish could work out enough. It turns out the Foreign Office was right, after all. Alvarez *was* working for the Americans. Looks as though he'd been working for them for some time.'

'Interesting.' Jerusalems was nodding and peering at the volumes he had just moved, as if surprised to discover them in their new location. 'And you are telling me this, Thomas, because . . .?'

Staveley attempted to look nonchalant.

'Well, it's rather your area, isn't it?'

'Of course.' Jerusalems looked at him then; a steady gaze that made Staveley take notice. 'And I assure you, Thomas, that I take no pleasure in the fellow's unfortunate fate. But presumably he chose such a hazardous occupation of his own volition. He would have been aware of the risks.'

Jerusalems' sympathy for the dead man seemed earnest and unfeigned, and it caught Staveley slightly off balance.

'But there was something else that brought you here today, wasn't there, Thomas? I can see it in your face.'

It was true, but Staveley still felt ill at ease.

'Just something I wanted to ask you, John.' He paused, choosing his words carefully. 'You see, about a year ago when I was arriving here quite late one evening, I bumped into someone I'd known as a boy. He told me he was an old acquaintance of yours. Said he was only in London for a few days as he was almost exclusively resident in America. I thought of him again when young Wyville told me the story about the Cuban spy. My old friend's name was Henry Masterson.'

Jerusalems nodded. That moment of stillness had passed and he was in motion again, prodding the pile of books with his toe as if to test its stability.

'Yes, I know Masterson. A very reliable fellow. What of him?'

'Henry *Preston* Masterson. It was the initials that struck me, that was all.'

Jerusalems considered this for exactly the right amount of time. Less would have seemed hasty and awkward; more would have appeared theatrical and inherently false.

'HPM? Not such a coincidence, surely?' He bent down and selected from the top of the pile a volume written in German. 'But an interesting observation, Thomas. Were your friend *actually* involved in some sort of espionage activity, he would be well advised in future to be more imaginative with his fictional persona, would he not? Now tell me, is it too late to offer you tea? Too early to offer you whisky?'

But Staveley felt uncomfortable and did not linger. He had been hoping for some sort of reassurance, and was not at all sure he had received it. Of course he'd long been aware that

Jerusalems swam in stormy waters, but for all the fellow's eccentricities, he liked the man. Perhaps better not to speculate precisely how deep the currents ran in which the little man immersed himself.

XXII

Two months into his new posting, Backhouse was still aware that things had not settled down quite as he'd hoped. His work with the Mixed Commission in particular was a source of great frustration. His difficulties had become abundantly clear to him a month after his arrival when a Spanish merchant vessel was seized carrying a hugely excessive number of water casks, and with special hatchways for the laying of a slave deck: both unmistakable indications of slaving.

But Backhouse's fellow judge disagreed. The Spanish government's appointee to the Mixed Commission was invariably a man of consequence in Cuban society; in this instance he was also a prominent slave-owner, a man whose considerable fortune depended on a steady supply of new labour to the island. His position on the Commission was therefore little short of farcical, but with the two men in disagreement, Backhouse was powerless: there was every chance that a local arbiter would now be appointed, and the ship released. That possibility was, to Backhouse, both bitter and humiliating.

He was not helped in these matters by the behaviour of his assistant, Dalrymple. The man's eagerness to assist when Backhouse first arrived on the island had seemed invaluable. As the days passed, however, Backhouse began to suspect that Dalrymple's helpfulness was not entirely altruistic. The rather expensive suppliers he arranged for them, the laundress who was sloppy and slow to return their clothes, the establishments they patronised initially on his recommendation – Backhouse wondered if perhaps Dalrymple was not without a stake in these ventures, or at the very least stood to gain financially by delivering their custom.

And as an employee he was incorrigible. His work was careless, his attendance patchy, his punctuality lax. Too many months unsupervised seemed to have left him unfit for any form of supervision whatsoever. Worse still, he pestered Backhouse constantly about his salary and seemed always to be seeking advances.

Alarmingly, he seemed aware of Backhouse's conversation with Lavender almost as soon as it had happened.

'Small island,' he explained dismissively when Backhouse asked him how he came to know. 'So how did you two meet, as a matter of interest?'

George, taken aback by such impertinence, muttered something about a personal recommendation, then attempted to bring the conversation to a close.

'What did you make of him?' Dalrymple persisted. 'Dry old stick, isn't he?'

'I found him straightforward and honest,' Backhouse replied stiffly.

'Did you? Shouldn't be fooled if I were you. Nothing straightforward about Lavender. All that buying and selling, for instance. No one seems to know what he buys or sells, but I'll wager it's nothing respectable. The favours of little brown boys, I should think, if I've read him aright.'

Backhouse considered this an obscenity that deserved no response and decided a stern silence would be the best reproof. If the truth were told, however, the conversation made him uncomfortable, and perhaps a little less inclined to seek out Lavender's company.

It was some relief to Backhouse that his domestic arrangements at least were more settled. With Dalrymple's help a home had been found in the quiet suburb of El Cerro, a light and airy affair with verandas and large windows, and views across the main road to the ships in the bay beyond. The rent, George felt, was extortionate, but Dalrymple assured him it was quite reasonable by the standards of Havana.

'For nothing here is cheap, you know, old man. The labour's all in the sugar plantations and whatever's left over commands a fortune. Just you wait till you start to get the bills! Whatever salary you agreed in London, it won't be enough. It never is.'

And it was true that daily life in Havana was proving neither as comfortable nor as cheap as Backhouse had anticipated. However, under the terms of the treaty, his rent was to be paid by the Spanish authorities, leaving him and Grace free to set about furnishing their new home in the style, and to the standard, it demanded. He felt reassured too by the well-being of baby Alice, who had recovered well from her insect bites and appeared once again to be thriving.

Even so, life in El Cerro was far from relaxing. Backhouse strongly suspected the tradesmen of inflating their prices simply because he was English. And to make matters worse, Grace was having trouble with the servants. There seemed to be a great deal of quarrelling among them. And their English nursemaid, bewildered to find herself among so many speakers of Spanish, spent a very significant proportion of her time in tears.

Life was made no easier for any of them by the fact that Backhouse's relations with the consul, Crawford, remained so cool. His work at the Mixed Commission did not in theory require very much contact with the consul's office, but in practice, in a very small British community, the Crawfords decided who received invitations and who did not. Mrs Crawford, George acknowledged, seemed pleasant enough – she fancied herself a singer and enjoyed an audience – but Backhouse felt nervous that their place in society depended so entirely upon the goodwill of a man he did not much like.

He took great pains in all these matters to hide his anxieties from Grace, even excluding from his own diaries any details he feared might upset her were she to come upon them inadvertently. And when, two months after their arrival, Grace announced that she was pregnant, he expressed his delight volubly and without reservation.

In the matter of naval secrets, he heard nothing.

Callers at Backhouse's offices near the docks were infrequent. Dalrymple, as his gatekeeper, generally intercepted those without appointments and sent them packing. Those who made it past him were more often than not individuals convinced that the British judge in Havana must require their services for the provision of carriage hire, office supplies, gentlemen's tailoring – even once a man who wished to sell him a donkey. Backhouse used to wonder idly whether Dalrymple took bribes to let them through or whether he was foolish enough to accept a commission on any sales that might result.

So it was with a good deal of annoyance that he arrived at his offices one morning in late May and saw through the glass that his own room was already occupied. Looking around he realised that Dalrymple was again absent without permission, and that he had no way of knowing the caller's business. A glimpse of pale blue muslin told him his visitor was a woman. Other than that, he had no information.

Leonarda had first heard about the new British judge from Marty. 'He comes with a reputation for honesty,' he'd told her, 'which, if true, means he is unlikely to find his time in Havana particularly comfortable.'

It did not occur to her that the new arrival might ever prove of interest to her. She had seen him drinking coffee one morning at a table near the waterfront, and had thought he looked honest in that upright, unbending, slightly pompous way of the English – the quality that made that country's sinners so much more attractive than its saints. He alone, of all those lounging in the shade, looked ill at ease, as though the very act of taking coffee on such a morning in such a city was questionable behaviour.

Then, in conversation with the captain of police, she had thought of the new British judge again. This time his awkward respectability struck her as less comical. An honest Englishman, new to the island, not yet corrupted by it . . . Officially, in diplomatic terms, he had a certain status. An informal note from him, were it to land on the right desk, might give a young police officer the excuse to make certain enquiries. Of course a burglary so long ago, even one that led to murder, would mean nothing to the new arrival. But if he truly believed in justice . . . And after all, she had nothing to lose.

Backhouse, however, disappointed her. He was irritable that morning: annoyed that Dalrymple had once again flouted his authority, annoyed that he would be forced, after so little time on the island, to address the matter officially; annoyed because all his efforts at the Mixed Commission were proving pointless; annoyed that his clean collar was not clean nor his pressed shirt pressed, that he had been woken by his servants' arguing, that his vintner's bill was twice as high as it should have been. Annoyed that there was a stranger in his office.

It was only a minor consolation that his visitor spoke good English. With an accent, it was true, but accurately and with a command of English idiom that told him she must have learned from a native. She laid out the reasons for her visit very calmly, with great care, telling him about a break-in at the consul's office and the death of a night-watchman, explaining that the authorities had long since considered the matter closed. No further interest would be taken by the Spanish unless perhaps a British official requested it. It wouldn't even need to be an official request, simply an informal note, perhaps to a particular police officer . . .

To Backhouse it all seemed absurd and bizarre. The matter was nothing to do with him. He was not in Havana to do favours for its citizens, however politely expressed. She was wasting his time, and he resented it. As a result his reply was curt.

'I fear, madam, I must disappoint you. If you are unhappy with the conduct of the Spanish police, that is a matter to raise with them. I have quite other duties to attend to, and a burglary at the consulate so long ago would not concern me anyway.'

His tone was dismissive and impatient. If anyone was to take an interest in the affair, he told her, it would be the consul himself, Mr Crawford.

'Mr Crawford, señor,' she replied with calm, quiet dignity, 'does not like to grant interviews to Negroes.'

Something in the way she said it made Backhouse pause. The implication was clear: that Crawford was no friend to the island's black population; that he was not someone to whom Havana's slaves or *emancipados* would turn in the pursuit of British justice. Whereas he, perhaps . . .

He didn't like Crawford. He certainly didn't want to be considered a man of the same stamp. When he replied, his tone was noticeably milder.

'Madam, I am sorry to say that I cannot help you in this matter. It is simply none of my business. But if it is any help to you, I would say the incident you describe sounds like one of common lawlessness. If the Spanish police could not catch the perpetrators at the time, I feel it is doubtful they will do so now. And of course there can be no question that any British citizen might have been involved in the incident in any way.'

It was the end of the interview, but as he held the door for her and watched her go, he wished he had adopted that more mollifying tone from the beginning. A little more patience would not have hurt and would not have been out of place. After all, she was dressed quite like a lady.

He returned to his desk marvelling at what a very strange shore he had chanced upon.

Two days later, at his home in El Cerro, Backhouse's dinner was interrupted by a very loud disturbance at the front door. Eventually forced to investigate in person, he discovered that the caller was a large black woman calling herself Maria Guadalupe, accompanied by a very skinny man whose name Backhouse never learned. Maria Guadalupe declared loudly and persistently that she was Dalrymple's mistress. She had come to fetch help. There had been a theft from the office of the British consul. A huge sum of money had been stolen. Dalrymple had been arrested near the scene of the crime and was being held by the police in an appalling dungeon. But he was innocent. Maria Guadalupe was sure of it. If only the British judge would intervene on his behalf . . .

Cursing inwardly, Backhouse called for his cane and went with her.

XXIII

In Havana, dress mattered. By choosing the plain clothes of a servant, Leonarda could go almost wherever she pleased, enjoying an anonymity and a freedom of the streets unknown to the island's white women, who were forced to peep out at the world through drawing room windows fitted with iron bars, placed there expressly to protect their honour.

She was seldom recognised. Her progress from street urchin to the luxuries of the Calle Chacón had been a rapid one: she had left barely a footprint behind her. And for three years or so she had been away. That was a long time in the busy avenues of Havana, where faces were quickly forgotten. So when she began her search for the men accused of Hector's murder, she aroused little curiosity. Somebody was always looking for somebody else in Havana: there was nothing strange in that. The city was a good place to hide. If anything these were lucky men, to have such a comely pursuer.

She began at the Anchor, a small tavern on the waterfront not far from the San Francisco depository. Although hardly salubrious, it was not the most intimidating of Havana's drinking dens. Its position ensured it a mixed clientele – sailors, travellers and fishermen, as well as the more usual collection of Havana's down-at-heart and down-at-heel. Leonarda was able to slip largely unnoticed into its crowded interior.

There the pot-boy, scenting a tip, led her briskly through the standing crowds of drinkers to a table still laden with the jugs and pots of recently departed customers. These he scooped up deftly under one arm while, with the other, he used the hem of his apron to give the tale a cursory wipe. He knew Antonio Canaria by name, yes. The old men on the benches still mentioned him sometimes. But he had never seen him, and he had been pot-boy at the Anchor for more than a year. The mention of Canaria's friend, Tartuffo, elicited only a shrug. If the lady would wait, he would bring her canary wine or brandy, and would send over Old Nicolas. Nicolas had been drinking at the Anchor since the dawn of time.

The generosity of Leonarda's tip ensured she did not have to wait long. The old man who elbowed his way to her table must have been at least sixty years of age and cadaverous, his brown skin cracked by time. At the sight of Leonarda, he paused to brush away the crumbs from the front of his smock.

He would be delighted to help, he assured her. To help a lady was a pleasure as well as an honour. But when she asked her question, he looked surprised.

'Antonio Canaria? Yes, I remember him.' His voice was hoarse with age. 'But he's gone now. Gone from Havana.'

He paused as the pot-boy returned with wine in a flask for Leonarda and, with it, a generous pot of rum. Before continuing, the old man insisted on filling Leonarda's glass and then his own.

Antonio Canaria, he told her, had left the city at least a year before. A friend of his had been beaten to death in an alleyway and Canaria believed the same fate awaited him. Besides, he had many debts in Havana, so he had signed papers on a ship bound for the Yucatan, and no one had heard of him since. It seemed unlikely he would ever return. He had no reason to come back, and many reasons to stay away.

'And did you know a friend of his called Tartuffo?' Leonarda asked. 'His real name was Felipe Martinez.'

The old man nodded.

'Yes, Tartuffo was the one. Canaria's friend, the one who was killed. The two had been very close.'

Leonarda couldn't pretend the news was not a blow. It seemed she would not, after all, question the men accused of killing Hector. When she asked Nicolas about the third man said to have been there that night, the old man shook his head sadly, as though sensing her disappointment.

Pedro the Salt-Eater, he confirmed, had indeed died in prison, taken by the cholera. He had been well-known at the Anchor and it had surprised no one to hear that he had bludgeoned to death a night-watchman. Pedro enjoyed that sort of work. In laying him low, the cholera had done the world a favour.

'But tell me,' he asked, 'why does a beautiful lady ask about men such as these? I've been trying to guess, but I cannot.'

Leonarda's instinct was to evade, but the old man had helped her and the question was asked with kindness.

'I'd hoped to ask them about that night, when the night-watchman was killed. He was someone very dear to me.'

The old man's eyebrow lifted again.

'So it's vengeance that you seek?'

'No,' she replied quickly. 'Not vengeance. Only answers. I want to know the truth.'

'Answers . . .' There was suspicion in his voice now, and he no longer smiled as he had done. 'Are you certain it is not the reward that you seek?'

Leonarda's incomprehension must have shown in her face, for he carried on.

'For a year or more I have barely thought about Antonio Canaria and his friend. And now two people come here less than a week apart and ask the same questions . . .'

'Someone else was looking for them?' A little spark of surprise. She had told Moses Le Castre that she intended to start her search at the Anchor. Had he decided to help her after all? 'Was it a black man who was asking, a man with a little scar above his eye?'

'No, it was a white man. He told me the Captain-General had offered a reward.'

Leonarda shook her head.

'No,' she said. 'There's no reward.'

The old man shrugged. 'Yet he came. And only a few days before you did.'

Leonarda could see he did not entirely believe her. A reward was an easy concept for him to grasp: the idea that she might subject herself to the jostling of the crowds at the Anchor for no better reason than the truth was much harder for him to believe. In Havana, truth was a currency of limited value.

With no further questions to ask, Leonarda could think of nothing to do but to thank the old man for his time, and to make sure that his glass was refilled before she settled her bill. She left him at the table they had shared, his eyes fixed happily on the rum as though he had already forgotten her.

But he had not. Leonarda was already several paces along the harbour front when she heard him call.

'Señora!' Nicolas was holding on to the doorpost of the Anchor as though the rush to catch her had left him short of breath. 'Señora. There was one other thing. Something I did not tell the white man. He did not ask, and . . .' The old man shrugged. 'And I did not warm to him. So I didn't tell him that Pedro the Salt-Eater had a wife.' He paused and coughed uncomfortably. 'I don't recall her name, but she was a good girl. More of a slave to Pedro than a spouse. When he died, she disappeared, but there was a sister at the Dominican convent who took an interest in her. You'll find *her* on the waterfront every morning at first light, in the place where the whores gather. Ask for Sister Conchita.'

In the hour of sunrise, under a monochrome morning sky, Leonarda found the woman she sought. It was the place where the small boats put in, where the waterside prostitutes would gather for spiced rum after the night's work. When Leonarda asked if any of them knew the person she was seeking, her enquiry was received amicably enough. The sister came there every morning, they told her, offering bread and the Bible. She was not the worst of her kind, she did not preach, so no one chased her off. Besides, the men, the pimps, were superstitious about threatening a nun.

Leonarda found her standing a little apart from the crowd, distinct in dress and posture, looking down on the craft that manoeuvred below her. The water was already busy with fishing boats attempting to land their catch, and with the rickety dinghies from the bays along the coast, all laden with cargoes of fresh produce for the markets. On the harbour side, the street was noisy with the shouts of traders calling out prices, with men whistling and women laughing, with the squeals of outraged piglets being tossed ashore from hand to hand.

When Leonarda approached her, the nun turned, and her face brightened with welcome. There was warmth in her features, and kindness, and none of the severity that so routinely accompanies the giving of charity to the sinful by the virtuous.

'Can I help you, my child? I still have a little food in my basket, or if it is medicine you seek . . .' She paused and her expression changed slightly. 'But my apologies. I can see you are not in need in that way. There must be another reason for you to seek out an old woman such as myself so early in the day.'

Leonarda explained that she was looking for the widow of a man known as Pedro the Salt-Eater. Was it possible that such a woman had once sought the nun's assistance?

But Sister Conchita hesitated.

'Señora, the girls who come to me for help, they do so to escape their past. You can imagine, perhaps, that often there are individuals very anxious to drag them back to their former occupations. Perhaps, child, if you tell me what it is you seek . . .'

Again, as at the Anchor, Leonarda found her instinct to evade undermined by the simplicity of a stranger.

'I'm looking for her, sister, because I have lost someone very dear to me. Lost him suddenly, without ever properly saying good-bye. I think now, if I could find out the truth of how he died . . .'

The nun's expression did not alter, but Leonarda sensed she was listening.

'I think if I could find out the truth, I could perhaps begin to let him go.'

But Sister Conchita was shaking her head. Leonarda noticed that her eyes were as grey as the early morning sky.

'I cannot help you do that, child, and nor can this woman you seek.' The nun turned to face the water. 'To do that you must look inside yourself. Those other things – facts, explanations, what you call the truth – they are not your answer. They are the smoke that stops us from seeing.'

'Perhaps.' Somewhere near the horizon a tall ship was no more than a dark pencil point against the grey. Leonarda watched it disappear before she turned back. 'But if I could only find this girl, this widow, perhaps I would be a little closer to finding my answer. And I don't even know her name.'

For a few seconds Sister Conchita said nothing. When she spoke, she did not look at Leonarda.

'There *was* a girl like the one you describe, the wife of a ruffian called Pedro. I remember her well. She was little better than a slave, really. When he died, she came to me starving and without hope. Her body still bore the marks of his beatings. I sent her where she would be fed and clothed, and I found her rooms in a good Christian house. There they arranged for her to train as a seamstress, and I had great hopes for her. Then one day she was gone, without warning.'

She paused, but Leonarda could tell she had more to say.

'She had attracted the attention of one of the plantation owners. The San Isidoro Estate. He asked her to become his mistress and she went with him on the instant, just like that. No message, no hint of regret.' The nun turned back to Leonarda then and her smile was sad, slightly wistful. 'As far as I know, she is still there. Her name,' she added, 'was Seraphina.'

XXIV

The facts, as laid before Backhouse in rather florid English by the police officer at the city gaol, seemed straightforward. More than $3,000 had been removed from a secret drawer in the consul's desk at some point the previous day. It was money given to the consul for safekeeping by British travellers in the region. There had been many such travellers that month, which was why the sum was so exceptionally large.

No force had been used in the theft and it was thought a duplicate key had been employed. It was surely the case that only those very intimate with the workings of the consul's offices would have known of the drawer's existence. All servants had been searched, all employees questioned. It seemed that very few of them had ever had an opportunity to open the drawer or to spirit away the money.

But Dalrymple ... According to the porter, Dalrymple had arrived at the consulate in the late afternoon. He had been alone in the office for at least fifteen minutes. Yet, when questioned, Dalrymple had denied even being there. At first he claimed that he had been with Backhouse, then corrected himself and said he'd been in the company of Maria Guadalupe. But when the police called upon her, it emerged that his visit there had been much later.

'And his interview with me rather earlier,' Backhouse confirmed. 'It was a stormy meeting. I had reason to discipline him.'

'Just so.' The police officer smiled. 'A disgruntled man, a foolish and desperate act.'

Backhouse was shocked to discover that this was not Dalrymple's first experience of a Cuban gaol. He had been locked up at least twice before, the police officer revealed, on both occasions for debt. He was known in Havana as a man always in need of money.

'Take it from me, señor,' he concluded, 'your friend is not a man to trust.'

Shown into Dalrymple's prison cell, Backhouse was horrified by its dimensions. It was barely four feet by five, and hardly high enough for him to stand up straight. The interview was conducted with the two men standing facing one another at an uncomfortably short distance. Dalrymple, who had been lying curled on the floor when the door opened, leapt up on seeing Backhouse.

'At last!' It was a cry of joy. 'Am I free to go?'

Backhouse disliked Dalrymple, but he couldn't deny that he felt for his clerk then, as the door was banged shut again and all the elation drained from the man's face. It was replaced with anger; the self-righteous, self-pitying sort of anger that arose so quickly in Dalrymple. To emphasise his points as he protested his innocence, the dishevelled clerk banged hard upon the wall with the palm of his hand, a display of emotion that embarrassed Backhouse and made him wish he had not come.

'It's Crawford to blame, I tell you! Crawford! Crawford has always hated me. He has behaved like a blackguard to me and my family, and I know that he has, and that is why he wishes to ruin me. He wants no witnesses to his black-heartedness. You must believe me, Backhouse. You don't know what he is like . . .'

He rattled on without pause, cursing freely, frequently contradicting himself, blaming a great many people for his predicament, but principally the British consul. When Backhouse mentioned the evidence cited by the police officer, Dalrymple's anger grew suddenly fierce.

'I wasn't *there*, I tell you. Someone is *lying*. But there's nothing surprising about that, damn it. Havana's full of liars. Give me ten minutes of freedom and I'll find you a dozen different men prepared to swear on the Bible that I was with each of them for the entire day.'

'Which you were not,' Backhouse pointed out. 'As a matter of interest, if not at the consul's office, where were you?'

To Backhouse's surprise, Dalrymple mood changed again, as if he took the question as a sign that Backhouse was prepared to believe him. He seemed suddenly to relax.

'Yesterday afternoon? After seeing you? To tell the truth, I was giving myself to some nasty little whore down on the docks. You know how it is when you're angry. But don't for Christ's sake tell anyone. Not *anyone*. Do you know how prison works here? There's no food, and you have to pay for privileges – I mean the sort of things that make the difference between living and dying. I'm not joking, Backhouse! If Maria Guadalupe doesn't feed me I'll starve to death in here. And if she hears I was fucking some slut all afternoon, then she'll see to it that I starve to death anyway, even if they let me out.'

Backhouse was trying desperately hard not to allow his disgust to show.

'Could this . . . this woman you were with be found, do you think?'

Dalrymple put his back against the wall and let himself slide to the floor, his hand partly covering his face.

'Christ, I don't suppose so. There are hundreds of them down there, and they come and go like crabs. You'd have to ask them all, and even if you found her she'd almost certainly deny it. None of them would deliberately get caught up in anything that looked like trouble.'

'What did she look like?'

Dalrymple groaned and rolled his eyes, as if in disbelief.

'For Christ's sake, Backhouse, I wasn't looking at her *face*. She was black, skinny. What do you want? A description of what she looked like from behind?'

It was at that point Backhouse resolved to leave. He had heard quite enough, and Dalrymple revolted him. Even standing so close to him in a cell was repugnant. And yet, as he rattled the door to be let out, he was aware that Dalrymple's account and the way it was delivered – perhaps simply because it was so utterly shameless – was not entirely unconvincing.

Very coldly, Backhouse promised he would do whatever he could on his clerk's behalf.

'But you do believe me, don't you, Backhouse? Tell me you believe me!'

He raised himself up again, forgetting himself to such an extent that he even took hold of Backhouse's lapels.

Backhouse tried quietly to disengage himself.

'I'm afraid, Dalrymple, that nothing you have said convinces me that you are the victim of a plot by Mr Crawford. Be sensible. You haven't actually given me one cogent reason why he would stoop to such a thing.'

'One reason? One reason!' Dalrymple was enraged. 'I've given you a dozen. He hates me, for one thing. That's reason enough. And I know too much about him. I know he makes money from slaves. I know some of the deals he's been involved in. And what about this? I know someone's selling our navy's sailing plans, right here in Havana. Who else could that be, do you think?'

Backhouse had been about to rattle the lock for a second time but he paused then, turning back to Dalrymple with a look of astonishment that the other took for disbelief.

'It's true, I tell you. I had it from a whore in one of the brothels by the old wall. Oh, not a woman like the other one. This one's a good girl, a hard worker. She's got a mother and a sister to support. I've been seeing her for years.'

'And what did she tell you?' Something told Backhouse it was important not to seem too eager.

'She had it from a man called O'Driscoll. Part Irish, part Spanish. He runs labour gangs on the southern dock. He's a regular of hers too. He told her that all the slave captains know the British sailing plans. He's got friends among them. Says they get them from someone in the old city who is making thousands from it.'

'And you think that's Crawford?' Backhouse felt the conversation was hanging from a frayed rope. One word in the wrong place might send Dalrymple off into another of his rants.

But Backhouse's willingness to listen to him was having a soothing effect on the other man, and now his voice was quieter.

'Who else? He does a lot of business in Jamaica, doesn't he? They'd trust him with any amount of information over there. But I'm the only one who's worked it out, and that's why he wants me out of the way.'

'And if I needed to, could I find this man O'Driscoll?'

Dalrymple didn't seem to think the question a strange one. He was, Backhouse realised, too self-centred to imagine an ulterior motive.

'If he's the person I'm thinking of, he works out of one of the taverns on the south side. No idea which one. Shouldn't be too hard to find though, if you had a guide to take you round, someone who could translate for you. Do you know anyone?'

Backhouse suggested Lavender but Dalrymple rolled his eyes again.

'Oh, for mercy's sake, not the sodomite. He's probably in Crawford's pocket.' He mentioned the name and address of someone he considered suitable, then cleared his throat as if the mention of taverns had sent his thoughts off at a tangent. 'I don't suppose you could get me any liquor in here, could you, Backhouse? Rum would do, nothing fancy. As much as you can manage. I'm thirsty as a salt cod, and I'm going to need a drop or two to sustain me where I'm going.'

It was not a request that Backhouse regarded with favour, although two days later he rather regretted his rigidity. That was when he heard that Dalrymple had been transferred to the cells of the notorious Tacón gaol, and for three or four days was permitted no visitors.

137

XXV

In his chaotic drawing room in Lowther Street, John Jerusalems had pulled a chair close to the fire and was contemplating a document sent to him earlier that day by a contact of his at the Admiralty.

Outside, the pavements were deserted. It had been a pleasant spring day: cab drivers had rolled back their cuffs, sparrows had been gathering moss, old men had dozed on park benches. But at sunset the warmth evaporated, and now a sharp-edged moon was sitting in splendour above the streets.

For once, Jerusalems was not on the move. He had been on his feet most of the day with various visitors, talking incessantly, or else dictating letters in rapid, irregular bursts. But now, with the hands of the clock a little short of three o'clock, there was time for stillness. He read the document three times, slowly, nodding as he read.

It had taken him by surprise: an intelligent piece of work, and a perceptive one, not at all the sort of thing he expected from the Admiralty. Its author, a rising young man, had been asked to investigate – informally, from the Jamaica end – the security of the navy's sailing plans. He had concluded that there was nothing to suggest any breach in security.

And yet . . .

It was clear from his prose that the writer had his doubts. He was far too circumspect to state as much, but he had concluded his report by suggesting various measures that might be adopted 'in the best interests of all concerned', 'by way of reassurance'.

These included greatly limiting the circulation of the sailing plans to only a handful of senior officers; requiring the collated plans to be circulated only in cipher; and permitting ships' captains to submit altered sailing plans at short notice.

The report, of course, was not an official document. Officially the Admiralty had already scotched the idea that any problem could possibly exist. But, as Thomas Staveley pointed out in a separate note to Jerusalems, the author was well connected, and were the report to be given a wider circulation, some notice might be taken. What extra measures in Jamaica, Staveley asked, would Jerusalems recommend?

The little man considered the report for a final time, then took up his pen and added his reply to Staveley in neat letters across the top of the document.

No additional measures required, he wrote.

XXVI

There had been rain. A warm, wind-tossed downpour had swept across the city, turning the dust to mud, so that the southern docks seemed to steam in the heat. Backhouse picked his way through the market-day crowds as carefully as he could, anxious to avoid the rain-filled potholes. Ahead of him, Ezekiel, an interpreter, was making leisurely progress, pausing whenever it suited him to exchange words with passers-by in rapid, colloquial Spanish that Backhouse had no hope of following.

Ezekiel had been Dalrymple's recommendation, and Backhouse was already regretting that he had followed his assistant's advice. Ezekiel had struck him from the first as a disreputable fellow, probably one of Maria Guadalupe's many relatives to whom Dalrymple owed a favour. The almost servile respect he showed Backhouse to his face was noticeably absent the moment he turned his back and began to joke with his acquaintances on the market stalls. Backhouse felt certain that he himself was the object of these exchanges; and to make matters worse the fellow spat a very great deal, even by the standards of Havana. It was not a habit Backhouse cared to indulge.

The suspicion that he was being taken for a fool grew as they meandered around the docks, stopping every ten or twelve paces while Ezekiel engaged someone in conversation. After some of these instances the interpreter would turn to Backhouse and bow in a manner that the Englishman found rather embarrassing, reassuring him that he had been given *very excellent information* about the whereabouts of the man O'Driscoll. Backhouse, whose efforts to learn Spanish were in earnest, had been listening intently and grew more and more convinced that the Irishman's name had never even been mentioned.

The crisis came in one of the narrow streets that ran westward from the waterfront towards the city wall. Here Ezekiel led him into a small coffee house, empty but for themselves, where they were greeted with great warmth by the owner and ushered to a table near the window. Drinks were brought that Backhouse hadn't ordered while the owner and the guide chatted noisily.

'We need to wait here for a few minutes,' Ezekiel explained eventually. 'José has a nephew who will be here soon, who will most certainly know where to find this man you seek. So please, take comfort. The coffee here is excellent. All the English come to this place.'

That was so palpably a lie that Backhouse didn't even bother to contradict it, but sighed and resigned himself to a wait, only to be interrupted when a small boy emerged from the back of the shop with a tray of cigars that he held respectfully for Backhouse's consideration.

'No, thank you. No cigars.' Backhouse was too afraid of losing face in front of Ezekiel to attempt any Spanish.

'Are you sure, señor?' Ezekiel seemed pained. 'These cigars are very fine. José's nephew works at one of the factories. He is able to obtain these at a very special price.' He mentioned a sum that Backhouse didn't quite catch. 'That is for a box, of course. With such cigars one does not sell them singly.'

He said something to the boy, who disappeared and returned with a different tray, and it was then that Backhouse began to realise the true reason for this diversion.

'My word,' he exclaimed. 'I don't believe we are waiting here for news of O'Driscoll at all. I believe you have brought me here on commission, so your friend can sell me cigars.'

Ezekiel's protestations were loud and anguished, fluctuating between outraged resentment at such a slur, and rather sickly protestations of his good faith; and all the time he interrupted himself with attempts to reassure Backhouse as to the quality of the cigars, as if convinced that the Englishman's objections would vanish were the true nature of the bargain made clear to him.

But Backhouse had had enough. Rising to his feet, very red in the face, he threw a bundle of notes on to the table – rather too many, he realised later – and declared that he would continue his search alone. To his even greater annoyance, the interpreter had the effrontery to follow him, still protesting, into the street, and when Backhouse raised his voice to send him on his way, he realised the scene had attracted an unedifying crowd of spectators. To escape them he turned his back on the sea and strode off with great determination, turning right at the first opportunity in order to escape the onlookers' gaze.

Subsequent unplanned turns followed, and by the time Backhouse re-emerged on the waterfront, it was on a stretch of the bay that was unfamiliar to him. Calmer, he paused to take stock. The effect of such rapid progress had been to generate an uncomfortable amount of perspiration, and the shade of some of the taverns looked appealing. It was in places such as those that he had expected to search for O'Driscoll and, still buoyed by the momentum of his own temper, he marched with chin held high into the first tavern he came to.

It was true that his Spanish was not fluent. It was also true that no one in that particular establishment seemed to have heard of anyone called O'Driscoll. But he felt his first foray had been a success. And as the place had been almost empty, he determined to try another.

It was not until he entered the third tavern that he began to feel any misgivings. By then he had drifted a little distance from the waterfront, and this particular place was entered down a small flight of steps. It too was far from busy, but as soon as he entered he felt the attention of every drinker was focused on him. The proprietor, if not hostile, was certainly not welcoming. Nevertheless, he listened to Backhouse's Spanish patiently enough and even apologised that he was not able to help.

Had he been even slightly less accommodating, Backhouse might have given up his solo venture there and then. But his pride was not yet completely satisfied, and when he came to the next tavern, this one some thirty paces further from the water-front and down a somewhat longer flight of steps, he barely hesitated.

This establishment was busy. A little light filtered in from street level but it was still gloomy enough for lamps to be lit, adding to the intolerable heat. They burned with the smoky pungency of cheap oil, and by their glow Backhouse could make out various groups of men clustered around tables. On each one, large earthenware jugs held what might have been water, but was almost certainly rum.

As no waiter was in view, Backhouse felt obliged to advance further into the room, until intercepted by a small, balding man with an elaborate moustache, who appeared to be the proprietor. A Spaniard, Backhouse thought, but his unsmiling features projected no sense of European fraternity.

When Backhouse attempted to greet him in his best Spanish, he felt sure the tension in the room diminished a little, almost as though it were impossible for them to believe that anyone speaking their language in such a childlike manner could possibly pose a threat. But when he mentioned the name O'Driscoll the change was immediate. He saw the proprietor's eyes flick instinctively to his right, and he was aware that somewhere in the darkness two or three men had risen to their feet.

The desire to turn and look in that direction was very strong. Worse still, so was the urge to look behind him, to rehearse his route to the door. But he was an Englishman going about his lawful business. Backhouse had no intention of flinching.

The proprietor stepped back then, and another man took his place; also small, but solid and intimidating, with no discernible neck around which to put a collar. His skin was dark, his features coarse, his cheeks rough with stubble.

'Who are you?' he asked abruptly in English.

'I am a representative of the British government,' Backhouse replied. 'Are you going to be courteous enough to assist me?'

Someone in the darkness asked a question in Spanish and a tense exchange ensued. Backhouse thought he heard the word 'police'.

'And why do you want to see this Señor O'Driscoll?'

Backhouse drew himself up to his full height.

'That, sir, is between Mr O'Driscoll and myself.'

The urge to turn around was almost unbearable now. It was absurd, of course, to believe he was in any real danger. This was the middle of Havana, in the middle of the day. Nevertheless . . .

Further exchanges in Spanish were taking place around him. Before they were concluded Backhouse heard the door open again, and it gave him an excuse to turn his head. The result was not reassuring. Behind him, only four or five paces back and blocking his view of the door, five men barred his path. Their faces were expressionless.

'Come now, señor . . .' His interrogator was smiling. He had seen Backhouse look round. 'I think you could tell us a little more. If you do, perhaps it may turn out that someone has heard of this fellow you seek.'

But Backhouse had no intention of saying more. They would not prevent him from leaving, surely? He was the British judge to the Anglo-Spanish Mixed Commission. He had only to turn and stride out purposefully and they would part to let him pass . . .

From behind him he heard the scrape of a knife against a pocket stone. Very deliberately, as if he were meant to hear it.

Turn, and stride out.

Then, from the door, a woman's voice was speaking in Spanish. He turned to look but the men behind him still blocked his view. The speaker's voice was quiet but did not lack authority. To his surprise, the man who had confronted him replied to her directly, leaning his head slightly so that he could see beyond his own men. He spoke very quickly, almost irritably, and seemed to finish with a question.

The reply was only a few words, but another question followed from one of the groups at the tables. Backhouse waited and listened while a conversation developed between the newcomer and the men in the room. He heard the name O'Driscoll more than once, also his own name although he had not given it. At one point he even heard the name of Queen Victoria, a reference that was accompanied by merriment all round. By then Backhouse already knew the situation had changed, the danger gone. The men were enjoying the exchanges, making jokes at his expense.

Then suddenly it was all over. With a shrug and a wave of his hand, his main interrogator turned and moved back to his table. There was a general murmur and the scraping of stools as those who had been standing seated themselves. Suddenly no one was interested in Backhouse. He felt foolish and a little absurd as he retreated to the door.

As he approached it, he was better able to make out the features of the woman who had taken up his cause. She was smiling at him.

'You must forgive me, madam,' he began, holding out his hand, 'but I'm afraid I've forgotten your name.'

At his insistence, they repaired to a café on the waterfront, a place of Leonarda's choosing, famous for its ices, a place frequented by *habaneros* of various shades, where the English judge might go without exciting too much – *too* much – comment. There he insisted on ordering, testing himself with the pronunciations, unconcerned by blunders that would have been impossible to countenance in the company of Ezekiel.

But Backhouse found he didn't care. Perhaps it was relief: for the first time in his life he had felt himself in genuine physical danger. Or perhaps it was humility: he had snubbed a woman who'd asked for his help; he had blundered into an awkward and potentially dangerous situation from which she had nevertheless extracted him; she had seen him humiliated at the hands of some very low fellows; and on leaving the tavern she had not sought any advantage from the encounter. She had not even made any reference to their previous meeting. In the circumstances, his very poor Spanish did not seem such a significant failing.

Leonarda was pleasantly surprised. In his office, Backhouse had seemed to her the Englishman of a hundred Spanish jokes, all stiffness and self-righteousness and hypocritical morality. Even when intervening on his behalf, she had not expected thanks. The English did not like to be helped, she knew. It embarrassed them. The Englishman whose name she bore had been too broken to care, but there were few like him. For the rest, unsolicited help was something of an impertinence. And help from a woman – a mulatto woman – was surely more than could be borne.

But he had taken it well. Embarrassed, yes. Awkward, certainly. But his gratitude seemed genuine and was expressed frankly, even if the formality of his language conspired to obscure it. She had not been seeking to renew their acquaintance, and on leaving the tavern she had expected to leave him to his own devices. But he had shaken her hand and had pressed her – rather against her inclination – to accept some refreshment. And when a waiter appeared offering cigars, he explained with a self-deprecating smile why a flush had risen to his cheeks.

Backhouse found himself in a situation he had never imagined. He had left his home that morning expecting the day to be much like any other. True, he had hired an interpreter to accompany him on a certain piece of business, but that was not unusual. In investigating the case of the Spanish slave ship he had proceeded in a similar way.

But now he found himself in a café he had never heard of, eating an ice in the company of an unchaperoned woman – a mulatta, as the natives of the city would have it, using the term to cover every degree of mixed blood. Moreover, a mulatta to whom he owed a considerable debt.

But he was doing nothing actually improper, nothing he need be ashamed of. And after the appalling heat of that blasted tavern, it was good to sit there by the bay. The ice was good too, much better than the ones he'd had at La Dominica. He felt sufficiently relaxed to risk a question.

'May I ask, madam, what arguments you used to persuade my friends back there to part with my company?'

Leonarda laughed at that, and Backhouse found himself smiling too, although the humour was not entirely intentional.

'I told them that you were a very important man and that, if they killed you, the Captain-General would need to find a dozen people to execute in return, to keep the English happy. And as the English officials would most certainly know where you had planned to go today, the Captain-General's men would not find it difficult to decide where to search for the necessary victims.'

'And they laughed at that?'

She looked away, trying to hide her smile.

'They laughed because one of them said you had legs like a sparrow.'

'Really, madam!'

Backhouse felt his cheeks flush again. Beneath the surface of the good sport, Backhouse, like all other Englishmen of his class and generation, had been taught to cherish his dignity above everything, perhaps even above his honour. It grew from boyhood, heavier with every day that passed, heavier still with the acquisition of a wife and family.

And it seemed to Backhouse that ever since setting foot in Havana his dignity had been under attack. From Crawford, from Dalrymple, from Spanish officialdom, even from his own servants. Yet now, when he should have felt mortified, he felt oddly liberated. Sparrow legs, indeed! Outrageous that a woman should repeat such a comment, and to repeat it to his face . . . And yet he did not feel particularly outraged. Back in the tavern he must indeed have cut a ridiculous figure. Of course, were others to know of his humiliation – Crawford, for instance, or Lavender, or Staveley back in London . . . Were Grace to know . . . The thought appalled him.

But why should they? The woman opposite him belonged to a different Havana. And seemed . . . Backhouse couldn't really explain his instinct, but there was something strikingly generous in her behaviour that day. It was the first time since his arrival in Cuba that anyone had rendered him a service without attempting to profit from it.

'Would it be rude to ask what took *you* to such a place, madam? If I may say so, it does not strike me as any sort of place for a young lady.'

'Believe it or not, I was looking for a book. It's a long story. I can tell it another time.'

Backhouse was intrigued. It was his first ever prolonged social encounter with someone less white than himself, and he was a little embarrassed as to how to conduct himself. Of course he had already interviewed various sailors and *emancipados* as part of his official duties, but those had either been supplicants seeking favour or witnesses to be brought to the truth. This encounter was different. She did not call him *sir*, in English, as an inferior might; she called him *señor*, in the way a lady of Havana might address a gentleman. And then there was that English surname . . .

Unfamiliar with Havana's complicated system of social strata, he realised he had no idea how to categorise her. So he simply reverted to common courtesy, as he would have done had she been introduced to him in a London drawing room.

He realised she was watching him from behind her ice.

'May I ask you the same question, señor? What leads you to seek someone in such a tavern? It is a surprising place to come across the island's English judge.'

Relaxed he might have been, but Backhouse knew he needed to be careful. Clearly he could not betray the true reason for his interest in O'Driscoll, yet to offer no explanation would only encourage speculation. So he explained to her that another robbery had taken place at the consulate. Very different from the last, he emphasised. No forced entry, no violence. But the police had arrested his assistant – misguidedly, he asserted – and he had promised to locate certain individuals who might be able to contribute to his defence.

But Leonarda was not to be satisfied so easily. She wanted to know more about the robbery, about why Dalrymple had been arrested. Backhouse felt certain he was not entitled to share such information and was reticent at first, until he realised that anyone with a coin in their hand who applied to the officer at the gaol-house would elicit the full story without any difficulty whatsoever.

When he had finished, Leonarda was still looking at him, meeting his eyes with such directness that he blinked and looked down.

'So your assistant insists he wasn't there?'

'That is correct.'

'And you believe him?'

Backhouse hesitated. Dalrymple was a difficult man to trust, yet he had found his testimony oddly convincing. He felt certain that if Dalrymple were lying, he would have created a much more elaborate construction to hide his guilt, and one that would have shown him in a far better light.

'Of course I believe him. He is a British official. I understand he has lost his way out here somewhat, but he was raised a gentleman. His father was the British judge here once, you know. I cannot believe him a sneak thief.'

Backhouse sounded more certain – and a good deal more pompous – than he felt. But Leonarda made no reply. She was finishing her ice, apparently lost in thought. Noticing the delicacy with which she handled the long silver spoon, he wondered for the first time who she really was. Havana was full of things exotic and enigmatic. Hitherto he had tended simply to accept them as part of the scenery.

'This man O'Driscoll,' she mused aloud, 'the one you were looking for. At the tavern they were all a little afraid of him. They said he was a gangmaster – someone who trades in the labour of the *emancipados*. Such men are not known for their tenderness. I wonder how Señor Dalrymple's defence depends upon him?'

But Backhouse avoided the question.

'So they *did* know him?' he asked, and his interest was genuine. 'I don't suppose they mentioned where I might find him?'

'They said you wouldn't find him unless he wanted you to. And that he did not give interviews with strangers except by appointment.'

'But how the devil is one to make an appointment?'

She smiled.

'Fortunately, I asked them that too. They thought it was highly unlikely he would wish to see you.' She turned and said a few words in Spanish to the man waiting on them. 'However, if you wish to try, señor, I would suggest a letter would be a safer way to proceed.'

Paper was brought, and a pen, and he watched as she wrote down the address of a tavern where O'Driscoll's post might be sent. He realised as she wrote that their encounter was nearly over. He felt somehow that her departure came too soon, that he had not yet learned all he should have done. However, he had set out hoping to find O'Driscoll, and here it was, the address in his hand.

'Madam, that matter you raised with me. About that earlier burglary. I don't know what your interest is in the affair, and it is not really my place to raise it through official channels . . .' Those were the wrong words. He sounded formal and patronising. 'But if by chance I were to hear anything more about it, I would be happy to inform you. Is there an address at which I might write to you?'

He paused, awkwardly. But Señora Leigh did not look embarrassed. In fact she smiled, and added her address to the same sheet of paper as O'Driscoll's.

'Perhaps, señor, your friend Dalrymple may know something of that earlier burglary? He has been on the island many years. Unfortunately, given his current place of residence, I'm unable to ask him for myself.'

Backhouse bowed. He thought it unlikely he would question Dalrymple on the subject. The affair was none of his business, and Dalrymple would surely think it very strange. Perhaps

Leonarda was aware of his reluctance, for she smiled to herself as she took her leave. He watched her as far as the corner of the Calle Cuba, where she turned and looked back at him. She was still smiling, he thought. Not at anything he'd said, but as though he himself were the object of her amusement.

XXVII

The San Isidoro Estate lay in the region west of Havana, an area of forests and plantations on the fringe of the mountains, some two days' ride from the city. On hearing of Leonarda's plans to travel outside Havana, Marty had insisted on making his carriage available to her and eventually, worn down by his insistence, she had accepted; so she made the journey slowly but in comfort, with Rosa in attendance. She had written in advance to secure comfortable rooms along their route, including at the small roadside inn half an hour's ride from the plantation. If the proprietor was surprised that the English lady of the letter turned out in the flesh to be a young and striking mulatta, he made no comment. She tipped in gold, and gold was a glass through which every face seemed fair.

Leonarda had travelled in that region before. When Edward Leigh, the dying, drunken Englishman, had begged her to marry him, he had vowed he would go back to Jamaica, to his estates and his responsibilities, and live his life in a better way – if only she would go with him. He would quit Havana, he promised, and would drink nothing but water; and before leaving the island he would complete the study tour of the island's plantations that had brought him to Cuba five years earlier – a tour that had been quickly abandoned in favour of Havana's sweet oblivions.

She hadn't really believed his promises. She had heard the pleading of drunkards many times before. Yet there had been a quality of anguish in his pleas that was new to her, and strangely affecting; she had agreed, in the end, out of curiosity as well as out of pity. But he had been as good as his word. By the time they reached the district of San Isidoro, he had been barely able to stand – pale, gaunt, shaking uncontrollably, vomiting whenever he tried to hold down food. But there had been no liquor. From somewhere he had found the strength. She had held his hand as he lay in a local inn, sweating and shivering, scarcely aware of her presence, and she had wondered how she found herself there, with him, in that green, steaming, unexpected world.

Since then she had travelled to the English islands and beyond, had seen her name stamped and registered as the owner of an estate much larger than the one at San Isidoro; but the green of those valleys still affected her. It seemed almost impossible that whole lives, from birth to death, were lived in the glaring streets of Havana, coated in its brown and ochre dust, while all the time, at so little distance, the still, untroubled forest lay in silence.

The plantations were different, of course. There was little silence there, little comfort for the ear or the eye; to visit even for a day was to learn an unpleasant lesson about the meaning of suffering. Edward Leigh, the stranger who was her husband, had woken from the throes of his withdrawal to stare upon the sugar cane fields of Cuba with hollow, blinking eyes. And on their arrival in Jamaica, he had immediately set about placing all his affairs, and the running of his estates, in the hands of a young lawyer derided for his idealism, a man committed to God and to fair practices.

Leonarda arrived at the gates of the San Isidoro Estate unannounced on a morning heavy with heat. She made no pretence of calling at the plantation house itself, which she knew to be empty, but directed her carriage to the white-board house on the edge of the plantation where Ramón Hernandez kept his country mistress.

She was admitted by a maidservant who peered at her with suspicion but asked nothing more than her name before ushering her into an empty parlour. It was a pleasant room, small but airy, neatly furnished in the modern taste; but it gave no clue to the woman who lived there. Leonarda waited some minutes before the door opened and a woman who was little more than a girl appeared behind it. Seraphina, who had once been bound in marriage to the ruffian known as the Salt-Eater.

Leonarda's first surprise was how tiny she was. Slight of figure, her curves muted, and in height no taller than Leonarda's shoulder, from a distance she could easily have been taken for a child. And the expression on her face had something a little childish in it too – the suspicion and anxiety of one who fears she is about to be admonished for an unknown misdemeanour. But Leonarda could also see why the wealthy Ramón Hernandez had taken her as a mistress. Her skin was the palest of browns, much fairer than Leonarda's, and she had the face of a Madonna: eyes almost black beneath long lashes, every feature small and smooth and perfect. A beauty in miniature.

But she did not come into the room. She remained half hidden by the door, poised to disappear in an instant.

'Señora Leigh?' Misled perhaps by the difficult English surname she had clearly not expected her visitor to look like Leonarda. 'If you have come from him, from the man in Havana . . . If you have, I swear I have nothing more to tell you . . .'

Leonarda rose and held out her hand.

'I have not come from anyone else. I have come only for myself. I'm hoping you can help me. Please, will you not come in?'

She came, but only hesitantly, while Leonarda soothed her with trivial conversation about the décor of the room, the heat of the morning, her dread of hurricanes. Only when the two were seated did she begin on the subject that had brought her to San Isidoro, and even then she was careful to begin with her own story – her journey abroad, the death in her absence of a very dear friend. When she first mentioned the burglary at the office of the British consul, she saw Seraphina draw back a little, saw the fear return to her face.

'I knew it. I knew you'd come to find out more. But I know nothing. I told him everything I knew.'

Again Leonarda tried to soothe her.

'I give you my word, no one else has sent me. Whoever has been here asking questions is a stranger to me.' She paused. 'Three men were arrested for the murder of my friend, and all of them are either dead or gone from Havana. One of them was your husband. Please, I beg you, did he ever tell you anything about what happened that night?'

'No!' Seraphina almost shouted the word. 'Pedro never spoke to me about such things. He never really spoke to me at all. I was his slave. I hated him.'

The memory of that time clearly distressed her, and even though Leonarda pressed, she continued to protest her ignorance. Pedro the Salt-Eater had gone out that night and had never returned. Only later had Seraphina learned that a watchman had been murdered and that Pedro was accused of it. She had never even wondered whether or not he was guilty. His arrest had left her alone and destitute; to her, that had been the only truth that mattered.

'So tell me about your other visitor, the man who's been asking the same things. What did he want to know?' It was a question that puzzled Leonarda more than she cared to show.

But Seraphina had been too alarmed and too afraid to remember his name, and had asked him nothing. She could say only that he was white, a hard-looking man, she said. She had been terrified of him, terrified he might tell her beloved Ramón about the life she'd once led.

'He said Ramón would never touch me again if he knew I had been used by such a man as Pedro. He said no white man would touch a black man's whore. So I told him everything I could – but I had so little to tell. I just told him over and over that I knew nothing about what happened that night, until in the end he seemed satisfied and went away.'

'And so,' Leonarda concluded, 'there really is no one left who can tell me what happened. You were my last hope. Of Pedro's two comrades, one is dead and the other gone abroad.'

Leonarda sensed rather than saw the reaction in the young

woman. Nothing obvious. Perhaps just a momentary tensing. But she knew at once there was more.

It took another quarter-hour for her to elicit the truth. Perhaps the isolation of that estate house had started to tell upon its occupant, but Leonarda began to feel that Seraphina *wanted* to tell her, that the strain of keeping an extra secret was too great for her. The previous caller had frightened her; Leonarda did not.

So Seraphina gave out the story in fragments. It was not hers to tell. She had promised to tell no one and she had kept her word. She would never betray a friend. Yet as the rain began to sweep across San Isidoro, the truth emerged. Tartuffo was not dead. It was true he had been stabbed and beaten in an alleyway and left for dead. But he had not died. He had been smuggled from the city barely breathing, by a friend, a fisherman, whose sister had tended him while he recovered his health. Seraphina knew this because Tartuffo had travelled to San Isidoro when barely recovered, still pale and gaunt, and had begged her for money.

'He is a good man,' she insisted. 'Not like Pedro. A thief and a pickpocket, of course, but not a violent man. Not a murderer. He was often kind to me. So I gave him what money I had here and made him promise never to come again.'

'And do you know where he went?' Leonarda heard her own voice tremble slightly.

The trace of a smile lit up the younger woman's face.

'There is a Spanish missionary in San Miguel, a little further down the valley. He has a very pious assistant, a grey-haired Negro who walks with a limp. I saw him from my carriage one day. I couldn't tell you what name he goes under, but he looked very much like someone I once knew.'

Leonarda did not remain much longer at the little white-board house. She could see that Seraphina was growing restless. As she said her farewells at the top of the steps, she asked if there was anything she could send from Havana, or any service she could perform – anything at all that might give Seraphina pleasure. But the young woman shook her head.

'No, there's nothing. Nothing at all. I'm happy here. Ramón gives me everything I need.'

So Leonarda took her hand and thanked her, and drove away full of the sadness of the place, leaving Seraphina clinging tightly to her loneliness.

XXVIII

To Backhouse's astonishment, his letter to O'Driscoll received a reply.

Not a prompt one. Days had passed and had brought nothing, and he had begun to steel himself for another expedition to the docks when a terse note was delivered by hand to his office. If Mr Backhouse still wished to talk to Mr O'Driscoll, he could do so at the Golden Flag that afternoon at four o'clock.

The Golden Flag was an establishment that Backhouse knew by name. It had a reputation for rowdiness, but it was near the centre of the old city, and was open to the street, with large, reassuring windows; so, if not exactly respectable, it was at least considered a safe place for an honest man to visit.

At four o'clock it was almost empty and Backhouse had little difficulty identifying the man he was seeking. He'd imagined O'Driscoll as a young man, probably something of a common ruffian. But the man sitting alone at a small table in the shadowy interior was in his late thirties, his close-cropped hair already steely grey, and he wore a European suit of respectable cut, the collar high in the style that was in vogue in Havana that season.

These superficial signs of respectability cheered Backhouse, but on closer inspection O'Driscoll appeared less welcoming. His face was lean, all taut flesh and hard angles, and he did not smile when Backhouse introduced himself. His eyes were cold, and not without a hint of menace.

'You wished to see me, Mr Backhouse?' he began. He spoke English with an accent that sounded part Irish and part American.

'About the British navy's sailing plans, you said. Forgive me if I tell you that your letter was a little vague.'

He had not risen when Backhouse approached, nor had he offered him a seat, so Backhouse selected one and sat down anyway.

'I heard a rumour that you'd witnessed them being bought and sold.'

'Is that so?' O'Driscoll raised an eyebrow but did not seem surprised. 'This is a city of rumours, Mr Backhouse. You shouldn't believe them all. What exactly was it you wanted to know?'

'Whatever you can tell me.' He was playing for time a little, wondering what cards he held, what he could offer a man like O'Driscoll in return for information.

But to his surprise the gangmaster did not haggle. After a few moments of thought he simply shrugged.

'Why not? If it stirs up a bit of trouble for Her Majesty's navy, I'm in favour. It's an Irishman's duty, if you like, and a Spaniard's too. I can't tell you who does the selling though. I've never known that. But the information gets through to the slavers all right. I know. I crewed those boats for years and I know plenty who still do. Listen. This is how it works.'

As he talked, Backhouse wondered at his helpfulness. O'Driscoll's candour only made sense if he believed that a Briton was involved, and involved deeply enough to cause a scandal.

While Backhouse listened, O'Driscoll described a system of complicated business transactions whereby the masters of slave ships could purchase information about British patrols. The individuals who provided this information were no more than simple intermediaries. They too had purchased it, rather more expensively, from contacts of their own, who had in turn paid larger sums still.

O'Driscoll seemed to rather admire the way it all worked. The man at the apex of the triangle, he calculated, must be making thousands.

'But you don't know who he is?'

'I honestly don't. My acquaintance used to buy the information from someone near the fish market. It cost him a king's ransom, but he turned a tidy profit from it. And that, Mr Backhouse, is all I can tell you. If you can use it to hang a British admiral, all well and good.'

Backhouse was pleased. This was at least something he could report to Staveley, corroboration that naval secrets really were reaching the slavers through Havana. And despite himself, he kept recalling Dalrymple's denunciation of Crawford. Crawford had contacts in Jamaica as well as in Havana. And he certainly enjoyed a very comfortable existence . . .

When O'Driscoll made it clear that he had nothing further to add, Backhouse was quick to escape from the Golden Flag. He would write to Staveley at once. And he would confer with Lavender, to see what his next step should be. While it was true that he was achieving nothing of significance at the Mixed Commission, in this other matter, at least, he had made a little progress.

When he visited Dalrymple in prison three days later, Backhouse was shocked by his clerk's appearance. The prisoner looked haggard and unwashed, and an anaemic grey stubble had spread over his chin and cheeks. The odour of stale sweat accompanied him into the narrow-windowed interview room, along with another smell, more pungent, which Backhouse rather feared was stale urine. Worse than all, Dalrymple seemed sullen, as though his brimming store of indignation had been drained dry by the hardships of incarceration.

But he brightened considerably when he saw the items Backhouse had brought with him: money, tobacco, brandy, a pile of clean shirts and, rather optimistically, a Bible. Dalrymple seemed genuinely touched.

'It really is hell in here, old man. I can't tell you. Look.' He pointed to a scratch on his cheek. 'I got that simply getting out of the way of a fight. But these things will help. If you can pay enough in here, it's not too bad.'

When Backhouse tried to talk about the charges against him, Dalrymple seemed barely interested. Informed that Crawford was not agitating for his prosecution – that he had in fact written to Cuba's Captain-General requesting his release – Dalrymple shrugged wearily.

'That's just words. He knows I'm finished. He can afford to behave like a decent human being for once. Whatever makes him look good. I don't suppose you had any luck finding that whore, did you?'

Backhouse, having taken Dalrymple's word for it that the task was impossible, had not even tried. So instead he told him about his interview with O'Driscoll.

'It's Crawford behind it, old man, I'm telling you.' Dalrymple seemed to think further discussion of the subject was pointless. 'It has to be someone with good connections in Jamaica, doesn't it? And there aren't many people in Havana who can claim those.'

He thought for a moment.

'If you say the information is coming from somewhere near the fish market, then I suppose Marty might be able to throw some light on it. You know who I mean? Francisco Marty, the theatre man. Marty controls the fish market, and he keeps his ear to the ground. But you can't just walk in and start asking Marty questions. He's like royalty here in Havana. You'd need a proper introduction. Tell me, what's happening about that porter? You know, the one who says he saw me?'

Backhouse told him as gently as he could that the porter was adamant, and that the police thought him an honest man.

'Of course,' Dalrymple sneered. 'Honest enough to stick to the story he's been paid to tell.'

Backhouse was afraid the longer they lingered on the subject, the more desperate Dalrymple's plight would appear, so, almost without thinking, in an effort to change the subject, he asked Dalrymple if he remembered the previous burglary at the consul's office.

At first the prisoner showed little interest in the question, merely nodding listlessly and continuing to examine the shirts Backhouse had brought him. But then, as if a thought had struck him out of the blue, he looked up.

'Good lord, there was something fishy about that one, too, wasn't there?' He narrowed his eyes. 'It was a funny business, you know. Apart from the jewels, most of the stuff they stole was worthless. And there was money in one of the drawers that they didn't even find.'

Backhouse waited while Dalrymple delved back into his memory.

'Could Crawford have cooked up the whole thing? No, I hardly think so. Not his style. But he did behave strangely about it though. I remember going over there the following morning to have a snoop around and finding Crawford in the garden. Came across him by the sundial and saw he had a small velvet case in his hands. You know, a jewellery case. He said it was the one the jewels had been in and that he'd found it under a bush where the thieves had thrown it.' Dalrymple was shaking his head. 'The thing is, I'd already had a good look around – just in case they'd dropped anything, you know – and I remember being surprised I'd missed it. You don't think . . . ?'

But his interest began to fade as quickly as it had flared up.

'No, it doesn't make any sense. If Crawford had arranged for someone else to steal the jewels, he wouldn't have been out there tidying up after them, would he? There'd be no need. And if he'd stolen the things himself, he wouldn't have needed to hit his own night-watchman over the head. He's far too fastidious for that sort of thing anyway. He wouldn't have the stomach for it.'

But it occurred to Backhouse that a horror of bloodshed did not necessarily make a man honest, and that history probably contained its fair share of fastidious villains.

XXIX

The Spanish missionary was away. Somewhere in the east, Leonarda was told, preaching the gospel to slaves fresh from Africa. The plantation owners, she knew, tolerated such missionaries with a degree of suspicion. Zealotry was distrusted and so were peninsular Spaniards, whose European arrogance might easily turn out to conceal dangerous liberal leanings. But the overseers would keep an eye on him, and the Bible message was always encouraged on the plantations. In the sugar fields, the owners felt, the gospel of humility could not be preached too loudly.

In the missionary's absence, his assistant looked after the mission house. It stood in a grove of *tam-tam* trees, on the edge of the little village of St Miguel, only an hour further by road from the San Isidoro Estate, and was in reality little more than a wooden hut with a cross whitewashed on its wall. In front of it, in a poorly tended garden, two lines of dusty vegetables were being strangled by weeds. When the Spanish missionary was resident, the shack served as a schoolhouse to a handful of children rounded up from the fields; but when the missionary was away there were few visitors, and the peace of the grove remained largely unbroken.

Leonarda's carriage was too wide for the rough track that led up to her destination so she left Rosa sitting in the shade and completed her journey on foot, parasol in hand, placing her feet carefully as she climbed. It was still early in the day but her white dress caught the sunlight, a pale scratch on the green skin of the forest.

The missionary's assistant must have heard her approach because before she emerged from the trees he had appeared in the doorway of the mission house, a grey, slightly stooped figure, his hair short, his hands clasped in front of him as if ready for prayer. He was, Leonarda noticed, barefoot.

She had expected evasion: nobody seemed particularly eager to talk about Pedro the Salt-Eater. But this time it was as if the person she sought were waiting for her, ready to speak. He remained in the doorway as she approached, but when she held out her hand to him he took it and bowed.

'Tartuffo?' she asked.

He did not deny it.

'You have come from the city,' he told her. 'I can see it in your face.'

'So you *are* Tartuffo?'

He bowed his head again, the barest movement.

'I have seen you before,' he went on, although the eyes turned towards her did not seem entirely focused. 'In St Simeon. When you were a girl. I recognised you at once. You lived near the waterhole. Everything else is different, but your face is the same.'

'Yes,' she confirmed. 'I grew up in St Simeon. In the house of Hector, the night-watchman.'

But the name seemed to mean nothing to him. His hand remained in hers, gentle, if rough to the touch.

'I do not think you mean me harm,' he concluded, as if speaking his thoughts aloud.

With that he turned and led her into the sparse room of the mission house. For furniture there was one short bench, a wooden stool and a low table with a Bible on it. Gesturing Leonarda towards the missionary's stool, he moved to the bench and sank down upon it. Watching him, Leonarda realised it was not age but injury that made him stoop. One shoulder was pushed forward at a strange angle and frozen there as if the bones, once broken, had healed unevenly. It did not surprise her that his enemies, their work apparently done, had walked away from the alleyway and left him for dead; looking again at that strange, dreamy gaze, she wondered if the injuries he had carried away with him were not all physical.

Having settled himself on the bench, he seemed content to wait in silence, watching her, so she told him her name and said that old Hector, who had sheltered her as a child, was dead, murdered by night at the house of the British consul – a crime for which he himself had been arrested.

Again she expected a reaction, a protestation of innocence perhaps, but the man in front of her continued to sit with his hands together in his lap, his head nodding very slightly as if listening to the sort of familiar tale told to a child. Uncertain how to go on, Leonarda added that she had come to St Miguel because she wanted to understand better the circumstances of the old man's death.

'For vengeance?' he asked. His voice was oddly high-pitched, at odds with the thickness of his frame.

'For the truth,' she told him. And she meant it. Vengeance, justice . . . These were things Leonarda had barely even considered. But until she *understood*, until she could see the picture clearly, she knew she would not rest.

'I do not know who killed your father.'

It was not a word she had used, not a word she had ever used in relation to the night-watchman, and her instinct was to correct him. But Tartuffo was carrying on, his phrases falling into a lilting, dream-like rhythm.

'I do not know who killed him, but it was not me. It was not Pedro, though Pedro would happily kill a man, a woman, a child. But he did not kill your father. Pedro was with me. We were not there. Listen, I will tell you . . .'

It was a strange and unlikely tale, but Leonarda found herself believing it. In those days, Tartuffo told her, he had spent his days playing cards with his friend Antonio Canaria at the Dragon, his nights drinking with him at the Mermaid. From time to time, when in need of money to carry on drinking, they would rouse themselves to carry out any simple crimes that presented themselves;

burglary mostly, but if offered an easy target – a drunkard, say, or an unarmed foreigner – they were not averse to a little street robbery. If their victim was a foreigner, Tartuffo might be required to slam him up against the wall, just to make a point. But he and his friend were not fighters, they did not carry knives.

They knew Pedro from the Mermaid, and like all his acquaintances they were afraid of him. He would often come to the tavern looking for accomplices, and if no one more adept was available he would choose the two friends. They never said no. You did not say no to Pedro the Salt-Eater.

Pedro was a criminal of a very different kind. If you needed someone to be taught a lesson, or a rival to be warned off, or an enemy to vanish altogether, Pedro was your man. He had a reputation for thoroughness, and for enjoying his work.

'We saw men die. Often. Bleeding like pigs.'

Tartuffo's eyes were turned away from Leonarda as he talked, turned towards the single, high window, a simple square of unblemished blue.

'Pedro always smiled, and afterwards he cleaned his knives as though he loved them.'

The night that ended in their arrest began in the usual way. He and his friend Antonio had been drinking at the Mermaid since dusk and it was midnight when Pedro came in. He had a job, he told them. A white man wanted some goods recovering from a friend. An alley robbery. No knives, no killing, nothing difficult. Of course they knew that Pedro didn't usually need help for that sort of thing, but his victim being white, and white men sometimes showing remarkable foolishness in such situations, a couple of accomplices would make things simpler.

'We knew where to find this man,' Tartuffo recalled. 'A drinking place on the docks. Two o'clock was the time, and he'd be alone. He'd have a sailor's bag, a small one. It was that bag we were after.'

At that hour, the place had been almost empty. The white man had stood out, an unusual sight in such a place and at such an hour. The bag was at his feet. Not even particularly close to him.

'It was easy. Pedro wanted to wait because he wanted to get some exercise, use his fists. But there was no need. I went over, asked the man for a match, asked him if he was lonely, asked him if he liked African girls, and while I talked my friend Antonio walked out with the bag. So easy. So easy.'

They had retired to the Mermaid to examine their loot. Their instructions were to report at dawn to the Dragon tavern where they would hand over the bag and be paid for their efforts. But of course they wanted to examine the merchandise for themselves, just in case the contents of the bag were worth more than they were due to be paid.

But it proved a disappointing and perplexing haul. Laid out on a table at the Mermaid, the items appeared to have no value to anyone: an ebony paperweight; a leather blotter; a box of small cigars; a china figurine; some playing cards; a plaster bust of a young woman with a garland in her hair. No, he insisted in answer to a question from Leonarda, no book. And no watch. He would have remembered a watch.

A small crowd gathered around their table at the Mermaid to peer at this strange collection, and it was universally agreed that there must have been a mistake – that Pedro must have got the wrong victim or else the wrong bag.

He was adamant however. And it was not a problem. He would be paid as promised or there would be blood spilled that night after all. It was not his fault if the bag contained rubbish. The white man who had hired him would pay – one way or the other. Pedro seemed inclined to blame Tartuffo for stealing the bag by stealth. Had he been allowed to get to work with his fists, perhaps more valuable items might have been brought to light.

But the incident had put him in a bad mood, and the three men did not linger at the Mermaid. Repacking the bag, they decided to go directly to the Dragon to wait for their money. There, over a desultory game of cards, they waited until dawn and beyond.

'But no one came. Antonio wanted to wait longer but Pedro said he had a bad feeling about it. It was still early in the morning when he took the bag and dumped it in the alley outside.'

To Tartuffo, it had felt like a poor night's work, but it very quickly felt a good deal worse. Even before he reached his bed the police had come for him. The charge was theft and murder. Many people at the Mermaid had seen him with objects stolen from the British consul. Most of them had assumed the Salt-Eater's story was a fiction, that he had killed the watchman and stolen the first things that came to hand. Pedro was a good fighter but a poor thief. It was quite possible he really had stolen such rubbish.

Fortunately for Tartuffo, those at the Mermaid who were happy to gossip freely were less inclined to bear official witness against their fellows, especially when one of them was Pedro the Salt-Eater. By the time of Pedro's death in gaol, the number of witnesses to the scene at the Mermaid had dwindled to none. And so, having survived the horrors of prison, Tartuffo and his friend eventually walked free. But with Pedro dead, the situation in the streets around the docks had changed. All those beatings, all those quick, deft killings . . . Pedro had enemies, and now those enemies had become the people to fear. As Pedro's occasional accomplices, the two friends quickly realised they had been safer in prison; and both, in the end, had found their own method of escape.

Only when he had finished his tale did Tartuffo lower his eyes from the high window and turn them towards Leonarda.

'So I don't know who killed your father. But I think one of the white men killed him. It was planned that we should take the blame. Had Pedro not thrown away the bag, we would none of us have left that prison.'

She pressed him then about the man who had commissioned the theft. What had Pedro said about him? Had Pedro ever worked for him before? But Felipe looked at her with that strange gaze and could tell her nothing. He had not asked questions. You did not ask questions of Pedro the Salt-Eater. And Pedro told you nothing. Discretion was good for business.

'But what about the man with the bag?' she persisted. 'What was he like? You talked to him. Was he old or young? Spanish or Creole?'

'Neither old nor young. He spoke good Spanish, Havana Spanish.'

When she pressed him further, his answers became less helpful. He was neither tall nor short. He looked like other white men. He wore a European suit of clothes. He had a bag but he did not keep it close to him, which suggested that perhaps he was no true *habanero* after all.

'But would you recognise him?' It was the question she had to ask. 'I know it was only for a few moments and a long time ago, but if you were to see him again would you recognise him?'

Perhaps she imagined it but his eyes appeared to clear a little, as if focusing more closely on her face.

'Oh, yes,' he replied. 'I recognised you, didn't I? After many years. And you a woman now, all covered up in finery. Yes, I would remember him. I would remember him.' He smiled for the first time. 'I never forget.'

Leonarda returned to Havana the following day. As her carriage rolled through the gates into the old city and the familiar sounds and smells rose to greet her, she felt strangely comforted. The green of the countryside was soothing to the eye, but there, in the old streets, despite the heat and the noise and the dirt, she felt at home.

At the apartments in the Calle Chacón a message awaited her – a letter from the captain of police.

XXX

The hours of work expected of Backhouse were not demanding, and it was his custom to return home promptly to the house in El Cerro when his duties were concluded. But that day he felt reluctant to make the journey. Grace, he knew, had plans. She had been invited to spend the afternoon with some other Englishwomen, people they had met through the Crawfords. Backhouse was pleased – it was the sort of social connection they needed – but he had no desire to return home alone to listen to the quarrels of his servants.

Instead, on a whim, he headed to the waterfront, remembering how pleasant it had been to take an ice somewhere shady, with the blue water at his feet. At a respectable-looking establishment near his office, he took a seat in the shade and, in his best Spanish, ordered an ice. It arrived without discussion, without fuss, and he felt pleased with himself. For the first time it occurred to him that it might be possible to enjoy life in Havana for what it was, rather than always to be dwelling on its shortcomings. He knew, of course, he had not come to Havana to *belong*. That was not the purpose of his posting. Even so, for a few moments to sit back and watch the people pass was not unpleasant. Not unpleasant at all.

He had finished his ice and was contemplating further refreshment when he became aware of a large man with a face like a prize-fighter's approaching him from the street, squeezing between the small tables with some dexterity.

'Mr Backhouse? Mr George Backhouse?' He came alongside and extended his hand. 'I wonder if I may introduce myself. My name is Jepson.'

Backhouse was instantly suspicious. Men who introduced themselves in cafés were generally to be avoided, and this one appeared to be American. But he couldn't help being impressed by the stranger's clothing, which was impeccably cut and of the finest quality. From London, surely? The stranger was, Backhouse realised, the best dressed European he had encountered in Havana. Curious, and aware he was being impulsive, he took the offered hand and allowed the waiter to bring up another chair.

The American was all affability and good humour, explaining that he was on the island as a representative of the American government, mentioning the name of one or two eminent statesmen in a familiar, almost off-hand, way that Backhouse found reassuring; then venturing into all the usual generalities of Havana life – the heat, the hurricanes, the prices, the woeful sanitation. Only when his drink had arrived and he had taken a thirsty sip of it did his tone become more serious.

'I should confess, Mr Backhouse, that I'm not here altogether by chance. The truth is I've been hoping for an opportunity to talk to you for a few days now. I was hoping to ask you about your interest in a man called O'Driscoll. Oh, I know all about your meeting, so there's no need to be coy. We've been watching him for some time.'

'Watching him? What? You mean you were *spying* on us?' Backhouse straightened in his chair. Then, feeling that his response lacked composure, he corrected himself. 'Who *are* you precisely, Mr Jepson?'

'I told you. I work for the American government, keeping an eye on things over here. Looking after our interests. You know the sort of thing.'

Backhouse didn't, but he nodded anyway. His instinct was to stand on formality and to snub the man, but O'Driscoll's name was linked in his mind to the business of the stolen shipping plans and for once, without really meaning to, he allowed curiosity to get the better of his habitual caution.

'And what is your interest in Mr O'Driscoll?' he asked.

'To tell the truth, I'm not entirely sure. I'll be frank with you, Mr Backhouse. I think you and I may be able to help each other. I'm here because I want to prevent a war, and I figure you might also feel that's a desirable objective.'

A waiter appeared and brought Jepson a second glass. A brandy, by the look of it. Backhouse hadn't even been aware of him ordering.

'We're keeping an eye on O'Driscoll because he receives certain payments from various groups in the United States. Regular payments, from groups we know are up to no good. But we don't know *why* they pay him, or what he does in return.'

The American took a rapid sip of his drink.

'So when a British official meets up with him at one of his favourite drinking haunts, well, you can imagine why I'm interested. I hoped I was on to something. However I get the impression that O'Driscoll is as much a mystery to you as he is to me. Tell me about this business of the naval secrets, Mr Backhouse.'

But Backhouse was outraged, and had no intention of doing any such thing. Was nothing ever confidential in Havana? At first he attempted a denial but the American was having none of it.

'It is my business to know what you talked about, you see. Please don't take offence. Perhaps it would help if I told you what *I* know about O'Driscoll?'

He leaned back, his glass in one hand, and eyed Backhouse with almost affectionate amusement.

'O'Driscoll runs labour gangs from the southern docks. He pays people for the labour of their *emancipados*, which technically speaking is illegal – those people are meant to be *free*, for Christ's sake – but no one here cares in the slightest. Anyway, he puts them to work, pockets their earnings and does very well out of it. He also, though this is less well known, will provide you with other services if you ask him in the right way. For instance, if you need someone teaching a lesson, if you need someone's business burning down . . . That can be lucrative work. And it's certainly keeping him busy, because someone is paying very nice sums into bank accounts in New York. He doesn't need to touch them, but they're there.'

The big American seemed to be enjoying himself.

'You're interested in him, Mr Backhouse, because he knows something about an illicit trade in information that you want to put a stop to. Now that's not something I know much about – as far as I'm concerned it's a British problem – but I'm prepared to do you a deal. I will see what I can find out for you – and my resources are considerable – if in return you help me with something.'

'And what would that be?' Backhouse was still wary. He had no intention of cooperating with this stranger but he still wanted to learn what he could from him.

'I'm interested in knowing who briefed you about this naval business. You're very new to the island, Mr Backhouse, and I assume that before you sailed someone at your Foreign Office asked you to look into it. Just out of curiosity, I'd like to know who.'

Backhouse shook his head firmly.

'Any discussions I had before my departure were confidential, Mr Jepson. You must realise that. And even if I could tell you, I can't see why the information would help you.'

'Call it professional interest if you like. I have one or two old friends in London.'

The American waited, meeting Backhouse's gaze, and when he realised the Englishman would go no further his tone changed slightly.

'Perhaps I could ask a slightly different question then. Tell me, Mr Backhouse, whoever it was who briefed you, how do you explain the fact that they chose *you* to help them?'

Backhouse was indignant, but before he could protest, Jepson held up his hand.

'Oh, I'm sure they think you're a good man. And they've probably told you that they can't trust anyone associated with the consulate. That might even be true. But why *you*, when they already have their very own agent in Havana? Someone who knows a good deal more about the place than you do.'

'I don't know what you mean.' And it was true. What was the American hinting at? Did he mean Lavender?

'Let me tell you a funny story, Mr Backhouse. A year or so ago the Captain-General here drafted a confidential letter to Madrid outlining certain changes he planned to make, something to do with new regulations about non-Catholic worship. It was a deliberate poke at the British, and sure enough, the British ambassador in Madrid made an informal protest to the relevant minister. To his surprise, the protest was greeted with incomprehension. The officials in Madrid knew nothing about the Captain-General's plans. In fact, because of a storm off the Canaries, his letter didn't reach them for another two weeks.

'In other words, Mr Backhouse, the British ambassador in Madrid knows more about what goes on here than the Spanish government does. Your informant here is good, Mr Backhouse. He knows more than I do, which means he's *very* good. Yet they've asked *you* to look into the matter of naval secrets. Now why would they do that?'

But it was not a conversation Backhouse was prepared to enter into. He resented the implication that he was ill-equipped for the task assigned him. He resented the man's manner. And he resented the implication that he might join the American in some seedy alliance of convenience.

He rose to his feet full of disdain.

'I'm afraid, Mr Jepson, you have misunderstood my business on the island. I am the British judge to the Mixed Commission on the Slave Trade, and as such I am here to lead the fight against a rather vile activity – one that your government supports and encourages. Any other interests I have on this island are mine alone, and I do not intend to discuss them with you further. I wish you a good afternoon.'

And with that he bowed and turned on his heel. So pleased was he with the dignity of his exit that it was only afterwards that he realised, with some mortification, he had left his bill for the American to pay.

He went directly to Lavender's and found the thin Englishman in his office above the English bookshop. Something in his manner must have suggested a degree of perturbation because on seeing him enter Lavender rose to his feet, a look of surprise on his face.

'Is everything all right, old man?' he asked. 'Here, take a seat. Is it too early for a drink?'

Backhouse accepted the seat but declined the drink, and with little preamble described his encounter with Jepson. Having already taken Lavender into his confidence, it felt natural to share with him this additional development; and now Backhouse found himself in the mood to ask questions. He began by asking what Lavender knew of the big American.

'Jepson?' Lavender licked those dry lips of his before committing himself. 'Well, he's said to be some sort of spymaster. Spies used to be those little people in ill-fitting peasant garb we sent behind enemy lines before a battle. Nowadays peacetime spies are all the rage, and that seems to be Jepson's line of business. An abrasive chap, they say. He certainly seems to have upset you.'

'I'm not upset.' Backhouse spoke firmly. He was not going to let himself be patronised. 'But I confess I was taken aback when he knew all about my conversation with O'Driscoll. He must have had a waiter in his pay, someone who could understand English. But what about his idea that the Foreign Office has a spy of its own on the island? What's he getting at?'

Backhouse looked steadily at Lavender as he asked the question, but could see no sign that the other was rattled.

'Well, it isn't me, old man, if that's what you're asking. I run a few errands every now and then for our friends in London. Nothing more. It seems to me quite possible that the American was simply trying to rile you.'

'So you think you'd know if there was any truth in it?'

Lavender nodded breezily.

'Heavens, yes. I like to think I have a pretty shrewd idea what goes on here. I suggest you take it all with a pinch of salt.'

'That's all very well . . .' There was an intensity in Backhouse's eyes that Lavender hadn't seen there before. 'But it doesn't answer the American's real question. Why me, Lavender? Why did they ask me to investigate this business? Even if Jepson was inventing this spy of his, why me? Why not you?'

Backhouse watched as Lavender considered the question, his long fingers caressing the tip of his chin.

'You know,' he replied eventually, 'I've wondered that myself, old man. Believe me, I've wondered that myself.'

XXXI

A pleasant summer morning in Kensington Gardens after a week of rain, and the crowds were out to welcome it. On the edges of the Round Pond, where Thomas Staveley was waiting and feeling foolish, small children ran in packs, many of them armed with boats, some with penny whistles. The adults present at the scene were mostly there to oversee the children: governesses and nurses, and one or two delicate-looking mothers, all anxious that their charge should not be the first to pitch head first into the murky waters. Watching it all, Staveley felt he was intruding upon a complicated and timeless ritual.

To his relief, John Jerusalems did not keep him waiting for long. The little man appeared promptly on the hour from the Bayswater side of the park, neatly dressed and walking briskly, and carrying an object in his left hand that proved to be a punnet of strawberries. He extended this towards Staveley by way of greeting.

'Try one, Thomas. They're really very good. Bought them from a woman at the park gate. I always think strawberries go some way towards making summer in London bearable, don't you?'

'I'm not sure I've ever seen you out of doors before, John,' Staveley replied, declining the proffered fruit. 'I was beginning to think you a phantom that had no existence beyond Lowther Street.'

Jerusalems chuckled gaily. 'Oh, I like to get out. In fact I'm just back from Paris. Hellish hot over there, you know. I suggested meeting here by way of antidote. Also, I knew I would be crossing the park between engagements and thought this spot might suit you too. Here, you really must try one.'

But Staveley disapproved of eating in public places, especially when also in motion; for Jerusalems was showing no inclination to linger by the pond, and Staveley had no choice but to fall into step.

'You mentioned you had a question for me, John,' he reminded his companion. 'You're not still fretting about Cuba, are you? There's been no sign of aggression against any American ships, you know. The Foreign Office thinks it's just one of those rumours that blows up in the Caribbean, then simply blows over.'

He glanced across at his companion and saw Jerusalems smile.

'I'm sure that is what they hope, Thomas, but you'd be a fool to think it's true.' He seemed about to add something, but changed his mind. 'No, I wanted to talk to you about diplomats, not ships.'

'Any particular diplomat?' Staveley enquired. They were approaching a bench occupied by two respectable-looking matrons who, from their movements, were about to leave. Jerusalems stopped in front of them and raised his hat, as if to hasten their departure.

'There's a new Captain-General of Cuba to be appointed soon. I've heard one or two rumours from Spain, but I wondered what you could tell me.'

Staveley looked around, instinctively cautious of discussing such matters in a public place. But the passers-by moved around them as if unaware of their existence.

'Well, they say it's going to be Pezuela. He'd be very different from the usual type of governor. Honest, for one thing, and no connections with the island, so no friends or creditors among the plantation owners. Anti-slave trade, certainly, and they say at heart he's an abolitionist.'

'I see.' Jerusalems was still beaming at the matrons on the bench, who now seemed to be gathering up their possessions with greater urgency. 'I heard a similar rumour. Tell me . . .' He seemed genuinely perplexed. 'Does the Foreign Office have any idea what the effect of someone like Pezuela landing in Havana is likely to be?'

'You mean he'll probably stir things up?' Staveley was aware that the appointment, which seemed all but certain, would be controversial in Cuba.

'Stir things up? Stir things up, Thomas?' The little man waved his hands impatiently, apparently forgetting all about the ladies in front of him, even about the strawberry he held between his fingertips. 'We are not talking about a cook making porridge. We are not talking about a boy with a stick in a pond. If Pezuela were really to enforce every one of Cuba's slave laws, the plantation owners would be up in arms, and I don't mean the phrase figuratively. And how long do you think the Americans are going to tolerate an abolitionist governor on their borders? The Spanish could make no more provocative appointment if they tried.'

The two elderly ladies finally moved off and, after a decent pause, the two men seated themselves.

'But, John,' Staveley reminded his friend, 'Great Britain is committed to ending the slave trade. The Foreign Office can hardly object to the appointment of someone who shares that goal, can it?'

'Object, Thomas? I never suggested that. I was merely wondering if our lot properly understand what's happening.' His tone changed. 'For myself, I'd be delighted to see Señor Pezuela appointed. He has very charming manners and collects butterflies, you know. Meanwhile, what other news from Havana?'

He asked the question looking down, apparently in earnest contemplation of his strawberries.

'Very little from Backhouse yet, if that's what you mean,' Staveley told him. 'Still settling in, I suppose.'

'Look, Thomas, this one is hardly ripe. Here, see for yourself.' He passed the offending fruit to Staveley. 'Not to worry about Backhouse. I'm sure you'll be hearing from him shortly. It will be fascinating to discover what he has to say. Are you sure I can't tempt you?'

He held out the punnet to Staveley again. This time only one rather battered little fruit remained, but when Staveley declined with a shake of his head, Jerusalems took it up, hulled it with a dexterous twist, and popped it into his mouth.

'Superb,' he declared. 'How does one survive the winter without them? On the subject of Backhouse, by the way, I was wondering whether he might be willing to take on one or two extra little errands for us?'

Staveley looked across at his friend then, some doubt in his face.

'What sort of errands did you have in mind, John? Backhouse is a very upright fellow, remember.'

'Yes, yes, yes. Of course.' Jerusalems sounded pained. 'I wouldn't suggest anything unsavoury, Thomas. Just some help with the unofficial post, perhaps delivering one or two things to America. The sort of tasks my friend Lavender sometimes undertakes for us.' The little man sighed and shook his head. 'You see, I'm afraid Lavender's personal conduct is becoming a bit of a problem, and it's causing me a little difficulty. For his own sake it might be time for him to think about leaving Cuba.'

Staveley raised his eyebrows. He knew Lavender had been working for Jerusalems for a very long time; indeed he had often wondered whether Lavender was a rather more significant presence in Havana than Jerusalems ever let on. But now, it seemed, things were to change.

'You think Lavender may be in some kind of trouble?' he asked, wondering at the same time what sort of trouble it might be.

'He is behaving with less and less discretion, and yet is resisting all my suggestions that he leave Havana. It seems he has formed an attachment to the place.' Jerusalems rose suddenly to his feet. 'It is a worry, I confess. Remember what happened to that man Alvarez, the one who was working for the Americans? I wouldn't like to leave one of *my* men dead on the docks. But of course' – he brightened visibly – 'I do have a plan. No, no, don't get up,

Thomas. It's such a nice day, it would be wrong to make you hurry back. We shall say our farewells here.'

And with the smallest of bows, he was gone, threading his way southwards through the crowds, leaving Staveley once again feeling foolish, this time clutching a single white-tipped strawberry in the palm of his hand.

XXXII

The captain of police was looking pleased with himself.

'You see, señora, a man with boots – proper leather boots – cannot do business in the taverns in the way of a common thief. Not without attracting a great deal of attention to himself.'

They were walking in the deep shade of the lemon trees which in those days still ran the length of the Cortina de Valdés. Away to their left, too bright for the eye to linger on, the waters of the bay danced diamond-white patterns under the morning sun. It was possible, in such a place – glimpsing the distant sea, breathing unsullied air – to forget for a moment the turmoil of the city behind them. Certainly it was a meeting place that suited the captain of police much better than their previous rendezvous; the sort of place where a sophisticated young Spaniard might comfortably flout convention by walking with his mistress of a morning. And it was undeniable that to be seen promenading there with a woman as striking and as immaculately attired as the enigmatic Señora Leigh would do no harm at all to his reputation among his colleagues.

Leonarda, of course, was not unaware of the young man's reasoning, but did not greatly resent it. After all, the Cortina de Valdés was convenient for her too, and she liked to be close to the water. Besides, such a pairing in such a place was not as unusual as the captain thought it; they would, she knew, go largely unnoticed.

'Since I saw you last, my thoughts have been returning to those jewels, señora. If a man rich enough to own boots found himself in possession of stolen gems, how would he dispose of them? He *could* try to find a buyer in one of the waterfront taverns, but he would realise only a fraction of their value and, as I say, such an attempt would be certain to excite unwelcome curiosity. Such things have a way of becoming widely known.'

If it amused Leonarda to have the workings of Havana's underworld explained to her by a young man still wearing the pomade he had brought with him from Madrid, she did not show it. Her expression remained solemn, her eyes on the avenue ahead of her.

'No,' the captain of police went on, 'for discretion, and for any sort of price, he would surely turn to the jewellers on the Calle Ricla. So, señora, I took it upon myself to make certain enquiries.'

Was that a frown or a smile? Glancing at her profile silhouetted against the glare of the water, he couldn't be sure.

'I hope you have not put yourself to any trouble on my behalf, Captain.'

'On the contrary, señora. It is no inconvenience at all. These things should have been considered at the time.'

Leonarda knew enough about the imperial police to know that scrupulous investigation was not something in which they generally engaged; but again she chose to remain silent.

'And were your investigations fruitful, Captain?'

'I believe so. As you know, señora, the jewellers on this island are mostly Dutch in origin. I have had some dealings previously with one of their number, an old man called Michaels.'

And as he paraded along the Cortina de Valdés, there was a certain pride in his step. He explained that the Dutchman thought it highly unlikely that any jeweller in Havana had been offered the items stolen from the British consulate. If they had, he was convinced, news of it would have spread. The gems were too fine to keep quiet.

In that case, the captain of police had asked him, what had become of them? To which the old jeweller had shrugged. Perhaps they had gone abroad. Ships and sailors were leaving Havana every hour. In America they would be much easier to sell. He would ask among his contacts.

Alternatively – and here Michaels had paused and eyed the captain of police shrewdly – there was another theory common on the Calle Ricla. Perhaps *no* attempt had been made to sell the gems. Perhaps the thief, for reasons of his own, had chosen to keep hold of his booty. But when the captain of police asked why a thief might do such a thing, Michaels had smiled enigmatically. They had belonged to a young Englishwoman, he pointed out. A beautiful young Englishwoman, with an elderly husband. Such situations were complicated, and thieves were not always strangers.

As the captain of police relayed this theory to Leonarda, he saw she was listening carefully, and the knowledge cheered him. When he finished, she remained silent for a few moments, as though placing what he had told her into a framework of ideas she already carried in her head.

'Thank you, Captain. That is very interesting.'

In the captain's imagination when anticipating this meeting, they had walked close to one another, her hand resting softly in the crook of his elbow. But in reality, she had remained from the outset formal and polite, untouchable beneath a carapace of brisk practicality. So they walked a foot or so apart, like two solemn gentlemen discussing business, and he had no idea how to bridge the space between them.

So perhaps it was the effect of the soft shade in which they walked, the dappled blurring of the shadows, that made the captain of police suddenly courageous.

'Señora, if I may be so bold to ask . . . You have never explained to me your interest in this matter.'

And it was true, she had told him nothing. But even then, in that quiet, honest moment when she had no desire to evade, she could find no answer for him.

'Once . . .' she began, then almost imperceptibly shook her head. 'Forgive me, Captain. It is all foolishness on my part, and it is wrong of me to bother you with my questions. After today you must think no more about it.'

And she meant it. As the nun had told her so firmly, the details of Hector's murder were an irrelevance, a distraction from the truth of his death. She knew it was time to grieve for him properly, as he deserved. But the questions that rose unbidden and persistent in her head would not be silenced; however hard she tried to swat them away their buzzing drowned out her grief.

The captain of police returned to his tiny room that evening fiercely determined to pursue the matter further.

XXXIII

That night Leonarda dined with Marty at Domingo's. His choice of venue was perhaps a mixed compliment: Domingo's was the finest restaurant in Havana where a gentleman might dine with his mistress. Marty the entrepreneur, having noticed an unsatisfied demand, had created Domingo's in order to satisfy it, and had done so with his usual aplomb. Domingo's was more expensive than anywhere else in the city, the food was finer, the décor more lavish and more decadent. The chef had been summoned from France, where, it was said, he worked for a duke. It was a place where Havana's strict codes were forgotten; Marty's rules applied at Domingo's, and demand for tables comfortably outstripped supply.

And yet, Leonarda noted, Marty had not chosen his usual table at the centre of things. They were shown instead to a corner discreetly screened from the main body of the room, as though deliberately chosen to avoid the public gaze. This surprised her. Marty had always liked to show off in public with a young woman on his arm.

But that night he seemed intent on nothing more than enjoying her company. He talked freely, of his day-to-day tribulations, of island gossip, of his plans for the opera. And he asked her about herself – nothing personal or inquisitive, she noticed, but questions about her travels; what she had seen, what she had observed. And he seemed interested in her answers. He appeared, quite simply, pleased to see her.

Leonarda had realised very early in their acquaintance that Marty was not an easy man to know. He kept too much hidden for that. Yet she thought she understood the things that drove him: the reassurance he found in wealth, his pleasure in power, his desperate desire to force the island's aristocracy to acknowledge him their equal. His relationships, she thought, were all transactions – he was more comfortable that way – and he would happily amuse himself playing games of the most devious kind if he felt they would lead to the confusion of his enemies. It was said that once, in his youthful pirate days, having handed himself in to the Spanish authorities under an amnesty, he had then claimed the reward on offer for his own capture.

Leonarda had no way of knowing if that story was true, but it was already part of the island's folklore, and Marty neither confirmed nor denied it. All that was certain was that he had begun his business career in Havana with a small fortune already at his disposal. Whether he had amassed it through piracy or trading in slaves, or in something equally nefarious, history did not record.

By the time he first encountered Leonarda, he had long been one of the richest men on the island. But that night at Domingo's it struck her for the first time that perhaps Marty was *lonely*. Lonely for someone to whom he could talk freely, someone who accepted his invitations because they wished to, who had nothing to gain from his patronage. There were very few in Havana of whom those things could be said.

She therefore broached the subject of the British consulate with care, anxious not to alter his expansive mood.

'Ah, yes!' He regarded her shrewdly. 'Your interest in all things English. But I know so little, my sweet, and what I know I've told you.'

'A little while ago, Marty, not long after I went away, there was a robbery at the consul's office. A man was killed and some jewels were stolen. I was wondering if you remembered it?'

He furrowed his brow.

'I remember the jewels, yes. I remember wondering who had achieved such a delightful *coup de main*.'

'And did you ever find out?'

Marty turned up his palms as though the answer were obvious.

'The culprits were caught, were they not?'

'Three men were arrested,' she confirmed, 'but never convicted. And those men didn't steal the jewels.'

Marty leaned forward slightly.

'Indeed? What makes you so certain? As I recall, there was little doubt at the time.'

Cautiously, picking her words with care, she told him about tracking down the man known as Tartuffo, and repeated the tale he'd told her. She had expected Marty to greet the story with some scepticism, but to her surprise he listened carefully and nodded when she had finished.

'So you think someone else – perhaps even someone from the consulate – used this Tartuffo and his friends as scapegoats?'

'Yes, I do. But what do *you* think, Marty? You know Crawford and his colleagues better than I do.'

Marty leaned back in his chair and considered for a moment, then pulled a face and shook his head.

'It's an attractive theory. A scandal in the English house is always to be relished. But the English officials here . . . Crawford, Dalrymple . . . No, I cannot see them spilling blood. They surely lack the . . . the *manly attributes*, let us call them, for such a brutal scheme.'

Marty seemed to be thinking hard. On the other side of the screen, just visible through the fretwork, a new party was taking its seats: a notable plantation owner and three very beautiful, very dark-skinned women.

'There's a way to find out,' Leonarda told him. 'Tartuffo is certain he'd recognise the white man whose bag he was told to steal. If I could tempt him back to Havana . . .'

'You think he might identify your villain?' Marty considered this, looking down at his fingernails. 'Yes, I suppose it's worth a try, although the person you're looking for could be long gone by now. But tell me again, my dear, what is your interest in these jewels? Something to do with your husband's estate, you said?'

She didn't correct him.

'There's another thing, Marty. Someone else has been asking about that robbery. He'd been at the Anchor a few days before I went there, asking about Tartuffo and his friends. And I think the same man has been out at San Isidoro too. Can you imagine who else in Havana might be interested in the affair?'

Marty shrugged. 'Where there are jewels involved, people will always be interested. Those gems were never recovered, were they? It doesn't surprise me in the least that people in Havana are still looking for them.'

'But why now,' Leonarda persisted, 'just when I happen to be asking the same questions?'

He shrugged again, more theatrically this time.

'Life is full of coincidences. Without them there would be no novels, and my theatre would close for want of plays to perform. But I make it my business to know some fairly unsavoury characters in this city. I will enquire on your behalf, to see what I can find out.' His brow remained furrowed. 'Tread carefully though, my sweet. The person asking these questions is probably not someone you would wish to know better.'

Then he looked up at her and smiled.

'But what peculiar company you have been keeping since your return. The widows of thugs, and retired robbers on the run. You must promise me, my dear, that you will not start bringing them all to the opera. My reputation can only withstand so much.'

And at this Leonarda laughed, choosing to ignore the mild rebuke that lay behind the words.

XXXIV

The bundle of papers delivered to Backhouse's home in El Cerro while he breakfasted contained no return address, nor any mark to indicate its sender.

It was given into the hands of Martha, one of Grace's temperamental maids, who afterwards was unable to recall any aspect of its arrival and who, when pressed, was inclined to grow hysterical. The bundle itself offered no clues; the papers were tied with cheap string and wrapped in a piece of rough cotton rag. At first glance it was an unremarkable delivery.

It reached Backhouse's desk at a time when he'd begun to despair at his own inactivity. The work of the Mixed Commission was proving as fruitless as ever, and his plans to obtain an interview with Francisco Marty about the sale of the naval secrets had been thwarted, not by the Cuban adventurer's refusal – Backhouse's letter requesting an audience had received a surprisingly affable reply – but by a tropical fever. It was perhaps inevitable that the Backhouse family, as newcomers to the island, could not escape such fevers indefinitely and, over a period that stretched into weeks, first Backhouse then little Alice were laid low. To his great relief, Grace, now very visibly pregnant, seemed to escape the worst of it, but even she was far from well.

The result was that for a time Backhouse had struggled simply to keep up with the day-to-day paperwork of the Mixed Commission, futile though it was, and he had felt it necessary to write to Thomas Staveley in London, explaining that his investigations were temporarily delayed, but that he had real hopes of learning more about the sale of the sailing plans as soon as his strength returned.

Ill health had also prevented him from sending Señora Leonarda Leigh the note he'd intended, repeating Dalrymple's recollections of the first burglary at the consulate. And by the time he felt quite well again, he felt tolerably certain the moment had passed. A prompt letter would have appeared courteous and helpful, but, as the days turned into weeks, so tardy a communication began to seem more ill-mannered than no letter at all. When he finally sat down to write, he found he didn't know where to begin.

And while Backhouse was still fretting, Dalrymple's release from gaol was announced. The reason given by the authorities was lack of evidence against him, but the porter's testimony remained unshaken and Backhouse suspected a certain amount of diplomatic pressure must have been brought to bear.

To his surprise, the lengthy incarceration seemed to leave no lasting mark on Dalrymple. In fact Backhouse was astonished by the clerk's ability to put the entire ordeal behind him. Within hours of his release he had reported to Backhouse to request an increase in his salary, apparently in the belief that the Foreign Office had a duty to recompense him for his recent hardships. The sense of sympathy between the two men that Backhouse had felt briefly during his visits to the prison house had clearly not burned very brightly in Dalrymple's breast: his attitude to Backhouse reverted almost instantly to one of insolence tinged with resentment. Backhouse noted that the clerk made no further reference to the gifts he'd received, nor did he offer to repay the money Backhouse had given him from his own pocket. It was as though those visits had never taken place.

Whether or not Crawford had assisted in obtaining Dalrymple's release, Backhouse couldn't be sure. His disapproval of the consul had hardened into firm dislike; and when it became evident that he and Grace had been deliberately excluded from an important social occasion organised by Crawford's wife, Backhouse was both hurt and angry. Nevertheless, the incident made him less inclined than ever to cross Crawford openly. It would be unfair to Grace to break completely with the one man on whom their position in society depended.

So Backhouse, when the fever had left him, found himself uncertain what to do. Until, as if to raise him from his torpor, the bundle of papers appeared from nowhere and challenged him to act.

At first he assumed they related to some case that was to come before the Mixed Commission. His next thought was that perhaps they had been delivered to him in error, that they were intended for Esteva, the Spanish judge, and that a mistake had been made by the person charged with their delivery.

But his name had been inked on the cotton wrapper in bold, simple script that left no room for doubt.

There were about a dozen letters in total, all of them written in Spanish on similar sheets of unmarked paper. It struck him at once that there were no addresses – neither the recipient's nor the sender's – but each one was dated, and they had all been written over the previous six months. The writer had used black ink, and the handwriting was so exaggeratedly simple as to appear child-like, as though in a deliberate attempt to conceal the sender's identity. Each was signed, in English, with the words 'Your English Friend' but there was no further signature or mark.

It was this last detail – the deliberate mysteriousness of it – that convinced Backhouse the letters had been sent to him for a reason, and he settled down with real concentration, his Spanish dictionary at his side, and studied every line, determined to extract the meaning.

For all his persistence, however, the detail eluded him. Too much of the language remained confusing to him. He could infer the gist of the correspondence, but no more.

Yet that was enough to persuade him that the papers he held in his hands were devastating in their implications. If he understood correctly – and he was sure he did – he had before him the deadly charge that would spark war in the Caribbean. A war that would not only be fought right there, in Cuba, but all along the Atlantic seaboard, on the borders of Canada, deep into the Gulf of Mexico – wherever British and American interests clashed.

And at a time, Backhouse knew, when his own country was hopelessly unprepared, entangled in a war on the other side of the globe. The best of men and ships were committed to the Crimea: they could not now be withdrawn. It meant that a full-blown war between America and Spain, between America and Britain, would be disastrous not only to Britain's national interests, but to the whole cause of abolition. A victorious America, hoisting its flag over Havana, would guarantee the rights of slaveholders in Cuba as securely as if they were in Georgia or the Carolinas, and the slave trade would be allowed to flourish without check. It was not just the lives of Britons at stake, Backhouse realised, but of a generation of Africans too. The very people he'd come to Havana vowing to defend.

The letters were, he felt certain, written by a Briton who was actively engaged in passing information to the Spanish authorities. More than that: the same man appeared to be deeply involved – with Spain's connivance – in other acts of espionage against America. There were frequent references to London and Washington, some mentions of money – substantial sums – and many references to what Backhouse took to be the planned destruction of an American ship.

He spent three hours poring over the papers that morning, refusing all interruptions, desperate to make them yield up their full meaning. But eventually he had to accept defeat. He could decipher only so much of the whole. To understand more he would need assistance.

Which was a problem.

Clearly he could not take such material to a commercial translator. It needed to be someone he could trust. Someone discreet, who had no direct interest in the issues raised. Crawford would no doubt recommend someone, but would want to know why. Dalrymple certainly would. Lavender would perhaps volunteer to act as translator himself. Backhouse instinctively shied away from any of these choices. The papers had been sent to him, not to Crawford or Lavender. He felt extremely reluctant to surrender them to anyone who might want to claim a share of ownership.

So who then? Backhouse did not consider himself an impulsive man, nor one inclined to take risks. But try as he might, he could discover very few options. And, strangely, the solution he alighted upon did not feel like a risk at all. If anything it felt safe. Far safer than sharing the information with his compatriots. So it was with surprising confidence that he finally took up his pen and addressed himself to Mrs Leonarda Leigh on the Calle Chacón.

He went the same afternoon. Leonarda received him in her lavishly hung drawing room. She had cleared the surface of a small writing bureau that stood in one corner and had drawn up to it two small chairs.

His first reaction on being ushered in was one of horror. He had not paused to wonder at what sort of address he was calling, just as he had never paused to ask himself any questions about Leonarda's past. But it was clear to him at once that the apartment he'd blundered into was not the respectable salon of an Englishman's widow; and in such a setting Leonarda no longer seemed quite the reserved, decorous individual he'd thought her. Here she seemed more relaxed, more casual. Her day dress, for instance, was impeccable, but she wore it with such informal ease that to Backhouse it seemed somehow less discreet than it should have been. Almost a little risqué.

And her hair . . . He had never noticed it before. She had simply been a specimen of Havana life, albeit one who had helped him, who had somehow inspired his trust; but she had been as far removed from him in any personal sense as the man who cleaned his windows or the sniffing housemaid who brought him luke-warm tea every morning. Now, with her hair hanging loose, her throat bare, her fingers free of any gloves ... Now it was impossible not to see her in a very different light.

His response was alarm, perhaps even a pin-prick of panic, and his first thought was to apologise for his intrusion and to withdraw, as if he had surprised her in a state of dishabille. But the papers were there, under his arm, and he realised that by hesitating he must look ridiculous. And when she spoke it was with precisely the same calm, measured tones that he remembered; she, clearly, did not feel embarrassed. The patient ease with which she performed the rituals of tea-making made his own reservations seem prudish and rather absurd.

At first they sat apart, he in the armchair, she on her day-bed, while he explained the reason for his lengthy silence, then went on to share with her Dalrymple's account of the earlier robbery at the consul's office: the money untouched in a drawer, Dalrymple's discovery of Crawford in the garden, Crawford's finding of the jewellery case after the police had left. Leonarda listened in silence, and when he'd finished she thanked him for the information but did not share with him any of her own discoveries. She simply moved on to the other subject of his note.

'You mentioned some papers, señor?'

'Yes. Yes, indeed.' Once again he felt himself embarrassed. 'They're written in Spanish. I feel certain they touch on matters that are ... That need to be treated with great discretion.'

'And you thought of me?'

She was genuinely intrigued. Did this awkward Englishman really have no one else to turn to? There were not many English in Havana, it was true, but in all that dry, stiff community of upright husbands and snobbish wives had he found no one to help him? And he must have staff, clerks, people paid to assist with such things. Of course they were not his own people, just strangers whose services he had inherited; but even so, was it possible he was really so alone?

For him to seek her out was more than unconventional. It revealed, beneath Backhouse's outer skin of ordinariness, something unorthodox and surprising. At their previous meeting he'd seemed to find an ice at Lippi's something of a radical departure. But now there was this . . .

Long before he did, she began to understand his loneliness.

Meanwhile, his own explanation of his conduct was not particularly coherent.

'I simply wished . . .' He was speaking hurriedly. 'Simply wished to enlist the help of someone unaffected by the issues in these documents. As all my acquaintances tend to have been made through official channels, I found that much harder than I expected. And I know so few people on this island . . .'

He thought she was about to question him further, but instead she rose from her day-bed and indicated the writing bureau.

'Shall we begin, señor? There is more tea if you require it, and you must feel free to ring the bell should you wish for anything else.'

At first Backhouse was uncomfortable at the bureau. It was a small piece of furniture, clearly intended for one. The two chairs were placed so close together that, had he not edged away, his shoulder must have rubbed hers. To compensate, he moved his chair too far, so that only by leaning forward and to his right could he see the papers they were discussing. As a result Leonarda had to tilt them awkwardly in his direction until, aware he was inconveniencing her, he finally edged closer.

They worked line by line, Leonarda reading the words aloud in Spanish, then again in English, moving her finger as she went so that Backhouse could see how the translation fitted the original. Rather than simply translating, she explained the Spanish to him, and he fixed her explanation in his memory as she went. Only when he came to something particularly difficult did he stop to make a note.

It was quickly clear to him that the content of the papers was every bit as shocking as he had feared. They had in front of them one half of a correspondence between an Englishman based in Havana and a Spanish official, someone senior. Someone in the secret police, Leonarda told him, although the letters did not say so explicitly.

The English Friend, as he signed himself, appeared to be involved in various legitimate trading interests, and that in itself helped Backhouse narrow down the field. In addition he seemed to have access in some small way to information coming directly from London. Much of this, Backhouse could see, was little more than tittle-tattle, of little or no real value to the Spanish authorities, but couched in terms that made it seem more significant than it was. As he listened, he tried to recognise the voice behind the writing. Was that Crawford's slightly disdainful turn of phrase? Was that Lavender's dry humour?

Of course he could not be certain it was one of those two men. There were, in theory, other merchants who could have been the English Friend, people who came and went from Havana, sometimes staying six months at a time. But the resident British community was a small one, as Backhouse was painfully aware. As Leonarda continued through the documents, the conviction grew in him – unwanted but undeniable – that he needed to look no further.

But speculation was not enough, for the letters were about much more than just petty gossip. The English Friend, it seemed, had some manner of debt to pay to his correspondent, and to do this, apparently at his own suggestion, he had entered into various schemes, not against Britain, but against America.

The likelihood of an American invasion was a theme that ran throughout the correspondence, and it was clear that the Spanish official was eager for the writer to do anything in his power to inconvenience the invasion force and its leaders. It was a brief that the Englishman seemed happy to embrace.

The correspondence showed that between them the two men had plotted and executed numerous anti-American actions, all of them suggested and organised by the Englishman but approved by his mentor. Many of them were mentioned only in passing, with too few details for Backhouse to know exactly what had taken place: 'the incident at New Orleans', 'the accident that befell Colonel Buckley', 'the theft of Quitman's memorandum' and various others.

But three were described very clearly: a munitions explosion in Louisiana in which four soldiers of the unofficial invasion force had been killed; the interception and subsequent beating of a messenger boy in New Orleans; and a proposal to attack a ship referred to as the *Pilgrim*. In the latter case, an explosion was to be engineered by someone in the Englishman's pay and the writer discussed the likely outcome quite dispassionately. He estimated the detonation, if achieved when the ship was fully crewed, would cost the lives of at least one hundred American sailors. What the response had been to this particular proposal, it was impossible to tell.

If the documents were genuine – Backhouse could not yet fully believe they were – and if the contents were made public, the first two incidents might in themselves be enough to start a war. The American public was already suspicious of imperial Spain. To discover that the Spanish were actively commissioning acts of sabotage on the mainland of the United States – acts that had led to the deaths of American citizens – would cause uproar beyond measure. And were they actually to sink an American ship . . . Well, there would be no halting the invasion of Cuba after that.

And what then? British action in support of Spain was inevitable. Hundreds, probably thousands, of lives would be lost. As Leonarda continued to work through the letters sentence by sentence, Backhouse found himself dry-mouthed. The implications of the papers appalled him. And the decision as to what to do with them was his.

By the time Leonarda started on the last document, the room was growing dark. Rosa had been in twice, once to light the little lamp above the bureau, later to bring a platter of tiny pastries and to half close the shutters. Without Backhouse realising, the small pool of lamplight had made him draw closer still. Their heads were only a few inches apart.

Outside, the abrupt Havana dusk was already thickening into night, and as the light faded the dirt and grime of the city faded too. On the streets around the Calle Chacón, clearly visible from the window, dozens of soft lanterns touched the cobbles with a beguiling glow, and music drifted up from the streets like smoke. Beyond it all, beyond the sprawl and spikes of the city, the waters of the bay lay motionless, the dark blue yielding silently to the black.

When the last words had been picked over, Leonarda sat back a little. Backhouse was aware of her dark eyes watching him, searching.

'And so?' she asked.

But he could think of nothing to say. He had no idea whether or not the papers were genuine. He sincerely hoped they were not. If they were, life and death were balanced in the palm of his hand.

'It's curious that someone wanted you to know all this.' Her voice was low and soft.

'Yes.' He had no idea who might have sent them, nor why. 'I suppose someone feels the writer of these things needs to be exposed. They must feel I can be trusted to do it.'

'If you do not, and if they go ahead and sink that ship, many people will die. Many young men.'

He returned her gaze then. They were still very close to one another. He was aware for the first time how gentle her eyes were.

'And if I do, if I alert the Americans to the danger and bring all this into the light, then many, many more lives will be lost. And not just here in Cuba, either.'

She nodded. 'Yes. War. It is not hard to see.' A pause. 'Is there a middle way? Could you somehow put a stop to what he's doing without making these things public?'

'I suppose it's possible.' Backhouse spoke without enthusiasm. He couldn't for the life of him see how. 'But of course there's probably not going to be an attack,' he added more eagerly. 'This proposal must have been rejected out of hand. The Spanish don't want to start a war.'

'The Spanish government in Madrid doesn't.' It was said so softly, so quietly, that at first he didn't understand what she was suggesting. 'But there are many big families and rich planters here in Cuba who think an American invasion would serve them very well. It might be the only way they can be sure of keeping their slaves. The person receiving these letters here in Havana . . . Let us imagine it is someone senior in the secret police, someone like Colonel Aguero for instance . . .' She paused. 'Well, Aguero is a *habanero* himself, with family estates all over the island. It is not impossible someone such as he might secretly put his own interests above those of imperial Spain.'

'Perhaps they're not genuine?' Backhouse desperately hoped she would find some reason to agree with him.

But she shook her head. 'No, I think they are real. Did you notice, sometimes when he is excited by something, the way his writing changes? His letters begin to slope, as if he's writing faster.'

Backhouse leaned forward to look again. It was true, he thought. A convincing detail. And why would anyone go to so much trouble just to fool him?

'I shall send these to London,' he told her.

It was the obvious course of action. He was not a diplomat. His duty was to pass things up and to pass things down.

But they both knew London was a long way away. Before a reply came back, the *Pilgrim* might be under water, her crew with her. He wasn't even sure how he would send the papers. Through Crawford and the diplomatic mail? Through Lavender? Neither route seemed advisable. Better to do it discreetly to Thomas Staveley's home address through the standard post. But that might take longer still . . .

He realised she'd looked away, and he felt he'd disappointed her. By passing on the papers, he was avoiding their implications. His hands would be clean in official terms only. But what else was he to do? It was not his job to prevent maniacs from attacking ships.

His hand was still resting on the last of the papers and while he was looking down, at a loss how to proceed, he felt Leonarda's fingers touch his. It was only for a moment, the lightest of touches, but the intimacy shocked him.

'You must do what you think is right,' she told him, her voice still low. 'No one can ever blame you for that.'

'No, of course not.'

But he could feel himself flushing, embarrassed by her behaviour. No respectable woman would ever have forgotten herself in such a way, and it placed him in a very difficult position. They were alone together, and had been for nearly three hours. That was questionable enough in itself. To remain a moment longer, now that line had been crossed, would be to condone its crossing. It would be a betrayal of his family.

He rose to his feet, only to find that she too was rising.

'You have difficult questions to ponder, señor. I do not envy you. And of course if I can ever be of any further assistance, you are welcome to return.'

She wasn't sure why, but she meant it. He was, in so many ways, an awkward and ungainly man, not even particularly gracious, trapped under such a deep layer of English anxieties that it was hard to see the real person beneath. But she could sense he was bewildered, perhaps even overwhelmed. Friendless in a crowded, noisy place.

A place, she suspected, as she re-tied the string around the papers, less kind, more treacherous than he knew.

When Backhouse stepped back into the Calle Chacón the street was crowded with couples walking arm-in-arm. There was laughter in the air, and noise and shouting, and at one end of the street a drum had settled to a low, rumbling rhythm. All afternoon he had found the dark hangings of Leonarda's boudoir oppressive and discomforting, and had looked forward to his walk home. But out on the street, as the people parted to pass him, he felt less relief than he had expected.

He carried the papers tightly under his arm, but the feeling of them there filled him with a dull despair. The truths they contained were horrifying. Someone in the city – an Englishman – was conniving at murder. No, it was worse than that. Was commissioning it. And doing so in such an off-hand way it seemed no more significant to him than a routine business transaction. He was betraying his country too. Backhouse's country. And Backhouse had the proof.

The sinking of the *Pilgrim*, were it to happen, would claim the lives of a hundred young men. It might happen at any time. But the consequences of raising the alarm were unthinkable.

It was then Backhouse thought of Jepson. What had the American said? That he was in Havana to prevent a war. To prevent a war . . .

As Backhouse walked, the words drummed in his ears.

Only later, unable to sleep, restless in the heavy darkness, did his thoughts return, reluctantly, to the room above the Calle Chacón.

She had touched his hand. No gloves. Bare fingers upon his. Grace apart, his mother apart, he could not remember any woman ever touching him so freely. Most shocking. But he had behaved correctly. He had left at once.

So why did he feel so ashamed?

Perhaps because he had hesitated. Perhaps because he had not complained. Perhaps because the touch of Mrs Leonarda Leigh's fingers upon his own had affected him so differently – so very differently – from any other touch he could remember.

XXXV

It was after midnight, and Leonarda was already undressed and preparing to retire when the captain of police came calling. There was something a little ragged about his knock, and when the porter at the front door denied him entry she recognised the voice raised in protest. Reaching for her over-gown, she sent Rosa to bring him up, afraid that otherwise he might make a scene, might get himself into trouble on her account.

But when Rosa finally ushered him in, the young man appeared as collected and as neatly turned out as always, only a very faint flush in his cheeks suggesting that he might have come to the Calle Chacón directly from one of the many bars around the Plaza de Armas.

She received him in the richly hung drawing room with its drapes of dark, velvety hues. Her boudoir, as Marty insisted on calling it. At the sight of the décor, she saw the flush in the young man's cheeks deepen, but when he spoke he seemed himself.

'Forgive this late hour, señora. I called earlier, you see, but was told you had gone out and was determined to wait. I'm sure I should have left a note, or called another day, but I confess I was eager to see you in person.'

He flushed again, aware of her over-gown. She had been undressed, he realised, and the thought embarrassed and fascinated him in equal measure. So he hurried on.

'I have news, you see. Something I was sure you would wish to hear as soon as possible.'

Leonarda understood then that his excitement was not purely

the effect of liquor. He was attempting to appear calm and sophisticated, while bursting with untold news.

'You will remember, señora, that I spoke to my friend Michaels, the jeweller, about those items stolen from the British consul's office.'

She had seated him in the armchair opposite her day-bed, where, a few hours earlier, Backhouse had looked so uncomfortable. The captain of police did no more than perch on the edge of the cushion, too full of his tale to sit back and relax. While he talked, Leonarda prepared him a drink of brandy and mint leaves, performing the familiar ritual of sugar, lemon, mint and brandy with serene, unhurried movements.

'Well,' the captain continued, 'I had a note from Michaels last night and called on him this morning. He had just returned from a few days in New Orleans. The Dutch do a lot of business there. And what he told me is significant, I think. In fact I'm sure it is.'

He took the glass she offered him but did not drink, while Leonarda settled herself on the day-bed. For all her apparent serenity, she was not immune to the young man's excitement.

'In New Orleans, when Michaels asked about the stones, his contacts were adamant that they'd never come across them. But there was one old man, Vermeulen by name, a dealer from New York, who said that a friend of his had been offered certain gems. He'd shown them to Vermeulen, and both men had agreed the stones were unusually fine – but both felt certain they were not a safe investment. Apparently men like Vermeulen can just smell when a stone has trouble attached to it.'

He waved his glass beneath his nose as if to illustrate.

'So when, some time later, news reached Vermeulen about the theft in Havana, he thought about those stones again. He'd have been certain from the descriptions that the Havana stones were the stones he'd seen in New York were it not for one thing.'

With an air of great satisfaction, the captain of police sat back in his seat.

'You see, señora, he had been offered those stones – already out of their settings – in June. But as you know, the theft from the British consul's office did not take place until a month later.'

He delivered this news triumphantly, but at first Leonarda said nothing, sitting very still, as though working through the implications.

'So either this man Vermeulen was mistaken . . .' she began, 'or else the jewellery given to the consul for safekeeping contained stones that were not the originals . . .'

To the captain of police, watching her, his usual inhibitions vanquished by several glasses of rum, she had never looked more beautiful. Her hair hung loose around her face as he had never before seen it, and cascaded down over her shoulders. Beneath the studied modesty of her over-gown, he realised with a little shock that her feet were bare. When she lifted them and curled them beneath her on the day-bed, he caught a glimpse of ankle, of soft, brown skin stretching flawlessly upwards.

At that moment the news he had brought, the news that had so excited him, suddenly seemed less significant. What mattered more, he knew, more than anything else in Havana, was that ankle, the hidden nakedness beneath that gown.

'Señora,' he began, sitting forward again. 'Señora . . .'

Afterwards, in the sober, aching dawn, he shuddered to think what hopeless, hapless words might have followed had he been allowed free rein. Even that first word, with its unconcealed earnestness, made him groan. But Leonarda had risen, all brisk formality, before anything else could follow; and it seemed only moments later that Rosa appeared with his hat and gloves. He was aware of being thanked – graciously and charmingly – and invited to repeat his visit at another time. His hand was shaken, he was thanked a second time, and before he really knew how it had happened he was once more alone on the cobbles of the Calle Chacón.

He walked home that night feeling deeply aggrieved. Her brusqueness, her insufficient gratitude, her haste to be rid of him . . . These things were unforgivable.

He woke the next morning, dry-mouthed and deeply ashamed of himself, giving thanks to heaven for Señora Leigh's exemplary tact.

XXXVI

It took Backhouse a little while to find Jepson. Enquiries at the American consulate were met with perplexity. Mr Jepson, he was informed, was not a member of the consul's staff and they seldom saw him. They had no address for him. Eventually it was suggested that he might contact a man called Dale, although Dale was away from Havana and might be gone for a number of days.

Backhouse was in no mood to wait but had little choice. He occupied some of his time writing to Thomas Staveley. He had decided, on reflection, that the documents in his possession were too important to be entrusted to the post. So he made a careful précis of each one and enclosed these with his letter. After much thought, he sent them in a plain envelope by way of Boston.

The wait was not made any more restful by his domestic situation. Grace was now approaching the last days of her pregnancy – the child might come at any time – and although the doctor was happy with her condition, and although Grace herself tried very hard to reassure him that all was well, he could not shake off a sense that in every direction events were running out of his control.

When Dale finally contacted him, Backhouse had begun to think he would never find Jepson. He had even taken to spending his afternoons in the cafés frequented by Havana's American community, but he saw no sign of the man he was seeking. It seemed impossible to Backhouse that such a distinctive figure could be so hard to locate.

Dale's note when it came was apologetic. He had been away on business. When he next saw Jepson he would pass on Backhouse's message. Two days later, when Backhouse was still at his breakfast table, Washington's special envoy to Havana was announced.

Although taken by surprise, Backhouse felt the timing of this visit was fortunate. Grace was resting, the servants were relatively quiet and a shortage of business for the Mixed Commission meant it was not imperative that he should leave for his office at any particular hour.

His breakfast room was a pleasant place, with long double doors opening on to a veranda, and a view of the bay beyond. Backhouse welcomed Jepson into it with a handshake and an offer of tea that was declined with a shudder, a reaction that Backhouse noticed and considered ill-bred. The American settled into a chair opposite Backhouse with the air of one intending to linger.

'I dare say you were surprised to get my message, Mr Jepson,' Backhouse began awkwardly. 'I'm aware I was rather short with you at our last meeting.'

'On the contrary, Mr Backhouse. You'll think it impertinent, but I've been expecting you to get in touch.'

'Oh?' Backhouse couldn't help but sound rather cold. 'And why was that?'

Jepson stretched out his arms so that they rested across the backs of the chairs next to his own. He looked totally at ease.

'Because you're out of your depth here, my friend.' He moved one arm and wiped at the air in front of his face like a lazy man swatting at a moth. 'Oh, it's not a criticism. It's not your fault. But you're new to the island, and you're new to the games being played here.'

'Games, Mr Jepson?' Backhouse felt, and sounded, contemptuous.

'Big, rough games. Not many rules. You may not want to believe it, but that's where you are.'

It sounded like a lot of grandiloquent nonsense. Backhouse glanced around him at the reassuring tidiness of his breakfast room, all white wood and clean panels, with rather good china on the table. Jepson talked like a character in the sort of cheap novels that decent people didn't read.

But Backhouse had to talk to him. He had no choice.

'It may be true that my experience of overseas postings is very limited, Mr Jepson, but the British government stands for honour and decency. Yours may be the American view of things, sir, but the British do not engage in the sort of activities to which you allude.'

'No. No. Of course not.' Jepson examined his nails. 'You must forgive my country for its boorish manners. But if you're not in trouble, my friend, then why am I here?'

Backhouse felt he had come out of these first exchanges at something of a disadvantage. He had expected the interview to be very different from their earlier encounter. After all, he had in his possession papers that were, potentially, of enormous value to his visitor. It was clear who should be in charge. But the American was stretching himself out in his chair, apparently more comfortable than ever, while Backhouse's shoulders were hunched and stiff.

'When we met, Mr Jepson, you told me you were in Havana to prevent a war.' Backhouse leaned back a little and tried to relax. 'What did you mean by that?'

'Exactly what I said. Some of my compatriots think a war with Spain would be a good thing. They would like to see Cuba taken by force. My own view, however, is that a war now would not be in my country's best interests.'

'You think you might lose?'

Jepson responded with another, rather dismissive, wave of his hand.

'Win or lose, it would be a disaster. We are a young nation, Mr Backhouse. We have a great future ahead of us. But we have our weaknesses, our divisions, and a war about slavery is not what we need. And believe me, this would be a war about slaves, about who loses them and who gets to keep them. If we win, the cause of slavery in the Americas will stand stronger than ever. If we lose, those who seek to hasten its decline will have the whip hand. I happen to dislike both outcomes.'

'You have no view of your own, Mr Jepson?'

'My views are irrelevant. And to be honest I don't really give a Spaniard's fart about what happens here in Cuba. What I want to avoid – what I really, really want to avoid – is one group of Americans fighting another.'

As he spoke he was looking around Backhouse's breakfast room, apparently more interested in its furnishings than in his own argument.

'A nice place, this,' he went on. 'Good silver, very good china, and tea from Seddon & Moon's. All very pleasant. But living well in Havana is an expensive business, Mr Backhouse. I hope they're paying you enough.'

Backhouse ignored him.

'Mr Jepson, if I had evidence of a Spanish plot to sink an American ship, could I trust you to take steps to prevent it without any wider diplomatic repercussions?'

Jepson made no alteration to his posture, but he did raise an eyebrow.

'That would depend on the circumstances, of course. But I'd certainly hope so. You have such evidence?'

'I do. I feel sure it could start a war.'

'Frankly, Mr Backhouse, at this precise moment it would prob-ably take a good deal less than that.' The American pursed his lips as if in contemplation. 'Tell me, have you shared this evidence you mention with your superiors?'

'I have written to London describing the contents of the papers. But by the time I get a reply, it may well be too late.'

'And the originals?'

'The originals remain with me.'

Jepson stretched his legs in front of him.

'Why don't you start at the beginning, Mr Backhouse? The more you tell me, the easier this will be.'

So Backhouse explained, starting with the arrival of the documents. Jepson listened very quietly, the tips of his fingers resting together below his chin. When Backhouse had finished, he nodded slowly.

'Very interesting. Very interesting in a number of ways. Where are these documents now?'

'I have them in a safe place.'

'May I see them?'

Backhouse reached into his pocket and produced a single sheet of paper.

'An example. It is representative of the whole. It tells you all about the plot against the ship.'

The page was not densely written – the exaggeratedly simple handwriting prevented that – but Jepson spent a surprisingly long time studying it. Backhouse had finished his tea and was beginning to feel restless before the American looked up.

'The *Pilgrim*, eh? Do you have brandy in the house, Mr Backhouse? They say if you drink enough of it, it prevents the fever. I don't know *who* says that, and I don't believe a word of it, but I'd still like some brandy if you have it.'

Backhouse fetched the decanter himself. Brandy at breakfast time was a decadence he'd never before encountered, but if it made his guest more inclined to help . . .

When he returned he found Jepson pacing by the window.

'So what do you reckon, Mr Backhouse?' he asked, pausing by the head of the table. 'What do *you* think is going on?'

Before replying Backhouse placed the decanter and glass on the table, next to the water jug. He knew Jepson thought him naïve, an innocent. But he wasn't prepared to subscribe to the American's view of the world.

'One of my countrymen has gone to the bad. I suppose, in a place like this, that sort of thing does happen. He seems to have contacts of some sort in the British Foreign Office and apparently very good contacts in your country too.'

'Yes, yes.' Jepson sighed impatiently and flopped into a seat by the decanter. 'All that's obvious. But what's *really* going on?'

Again Backhouse experienced that intense feeling of dislike.

'I don't understand your question,' he replied curtly.

'Of course you don't. That's my whole point.' The American sighed again, as if his tolerance of fools was being stretched to its limit. 'But think about it. Who wants this Englishman exposed? Why? And why have you been involved?'

'I suppose someone trusts me to do what's right.'

'Namely?'

'To inform my superiors. To make sure this man is found and exposed. To use the information properly, without seeking any personal advantage from it.'

'And what about talking to me, my friend? Is that something they'd be expecting you to do?'

That was precisely the question worrying Backhouse. Confiding in Jepson was an initiative he was in no way entitled to take. Staveley would certainly have been shocked at such disregard for proper procedure.

The American smiled. He had poured himself rather a large glass of brandy and now he was holding it just below his nose.

'You see, Mr Backhouse, I think you have departed from your script. Were you the simple functionary you're supposed to be, you would have passed those papers on, said nothing, and got back to your desk. But by inviting me here you've done something pleasingly unpredictable.'

The American seemed to intend it as a compliment.

'There are lives at stake,' Backhouse pointed out defensively. 'A man cannot sit back and do nothing.'

'Mr Backhouse, a great many men would think that by reporting it to their superiors they had done all they could. Besides, this is a case of Spaniards killing Americans. Nothing directly to do with you at all. If you were truly a mere shuffler of papers you would have felt that fact absolved you. And you would not now be breakfasting with an American special envoy,' he added, taking another sip of brandy.

Backhouse took his jacket from the back of his chair and began to put it on.

'Mr Jepson, I find nearly every word you say, and the manner in which you say it, tends towards the offensive. But I have satisfied my conscience by warning you of the danger to the *Pilgrim.*' His jacket on, his tie straight, he felt strangely confident. 'I have no reason to trust you, but for some reason I believe that you feel as strongly as I do that a war should be avoided while, if possible, these lives should be saved. Now, if you have finished your drink, perhaps you will allow me to call a servant to show you out?'

Jepson listened to this without emotion, his attention apparently focused entirely on his brandy.

'Your conscience can be clear, Mr Backhouse. I'll do what's necessary. In return, let me give you two pieces of advice. The first . . .' He indicated the decanter. 'Go easy on what you spend here. This is an expensive city and an official with money problems attracts the wrong sort of friends.'

Backhouse made no reply. He remained standing very stiffly by the back of his chair.

'My second piece of advice, Mr Backhouse, is this. Do nothing about finding out who wrote these letters. In as far as you can, forget the whole affair. Make it clear to everyone, here and in London, that your time and energy are solely devoted to the work of the Mixed Commission in its narrowest sense.'

'And why should I do that, Mr Jepson?'

Backhouse took pains to make the question sound amused – the polite enquiry of one who humours an eccentric.

'Someone is drawing you into something you don't understand. Don't let them. Keep yourself out of it.' The American drained his glass and rose, indicating the door that led to the veranda. 'Forgive me for sounding trite, but I think I'm able to find my own way out, don't you?'

Backhouse allowed him to go. He was already wondering if taking the American into his confidence had been a terrible misjudgement. The action was, as Jepson had pointed out, completely unauthorised. He was guilty of indulging his conscience without properly considering the limits of his authority. He had not waited for, nor had he sought, permission. Were his actions to be examined in a critical light he would certainly be censured; he might even be disgraced. What had he been thinking? Spaniards killing Americans. He had no licence to interfere. What on earth had made him consult his conscience in the matter?

And the answer to that question was the most worrying thing of all. It lay, he knew, not in his training at the Foreign Office, not in his instincts as a gentleman, but in the darkness of the boudoir on the Calle Chacón. In the way she had looked at him with those quiet questions in her eyes.

Dale had waited outside the Backhouse residence, patient as a coachman, for Jepson to reappear. He had pulled his buggy into the shade and had sat quietly, smoking, uncertain why he had offered to drive the big American in the first place. Curiosity, he supposed. The same macabre fascination that makes respectable citizens follow the careers of particularly brutal prize-fighters.

When his compatriot appeared, Dale noticed at once that he was not smiling. He came down the steps quickly, a frown between his eyes, and climbed up beside Dale without saying a word.

Amused rather than offended, Dale said nothing until he had turned the carriage and had set them on their way, back into the city.

'Problems?' he ventured at last, worried that Jepson might say nothing at all if not prompted.

The other man blinked as though Dale's presence surprised him.

'Problems? Yes and no. Our little friend up there has documents that betray one of his countrymen. Someone who's been up to no good with the Spanish, and who wrote it all down. Who didn't even use a cipher.'

'And is that a worry?'

Jepson shook his head. 'Not at all. What worries me is the way those documents have come to light.'

Dale shook the reins and waited.

'It puts me in mind of someone I worked with once. Tell me, Mr Dale, have you ever heard of a man named John Jerusalems? He's a clever fellow, the cleverest Englishman I know. I worked with him in London, a long time ago, over a small matter relating to the French. I learned a great deal from him. A very great deal.'

'And is he in Havana?' Dale asked.

Again Jepson shook his head. He was looking ahead at where the walls of the old city faced him.

'He doesn't need to be. I may not know the identity of my rat, Mr Dale, but I have an inkling that someone in London is feeding him scraps. If I'm right then the British are playing a far deeper game than I thought.'

He remained silent for a moment, still looking ahead.

'Oh, and there was one other thing, Mr Dale . . .' He threw it in as though it were the most trivial matter in the world. 'We have a name for our warship. The one they're planning to sink. So I need to get to work.'

Dale turned to him astonished, taking his eyes off the road ahead.

'But that's excellent news, isn't it?'

'Well, it would be,' Jepson confirmed, 'and my job here would be almost over, if only our navy happened to have a ship by that name.'

XXXVII

Backhouse's invitation to meet Francisco Marty arrived only a few days later. He had written to the Cuban a second time on recovering from his fever, and by way of reply received a thick, gilded card requesting the presence of the English judge at an evening gathering to be held a little to the west of the city.

The venue was an unusual one. In those days, beyond the suburb of El Cerro, where the natural vegetation had not yet all been cleared, there remained a little glade with a stream running through it. It was to this place, at a late hour, that Backhouse was directed.

He was not alone. When Marty entertained it was very often on a lavish scale, and that night the glade had been transformed into a fairy glen, the trees lit up with countless strings of lanterns, and below them an array of pavilions where food was served and where dozens of bottles of real French champagne were packed into silver troughs of ice. Unseen behind the bushes an orchestra played, and couples danced wherever they wished, in and out of the trees, sometimes disappearing into the darkness altogether, to emerge later, flushed and giggling.

So it was not, Backhouse realised, a conventional gathering, and he felt relieved he had not brought Grace. She had been included in his invitation but her condition made it impossible for her to attend; and besides, it was not generally done for the English community to socialise with the Spanish except at the very big formal occasions. The Crawfords would undoubtedly have disapproved.

On arriving, Backhouse was greeted by an interpreter, a young Creole who had been enlisted by Marty to accompany his guest throughout the evening as required. At first, with no one to talk to, and with no host evident to make introductions, this proved a blessing. There seemed to be no structure to the event, no formalities, and Backhouse was displeased as well as a little bewildered. Around him the dancing was energetic, wild even, and there seemed to be no one present – no respectable cohort of elders – to police the conduct of the dancers. He had expected a respectable ball; he had stumbled into something more like a Roman bacchanal.

He could not deny that his eyes scanned the crowds for Leonarda. When he could not find her he was both relieved and disappointed. He had learned at their previous meeting that she was acquainted with Marty, but such an event, he thought, was surely beneath her. Yet without her there, and with no one else to talk to, he felt utterly at a loss. After half an hour of desultory conversation with the young Creole he decided to leave. Only the urging of his interpreter and a second glass of champagne persuaded him to stay a little longer. When that glass was drained, just as he began to plan his departure, he heard her voice.

She had come up behind him, out of the darkness, and he saw at once she was not dressed for the excesses of the evening. She wore a very simple gown in a muted shade of blue or green – in the half-light of the glade it was hard to tell. In it she looked sober and serious, an observer of the rites, not a celebrant.

When she held out her hand to him, Backhouse bowed over it, but once again he found himself embarrassed in her company. Unnoticed by the crowds around them, this meeting in the shadows felt to him oddly surreptitious, almost illicit. And when he noticed that the young Creole had slipped away, he realised they were once again unchaperoned.

'Marty told me you were coming,' she explained. 'It's very brave of you. He has invited you with the intention of shocking you, I think.' She paused. 'Has he succeeded?'

'Everything on this island shocks me, madam.'

He spoke without really thinking, with an openness and honesty that surprised him. It was a truth he had not previously admitted, not even to himself.

'And you, madam? Are you shocked by such a spectacle?'

'I'm used to Marty,' she replied simply. 'But he likes to unsettle people whenever he can. I sometimes think it is his only pleasure. For myself, I came here because . . .'

She tailed off. She was there because she knew he might be made to wait several hours for his interview with Marty were she not present to take his part. But to state that she was there purely for his benefit would surely discomfort the awkward Englishman who stood before her.

To her surprise, however, Backhouse seemed to understand, because he bowed again, and seeing no waiter in their vicinity asked if he might go himself to fetch her some champagne.

With Leonarda beside him, he did not have to wait very long before his host appeared and introduced himself. Backhouse had heard a great deal about Marty – it was impossible to spend very long on the island without being told the tales – and he was perhaps a little disappointed by the portly, rather ordinary-look-ing man who shook his hand. But the Cuban seemed friendly enough and to Backhouse's surprise spoke very fair English – enough for Leonarda to retire discreetly and leave them alone together. On the subject of the Royal Navy's sailing plans, Marty declared himself mystified. He was, he stated, shocked at the continuing trade in human souls, one that he himself was attempt-ing to render redundant by bringing to Cuba many willing labour-ers from the Yucatan. Perhaps the British government might wish to support him in this initiative? He would be happy to provide Backhouse with more information about the scheme . . .

Had Leonarda remained, she would have recognised this as a typical Marty performance – impudent, charming and menda-cious. It was not until the very end of the conversation that Backhouse heard anything of interest to him. Surely, Marty spec-ulated, it was highly likely that any person selling official British information in Havana would be British himself? To discover the information in the first place would require excellent contacts in Jamaica. In which case, the Cuban reasoned, Havana did not contain many likely culprits. To make his point, Marty began to list names, counting them off on his fingers. He began with five or six English merchants whose names Backhouse recognised, then moved on to people associated with the consulate.

'Señor Crawford, for instance. A tricky fellow. The sort of Englishman who wears his watch close to his heart because it is a gift from his wife, but keeps his mistress's hair tucked within it so as not to favour one party over the other. But for all that, he is well connected to some important individuals, both Spanish and English. As, of course, is Señor Lavender.'

This surprised Backhouse, who had never thought of Lavender as particularly well connected with the Spanish.

'Why, yes, of course.' Marty seemed to think it was obvious. 'My friend Colonel Aguero, for instance, who is very close to the Captain-General, always speaks fondly of Senor Lavender. My English friend, he calls him. Yes, that's the phrase he uses. Usually he says it in English. *My English friend*. Like that. And always he says it with a smile.'

When Marty had bowed and excused himself, Leonarda accompanied Backhouse back through the glade, to the point where the carriages were waiting. He was unusually silent. Anxious, she thought, and weary. And again she was surprised by a rush of sympathy for him. A man without friends; one whose conscience weighed heavily upon him. One who did not know how to share the burden.

For his part, Backhouse was barely aware of her until they had almost reached the place where servants were waiting to arrange transport back to the city. His should have been a straightforward posting. He had come to Havana to do right. There was nothing complicated about it. Every day in his diary he recorded the experiences of a simple Englishman abroad. So how had he become mired in a world of such duplicity, a world where nothing was clear or honourable or honest? With every day that passed, he seemed to drift a little further from the ordinary and the decent, further into complexity and confusion.

Señor Lavender. My English Friend.

Before his conversation with Thomas Staveley that night in London – how long ago it seemed! – he had never kept a secret from Grace. And now he found himself walking through an unfamiliar forest with another man's fate heavy in his hands; and at his side, alone with him, a woman he barely knew, a woman whose existence he had never even mentioned to Grace. And when her eyes met his, when they reflected back the light from the lanterns . . .

His farewell was brusque. He returned to El Cerro in a state very close to despair.

XXXVIII

A great squadron of flies had gathered around the wooden outbuilding at the back of the police yard. Most turned and twisted lazily in the air, humming quietly, but a good many had alighted on a sticky brown mark near the foot of the door, crawling between and over their brethren in their eagerness to reach it.

The stink of the dead body was unmistakable even from a dozen yards away, and, as he fumbled for the key, the captain of police wondered if it was too soon to reach for the scented hand kerchief in his pocket. But his companion, an older man, a Catalan and tough as leather, showed no sign of flinching.

'Yes,' he was saying serenely as if the smell barely affected him, 'I remember the incident you mean. We had to tread carefully because the British were involved. A political job.'

The captain of police had found the key, but had no desire to open the door until the other man was ready to go through it. The less time close to the corpse the better.

'It was you who made the arrests?' he asked.

'That's right.' A fly had alighted on the side of the Catalan's wrist but he appeared unaware of it. The captain of police watched it crawl beneath his cuff. 'They were three familiar faces, and stupid enough to show off some of the stolen stuff in a tavern, so it wasn't hard. I'd been trying to get one of them for months, so I was happy enough. But it was an odd business. There was a funny smell to it.' The remark was apparently made without irony. 'At the time it didn't really look to me like a robbery at all.'

Despite the slight queasiness in his guts, the captain of police was interested.

'So in your opinion it looked like . . . Like what?'

'I thought it looked like murder,' the older man concluded. 'Shall we go in?'

When the captain of police threw open the door, the stench was so great that at first he wanted to retch. Uncertain of his stomach he stepped back, and the other man, taking it as a courtesy, entered first. Inside there was no furniture, just bare wooden boards, stained and mottled with disturbing patterns, and it was on these that the body lay. Somebody had thrown a grey blanket over it, and flies already swarmed across its surface. When the Catalan officer pulled it away, a further cloud of flies, buzzing and angry, rose from the corpse. The policeman peered down at the dead face without repugnance.

'That's the fellow,' he declared with evident satisfaction. 'Saves me a job. Knifed a plantation owner over in Santiago a couple of months ago. Found him outside the front door, did you say?'

'That's right.' The captain of police remained on the threshold of the hut but now he risked a glimpse at the body. It had been dumped by night where the police could not help but find it, a piece of summary justice achieved with minimum fuss. Nobody since had bothered to untie the man's hands or feet.

'Fortunate I happened to be over this way,' the Catalan remarked. 'Means you can get him underground straight away. I'll sign the papers tomorrow and bring them over. Anything else I can do for you before I go?'

But the captain of police waited until they were back in the yard before returning to the subject of the burglary.

'You say it looked like murder . . .' He wanted to hurry inside to wash himself but realised that his companion was not going to linger. 'What did you mean by that?'

'Only that there was something odd about the rubbish they stole. As if they grabbed stuff any old how, without any thought of the value.'

The Catalan wiped his fingers down the front of his uniform. The captain of police was horrified to notice a grey smudge left behind. He tried not to wonder what it was.

'But what about the jewels?' he asked.

'Well, that was odder still. If you've got that necklace and stuff in your hands – thousands of dollars' worth – why bother with a cheap bust of the Queen of England? You'd just slip the jewellery case under your shirt and disappear, wouldn't you?'

The captain of police felt sure this was true. 'And they didn't even take the case,' he commented, then realised the other man was looking at him blankly. 'The jewellery case,' he explained. 'I heard they dropped it in the garden.'

'Did they?' The Catalan shrugged. 'First I've heard of it. I never saw it, at any rate, and I had a good look around. As I say, there was a political side to it all so I wanted to be on the safe side. No,' he concluded, 'I don't think they left the case.' His frown suggested that the whole business still bothered him slightly. 'Tell me, my friend, why are you interested?'

The captain of police muttered something about a young lady, and the older man laughed.

'Ah! Be careful, my friend! Don't let a pretty face get you into trouble.'

And he slapped the captain of police firmly on the back. With the same hand, the young man noted, that still bore traces of that nameless grey sludge.

XXXIX

Backhouse's son was born, small but healthy, a few days later. It proved, despite his forebodings, a relatively uncomplicated birth, and for all the discomforts and dangers of the tropics, Grace emerged from it with her spirits intact and her strength unimpaired. Backhouse, as was traditional, was kept well away from the birth chamber throughout, and found himself, as he had been at the birth of Alice, strangely removed from the whole event, isolated amid a chaos of activity. By the time he held the child, it seemed to him he was the last in the building to do so.

His first reaction on hearing of the successful delivery had been one of relief. Alice had been born into a world of fussing aunts and hectoring grandmothers, and it had never entered his head to fear for the outcome. But this time nothing was familiar or safe or reliable. Havana entertained no certainties. Bringing an unborn child to such a place had surely been a selfish thing, and the thought tormented him. Only when word reached him that all was well, when he felt a rush of relief that almost overwhelmed him, did he really understand how great the guilt had been that was weighing on his shoulders.

And although he held the new arrival only very briefly before being hurried from the room, he found in that tiny bundle a different sort of relief. Looking down upon the crumpled, sleeping face he was reminded of everything he held dear. The boy was faultless, pure, a little piece of England sent to remind him of all that was good in the world. Lavender and Jepson, and frolics in woodland glades, these things were not real, they were Havana things, distractions, hindrances in the performance of his duties.

He would rise above them all. He would make his son proud.

The child was named John in honour of Backhouse's brother.

Perhaps inspired by this new taste of fatherhood, Backhouse was swift to confront Lavender. By then he'd had an opportunity to compare the simple child-writing of the pages he'd been sent with a sample of Lavender's neat script. The result, however, had neither convinced him that the two were shaped by the same hand, nor persuaded him that the two writers were different. His course of action was therefore clear: he would simply put it to Lavender and see what happened. This time, however, he did not visit him above the bookshop, nor arrange a meeting in some public place: he summoned the man to his private study in the villa in El Cerro. And, after some demur, Lavender came.

Backhouse's study was a small room at the corner of the house, with a single window looking out across the bay. It contained only two chairs, neither of them very comfortable, and Backhouse made sure to offer Lavender the lower of the two. The thin Englishman must have been aware that something unusual was in the air, for he looked wary and licked his lips, and fiddled rather awkwardly with his cuffs.

'What is all this, Backhouse?' he asked plaintively when he was finally seated. But Backhouse had no intention of letting the other man seize the initiative. He had prepared his ground carefully, and he began with the papers, placing a sample document in front of his visitor and watching his reaction.

If he'd had any doubts at all about the letters' authorship, that dispelled them. At the sight of the paper, Lavender tensed visibly, his usual sardonic ease replaced instantly by a sort of beady watchfulness. Backhouse thought he looked paler; he certainly looked shocked.

Yet as Backhouse made out the case against him, Lavender's unease, instead of growing, appeared to diminish. By the time he had confronted his visitor with the fact that he was routinely spoken of by one influential Spanish official as '*My English Friend*', Lavender had staged something of a recovery.

'So tell me,' he began, when Backhouse gave him a chance to respond, 'now you have finished drawing your own conclusions, just what do you propose to do next?'

'So you don't deny that these letters are your work?' There was in Backhouse's tone a sternness and authority that his acquaintances in London would not have recognised.

'I deny nothing, I confirm nothing. I don't think your evidence is quite enough to hang me, not in a British court at any rate. And here in Cuba it would probably earn me a state pension.' He licked his lips once more. 'So, I ask again, what do you plan to do now?'

'I have already written to Thomas Staveley describing the content of the letters I've received. Now I intend to write again, stating that I have reason to believe you to be their author.'

Lavender shrugged. 'You must do what you think right, of course.' To Backhouse's astonishment he was preparing to leave.

'You have nothing to say?'

'Nothing at all, old man.' Lavender rose to his feet. 'I'm just sorry you've had to go to all this trouble.'

Backhouse rose too, wrong-footed by Lavender's response.

'You will understand if I do not shake your hand,' he said coldly.

'As you wish.' Lavender turned to the door, then turned back again, his expression more sorrowful than defiant. 'I know all this must seem pretty extraordinary to someone like you, Backhouse, but believe me, I am not quite the villain you think. There are people in London – influential people – who need certain things done. They pay people like me to do them. So you can write to Staveley all you like. It doesn't worry me.'

'Are you suggesting, Lavender, that someone in London actually *encouraged* you to collude with the Spanish in this way? That is frankly preposterous.'

But Lavender only shrugged again, and Backhouse was in no mood to be swayed in his certainties. Murder, deceit, treachery . . . He didn't know how he could bear to remain in the same room.

'I shall certainly write to Thomas Staveley,' he confirmed, 'and to Lord Clarendon too.'

The remark, intended to intimidate, provoked only amusement.

'The Foreign Secretary? Steady on, old boy. You'll only make a fool of yourself by writing to Clarendon. He doesn't want to know about this sort of thing. Don't you understand? People like him don't want to know the detail of what goes on out here any more than they want to know the names of the people who sweep their chimneys or deliver their coal.'

Lavender shook his head.

'Don't misunderstand me, Backhouse, you can write to him if you want. I doubt your letter will ever reach him though. There are people in Whitehall who make sure such letters go to the right place. And no one will thank you, you know. You probably won't even get a reply.'

But Backhouse was in no mood to exchange thrusts with a man he considered beneath his contempt. He merely remained where he was, standing very stiffly, waiting for his guest to leave. And when Lavender was finally gone, Backhouse flung the study window open wider. He felt unsettled and a little anxious. All this was very far from the London drudgery he'd been so eager to escape.

That night he retired late but could not sleep. He had hoped that a second brandy might prove soothing, but even after a third he remained wakeful. Telling himself it was no more than a bout of paternal anxiety, he allowed himself to listen at the door of the nurse's room; but all was quiet, his little son apparently at peace. On venturing upstairs, there was enough moonlight to show him Grace's sleeping form in soft, pale detail. She slept peacefully behind the nets, her face wiped smooth of the small frowns that had become a fixture by day. Had she frowned so much at home? He didn't think so. But he couldn't be sure.

Her diary lay open on the little writing table near the bed. It was her habit, since the first days of their marriage, to leave it thus; for a good wife, she told him, had no secrets from her husband. A good husband, he suspected, would have considered such open-ness reassurance enough, yet from time to time, pricked by curi-osity, he allowed himself a glance through the pages: more often since their arrival in Havana than before.

Yet he had never found anything there to alarm or worry him. Her honesty touched him, and if she had any secret fears or regrets about their migration to Cuba, they made no appearance in those pages.

Had she been awake that night, he would surely have confided in her. The unpleasantness with Lavender weighed heavily upon him and he felt suddenly too weak to bear it alone. Indeed, he would have confided in her sooner had it not been for the promise he had given Staveley to tell no one, not even Grace, about his special instructions. That decision pained him now, and he should never have agreed to it. A secret, once concealed, has a way of spreading its poison. Now he was ashamed to tell Grace that he had so enthusiastically and naïvely accepted the role of spy for his friend back home. For that is what he had done, he could no longer deny it.

And there were other things too, other obstacles that made him reluctant to confide in Grace. Lavender's rumoured sexual pref-erences, for instance, were something he couldn't imagine discuss-ing with his wife. And how to explain the presence in this sorry tale of the exotic Mrs Leigh? Had he thought to share with Grace the details of their first encounter, it would be simple to mention her now. But her first visit to his office had seemed too insignifi-cant to mention; and their second meeting, when she had come to his aid in that grubby tavern, had been part of an episode that he'd been too ashamed to share with Grace. And of course his decision to turn to Leonarda with those anonymous papers would most certainly be awkward to explain.

No, he would not wake her. She had worries enough of her own, and it would be selfish to burden her with more. A husband did not weigh down his wife with his problems, especially not in the middle of the night. He had done what was right in his reports to Staveley, and he had done what was right in warning Jepson about the likely attack on the American ship. If his actions left him feeling ill at ease with himself, that was the burden he must carry.

Besides, the whole affair was over as far as he was concerned. He had confronted Lavender with his suspicions and that evening he had written the necessary report about their exchanges. Now he would get on with his job. He would mend his fences with Crawford, would be more careful about the company he kept, and would endeavour to enjoy the life of a British expatriate.

With these resolutions burning strongly in his breast, he stripped to his underwear and joined his wife beneath the mosquito nets.

The next day he received a letter from Leonarda. It asked him for nothing and assumed nothing. It merely stated in a precise, factual way the further information she had acquired about the first burglary at the consulate: the evidence of Tartuffo Martinez, the recollections of the Catalan officer and the rumours circulating among the jewellers of New York. She told him, she said, because he was a colleague of the consul and it was hard not to believe that Mr Crawford had certain questions to answer.

Which was, Backhouse reflected, the very last thing he wanted to hear.

XL

Leonarda next saw Marty at his offices above the fish market. She found him leaning over his desk at one end of his light, spacious study, examining a complicated diagram of lines and arrows sketched over plans of the Teatro Tacón. He seemed delighted to see her.

'Come in, my dear, come in. Please, take a seat. Or better still, take a look at this.' He gestured at the paper in front of him. 'They were sent to me by an Italian who used to work here. He claims that instead of sending messengers from the wings here . . .'

He paused to locate a particular place on the diagram.

'Instead of sending messengers down to the dressing rooms, he could run a cable of some sort that would allow you to speak in the wings and be heard on the other side of the building.' He looked up. 'Is that possible, do you think?'

Leonarda had remained near a window on the other side of the desk, where the morning sun fell full on her face. Beneath her, the fish market crowds were at their peak, pointing, pushing, haggling. From Marty's office, their cries were strangely muted.

'Is the man honest?' she asked.

'Quite possibly,' Marty conceded. 'But also quite possibly insane.'

He shuffled the diagram and some other papers into a pile and looked up at her. She was, he thought, looking particularly fine in a pale morning dress so simple that the pampered ladies of Havana would never have thought of attempting it.

'Please, my dear, do take a seat. I shall ring for coffee. To what do I owe this delightful visit?'

'You sent me a note, Marty. Remember? You said you had news.'

Leonarda settled herself into a chair by the window. She knew there was nothing bumbling or absent-minded about Marty, only ever an act intended to disarm.

'Ah, yes! But I confess that note was little more than a ruse to see you again.' He helped himself to a cigar from the box on his desk, then seated himself opposite her. 'If you remember, you asked me to find out who else in Havana might have an interest in that jewellery theft at the British consulate. But my investigations have proved fruitless.'

He paused while a servant entered and poured coffee. He did not continue until they were alone.

'The theory in the taverns is that some associate of the men arrested, perhaps the person who commissioned the robbery, must be back on the streets – possibly after a period of incarceration. But that is speculation. My apologies that I could not find out more.'

Leonarda sipped at her coffee. Marty's note was not the only thing that had brought her there that morning. She had certain questions she wished to put to him when a suitable chance arose.

'Tell me,' he went on, 'that man you found, I think you said his name was Tartuffo, the man accused of the robbery. You hoped to lure him up to Havana, did you not? To take a look at Crawford and company. Did you have any success?'

Leonarda shook her head. She had sent a messenger out to the mission house to find him, but Tartuffo had been away and the mission deserted.

'The reason I enquire, my dear, is that I took the liberty of asking a few questions about him too, and the man is generally considered a compulsive liar. It seems he's always had that reputation, almost as if there were something not right in his head. Out there by the southern docks, no one seems in any doubt that he and his associates murdered that watchman.'

Leonarda listened quietly, and acknowledged Marty's words with the very slightest tilt of her head.

'All the more reason to see him again,' she concluded.

'If you think so.' Marty appeared unconvinced. 'Let me know if he turns up. He might be dangerous. In the meantime, I confess I'm intrigued. You hinted that your husband's estate had some claim on the stones if they could be recovered. But it seems to me an odd matter in which to concern yourself directly. I'm sure your honest executors in Jamaica will pursue any outstanding claims.'

'Of course,' she agreed. 'But they do not know Havana as well as I do. Nor are they personally acquainted with the person on this island who best knows what goes on here.'

The compliment was deliberate and Marty looked suitably flattered.

'Well, of course, if there are any other questions I can help you with . . .'

Leonarda put down her coffee cup and leaned forward a little, as one who invites a confidence.

'Since I saw you last I've been asking one or two questions of my own. Word has it that you have done a little business with the English consul's family. Something to do with slaves from the Yucatan?'

Marty sat back and sighed, an expression of intense, theatrical pain passing over his features.

'Labourers, my dear. Labourers, not slaves. Slaves, of course, would be illegal. I wonder who you've been talking to? People are so indiscreet, are they not? However, I for one always honour a confidence. I couldn't possibly reveal the names of those who invest in my schemes.'

But Leonarda could see he was smiling, enjoying the game.

'Oh, come now, Marty! You'd reveal their names in an instant if you thought there was a profit in it.'

'And is that the case?'

'You will have the satisfaction of pleasing a friend. There are people who say altruism is its own reward.'

'Very miserable people, I suspect. However, Mrs Leigh, for you I would be happy to oblige. Although in truth there's little to tell. It was not the consul who invested in my scheme, at least not directly. It was the family of his wife. All the British, even if they style themselves as gentlemen, are merchants at heart. And they do not necessarily share their government's lofty opinions of what constitutes legitimate trade.'

'So it *was* slaves. I thought it must be.'

'Really, my lovely, as you know, trading in slaves is illegal. It is my task to find other ways of providing the labour our plantations are demanding. In the Yucatan there are many poor natives anxious for work.'

'You mean indentured labourers. Slaves in all but name.'

'Some form of contract is necessary in these cases, of course. It is beneficial to all parties.'

'So . . .' She paused, trying to find the right form of words. 'The consul's family are not averse to a dirty profit?'

'Of course not.' He smiled a rather lopsided smile. 'Your wording may cut me to the quick, but I can only concur with your conclusion.'

'Is the consul in need of money?'

Marty seemed to consider the question superfluous.

'We are all in need of money, my dear. If you are asking whether his needs are acute, I couldn't say. I should imagine Crawford's business ventures are largely successful, but they live well and they have expenses. Havana is an expensive city.'

His eyes narrowed slightly.

'Tell me, my sweet, do you honestly believe Crawford was behind the theft of those jewels? I confess I'd like to believe it, but those items had been left in his care. Crawford would probably have no compunction about selling his friends a failing plantation, but actually pocketing their valuables? No, an English gentleman has a code of honour that lays down very neatly the ways in which he may rob you.'

Leonarda rose and returned to the window.

'And yet,' she concluded, 'I will ask Tartuffo to look at Mr Crawford anyway, just in case. After all, Marty, if we don't trust the liars in this city, we trust no one.'

And Marty, impressed by a cynicism he felt rivalled his own, could only concur.

XLI

The line of cafés on the waterfront south of the Cortina de Valdés were crowded at dusk, at the hour of the promenade, but by nine or ten o'clock numbers had thinned as the crowds moved away from the sea to the bustle and music of the main squares and to the streets around the cathedral. Then it was not so difficult to secure a good table near the water where one could enjoy a quiet glass of Canary or a drink of rum and mint leaves served stiff with ice.

Jepson, advancing from the northern end of town, had passed two or three such establishments before he found Backhouse, alone and seated in shadow. The drink in front of him, Jepson guessed, was not his first.

'Not yet home, my friend?' the American asked, pretending surprise at the encounter. He remained standing until Backhouse waved him towards an empty seat.

'I've been home. Came out again. Work to do.' The Englishman's tone was far from welcoming, but then he seemed to stir himself. 'Brandy, isn't it?'

'Brandy will do very nicely.' Jepson chose a seat not quite opposite the other man, one with a view of the sea, and waited while a waiter fussed around him with a bottle and glasses and a bowl of dusty oranges sliced into segments. 'I hear you have a new arrival at your house, Mr Backhouse. My congratulations.'

He raised his glass, but Backhouse didn't join him.

'You really do know everything about me, don't you, Jepson?' He sounded more resigned than irritated. 'I can't see why you bother.'

The American shrugged. 'People tell me things. Is the boy well?'

Backhouse allowed himself a smile. 'Yes, and has fine lungs. That's why I came out. I was in the way.'

'Congratulations,' Jepson said again, and this time Backhouse, slightly grudgingly, joined him in the toast.

'To tell the truth, Mr Backhouse, I came looking for you tonight. I wanted to thank you. A few days ago some of my men searched a small US training vessel called the *John Bunyan*. She'd called at Cartagena with a crew of thirty-five cadets on board. *John Bunyan. Pilgrim.* You see? I was rather pleased with myself. And we were just in time. We found a large quantity of explosives in the hold, all ready to blow. We were able to dump them at sea very discreetly, without mishaps.'

Jepson raised his glass again.

'So it looks as though our little chat has saved the lives of some fine young men, Mr Backhouse, and prevented a war into the bargain. Which is something we should both be proud of. Had you done nothing, my friend, the only winners would have been those who wish to see the enslavement of the Negro defended by American force of arms. And it sickens me to think of American soldiers laying down their lives so that the land-owners here can still have slave-women to rub their dicks. So here's to you, sir.'

Jepson had expected the news to be warmly received, but Backhouse simply nodded and looked down at his glass.

'In addition, the affair has also convinced the turkeys who run the US navy that my warnings might actually be worth some-thing.' Jepson chuckled to himself. 'My name is no longer quite the laughing stock it was a month ago. All in all, a very pleasing outcome.'

'Yes.' Backhouse hadn't particularly wanted Jepson's company, but he hadn't been enjoying his own either. Now, he knew, he was behaving churlishly. What the American said was true, it *was* a good outcome, and when he managed to place that month's events in a proper perspective he knew he would take comfort from those saved lives, and from the fact that he'd managed at least one action in Havana of which he could be proud.

'You must forgive me, Mr Jepson,' he explained. 'I'm grateful to you for telling me. But yesterday I drafted a letter accusing one of my compatriots of treachery. It was not the sort of letter I ever thought I'd write.'

'I see. Lavender, is it?'

Backhouse smiled, but without any humour.

'So you know that too, do you?'

'It isn't hard to guess. Rumour has it he enjoys the company of small boys, and I don't mean playing hoops with them. That's a capital offence, although it doesn't prevent the male brothels on the docks from doing good business. But there's nothing the Spanish like more than taking a stand against buggery from time to time. Especially when practised by a foreigner. Makes them feel good about themselves. So friend Lavender would ultimately have been easy prey, and very simple to manipulate.'

Backhouse shook his head.

'It's all so bloody sordid. All of it. I hate this island.'

'It's a kind of fragrant cesspit, isn't it? Funny how many people are desperate to get their hands on it.' Jepson contemplated his brandy. 'Tell me, did Lavender happen to mention to you who was giving him his orders over here?'

'Apart from the Spanish, you mean?' Backhouse's lips curled. 'He had the cheek to suggest that everything he'd done was at the suggestion of someone at home. Someone in the Foreign Office, even.'

'But here in Havana? He must have been taking direction from someone here. Lavender is a *little* man. I know his type. He surely couldn't have organised the attack on the *John Bunyan* by himself.'

'So you are still convinced the British have some sort of master spy here, Mr Jepson?' Backhouse sounded scornful. 'Well, he didn't mention anyone like that. In fact, he didn't really admit to anything. But he didn't deny anything either.'

Jepson pursed his lips for a moment, then smiled.

'If it cheers you up any, I have another bit of news. I said if you helped me, I'd see what I could find out for you about the theft of your navy's sailing plans. Remember?'

'Oh, that.' Backhouse was almost disappointed. The whole business of the sailing schedules, which had seemed so scandalous back in London, felt less important now, a bit of self-serving opportunism that was almost insignificant compared to the reckless, cynical acts of sabotage that Lavender had commissioned.

But Jepson continued regardless.

'You see, I've asked a few questions on your behalf, Mr Backhouse, and someone I know seems to know a bit about it. He's convinced that the person making all the money out of the scheme is Cuban, probably a *habanero*. He's got some friend very close to the whole business who drops hints. When I suggested that someone like Crawford or Lavender might be behind it, he just laughed. He said the person running it knew every detail about every ship captain sailing out of Havana. He refused to believe it could be an Englishman.'

'So who then?'

'I've no idea. Does it really matter? To be frank, my friend, if London was truly bothered they could block up the leak at the Jamaican end. Change their codes or something.'

'The funny thing is,' Backhouse confessed, perhaps lulled into a confidential mood by the warm night air, 'I'd rather hoped it was Crawford. I don't like the man. He's so damned contemptuous of everything I do. And you know, I half suspect him of robbing one of his own countrymen. In a particularly violent and underhand way.'

The unaccustomed liquor felt warm inside him as he outlined for his companion the information sent to him by Leonarda, as well as Dalrymple's tale of finding the consul in the garden, the morning after the robbery, mysteriously clutching a jewellery case. As he spoke, he was aware Jepson was enjoying the story. When it was over, the big American nodded in satisfaction.

'Well, well, well. It does sound as though our friend Crawford has been up to something, doesn't it?'

He didn't feel the need to add that such stories were the scraps upon which he fed, the tiny cracks in another man's armour through which a carefully guided blade might find a way. Jepson was not particularly interested in Crawford – he felt fairly sure the consul was irrelevant to what the British were up to on the island – but the opportunity to turn a thumbscrew on a British official was never to be neglected; it was almost a matter of pride.

And of course it was possible, just possible, that Crawford might furnish him with some small piece of helpful information. That was the joy of thumbscrews: you often had no idea what riches your victim would reveal.

XLII

In London, where summer stretched languidly into September, those who had any choice in the matter delayed their return to town for as long as possible. Staveley spent the summer between town and country, his work at the Foreign Office never quite letting go of him. His encounters with John Jerusalems in those months were infrequent and always brief. It was not until the new term was already drawing to a close that two letters from Havana sent him hurrying to Lowther Street.

There, it was as if summer had never happened. On being shown into Jerusalems' presence, he found the fire roaring, the shutters tightly closed, the tottering piles of books apparently unaltered. Even the half-cleared platters of cold meats and bowls of fruit seemed exactly where he remembered them. Only when he looked more closely did he perceive some changes. The maps on the walls, for instance, were re-ordered and altered, presumably to reflect Jerusalems' changing interests. Two or three large ones – Canada, Alaska, Mexico and the Pacific coast – seemed more prominent than he remembered them. And to his surprise he could see no chart of the Crimea, although the conduct of the war was now the most common talking point in London.

Jerusalems too seemed unchanged, although where there had been strawberries at the Round Pond, he was now gesticulating his welcome with the core of an apple. He seemed pleased to see his visitor, if not particularly surprised.

'Well met, my friend, well met. I was thinking of you only yesterday. So tell me . . .' He indicated the leather portfolio Staveley was carrying under his arm. 'What have you brought me?'

'News from George Backhouse in Havana,' Staveley replied bluntly. 'You were right in guessing he'd be in touch. But you'll never guess what he's got to say.'

Jerusalems placed the apple core on the mantelpiece and threaded his way between the various obstacles that separated them in order to take the portfolio from his visitor's hands.

'Well, enlighten me, Thomas. In summary . . .?'

'In summary, Backhouse has got hold of some papers. It seems someone, almost certainly someone we know, is collaborating with the Spanish in some unsavoury ventures. That's the first letter. In the second, he states his belief that Lavender is the culprit.'

'Indeed?' Jerusalems had taken out the letters and was looking at the dates on them. 'These have got here extremely quickly,' he observed.

'Backhouse sent them via Boston. They caught one of the Cunard boats,' his visitor explained. 'Transatlantic mail can arrive in a blink nowadays, John.' Staveley liked to cast himself as a man of his times.

Jerusalems cleared himself a seat at one of the cluttered tables, then continued his inspection of the letters. Staveley filled the time by examining the contents of the nearest bookshelf: a Spanish dictionary, various gazetteers, a history of the South American republics and, rather surprisingly, a very recent edition of *The Scarlet Letter*.

'As you can see, those letters are serious stuff, John,' he remarked after a suitable time had elapsed. 'Treacherous intercourse with a foreign power – the sort of thing I really have to report. And the attacks on Americans, on American soil too . . . Things are looking rather grim for your friend Lavender, I'm afraid. If he really wrote those things.'

'Oh, he wrote them.' Jerusalems said it without hesitation, rising abruptly. 'I'm sure of it.' He took up position with his back to the fire. 'But more importantly, Backhouse is sure of it too. And once an honest fellow like Backhouse knows of something unsavoury, there's no hushing it up. He'll expect you to take things further.'

Staveley nodded. 'Yes, the man has a conscience. But are you *sure* Lavender's responsible? The evidence is largely circumstantial.'

'It would seem that Lavender is refusing to deny it.'

'That's true.' Staveley frowned. 'But hang it all, what's he play-ing at, getting mixed up in stuff like that? He's asking for trouble. And can he really be so stupid as to plot against an American ship?'

Jerusalems dismissed this question with a flutter of his fingertips.

'Oh, I shouldn't place any credence in that, Thomas. I imagine he's heard the same rumours we have, and wants to impress his Spanish friends. For a start, I don't believe there is a ship called the *Pilgrim* in the American navy. If you want to check, there's an up-to-date list on the shelf behind your head.'

Staveley was prepared to take his word for it.

'But those other things. The explosion that killed four Americans, for instance. There's no escaping that.'

Jerusalems nodded, then paused for a moment, balancing on the ball of one foot, tracing the pattern of the carpet with the toe of the other.

'I'll be honest with you, Thomas, I think it would be better for Lavender to leave Havana. His personal conduct is putting him at risk and I think he's a danger to himself. But I'd be sorry to see him brought home in chains. This incident with Backhouse should be the spur he needs to leave. If he's too stupid to see that the game is up now, then he deserves what he gets. So a little time would be appreciated.'

Staveley nodded. It was not the first such request he had received from Jerusalems.

'Very well. I think I can manage that. But not too long. We can't have him carrying on in this way, John.'

'No, no. Of course not. Now, Thomas . . .' He stopped pacing and faced his visitor. 'These letters Backhouse has received, has he sent them to you?'

'Not the originals, only a précis. Did you want to see them?'

Jerusalems resumed his pacing.

'I should certainly like to have the originals in my hands. With the pious Señor Pezuela about to take up the post of Captain-General, the situation is delicate enough already.'

Finding himself next to one of the many bowls of fruit, Jerusalems stopped and selected a pear.

'And just remember, Thomas, if the new Captain-General is as hostile to the slave trade as everyone expects, no one will need to sink a battleship to start a war. The Spanish will have managed that all by themselves.'

He bit into the fruit with great decision. Staveley, who was engaged to dine at his club, took it as his cue to leave.

XLIII

The period that followed his confrontation with Lavender was Backhouse's worst on the island. It was the dry season, when the roads turned to dust and the views to the bay from his house in El Cerro were permanently hazed by the hot air that rose, unwashed by rain, from the city below. The nights were cooler, which brought him some relief, but having cursed the prickling humidity for months, he now longed for a tropical storm to clear the air and bring the blue waters back into focus.

Writing to London about Lavender had also left him feeling sullied: it was the sort of prim tale-telling that he had been brought up to despise. He'd had no choice, he knew that. But being right didn't make him feel any less uncomfortable. He hadn't come to Havana to spy upon his compatriots, nor to peddle rumours. And Lavender had a family in London, a mother and a brother whose lives would be blighted for ever by his disgrace.

Writing such a letter had cost him a good deal, and now he needed a reply, one that would reassure and absolve him, wash him clean like a torrent of warm Havana rain.

So he waited, but nothing happened.

The English community continued in its usual way, dispensing its favours and its snubs with familiar *hauteur*, hosting hot, expensive dinners and stifling tea parties made unbearable by stiff dress and manners. Backhouse and Lavender took great care to avoid one another, but it was impossible for either to be unaware of the other's proximity. Lavender still dined with the Crawfords, still travelled on business to the British islands, still frequented Lippi's and La Dominica; in short, still enjoyed the status of decent

Englishman. Backhouse and his wife did not receive half so many invitations.

But Backhouse knew it was not his place to say or do anything against Lavender. He would wait to hear from London what actions he should take. The man's fate would be decided in Whitehall, not Havana, however frustrating that might seem.

Of course he had always understood there would be a delay. It took time for letters to reach London, and then time for decisions to be taken. But as the days passed, he began to feel that perhaps Lavender had been right. Perhaps no one back home cared what happened, for good or for evil, in a place like Havana. Thomas Staveley's silence started to nag at him. At night, he drifted in and out of sleep, uncomfortable and anxious, never entirely at peace.

And then, worse than anything, his baby son fell ill.

Perhaps it was the climate, perhaps the enervating effect of earlier illnesses, but Grace found she could not feed her son as she had previously fed Alice. He was, she insisted, a very hungry baby, and from his fourth month it became clear she could not satisfy him. The doctor, who spoke good English, insisted he must be weaned, but this solution seemed only to make things worse. The pulped tubers recommended by the physician were mostly vomited back, and his prescriptions of castor oil and barley water seemed powerless to stop the infant's decline. No matter what foods were tried, the child could stomach none of them and grew weaker by the day. As the decline become startlingly visible, Grace moved from horror to panic to despair.

To Backhouse, powerless to act as the tragedy unfolded, the guilt he'd felt during Grace's pregnancy returned horribly amplified. As things grew worse, he was increasingly pushed to the periphery, behind the doctors and nurses and midwives, not even allowed to hold the child.

And every day, the news did get worse. Backhouse, frightened by his own feelings, unsettled by the rawness of Grace's suffering, took to staying out late, repairing to the taverns on the waterfront where he could stare out across the bay at the darkness of the water. When he returned, usually well after midnight, more often than not he would find the house still and Grace dozing, only partly undressed, across their bed rather than in it.

On one such night he found himself unable to sleep, overwhelmed by the certainty that this night would be the last, that his son would not survive another. Disregarding the strict prohibitions laid down by their doctor, Backhouse rose and made his way in the darkness to the nursery where the infant lay. There, in unfamiliar territory, he relied upon the moonlight to show him the nurse asleep in her chair and his child, his little, pink-faced boy, ashen and shrunken in his cot. It seemed to Backhouse that the infant neither woke nor slept but lay somewhere between the two, on the outer edge of consciousness, no longer concerned with the world around him, as if quietly facing another place, where the fussing and the wailing and the pain would be no more.

Backhouse lifted him and cradled the fragile body in his arms. He did it inexpertly, but the child didn't stir, simply lay still, isolated in his misery, helpless and unhelpable. Backhouse sensed that the great struggle, fought so doggedly in such a tiny frame, was almost over. The tiny, failing creature seemed no longer to believe in the possibility of succour.

As he felt the child's warmth against his forearm, something in Backhouse changed. His had been a timid existence: he had relied unthinkingly, throughout its course, on the support of family and friends, on good luck and his own good nature, for whatever advancement he'd ever had. He'd never had to fight for anything as this little thing was fighting for its life. Had never been half so resolute, never a fraction so tenacious.

And to see so close to him such suffering, such uncomprehending suffering . . .

Nothing was worth this. No posting, no promotion, no special responsibilities. Not the lives of a thousand American sailors. Let the Spanish sink the whole US navy. Let them kill as many Americans as they liked. Let Lavender strangle them with his bare hands if he chose. Backhouse didn't care. He despised them all. But he despised himself far more.

Nothing would be the same after this. Nothing could be. He would be different. He promised God he would be different. He swore it to himself. If only, in return, a miracle . . .

With tenacity that defied Backhouse's stores of belief, his tiny son held fast to the last threads of life for three days more, while the doctors' increasingly desperate concoctions of yam pulp and barley water were vomited as swiftly as those that had gone before. Then, astonishingly, a note was received from an English lady they barely knew, an acquaintance of Mrs Crawford with a very young baby of her own.

Please disregard this if it does not please you, it is only something I thought of, and may be quite wrong for your little one, but there is nothing quite like mothers' milk and I was wondering, as I have so ready a supply at this time, if perhaps I were to try . . .

She came that very afternoon, and the child fell upon her as if he had never fed before, with writhing, pressing urgency. The transformation was astonishing; both joyous and humbling. Never before, Backhouse thought, had anything so small grabbed so hungrily, so avidly, at the chance of life. And with every famished gulp the great darkness receded. After three days of growing euphoria, Backhouse finally lay down to sleep.

From that day on, their path was clear. Wet nurses were sought and found. The child drank. One morning some weeks after the recovery began, Backhouse stumbled by accident into the presence of the newest wet nurse. She was holding the child naked to her breast, his pink paleness startling against her black skin, and she showed no embarrassment at all at Backhouse's intrusion. He excused himself hurriedly, of course, but in those brief moments – the first time he had been shown his son naked since the darkest days of his suffering – Backhouse saw that the skin which once had hung so loosely wrinkled was already smooth and full and perfect.

Grace, touched by a kind of ecstasy, blissfully afloat on a serene sea, sensed her husband's happiness and was delighted by it. Yet there was a fierceness to his joy that escaped her notice. In his manners, in his diaries, in his letters home, he remained the man he'd always been: measured, reasonable and respectful. But even as he performed the daily courtesies of life, he no longer felt them entirely natural. His son deserved a better father. That much at least Havana had taught him.

Perhaps that was why his relations with Crawford grew so much worse in the period that followed. Backhouse had always disliked the consul; now he found himself less willing to conceal his dislike. If he and his family were to be snubbed anyway, he would leave Crawford in no doubt as to what he thought of him. His correspondence to the consul became shorter, sharper, less conciliatory, yet he was shrewd enough never to overstep the mark. Crawford was unused to being treated with such undisguised contempt and resented it.

For the first time Backhouse had the satisfaction of seeing the consul unsettled, his air of rather supercilious superiority replaced with a sort of snarling annoyance. And he was careful to keep copies of all his correspondence, so that when Crawford complained to London about his manner, Backhouse knew he had nothing to fear. And when the people in Lord Clarendon's office sided with him against the consul, as Backhouse had known they must, he treated himself to a brandy at La Dominica, and allowed himself a long evening of petty satisfaction.

His attitude towards Lavender changed too. He no longer avoided events and places where he thought Lavender might be, but attended without embarrassment, making his intention to attend clear in advance. And this determination was rewarded. Lavender studiously avoided further confrontation and retreated to a smaller circle of friends. Within a few weeks of Backhouse initiating his more aggressive policy, Lavender seemed largely to have dropped out of sight.

Yet when the letter from London finally arrived, it contained no mention of Lavender, although Backhouse tore through it in his haste two or three times, certain there must be. But no. Thomas Staveley simply thanked him for his information, which, he said, had been read with great interest. Backhouse's excellent work was praised, he was exhorted to keep his eyes and ears open. And he was instructed, in the most forceful possible terms, to forward to London at the earliest opportunity the full correspondence of 'the English Friend'. Staveley's tone, if not his words, suggested surprise that Backhouse had not already done so.

Backhouse destroyed Staveley's letter as he was supposed to. Then, very calmly and deliberately, he sat down to consider his options.

PART TWO

XLIV

The new year in Havana found the city brown with dust. The mud of October had crumbled to powder and now rose in sullen clouds beneath the wheels of carts and horses' hooves. By day a sense of lassitude pervaded the streets, as though the old town needed the clammy heat of the wet season and all its lashing storms to feel itself truly alive.

But for Jepson the early months of that year were a period of immense activity. In Cuba he had been obliged to begin from the beginning, creating for himself a web of contacts and informers strong enough to pull down his prey. But as the spring advanced, his confidence was growing. He felt strong in knowledge. He had only to pull certain strings, to apply pressure in the right places, and the pieces would surely fall into place.

But first there was Crawford. Jepson had been busy in that matter too, and he was rather looking forward to his next move. He didn't expect the British consul to be of great use to him, but a consul was a consul, and it always paid to have a senior official in your pocket. Putting such people there was something Jepson always enjoyed.

At first it did not prove particularly easy to secure an interview with the Englishman. When his first correspondence was ignored, Jepson wrote again, this time allowing the consul a glimpse of certain cards in his hand. After that the reply was prompt. Jepson would be welcome to call at the consul's home after dinner the following day. The American had suggested the venue himself: he liked to stage these meetings somewhere his victim felt secure. Break a man on his own hearthrug, Jepson knew, and he would remain broken forever.

Crawford was entertaining friends that evening, and his guests had retired to the drawing room by the time Jepson arrived at the big villa in the southern suburbs. He could hear laughter through the open windows as he waited to be admitted.

When his knock was answered he was shown into the library, well away from the consul's guests, and Crawford joined him there, cigar in hand, after a wait of some minutes. The study was furnished like a little piece of London, all dark wood and gloomy-looking books. Of the two leather armchairs, the one next to the consul's desk looked the more frequently used. Without hesitation, Jepson appropriated that one for himself.

The two men had never met before, and Crawford knew very little about his visitor. He had heard something about a new American official on the island but he had never thought it necessary to learn more. Americans came and went, and were safe to ignore. So on discovering such a large and uncouth-looking individual sprawled in his favourite chair, he was undoubtedly disconcerted. Back in London, he thought, if he'd come across such an ugly fellow in his study, he'd have shot him as a burglar. The man had even had the gall to take his silver paperknife from the desk and was studying it intently.

'Mr Jepson?' The consul's voice was cold. A lifetime of snubbing Americans had made him rather good at it. 'I trust you have been offered a drink. We have beer, if that is your preference.'

'Thank you, sir. But they're bringing me some of your cognac.' Jepson had risen when the door opened but as Crawford showed no intention of offering him his hand he sank back into the armchair in the manner of one who intends to occupy it for some considerable time. 'A man like me rarely drinks very fine cognac,' he added mendaciously. 'I'm looking forward to it.'

Crawford nodded and dabbed at his brow with his handkerchief. This fellow seemed to think he'd been invited for the entire evening.

'You will forgive me if I rush you, Mr Jepson, but I should be getting back to my guests. You said something in your letter about a police matter?'

'Indeed, yes.' Jepson's voice became exaggeratedly formal. 'As a result of investigations taking place in the United States I've been asked to present the police here with a dossier of information. My intention is to deliver it tomorrow to Colonel Aguero in person.' His tone changed. 'But sometimes, you know, the Spanish police can be very tiresome. They jump to conclusions. They arrest first and think later, and, by Christ, the conditions in which they hold their suspects are beyond belief. Barbaric, Mr Crawford. A gentleman can barely imagine the indignities to which he would be subjected.'

Jepson had not relinquished the paperknife and as he spoke he was pressing its point into the pad of his thumb and twisting it very slowly.

'So I thought I would come and see you first, Mr Crawford, in the hope that we might be able to clear up the matter. Between gentlemen, as it were.'

Before Crawford could reply a servant entered with a decanter and glasses. The consul waited until he had gone before pouring the American a rather grudging measure. Then he remained standing by the second armchair, as if the matter under discussion was unlikely to detain him.

'You mystify me, Mr Jepson. But of course I will help if I can.'

'Excellent. Well, here's the gist of it. A little while back someone murdered a night-watchman and removed some significant items of jewellery from your offices. The jewellery belonged to a man called Wymondham, a wealthy Englishman. A ruby necklace and earrings. The rubies were distinctive and very valuable.'

Crawford nodded. 'I remember the incident, yes.'

'Then you will not be surprised to hear that those same rubies have subsequently been offered for sale in the United States.'

Again the consul nodded. 'I imagine that was inevitable.'

'Well, Mr Crawford, the good news is that we are now in a position to return them to their owner. An honest jeweller in New Orleans identified them and contacted the police.'

'In New Orleans, you say?' Crawford sounded surprised, and Jepson looked up from the paperknife.

'Of course. Why not?'

'Only that I would have imagined New York was a better market for that sort of thing.'

'Is that so?' Jepson took his time. He had been fabricating evidence to suit his own ends for his whole career, and he knew the importance of timing. 'You see, Mr Crawford, the man who tried to sell the rubies in New Orleans was after a quick sale because, he said, he was returning to Havana in a couple of days' time. Rather interestingly, the description of him given by the jeweller matches your own in every detail.'

At this Crawford simply looked astonished, then he laughed out loud.

'Is that what this is about, Mr Jepson? In that case I can assure you it is a matter of mistaken identity. You really need not have troubled yourself.'

'Yes, sir. That was my first thought too. But when I checked, I found that you were indeed in New Orleans that week. And the jeweller took the precaution of having two witnesses present when the man came back to collect the stones. When it became clear the gems weren't going to be returned to him the fellow fled, but not before the others had a good look at him. One of them, a retired Presbyterian minister who once spent three months in Havana, has signed a statement declaring beyond doubt that the man selling the rubies was yourself.'

This time Crawford hesitated before laughing.

'I should like to see that statement. A genuine mistake, no doubt, unless the fellow has some grudge against me. That sort of thing does happen.'

Having played this hand many times, Jepson expected some such response. It never failed to surprise him how people caught out in a lie of their own were always so willing to believe the lies he had assembled against them. There was no jeweller in New Orleans, of course, no retired minister; but Crawford couldn't possibly be sure. It was just possible that fate had made him the victim of an outrageous coincidence.

'So you are not concerned, Mr Crawford?'

'Of course not. I'm sure the Spanish authorities will accept my word that there has been a simple mistake here.'

'You will swear to them you did not steal the gems?'

'Certainly I will. The question is impertinent.'

Jepson nodded. 'It is, and I apologise for it. But there will be further questions of increasing impertinence, I'm afraid. You see, I would be ashamed to give these papers to the Spanish if they contained nothing but a couple of dim-witted allegations. So I checked out a few things for myself. And I now have a statement from one James Dalrymple who maintains that he saw you with the missing jewellery case the morning after the burglary, in the garden of the consulate.'

A peal of laughter rang out from the drawing room. The consul's friends were enjoying a very pleasant evening.

'Dalrymple?' The consul laughed too, but his laughter sounded strained and contrived. 'Nobody will believe a word of his. There is no more disreputable witness in Havana.'

Jepson's response was immediate.

'Yet his statement is supported by one Manuel Ramos, who was briefly employed as a gardener at the consulate. I don't know if you remember him? He says he saw you removing the case from a place of concealment in the old sundial. From a cavity behind a loose brick, to be precise. I checked this morning, and there is indeed a cavity exactly where he claims.'

Finally Crawford's defences were breached, and Jepson knew it. The consul flushed deeply, and mopped again at his balding pate. He seemed to have no idea how to answer the charge.

'Sit down, Mr Crawford.' All deference was gone from Jepson's voice. He knew he was in command. He was also very pleased with himself. The gardener Ramos had been an invention, a simple enough fabrication; but the hidden cavity was real, and discovering it had been a masterstroke of intuition. It had been the story of the bloodied boot prints leading into the garden that had put him on to it, and he had searched the garden the previous day. Jepson was good at finding things. It had taken him five minutes at the most.

'Sit down,' he repeated, louder this time. 'You see, you might convince a Spanish court that the gardener was mistaken, that Dalrymple was lying, that you never had the stones. But two highly respectable witnesses in New Orleans say you did. Were they mistaken too? They got the dates right, the sailing times right, even the hotel where you were staying. And the Spanish are funny about foreigners murdering Cubans, you know, even black ones. They don't like it. I believe they still use the garrotte here. A painful, squalid death, I've always thought. Now sit down and listen.'

The consul did as he was told, but was still attempting to muster a defence. 'Mr Jepson, I assure you, there has been a mistake. Those witnesses in New Orleans . . .'

The American held up his hand.

'You will forgive me for rushing you, Mr Crawford, but I know you want to get back to your guests. And I find your cognac isn't as good as I'd hoped. But hell, I'll try another glass of the stuff, why not? You have until I've finished it to tell me why the Spanish shouldn't have the dossier.'

He rose from the armchair and helped himself.

In the end, Crawford's tale was not a complicated one. There had been no jewellery theft in Havana, he insisted, despite his reporting it. And the murder, the break-in, they were nothing to do with him.

He began with the Wymondham jewels. He had known Edith Wymondham since she was a young girl. He was an old friend of the family. She was flirtatious and flighty and affectionate, and had always been a favourite of his. Her marriage to Wymondham had pleased him: her family was not well off, Wymondham was extremely wealthy, and Crawford hoped an alliance to a much older man would calm her down and force her to grow up a little. It would also remove her from the influence of her wayward younger brother, who from an early age had proved himself erratic and untrustworthy.

Crawford elaborated a great deal on the plight of his young friend but it came down to a simple story: Edith's brother had eventually fled his debtors and come to America. When his sister and her husband arrived in New York as part of a tour that was to take in Wymondham's Caribbean holdings, the young man had sought them out and had begged Edith for assistance. His financial plight was desperate, he told her. He faced ruin a second time. Wymondham would not help him further, but Edith could. She had her jewels. His plan was to replace the stones with replicas, so good, he assured her, that no one would ever know the difference. This was finally achieved with his sister's knowledge but, Crawford insisted, without her approval.

The necklace and earrings were rarely worn, but Edith Wymondham did not share her brother's confidence that the substitution would remain undetected for ever. She was due to wear them again at the Captain-General's ball in Havana, while she and her husband were staying as Crawford's guests. One night, shortly after her arrival in the city, she had confided tearfully in her old friend, and on investigating he saw at once that the necklace given to him for safekeeping was a fake that would convince no one. The young man might just as well have left the case empty.

And then, two days before the ball, someone broke into his offices. Crawford and his guest had been playing cards that night at a place near the waterfront. Wymondham had bowed out early, and had taken Crawford's carriage to get home; but the consul had remained until just before dawn. Then, rather than attempt the almost impossible task of finding a cab, he had gone instead to his offices, thinking he might catch a few hours' sleep in an armchair. In the half-light of approaching dawn he had discovered his office ransacked and the body of the night-watchman sprawled across the doorway into the garden.

At first he'd assumed that the Wymondham jewels were the reason for the intrusion, but on checking the bureau he had found the jewel case untouched, and he had cursed Edith Wymondham's poor luck. If only the burglars had taken the fakes with them . . .

The idea came to him almost at once. He simply broke the bureau's lock, removed the case and, finding it too bulky to conceal on his person, placed it in a cavity in the sundial, a hiding place he'd discovered by chance some months before. Then, rather than raising the alarm and risking questions, he simply left the scene as he had found it, using his key to let himself out through the garden gate. At the Puerta de Tierra he had been lucky enough to find a cab willing to take him home. The whole episode had delayed him by no more than ten minutes.

As for the testimony of the men in New Orleans, he assured Jepson it must be a genuine mistake. Whoever had ended up with the real gems must by purest chance have resembled himself, must by purest chance have sought a market for them in New Orleans rather than New York . . .

Jepson waved aside these protestations rather impatiently. On the whole he was inclined to believe Crawford's story. It made sense in a melodramatic way, and Crawford struck him as the sort of fool who would consider covering up a young lady's follies the height of chivalry. Besides, he couldn't imagine Crawford as a murderer, not even by proxy. Too spineless, he thought; a manipulator and a schemer, probably a bully, but at heart also a coward.

'So . . .' he concluded, still fingering the consul's paperknife, examining it carefully rather than looking at his host. 'So you expect me to believe that someone broke into your office, stole a small collection of valueless items, killed your night-watchman and failed to find a case apparently full of rubies?'

Crawford was nodding violently, perhaps hearing something in Jepson's tone that offered him the hope of escape.

'I know it's odd, but perhaps it's not too hard to believe. I imagine they were surprised by the night-watchman and panicked. And they did get my watch, which might have been enough for them.'

Jepson suspected there was much more to it than that. Someone had gone to considerable trouble to frame the thug called Pedro the Salt-Eater for that night's work, and you didn't go to such lengths just to steal a gentleman's watch. But the reasons behind the break-in were not Jepson's concern.

'Your defence, Mr Crawford, is a messy one. You will have to admit to making a false report and to interfering with the police investigation. I imagine at the very least that the Captain-General will insist on your removal from the island. And of course the reputation of your little married friend will be left in tatters . . .'

Jepson was offering him hope now, and Crawford could sense it.

'Of course, yes. I would obviously give a great deal to prevent the matter from becoming public . . .'

The American nodded, then drained his glass with an ostentatious flourish.

'I think you can leave this with me, Mr Crawford. I dare say the delivery of the dossier is not urgent, and over time such things have a habit of going missing, don't they? As a matter of interest, the more recent theft from your desk . . . Someone walked away with a lot of cash. Might the money possibly have gone the same way as the jewels?'

Crawford flushed deeply, and muttered something about waiting for the police to conclude their enquiries.

But Jepson, having made his point, had turned his attention back to the silver paperknife.

'I like to think I'm a reasonable man, Mr Crawford. Let us, for now, leave this as a matter between friends. I'm sure you will find the opportunity to help *me* out from time to time. Isn't that so? Now, I understand you have guests. It would give me great pleasure to meet them, sir. I have an insatiable appetite for company.'

The consul hesitated for only the briefest of moments, then he led the way.

XLV

Even for one who knew the city as she did, the tangle of back-streets off the southern end of the Calle Damas was a dangerous place.

The message summoning her had been delivered to the Calle Chacón by a small boy who had not waited for a reply. The porter repeated it to her apologetically, as if it were a saucy riddle.

The missionary's assistant has taken off his cassock. The pretty señora will find him by the beak of the gull.

But Leonarda knew it was no riddle. It was a message from a frightened man and she sensed danger. Something had happened.

She went that night, hidden beneath the tatty smock and hat of a street urchin, and she kept herself in deep shadow. The busy streets of the old town were easy. She was as invisible there as she had always been, and every cobble seemed familiar. But when she reached the point where she must leave the Calle Damas, it became less easy to hide.

Those alleys were the last vestiges of an older Havana, a place of narrow passages and hidden doorways, still redolent of smugglers and brigands, of summary justice administered by the privateer courts. The taverns there did not advertise their presence. To find them one needed to venture down poorly lit steps and knock at old wooden doors heavy with ironwork. Few strangers ventured there, and there was danger for any who did.

But she knew the Gull. She knew all those dark alleyways, though she had only ever ventured there with caution. There had once been an iron gate with a faulty hinge and behind it an abandoned courtyard that led in relative safety to an archway very close to the Gull. If that hinge were still faulty . . .

It was not. The old gate had been replaced by a formidable new one, higher and topped with spikes. She would have to go round, through some of the hidden yards, the refuges of men accustomed to doing as they pleased. It was not a safe place for an unaccompanied woman. There was no law there.

Yet it never occurred to Leonarda to give up her mission. She had her knife secured, out of sight, to her forearm, and if she had to defend herself she would. She knew from experience she would have surprise on her side.

Returning to the Calle Damas and continuing for another thirty yards, she found the opening she was looking for. It was no more than a narrow gap between buildings, really little more than an open gutter. At the far end a lamp burned feebly, casting its light over a high-sided yard. There were windows there, and voices, and steps leading up to doors. Three other alleys, little wider than the first, led out of it. She knew she must take the middle one but she lingered in the darkness until she was sure there was no danger in the yard. Then she slipped from her hiding place, and in two, three, four steps had crossed the open space. Her bare feet made no sound on the cobbles.

As she went, she was making calculations in her head. There were three more such yards to cross before she reached the Gull. The next one contained the Lantern, which she remembered as the most notorious of all the drinking haunts hidden away behind the Calle Damas. That would be the place of greatest danger, but if it was as noisy and disorderly as she remembered it, and if she passed through it at speed, she might slip away from the revellers before they even noticed her.

In the event, however, the Lantern Yard lay as quiet as the other, and fewer lights showed. Luck, she wondered, or simply proof that things changed, even in Havana? Her question was quickly answered, for the next yard teemed with drinkers in the way the Lantern once had. Taken by surprise, she almost blundered into a group of men coming towards her up the alley. A fraction of a moment more and she would have turned into their path, but a peal of laughter warned her and instinctively she stepped back, just in time to take refuge in a low doorway. Behind her she discovered a narrow flight of steps running upwards, disappearing into blackness, and afraid that she was still in the light, she climbed without thinking until she was certain she could not be seen from the alley below.

But the group of men did not pass as she had expected; instead they paused at the foot of her staircase where one of them was evidently intending to leave the party. From where she crouched she could see their faces, picked out by the lamplight. They were dark-skinned and their faces were scarred; but there was no African blood in them, she knew. She recognised them as belonging to that class of criminals, Spanish by birth, which imperial Spain had vomited out into its colonies. Even the fiercest *habaneros* feared them: these were cruel men, hardened by violence, who had no fear of the law. There would be no reasoning with such men. Should they come across an unaccompanied woman spying on them in the darkness, they would consider it their duty to show her the error of her ways. It would be a rare treat for them, a game, a piece of good fortune to round off a happy evening.

But even as she retreated further up the steps, her brain was still clear. If it was only one of them, she had a chance. He would be caught off guard.

Before she could consider further, she had reached the top of the steps and found that they ended in a door of solid timber. The darkness was total and she had to grope with her fingers to find a handle. When she turned it she heard the scrape of a latch lifting but the door did not give. Locked, she realised, and turned to face the danger below her.

There the man lingering on the first step was finishing some lengthy tale and his friends were laughing. One of them offered some swift reply and more ribald laughter followed. Then his companions began to drift away, leaving the one man behind, smoking in the archway. If they went far enough, she realised – if she could be certain they had turned a corner and were out of earshot – perhaps she wouldn't have to use the knife. A kick in the face, delivered from above, out of the darkness, even by a woman's bare foot, would be enough to topple him backwards down the steps. She could be past him and gone before he'd even come to rest. Even so, as he discarded his cigar and turned to climb the stairs, Leonarda unhooked the knife from her sleeve and transferred it to her right hand.

And then, halfway up the stairs, when he was no more than five feet from her, his face almost level with her feet, he stopped. She waited for him to look up. But instead he began to pat at the front of his blouson, slowly at first, then with increasing impatience, and she heard him swear. *His key*, she thought, and had she been less disciplined, less aware of the need for total stillness, she might have smiled. *He's forgotten his key.*

The danger however was not over. The dark figure below her seemed to reach a decision: he would carry on and knock instead. Resting one hand against the wall to steady himself, he felt for the next step.

This was the moment when she must decide. Knife or foot? Were his friends sufficiently distant? Would they hear him fall? He *would* fall, she knew it; the steps were steep and the walls sheer, offering nothing for his hands to catch at.

Very slowly she leaned back against the door and lifted her knee to her chin so that the underside of her foot was ready to snap forward into his face. It seemed incredible to her that he could still be unaware of her. He was so close she could smell the drink on his breath. Had he not been slightly drunk, he must surely have realised his danger. Another six inches and he would be in range.

Somewhere, in a different part of her brain, she was thinking that the fall would almost certainly break his neck.

And then, when every muscle in her was tensed in preparation, he stopped again. It was much too dark for her to make out the features of his face, but she could sense that he had changed his mind. She watched him turn very slowly, uncertain of his balance, and make his way down, leading every time with the same foot like a small child.

Gradually she felt her muscles relax, but only when he had reached the bottom did she begin to lower her foot. The urge to sit back then, to wait while her breathing settled, was very strong. But she knew the man would return. He might be away only a minute or two. And if she moved immediately, hard on his heels, she had an opportunity.

And so it proved. The return of the drinker to his den was a diversion that drew the attention of his fellows. Three men who had been sitting with a flask of rum in the next yard rose to greet him, and when a door opened to admit him into the tavern, the light that spilled out served to deepen the shadows around them. As the four men turned towards the noise and laughter, Leonarda was already past them. Twenty hurried paces brought her to the entrance of the Gull.

Unlike the other taverns she had passed, the Gull was not determined to hide itself. Its doorway stood open – the sound of music and boisterous voices was clearly audible – and above the door, painted roughly on to the stonework, was the flaking image of a seagull. Leonarda remembered it from her childhood and it did not appear to have been re-touched or repainted since she had last peered up at it. In one of the windows beside it, a low light burned.

Ignoring the open tavern door, she looked for a doorway or staircase that might lead her directly to the rooms above it. The message had been specific: *the pretty señora will find him by the beak of the gull.*

She found the steps she was looking for in the darkest corner of the tiny yard. They led her to an open walkway which ran along the back of the tavern and gave access to three closed doors, the middle of which, she calculated, must belong to the room closest to the painted beak.

The door was not locked. In fact, it stood very slightly ajar, and when she pushed it open Leonarda saw that the room contained two people: a broad, hugely muscular African of about forty, his face marked with intricate patterns of scarring, and a very small, very old, brown-skinned woman. They were working in silence by a single candle, working with quiet, almost reverent thoroughness. They were washing the body of Felipe Martinez, the missionary's assistant, the man once also known as Tartuffo.

XLVI

And they were expecting her.

When Leonarda stepped into the room, they showed no surprise. In fact the old woman greeted her with a silent nod, and a movement of her head that seemed to invite her to come closer.

Unsure what to do and reluctant to be the one to break the silence, Leonarda seated herself on one of the wooden chairs near the table where the body lay and watched them work. From where she was sitting, she could see very clearly that the dead man's throat had been cut. There was to be no second resurrection for Tartuffo Martinez.

When the job was finished, the old woman drew a sheet over the body up to the dead man's chin, just far enough to hide the fatal wound, then turned to Leonarda.

'You are the señora from the Calle Chacón? Tartuffo said you would come.'

Nodding to herself, she drew up a chair next to her visitor's, so close that their knees were almost touching. Leonarda found it impossible to guess her age. Her cheeks were deeply wrinkled, but the skin of her face was nevertheless drawn tight over the bones, pulling her lips into a permanent approximation of a smile. Behind them, the big man had retired soundlessly into the darkness at the corner of the room, where he remained motionless and almost invisible for the remainder of Leonarda's visit.

The old woman told Tartuffo's story concisely, without emotion.

'It was not long after your visit, señora, that the men came for him. Six of them, on horses.'

Leonarda recalled the solitude of the mission house, the quiet forest road that led to it. A good place to hide, perhaps, but once found, little better than a trap. He had faced his attackers all alone.

They had waited for him in the darkness of the trees, hidden behind the mission house so that he would not see them as he approached. But Tartuffo's instinct for danger had not deserted him, and he had gone cautiously. Something told him not to approach the mission house directly, so he had waited and listened, retreating noiselessly into the undergrowth so he could not be seen. In the silence that followed he was aware of the sound of horses standing, their soft, ruppled breath barely perceptible above the sounds of the forest.

The old man knew better than to attempt to escape down the path by which he had come. The trap was set, and on the track he was vulnerable. So he moved deeper into cover and waited.

He stayed there, barely moving, without food, licking leaves for water, for the entire day. During that time the riders came and went with growing impatience, less inclined to lie in wait, searching the road more frequently as their tempers frayed. From where he lay he was able to observe them closely. When, eventually, they decided that their quarry was gone, Tartuffo was pleasantly surprised. He had been prepared to lie there much longer.

After that he made his way eastwards, walking only at night, living off the country, until he reached Matanzas. He had a cousin there, and could have stayed. Should have stayed. But the lure of Havana was strong, and stronger with every month that passed. He still had friends there. They would help him hide.

'And we did,' the old woman concluded. 'He had been good to us, señora, to Arturo and myself. He hoped to hide here for two weeks, perhaps a month. He was dead within three days.'

Leonarda had listened in silence, aware throughout of the proximity of the man's corpse. When the story was over, she asked why he had sent for her.

'He was a thief, señora, and also sometimes a cheat, a liar, but he hated to be thought a murderer. Even many of his friends believed he had killed that watchman. He told us you were going to find the man truly responsible. So he wanted you to know about those six men who came looking for him. Five of them were black, he said. One of them was white. And he wanted to tell you, señora, that this white man, the one who came to kill him, was the man whose bag he once stole. He told me that you would understand what this meant.'

'Yes. Yes, I do,' Leonarda assured her. 'Was there anything else?'

The old woman hesitated.

'Only one thing, señora. He wanted to tell you that he did not blame you. Did not blame you for leading the assassins to his door.'

The old woman sent the man Arturo to escort Leonarda home.

'He does not speak,' she explained, although it was unclear whether this was through choice or through incapacity. Leonarda noticed that he led her back to the main streets by a different, more convoluted route than the one by which she had come, one that avoided the busy yards where drinkers gathered.

Leonarda knew she should be paying attention, memorising the route in case she were ever to need it, but her thoughts were else-where, recalling the silence of the forest around the mission house, Tartuffo Martinez waiting for her at the door. An empty place. Lonely. Only the sounds of the forest.

No one had followed her, she was certain. The road from Havana was often empty, and a pursuer would have been impossible to miss.

Yet someone *had* found the missionary's assistant, and only a few days after her visit. Not a stranger, either; Tartuffo never forgot a face. Someone who had beyond doubt played some part in the robbery from the consulate. In Hector's murder.

Hector had been a simple man, and she wanted to remember him simply. But now, whenever she thought of him, someone stood behind him in the lamplight, hand raised, waiting to strike him down. A figure whose face she could not see. But she knew there was no anger, no passion, behind that blow. It was murder coldly done.

And Leonarda still had no idea why.

XLVII

When Dale next saw Jepson, he was struck by the big man's good humour.

'The momentum is with us, my friend, the momentum is definitely with us,' he chortled. To emphasise the point, he slapped Dale on the back so heartily that the other man winced.

Their meeting took place in a small and rather grubby drinking hole at the southern end of the old city. It was not a place that Dale had ever visited before. In fact it struck him as a rather dangerous place for a foreigner to visit at all. The man behind the bar had an unpleasant look on his face and a scar beneath his ear, and the walls were decorated with busy and bizarre murals that seemed to depict the storming and sacking of an Inca city by imperial Spanish soldiers. It was hard not to notice that the painter had lingered unpleasantly on the scenes depicting the fate of the captured womenfolk and the executions of their husbands.

The hour was a little after ten in the morning, so they had the contemplation of these horrors to themselves, but even so the location made Dale uneasy.

'Are you sure this is a safe place?' he asked as Jepson pressed him to take a seat. 'Foreigners aren't always welcome in places like this, you know.'

'Fear not, my friend, they'll tolerate us here.' He lowered his voice. 'I practically own the place. No, really, I do. Somewhere I've the receipts to prove it. Makes sense in all sorts of ways.' He pointed to the man behind the bar. 'That means you can trust Don Juan over there. He's got a sister in the States and he knows which side of his bread I've buttered. Now, let me bring you up to date with developments . . .'

Dale listened carefully while Jepson described his interview with Crawford. The big man was clearly delighted at how easily he had established a hold over the British consul, and if Dale was rather shocked by his methods, he had to agree that there was little about Crawford to excite one's sympathy.

'As for my rat,' Jepson went on, 'we're here today to apply some pressure. You remember me telling you about a man called O'Driscoll? He's a gangmaster here on the docks, and a small- to medium-sized criminal. But someone is paying him some nice sums of money, and they're paying them into American banks. Those payments have the mark of my rat all over them, and this time I think he's been too clever.'

Jepson leaned back in his chair and put his hands behind his head. The position placed extreme strain upon the buttons of his waistcoat.

'Let's imagine that this man O'Driscoll does jobs in Havana for our rat. He's an unpleasant piece of work is O'Driscoll, but our rat needs men like that. Now, being cautious almost to the point of obsession, our rat decides that he will pay O'Driscoll indirectly through his pet committees in America. That way, he reasons, no one will be able to trace O'Driscoll's payments back to him. That's good in theory, but in practice he has drawn my attention to someone who otherwise I would never have noticed. He should have done the simple thing and left bags of cash on O'Driscoll's doorstep from time to time.'

Dale nodded. It still sounded to him like the stuff of tall tales, but he enjoyed hearing them told.

'So what now?' he asked.

'Now we give O'Driscoll a little squeeze, just to see what happens.' Jepson took out his watch. 'He's due in about ten minutes' time. I confess that to obtain his trust I've had to employ him to do one or two small jobs for me. Oh, don't worry, nothing too nasty. The important thing was to over-pay him. Now he thinks me both dishonest and a fool, which is ideal.'

Dale smiled, but Jepson was looking serious.

'Remember, this is a ruthless fellow. We need to be careful, Mr Dale. We need to be very careful indeed.'

It proved an interesting morning. O'Driscoll arrived on time, looking lean and unsmiling and every bit as unpleasant as Jepson had described him. But Dale saw at once that he was at ease, and understood Jepson's cleverness in his choice of venue and in his careful preparation of the ground. It was clear that the newcomer had formed a low opinion of the big American, and at times he struggled to hide his contempt.

In contrast, Jepson gave nothing away, and Dale had never admired him more. He was simultaneously brash and boastful and over-eager to please. He flattered O'Driscoll outrageously and whenever money was mentioned took pride in making clear that no figure, however high, would be a problem. He reminded Dale of those over-friendly householders who are routinely cheated by their tradesmen while all the time believing themselves to be fine and popular fellows.

O'Driscoll, it seemed, had previously been commissioned by Jepson to prevent a certain American trading vessel from leaving the port of Havana before a certain date. That was a minor piece of commercial corruption, the sort that required little more than a routine bribe and no special understanding of Havana's underworld. Dale could probably have done the thing himself. But Jepson appeared to consider it a miracle of criminal acumen, and O'Driscoll a genius for having achieved it. He spoke with naïve enthusiasm of the commercial advantages that had accrued to him as a result, and was now eager to commission further similar pieces of work.

The business did not take long to complete. O'Driscoll named an eye-wateringly high figure for his ongoing assistance and allowed Jepson to beat him down by a fraction. So confident was he, he even agreed to accept payment on a results basis, with only a very small deposit to exchange hands in advance. Not until their final handshake was imminent did Jepson appear to hesitate.

'Just before we conclude, Mr O'Driscoll, there was one small thing I wanted to ask you about. You'll appreciate that I have excellent contacts back home – people say the President can't cough without old Jepson knowing – and before I hand over any more cash I should tell you that I heard your name mentioned the other day by a man I know.'

Until that point, O'Driscoll had listened to all Jepson's ramblings with poorly concealed indifference but now he looked up, wondering.

'And who might that have been?' he asked.

'Oh, he's no one you'd know. He works for the government. My government, I mean. Involved in financial investigations of some sort or another. He seems to have your name on a list.'

'A list? Who is this man?' O'Driscoll was suspicious now, and already defensive. Dale knew that men of his sort liked to go unnoticed. They built up their unobtrusive little empires through quiet intimidation and carefully concealed violence. Such men do not like to be caught in the light.

But Jepson was all reassurance.

'Oh, I'm sure it's nothing. Nothing at all. I'm sure you needn't trouble yourself. Besides, how can he touch you over here? But obviously I'd like to be reassured that nothing's going to get in the way of the job in hand. For instance, if the Spanish authorities were to look into your affairs, might that jeopardise our little arrangement?'

'I'm being paid by results, aren't I?' It was almost a snarl. 'I'll get the jobs done for you, I assure you.'

'That's good, Mr O'Driscoll. That's what I needed to hear.' But his brow remained furrowed as though he had not quite heard enough. 'Look, O'Driscoll,' he went on, 'this may sound a bit forward, but if you do find yourself in any trouble from over the water, just let me know. As I say, I have good contacts. And I need a man like you over here. I'm sure I could make any trouble go away.'

But O'Driscoll showed no interest whatsoever in the offer of assistance, and again Dale found himself admiring Jepson's subtlety. The bait had been dangled and O'Driscoll had ignored it. But later, perhaps, he would remember it. That was when Jepson would learn a little more about his rat.

When O'Driscoll left them, Jepson seemed inclined to linger. He was clearly pleased with his morning's work, and promised to keep Dale informed of developments. Then, as Dale made ready to depart, a small boy, a common street urchin by the look of him, appeared with a message for the American señor.

'I was waiting on the docks as you told me,' he explained. 'So many weeks, señor! I think nothing will ever happen. But today your letter came.'

Jepson opened the envelope and studied the message carefully before slipping the boy a substantial tip. Then he handed the paper to Dale.

> *My friend, the person you were seeking has returned to Santa Maria. Come quickly. The man is very sick.*
> *Emilio*

When Dale gave the paper back, Jepson read it again and chuckled.

'Things just get better and better, they really do.'

He smiled again, then looked up at his companion.

'What do you think, Mr Dale. Can you spare a couple of days for a boat trip to Santa Maria?'

XLVIII

For Backhouse, one of the initial attractions of his new post had been the high salary attached to it. Although one or two rumours did reach him that Havana was an expensive city, it seemed impossible that a salary so generous might ever seem insufficient.

Even as the bills began to come in, he felt no great anxiety. Those first bills were a little alarming, it was true, but he assumed that was because he was ignorant of the best way of doing things. Over time more reasonable suppliers would be identified and he would be able to live more economically. After all, those around them seemed to live very well indeed, the Crawfords especially. In fact the Crawfords set the standards in terms of style and hospitality by which their compatriots were measured. And the cost of entertaining was beyond anything Backhouse had ever imagined. Yet it had to be done, and done well. One had no choice.

But eventually he could no longer evade the reality. Their bills routinely, and significantly, exceeded his income. They were living beyond their means. It had taken him almost a year to accept the fact.

It was not something he could keep from Grace, and she accepted his pleas for greater economy with a pleasing lack of drama. She knew things were very expensive. She would find ways to save on their household expenses. In the meantime, to prevent any serious embarrassment, they might write for help to her mother, to their families at home. They had nothing to fear. Everyone knew George had such a good post.

But first there was the piano. Every home to which they were invited had a piano, and the instrument more often than not provided the focus of the evening's entertainment. Within a few weeks of their arrival they had resolved that they too must have one.

With so many other things to buy, and then with Grace's pregnancy and the baby's illness, the matter had rather been pushed to one side. But now, with their little son recovering, Grace was longing to show him off, and her need for a piano was suddenly more pressing than ever.

Backhouse should have dismissed the suggestion out of hand. But since his son's narrow escape from death, an unfamiliar strain of recklessness had entered his soul. One evening, seeing the haughty Mrs Crawford at her own instrument, his mind was made up. They would have a piano, and hang the expense.

It cost him a fortune, but an instrument was secured. It gave Grace almost childlike pleasure.

XLIX

When Thomas Staveley next called at Lowther Street, the visit was at his own instigation. A good deal had changed since he'd last visited Jerusalems in his lair, and he could not deny a tiny spark of pleasure in the fact that his friend's dire forebodings about developments in the Caribbean now seemed unfounded, while his own more moderate predictions still held sway.

So, invited to dine at a house not far from Jerusalems', and finding himself homeward bound comfortably before midnight, he decided on the spur of the moment to see if his friend was receiving visitors.

He was in luck. Mr Jerusalems was taking some supper but would be very happy for Mr Staveley to join him. Staveley had expected to be welcomed a little sheepishly, for his friend rarely had to dine on humble pie. But the little man extended his hand with no apparent embarrassment.

'Will you join me, Thomas? There's a very nice ham from Chatsworth, and tea if you want it. Or a glass of hock at the very least?'

Staveley accepted the hock, and cleared himself a space at the table in which to drink it.

'So, John,' he began, 'I'm sure you'll have heard all the latest developments. It seems all the talk of war over Cuba is a thing of the past.'

Jerusalems looked at him over the rim of his teacup.

'Is that so?'

'You know it is, John. All those whispers about an attack on an American warship have gone quiet.' Staveley could not help but sound a little smug. 'The Americans have stood down all their extra watches.'

'Yes, I *had* heard that,' Jerusalems conceded, although his equanimity appeared unshaken.

'Meanwhile the mood in Washington has definitely shifted. The invasion army is being dispersed, you know. And better still, Madrid is recalling Captain-General Pezuela from Havana before he can cause any trouble. They seem to have realised that appointing a Captain-General opposed to slavery might not have been the best way of keeping the peace. Have you heard that they're replacing him with our old friend Señor Concha, who put down the last rising so ruthlessly? Concha's very friendly with the slave-owners, of course, but he can be trusted to take a very hard line against dissent. Once he gets to work rounding up Cubans with American sympathies, I imagine support for Yankee interference will go rather quiet.'

'And so, Thomas,' Jerusalems summarised, 'it would seem all parties are stepping away from the brink. *Bravo* to all concerned. It would seem the only thing that could start a war now would be if the Spanish really *did* sink an American battleship. But you'll forgive me if I point out, Thomas, that none of this good news does very much for our country's crusade against slavery. Señor Concha is the fiercest champion of the slave trade outside America, is he not?'

Staveley flushed slightly. He could not deny that the appointment of Concha as Captain-General would be seen as an invitation for the slave traders to renew their efforts.

'Well, obviously, John, our moral purpose and our actual strategies cannot always be perfectly aligned. You know that. And you yourself are always warning of the danger to our Caribbean interests if we have to compete there with the Americans.' He tried to muster a smile. 'So surely, for now, keeping American hands off Cuba is the important thing? If it sets back our campaign against the slave trade by a year or two, that is the price we must pay.'

Jerusalems stood still and looked at him with great seriousness. 'The words of a pragmatist, Thomas, and bravely spoken. I shall remember them.'

Again Staveley felt embarrassed. He hadn't expected to find Jerusalems, of all people, somehow assuming the moral high ground.

'I also need to talk to you about your friend Lavender,' he countered. 'He's still in Havana, John. It appears he's sitting tight. I think he must be expecting you to make the whole problem go away.'

Jerusalems sighed and nodded. 'Yet he must see that I cannot. It's as I said, Lavender's judgement seems to have deserted him. It saddens me to say it, but I think you have no choice but to set the wheels turning against him now.'

The little man said it without any particular regret, and Staveley was surprised.

'You've known him for many years, haven't you?'

'I have.' Jerusalems rose. 'And I say it with his best interests at heart. I think I told you Lavender's personal conduct is putting him at considerable risk, yet he refuses to leave Havana. But if the British authorities are pursuing him through formal channels, he'll have no choice. The Spanish authorities will hand him over readily enough if we request it. Would you warn him the knives are out for him, Thomas? Tell him that he needs to go somewhere out of reach. Mexico, for instance.'

'You won't tell him yourself?'

'Oh, I'm sure he'll take a warning much more seriously if it comes from you. Meanwhile, is there any sign of those documents from Backhouse yet? The originals, I mean, not his précis.'

His visitor shook his head. 'Nothing yet, John, but he knows we want them. You know how slow the official diplomatic mail can sometimes be.'

For once, Staveley did not hurry away. The two men stayed at the cluttered table talking for an hour or more. Staveley had expected Jerusalems to have trenchant views about the situation in the Crimea, but he spoke of the fighting there as if it were no concern of his, as if his interest in the affair had ended long before things descended into war. He was much more interested in other parts of the globe: Central Asia, India, China. He made no mention at all of the Americas.

Which was why, when Staveley finally rose to take his leave, Jersualems' final words took him by surprise. Both men were moving to the door and Staveley had promised to call again some time in the coming weeks.

'Thank you, Thomas,' the little man replied gravely. 'That will be greatly appreciated. And may I ask . . .' Here his eyes seemed to move past Staveley, to the handle of the door. 'I know how unlikely it is, but if you *were* to hear anything of an attack on an American ship off Cuba, would you let me know at the earliest opportunity? I would be eternally grateful.'

The request struck Thomas Staveley as a strange note upon which to end their evening, and as he travelled home through a blustery night he wondered why his friend had thought it necessary to return to the subject.

L

If Dale had been asked to accompany any previous Washington envoy on an expedition to an obscure fishing village some distance up the coast, he would undoubtedly have declined with alacrity.

However, since Jepson's arrival on the island, Dale had begun to feel his own existence to be rather an uneventful one, which was why, two days after witnessing the interview with the gangmaster O'Driscoll, he found himself sitting in the dusty market square of Santa Maria in the company of a grey-haired, elegantly attired Spaniard who was introduced to him simply as Don Emilio.

According to Jepson, Emilio was a peninsular Spaniard of good family who had come to Santa Maria forty years earlier to marry the only daughter – and only child – of the local landowner. On that gentleman's death, a year or so after the wedding celebrations, Don Emilio inherited a considerable fortune and had effectively ruled over Santa Maria ever since. But he had never sought common cause with the island's great families and since the death of his wife it was rare for him to travel beyond his own estates. He seemed to ask for nothing better than for Santa Maria and its people – himself included – to be left undisturbed.

Precisely how Jepson had won the Spaniard's confidence, Dale never discovered. He had evidently come to the village for the first time very soon after his arrival in Havana, and the two men now seemed at ease in one another's company. Don Emilio, with his clipped good manners, his rather gaunt profile and his stiff, uncomfortable collar, met all Dale's expectations of a Castilian aristocrat.

After welcoming his guests with a glass of Canary in the village square, their host indicated three horses tethered in the shade.

'I have taken the liberty of securing mounts for you, gentlemen. It is a ride of half an hour or more, but the road is not difficult.' He smiled at Jepson. 'You, my friend, had better take the largest of the three beasts.'

They left the village in late afternoon, with the heat rising from the road in a haze. The Spaniard positioned his mount next to Dale's and talked as they rode, his peninsular accent softened by the languid drawl of the Cuban provinces.

Vincente Delgado, he told Dale, had been a bright boy, the brightest the village had ever produced. His family were farmers and fishermen, and his blood was a mix of all the races that had ever been cast up upon the island's shores. His abilities being manifest, Don Emilio had arranged an education for him with the monks of St Peter in Havana.

'But as well as clever, Vincente was wilful,' the Spaniard explained with a shake of his head. 'When he left the care of the monks, we here in Santa Maria had only the vaguest notion of how he made his living. Clerical jobs mostly, I think, but always with an eye to his own advantage. There was a sense here that Vincente liked to play with fire. He would either soar with the eagles, people said, or he would crash to earth and perish young.'

They were climbing out of the village on a road that cut a path through deep undergrowth, where the trees cast patches of welcome shade. To the left, through a screen of leaves, Dale could sometimes glimpse the sea; but Don Emilio rode with his eyes ahead, barely looking at the road, letting his old chestnut mount find the way.

'I remember Vincente's last visit to the village very well. They told me he was a fugitive, that he'd come here to hide, and I waited for him to call upon me to explain. That much courtesy I expected from him. But he didn't come until I sent for him.

'He was twenty years of age then, but I thought he looked pinched and unhappy. He told me he had come to meet a man called Alvarez, a Creole who travelled the island maintaining machinery on the plantations. Vincente had something for him – a bundle of papers, he said. When I asked him what the papers were, he refused to tell me, nor would he explain how he had come by them. When I lost my temper and called him a thief, he had the effrontery to turn away from me. After giving them to Alvarez he would leave the island, he declared. He would go to Mexico or to Panama and live like a gentleman. He would never return to Cuba.'

They had reached a point where the road was a dark cleft in the forest, where its twists and curves left the traveller isolated and in shadow. On the seaward side, a drainage ditch had been cut parallel to the path, and it was next to this that Don Emilio reined in his mount.

'We found him about here,' he said. 'His hands and feet were bound and someone had opened his trousers to work on him with a knife. Also a blade had been driven under his fingernails. Then, mercifully, his throat had been cut.'

'Tell Dale about the white man,' Jepson prompted, and Don Emilio nodded, twitching his horse into motion once more.

'He appeared in the square the day Vincente went missing,' the Spaniard continued. 'He was asking a lot of questions, and when I heard about it I asked for him to be brought to me. But by then he'd discovered where Vincente was staying and had left the village. He took care never to come back.'

As he spoke, they emerged from the trees. In front of them lay the sea, a brilliant, startling sweep of azure and aquamarine, fading at the horizon into the palest turquoise haze.

'That's the place.' Don Emilio pointed to a lone shack below them on the edge of the water. 'Let's hope the man you seek has not yet followed his cousin to that place beyond our shores.'

But Luis Delgado was still alive. They found him sitting on a low bed in the only room of the house. He was dressed in loose trousers and shirt, and sat with a light blanket over his shoulders although the day was hot and the room hotter still. His cough, which came in horrible, debilitating bursts, could be heard well before they reached the house.

'Luis . . .' Don Emilio seated himself beside the invalid with surprising informality. 'These are the men I told you about. You are to tell them all about Vincente's papers.'

The invalid nodded. He had clearly been expecting them. 'Vincente . . .' he began, without looking up. 'Vincente was here, you know. In this very house. Before he died.'

Dale estimated Luis Delgado was no older than forty, but he spoke as an old man speaks, as one simply pleased to have an audience for his memories. Yet the incident he described was not so long ago. Perhaps the approach of death had altered the balance in his head, Dale thought, bringing close the things of childhood, pushing back the things that ought to be most clear.

'I knew he was scared, of course. He was jumping at shadows. But he was excited too. He felt sure he had made his fortune.'

The invalid looked around him, at the walls, at the sea visible through the open door.

'And then one day he did not come home, and that same afternoon the stranger came. I tell you, I understood at once why Vincente was frightened. As soon as he walked in, I knew I couldn't afford to cross him. Yet he never threatened me. Not in words. He didn't need to.'

Delgado's eyes turned to the door again. Next to him, Don Emilio was sitting very still, a picture of patience.

'He said he'd come to find Vincente, to get back some papers he'd stolen. When I said Vincente was gone, he seemed to believe me. I let him go through Vincente's things, but he didn't find what he wanted. And then he got angry. He didn't shout or anything. It was all in his eyes. That was when I knew, in my heart of hearts, that Vincente was dead and that this man had killed him.'

He had been coughing throughout his tale, but at this point he was convulsed by a fit that lasted a minute or more. When it finally passed, he sat back as if the story was at its end.

'What happened then?' Don Emilio asked, and Dale was struck by the gentleness of his prompting.

285

'The stranger said I had to help him find the papers. I said perhaps Vincente had them with him, but I knew it wasn't true. If he had, the stranger would have found them. He asked me where Vincente might have hidden them and I told him about the ruined mill.'

Another fit of coughing followed, and when it was over, Don Emilio prompted him again.

'The ruined mill, Luis?'

'It's on the other side of the village. Vincente used to play there as a boy. I told the stranger that was the place. But when I told him he'd have to ride back through the village to get there, he hesitated and said he'd no time for such an expedition. He told me I must go to the mill the next day and find the papers for him. He said I must bring them to him in Havana the day after that. If not, he would come back. I asked what to do if they were not at the mill, but he just looked at me and said, *two days' time*. And then he gave me money. If a man like that gives you money, you take it and do what he asks.'

He paused again and Don Emilio waited until the coughing was over.

'And you found the papers at the mill?'

'Of course. I knew they must be there.'

'And did you look at them?' The question was Jepson's. The eagerness in his voice could not be disguised.

'Señor, I cannot read.'

'Go on, Luis.' Don Emilio's voice was as calm as before. 'Tell him the rest.'

'The white man told me to take them to a certain tavern in Havana. But to reach the city on the day he wished, I would have to go with one of the big fishing boats, and they sometimes drop their catch well before dawn. It might be that his tavern would be shut up, I said. So he thought for a moment, then told me where I would find the offices of the British. He said the night-watchman there was in his pay.'

'Did he indeed?' Dale could sense Jepson's interest. 'And can you remember when this was? What time of year?'

To the big American's obvious delight, the fisherman didn't hesitate.

'It was the day before the procession of the saints. I remember the preparations.'

Jepson looked across at Dale. 'And that would be . . .?'

'Mid-July.' The answer seemed to give his companion a great deal of pleasure.

'And did you deliver the papers as instructed?' Jepson asked.

The invalid nodded. 'I said nothing to anyone, but I handed them in through the little window in the door. Then I ran away, back to the docks, and prayed I would never see the stranger again.'

'There, my friend.' Don Emilio looked up. 'There you have it. It seems the papers you seek did not remain here in Santa Maria. To discover the name contained in them, you will have to search in Havana after all.'

The three men did not leave immediately. Jepson and Dale waited for a few minutes on a weathered bench facing the sea while Don Emilio sat a little longer with the dying man. Then they rode back to Santa Maria in silence, as though such proximity to imminent death had sobered them. Yet when Don Emilio took leave of his visitors at the café in the square, Dale was aware that beneath Jepson's restrained composure there ran something very like elation.

'So, my friend, the gods of underhand dealings are smiling on us,' he declared, signalling for the waiter. 'Brandy, Mr Dale? To drink to the success of our journey?'

'I'm not sure how successful we've been,' Dale replied. 'I assume those papers were the ones Alvarez was pursuing, the ones that named your rat?'

'Of course, of course.' Jepson broke off to place his order. 'And now we know who our rat sent to tidy things up.'

'Do we?' Dale was doubtful. 'Havana contains any number of murderous ruffians, both white and black. It could have been anyone.'

'You think so? Really?' Jepson seemed genuinely astonished. 'With those murderous eyes? Come on, Mr Dale, I recognised him at once. That man was O'Driscoll, sure as sunrise. And our next step, my friend, is to make him regret it. Yes, O'Driscoll's days are numbered – here in Havana, or anywhere else. But first we're going to twist him. Twist him until he breaks.'

LI

Once a month, on the last Sunday, tables were laid out in the shade of the trees along the Paseo del Prado and the city's booksellers spread out their surplus stock – their old or cheap or battered volumes – in the hope of quick sales to those enjoying a stroll along the handsome boulevards of the new city.

Although few of the books were in English, Backhouse liked to be there. Compared to Havana's other markets, it was a restrained, civilised affair. He and Grace often chose the book market as a Sunday destination, wandering the length of the boulevard, one eye on the spines of the old volumes, the other on their fellow strollers in their Sunday morning finery. In his first weeks on the island, the bustle and general ungodliness of the Sabbath in Havana had rather shocked Backhouse, but he had grown accustomed to it more quickly than he'd expected. There was something about the easy informality of *habaneros* on a Sunday that he could not help but contrast favourably with the stiff-backed seriousness of the English at worship.

This particular Sunday, however, Grace was not with him. Alice had been unwell, Grace wished to stay with her, and Backhouse's presence, he was made to understand, was not required. Better that he should go ahead with his walk, Grace reasoned, than that he should fret around the house and annoy the servants.

So Backhouse went to the book market alone, a little disgruntled at being so lightly dismissed, but nevertheless relieved to be away from the rigid hush of an English expatriate Sunday.

At first he strolled through the shade paying scant attention to his surroundings. Alice's indisposition, although he was assured it was a perfectly trivial matter, reminded him of those fears, never entirely dormant, that had disturbed him ever since their first night in Havana. It had been clear from the very beginning that the city's climate was not the healthy and beneficial one he had been led to believe; and although his son continued to grow happily enough after his remarkable recovery, the fragility of a child's existence amid Havana's fevers and foul airs was not something Backhouse could easily put from his mind.

It was not until his second turn along the Paseo del Prado that Backhouse noticed Leonarda. She was standing in the shade, looking down intently at one of the tables, running a gloved finger along the lines of books. The width of the road was between them, and Backhouse was struck by her stillness, her concentration. She was, he realised, the only person browsing the books that day whose face was not white.

He had to wait for a *volanta* to pass before he could cross the road to join her. It was being driven very slowly, allowing plenty of time for its rich female passengers to be seen, and when it was finally gone Backhouse saw that Leonarda was no longer alone. A young man in the uniform of a police officer had approached her, and was hurriedly removing his hat. The two had clearly met before: there was a familiarity about their greeting that left him in no doubt. Yet it was not without formality. Conventions were being respected. The young man was asking a question and gesturing at the rows of books.

Were his attentions welcome? Backhouse remained on the opposite kerb, watching.

The young man was surely an admirer. There was something about the way he held himself, a slight tension in his shoulders that his determinedly cheerful manner could not quite masked. But the lady . . .? It was much harder to tell. She smiled, certainly, and there was warmth in her smile. Backhouse found himself unable to look away. Who was this young officer? By what right did he accost her in the street? And what was she thinking as she smiled back at him? He was a good-looking young man, Backhouse could see that. Was such a man the sort to capture the affections of the enigmatic Señora Leigh?

Backhouse found himself in two minds. To notice her without greeting her would most certainly look like a snub. But to interrupt her conversation was unthinkable . . .

He was spared the decision when a voice hailed him enthusiastically from his own side of the avenue. It was Callaghan, the clerk he sometimes employed when Dalrymple was incapacitated, and with him were three or four other young Britons, recently arrived on a visit from Jamaica. They were in high spirits and pleased to make Backhouse's acquaintance. By the time introductions had been made, compliments exchanged and farewells completed, the shadows where Leonarda had been standing were empty. Both the young lady and the captain of police were gone.

LII

The wall paintings at the Conquistador tavern appeared no less distasteful to Dale on a second viewing. He had travelled there rather reluctantly, it being a busy time for him with the wholesale markets for sugar and tobacco unusually volatile. But Jepson had been insistent.

'Come on, my friend,' he had urged when he called at Dale's offices on the Calle Obispo. 'Our story draws to a close. O'Driscoll has held out far longer than I thought he would, but it seems he's finally ready to ask for help. It would be wrong to use the word *beg* in relation to a murderous ruffian like O'Driscoll, but the note I received this morning came pretty close. He seems very eager to see me.'

So Dale had made the journey to that less savoury part of town out of naked curiosity. O'Driscoll had struck him as a hard man to crack. A dangerous man, Jepson had called him. A murderer, and worse. Bringing him to heel would be a considerable achievement.

Indeed, the man who strode into the Conquistador that afternoon appeared little changed from their last encounter; the same hard, lean, tanned face, the same purposeful stride, the same dark, nondescript suit of clothes. He was, Dale realised, angry rather than humble.

'Someone is playing games with me, Jepson.' There were no formalities, no niceties. He had barely seated himself. 'I've got fifty men out there on the docks and not one of them is working. My usual customers don't want to know me. People I've been working with for ten years. They've all heard rumours.'

'Rumours, Mr O'Driscoll?' Jepson looked concerned. 'Nothing that will jeopardise our little arrangement, I hope?'

'Rumours that the police are about to close me down. No one wants their labourers rounded up with their ship half loaded, do they? And there's worse than that.'

'Worse?' Jepson looked positively perturbed, as though he feared that a party of police were about to descend on the Conquistador there and then.

'My money in America. Something's happened. They're telling me it's gone. That I withdrew it all in person. Three different banks.'

The big American nodded sympathetically. 'Banks are so hard to rely upon, aren't they? I always prefer cash and a strong safe.'

'What's happening, Jepson? Who's doing this? There's no reason for them to come after someone like me.'

Dale watched his friend sit back and stretch, like a big cat, he thought, preparing to show its claws.

'Oh, no one's interested in you, O'Driscoll. You're nothing. You're nobody. You're less than nobody. You're dirt. You're *filth*. No, it's your employer I want.'

The change of tone was so abrupt as to be shocking. Gone was the affable, gullible trader, replaced by someone precise and ruthless. Duke saw O'Driscoll flinch.

'How *dare . . .*'

'Oh, please!' Jepson's voice was edged with steel. 'Spare me the righteousness.'

'Who *are* you?' O'Driscoll's manner was hostile, but his voice was quieter than Dale had expected.

'No business of yours. But I know enough about you to have you shot by the Spanish this very afternoon if I choose. How many people have you killed on this island? Dozens? More? There was a murder in Santa Maria a few years back. I've got you for that one. But I assume there are many others.'

'You're bluffing.' O'Driscoll rallied, as though finding himself on familiar ground. 'You'll never prove that. No one can touch me for that.'

Jepson smiled, a smile heavy with contempt.

'It's not murder that will put you up against the wall, you fool. Haven't you noticed that the new Captain-General's favourite pastime is sniffing out conspirators? Nice Señor Pezuela has been recalled to Madrid and the man who's replaced him has different interests. He likes an execution does Captain-General Concha. He's the man who had his wife's oldest friend garrotted for treason because of one indiscreet letter, remember? And when he sees the records of all those American dollars you've been banking, and then looks at one or two documents I'll be sending him that link your money to the invasion army – well, frankly, he isn't going to be very interested in your version of events. Don't expect a trial. Last week they strangled a priest for sheltering two conspirators. It turned out later it was the wrong priest, but Concha didn't mind. Summary executions send out the right signals.'

To Dale's surprise, O'Driscoll didn't attempt to argue. He was astute enough to grasp the position into which he'd been manoeuvred, and realistic enough to know where it might lead. There was something almost impressive about how quickly he shifted his ground.

'So what do you want?' Succinct, crisp, decisive.

'I want the man who gives you your orders. His name, and everything you know.'

O'Driscoll even managed a smile. 'The man you're after could send me to the gallows ten times over. If I were to breathe a word, I'd be finished here.'

He said it with conviction, but Dale could see he was already calculating where his best chance lay.

'You're finished here already, my friend. So you have a problem.' Jepson shifted his chair, as though preparing to walk away.

'He's protected me in the past,' O'Driscoll added hastily.

But Jepson shook his head dismissively. 'This is not some petty fairground test of strength, Mr O'Driscoll. This is serious.' He paused, and his eyes narrowed. 'I'm beginning to think you haven't understood the sheer power of the guns I have at my disposal. Enough to take out your friend with powder to spare. And at the moment, for want of a more worthwhile target, every one of those guns is trained on you.'

O'Driscoll held his gaze for two or three seconds, then shrugged. 'What would I get in return?'

Jepson was making no attempt to hide his contempt.

'To be frank, I don't really care what happens to you once I'm off this island. As far as your labour gangs are concerned, I might persuade a friend of mine in the Spanish police that you're not worth bothering about.'

O'Driscoll leaned forward eagerly. 'What about my money in America?'

Jepson sighed as if such undisguised avarice was distasteful to him. 'If I get exactly what I want from you, and if everything proves satisfactory, then I dare say some of it may be found. Banks are funny that way.'

Dale could see that O'Driscoll's brain was working fast, still making calculations.

'What guarantees do I have?' he asked.

'None at all, my friend.' The big man looked supremely unconcerned. 'None at all.'

The gangmaster hesitated for a fraction longer, then made his decision.

'Very well. But I want my money back. All of it.'

Jepson raised an eyebrow but said nothing.

'The man you're after passes himself off as a minor British merchant. When he first approached me about a job, I didn't take him seriously. He wanted me to intercept a brown dispatch.'

Jepson did speak then, turning to Dale as if to translate.

'From time to time, Mr Dale, when the Madrid government has something particularly sensitive to convey to the Captain-General, they entrust it to a special courier, someone who travels incognito. That's what they call a brown dispatch. It's all highly secretive.'

O'Driscoll nodded. 'Before that day I'd never really believed they existed. I thought the Englishman was probably mad. But he got it right in every detail. The courier was returning to Madrid with the Captain-General's reply. The Englishman was able to tell me exactly where he would be at a particular time, what he looked like, even where on his person he'd be carrying the dispatch. I confess I was impressed. After that I worked for him a lot. He pays well and he seems to know everything. I take care to keep on the right side of him.'

But Jepson held up his hand.

'Let's stop there, shall we? I take it you're asking me to believe that this Englishman is a man called Lavender? If so, my friend, that's not good enough. Lavender is a minnow. Somewhere in these dark waters there's a much bigger fish.'

But O'Driscoll was shaking his head.

'No. Don't you see? That's what he does. That's his plan. I've heard him boast about it, about convincing the Spanish authorities that there's a much more important spy, right under their noses.'

Jepson said nothing, so the gangmaster tried again, clearly anxious to be believed.

'Lavender works for someone in London. This man has people spying for him all over the Caribbean. It's how Lavender knows so much. He's receiving reports all the time. They come anonymously – no names, no addresses, just notes through his door. But he says they're always right.'

Jepson shook his head again, but Dale didn't think the gangmaster was lying. And he was clearly finding Jepson's scepticism exasperating.

'Don't you see? The man in London planned it,' O'Driscoll continued. 'He *wants* you to think there's someone else.' He ran a hand through his hair. 'He sees to it that there are always rumours flying around about some fancy British spy in Havana. Lavender loves it. He has a phrase: *When gold is stolen from the vaults, the pickpocket outside is never a suspect.*'

Now O'Driscoll was eager to talk. When Jepson questioned him about the affair in Santa Maria, the gangmaster's story was simplicity itself. Lavender had received an anonymous warning, written in the agreed cipher. It told him that a message from London had been intercepted which put Lavender and others at risk. A clerk in the administration, instead of handing it up the chain, had arranged instead to sell it to someone, someone willing to pay very good money.

Lavender's instructions to O'Driscoll had been straightforward: to retrieve the letter and to silence anyone who might have read it. It had been, O'Driscoll claimed, a fairly simple piece of work. He said it as though murder and torture were things of no moment.

Nevertheless, Dale believed him, although it was not until that evening, over a drink near the Cortina de Valdés, that he and Jepson sat down properly to share their thoughts on O'Driscoll's testimony. The smell of grilled meat, slightly charred, drifted to them across the water from one of the larger boats in the bay and reminded Dale how hungry he was. But his companion showed no sign of wanting to eat. He was cradling his glass and looking out into the darkness.

'So, Mr Dale, I take it that you found our friend's story persuasive?'

Dale confirmed that he had, but Jepson was still reluctant to recognise Lavender as his adversary in Havana.

'Oh, he *could* be. I accept that. It's *theoretically* possible that Jerusalems is controlling everything that happens here in Havana personally, all the way from London. Controlling Lavender as a showman controls a puppet. But it is surely too difficult a feat to sustain, even for Jerusalems. I cannot really believe it.'

Dale felt awkward. It seemed to him quite possible that Jepson's rivalry with his old acquaintance in London was clouding his judgement.

'No,' the big man went on, 'I won't be completely convinced that Lavender is my rat until I see some solid evidence. Something in writing, something I can read for myself.'

They were interrupted by the appearance of a small boy with a message for Jepson. It arrived at the same time as two further glasses of brandy, and Jepson waited till he'd sipped before slitting open the envelope.

At the moment he did so, Dale was talking about something quite different and at first he didn't notice the change in his companion's demeanour; but when he finally looked across the table he saw that Jepson's face had turned white. He was sitting quite motionless, looking down at the paper as though scarcely able to believe what he was seeing.

When he looked up, the expression on his face was not one Dale had seen there before. Shock, perhaps, or pain, or anger.

'Have you ever been outwitted, Mr Dale?' he asked quietly. 'Ever been made to look a complete bloody fool? Well, I have.' He rubbed a hand across his cheek. 'That training ship with explosives on board . . . It was nothing but a feint. A decoy.' His voice trembled. 'They've blown up a battleship, Mr Dale. A whole bloody battleship. The *Albany*, gone with all hands. And that's only the start of it. If I don't get over to Guantanamo faster than the bloody lightning, there'll be American gunboats bombarding Havana before the week is out. War, Dale. Bloody, disastrous war. We've talked about it like a game. This is not a game. This is it. The real killing is about to start.'

He looked down and read the message again.

'And when the war comes, Mr Dale, and when we end up taking this shithole of a city by force, I'm going to search every room and every cellar personally until I find the man behind this.'

He left within the hour on the fastest boat in the harbour. Dale watched him go, wondering precisely when the bad news would break.

LIII

After their confrontation at the villa in El Cerro, Backhouse and Lavender had taken care to avoid one another, each of them waiting, Backhouse supposed, for London's response to the letters he'd sent. And when they did meet again, the encounter took Backhouse completely by surprise.

For a number of months he had heard virtually nothing of the other man, and had been congratulating himself on vanquishing the fellow from the field. Then, one evening, after a quiet dinner with Grace, while Backhouse was still enjoying a cigar at the table, Lavender was announced.

Backhouse felt he had no choice but to receive him. To have him thrown out risked unwanted gossip, and Backhouse was not at all sure his servants were capable of carrying out such an order even were he to give it. However the prospect of facing the man again did not appeal. It seemed unlikely that Lavender had come to offer an apology and a full confession.

The visitor's first words confirmed this. Backhouse had risen from his seat when the other entered; as always when he dined at home, he was in evening dress, and the cigar he was smoking happened to be rather a fine one. The sight of him halted Lavender in the doorway.

Lavender was not in evening dress. In fact he looked dishevelled and had a wild look in his eyes.

'You smug bastard,' he began, then paused, and Backhouse realised he'd been drinking.

'I think perhaps you'd better leave,' Backhouse told him. 'Whatever it is you want to talk about, we can do it tomorrow.'

But Lavender was only beginning to warm to his theme.

'Look at you,' he went on, 'with your London suit and your Havana cigar, and your villa in the suburbs. Quite the little gentleman, aren't you? Well, let me tell you, *no one* here takes you seriously. Do you know that? You are *nothing* in Havana. They're all laughing at you. And not just here, in London too. In London they must be holding their sides. I'm surprised we can't hear them from here.'

'You'd better leave, old man,' Backhouse said again. He would have been embarrassed once, but now he was just angry. Even so, he had no intention of trading insults. Instead he crossed the room and reached for the bell.

'Wait! You may summon the minions in a moment.' There was something slightly different in Lavender's tone and Backhouse did indeed pause, turning to look at him, lowering his hand.

'Hear me out, Backhouse. George. May I call you George? I think when a fellow destroys your life, you're entitled to call him by his Christian name. Even if he is so confoundedly prim that his arse must hurt every time he shits.'

Backhouse reached for the bell-pull a second time.

'Wait! I want to tell you a few things first. Then you will never be troubled by my presence again. I leave tomorrow for Mexico. I'm getting out.'

It was the news Backhouse had most wanted to hear. He lowered his hand again and waited for Lavender to continue.

'But first I'm going to tell you what's really happening in Havana. It might make you a little less self-righteous. The world is not the place you think it, you know.'

Lavender moved forward then and took the chair recently vacated by Grace. Backhouse remained standing.

'First of all, you were right, of course. I did send those messages to Colonel Aguero. But I want to be clear about this: none of it was for my benefit. I was only doing what I was told. Do you hear me? It's important. I've got a mother and brother in London. I want them to know I've done nothing wrong.'

'You conspired to murder young sailors in peacetime.' Backhouse found it extraordinary that Lavender should attempt to justify his actions.

But Lavender barely heard him.

'Have you ever heard of a man called John Jerusalems, George? Well, *you* may not have done, but everyone important back home knows who he is. Even if they've never met him, they know who he is. He has very powerful friends.'

Lavender looked round as if hoping to find the table supplied with liquor. Disappointed, he returned his attention to Backhouse.

'I've only met Jerusalems twice, but for most of my life he's been paying me to do what he says. Paying me well. Too well, perhaps.'

The alcohol he'd already consumed was making him loquacious. Backhouse said nothing and let him continue.

'The first time I met him was in London, just before I came out here. He was interested in my plans and had contacts in all the islands. Just what I needed if I wanted to do well over here. I had a good business head but no capital. Jerusalems offered help.'

He shook his head.

'I suppose I'll never know how well I'd have fared without Jerusalems' money. Perhaps I'd have made it big, taken some risks. I'd have been hungrier, that's certain. I see now that his money was a curse. It was all too easy. Regular payments, enough to live on comfortably. My business interests ended up as a hobby, a façade of endeavour behind which I could do Jerusalems' dirty work.'

He reached forward and rather idly took up the salt pot.

'You probably think a spy is the lowest of the low, don't you, Backhouse? So did I. I thought spies were unshaven men in grubby clothes, the sort of people who'd been brought up to lie and cheat. But it's not true. You don't become a spy all at once. You don't sign the articles. You probably don't even know it's happening. First you agree to do something, something not very difficult which you believe is of benefit to your country. And then you take the money. You win both ways. It would seem absurd not to do it again. And again. And before you'll know it there's talk of blowing up munitions, assaulting messenger boys.'

He looked up from the salt pot.

'So watch yourself, Backhouse.' He spoke with urgency. 'They'll do the same to you. First the sailing plans. Next it will be something else. Then you'll realise you're short of money. That's inevitable out here. A little extra, they'll say? Of course. Before you know it, you're deep in, and you've no one to blame but yourself.'

Backhouse had never heard Lavender talk so fast or so freely. But his heart was hardened against the man.

'And in the end . . .' Lavender went on. 'You know what happens in the end? If you get into any difficulty, if you mess things up, they cut your throat. You don't really matter to them at all. There will be others. Jerusalems!' He looked as though he wanted to spit. 'He is made of stone. You know what I did wrong?'

Backhouse realised Lavender was going to tell him anyway. The man's self-pity was an outrage, but there was something slightly moving about it all the same.

'I have a weakness, George. The Greek vice, they call it. I cannot fight it. There are places in Havana where you can go to enjoy that kind of thing, where you can do whatever you like. They bribe the right people so they are above the law, and nothing can go wrong. Then one day Colonel Aguero's men came for me. He had a pile of statements in front of him. He must have been preparing it all for months. I was to be charged immediately and sent to the Tacón gaol to await trial and execution. The documents would also be handed to the British. My family at home would be disgraced too. But if I were to help him . . .'

Lavender still held the salt pot and now he turned it gently upside down and watched as its contents formed a neat pile on the tablecloth.

'He already knew I was gathering information for London. If I was prepared to do the same for him, then all action against me would be suspended. Suspended, you note. Not dismissed.'

The salt pot exhausted, he tossed it to one side. It rolled a short distance along the table then fell to the floor. Lavender didn't watch it go. He had raised his head and was looking Backhouse in the eye.

'Do you know what they do to people like me in the Tacón gaol, George? Before we're executed we're handed over to the inmates. It's a little tradition. We're held down by the mob, and our testicles are taken off with a knife while the rest of the crowd cheers. After that, it's a race to get us to the executioner before we bleed to death.'

Backhouse shuddered. From what he knew of the place, such barbarism was all too possible. He was trying not to meet Lavender's eye.

'So of course I promised Aguero everything he wanted. But I'm not a complete villain. I wrote to Jerusalems at once. Not directly, of course. You always write to some unheard-of name and address. But I told him what had happened and asked him what I should do. The reply came back loud and clear. I was to do whatever was necessary to win Aguero's confidence. I was to suggest ways I could actively help him take action against the American filibusterers and their army. I would be told what to suggest by letter. To make sure Aguero's complicity was clear, I was to contact him in writing whenever possible. There was no need to use a cipher.'

He looked down at the perfect cone of salt in front of him then angrily brushed it aside with his hand.

'Believe it or not, I was delighted. Relieved. I thought Jerusalems the finest man on earth. His instructions meant I got to keep everything I had here, while freeing me from any possible trouble with the authorities. Jerusalems knows a lot of people out here, and he used them all to help me. Messages would come to me anonymously, in Spanish, delivered by hand, detailing acts of sabotage being planned against the invasion army. I simply passed the details on to Colonel Aguero as my own suggestion, then took the credit for them when they happened. Aguero was delighted and Jerusalems seemed pleased too.'

303

Lavender pushed back his chair as though about to rise but then appeared to change his mind, remaining seated, a little back from the table, regarding Backhouse with a sort of loathing.

'And then you came along with all those letters neatly tied up in string. Someone had tried to betray me. I don't know who. Probably some miserable little Jesuit on Aguero's staff who knew what I got up to on the dockside and felt I needed to suffer for my crimes. The irony is that if you hadn't been such a prig, you might have understood that you and I were both on the same side. And even when you insisted on reporting the whole affair to London I wasn't too bothered. Jerusalems would sort it all out. Jerusalems can sort anything out if he wants to.'

Lavender paused. Backhouse saw his throat quiver and realised he was close to tears.

'But not this time. This time, it seems, he doesn't want to. He's thrown me to the wolves. Staveley wrote to me and warned me, God bless him. Said the game was up for me and that I needed to get to Mexico as quickly as I could with anything I could salvage. Meanwhile all my assets on Jamaica have been impounded. There's a warrant out there for my arrest. And apparently the consul here is to request that I be arrested and handed over to the Jamaican authorities.

'So that's what your letter has achieved, George. You've condemned me to penury and exile, and you know what? Nothing's changed. The world is no cleaner or purer. When I'm gone Jerusalems will find someone else. He probably has someone in mind already. You want to make damned sure it isn't you.'

Later Backhouse was to regret two things: that he hadn't asked more questions, and that he had showed Lavender no flicker of compassion. But he didn't want to hear Lavender's story. He didn't want any part in it. Staveley, Crawford, Lavender, they could all go to hell. They might mock him if they wished, but he would not play their games.

So he let Lavender rage and said very little in reply. And when Lavender finally left the villa in El Cerro for the last time,

Backhouse sank back in his chair and called for the brandy to be brought back to the table.

Yet Lavender's was not his final interruption that evening. A minute or two after he had joined Grace in their high-ceilinged drawing room, a message arrived for him addressed in a sloping hand.

> *Things move fast, Mr Backhouse. I'm sending this note ahead of me. By the time you read it I should be no more than a day or two from Havana. When I return, might I trouble you for five minutes of your time? Send me a line at the Conquistador tavern telling me when it would be convenient to call.*
>
> *Jepson*

The note was intriguing if melodramatic, but Backhouse did not reply as promptly as he intended. Before he could put pen to paper the following morning, news reached him of Lavender's arrest.

Only an hour after leaving Backhouse's villa, the Englishman had been seized in a male brothel near the waterfront. An hour after that, in the police station by the old city walls, before he could be transferred to the Tacón gaol, he was found hanging in his cell, strangled by a noose of his own devising.

LIV

The republic of Haiti is separated from the island of Cuba by a sliver of water so narrow that at night a watcher on Haiti's north-west shore can glimpse Cuba's lights across the water. The tiny village of St Pierre, however, lies back from the coast, cut off from the sea by folds of rock and shrouded in jungle. It is a village that looks only at itself.

And a village accustomed to bloodshed. Since the expulsion of the French many years before, civil war had swept across the island with the regularity of tropical storms, brutal and furious and without apparent meaning. After each outbreak, the villagers would emerge from the forest and attempt to rebuild what was left to them.

The armed men who patrolled their streets in the year the American came were not soldiers of the government, the villagers knew, but they were the government of St Pierre, which was all that mattered. And when that year three Spaniards were executed in the square – shipwrecked sailors, it was said – the villagers were neither shocked nor surprised.

The remaining Spaniard knew that he too was certain to die. He had broken his ankle when his boat hit the rocks, and had therefore been unable to join his comrades in their attempted escape. So when he was made to watch while his friends were put against a wall and bayoneted, he knew that one way or another he must share their fate. If the pain did not kill him, his captors would, and if they did not, then the infection would soon finish him. Already his leg was turning green.

So when the large American was brought before him, he felt no surge of hope, not even any great curiosity about the presence of a white man in such a remote and barbarous spot. He simply wanted to die. The pain in his leg was too great, too constant. Besides, Americans were the enemy. If this one had come for revenge, all the better. A swift execution would be a mercy.

But he answered the man's questions nevertheless, and answered them with pride. He was lying on the floor, his hands bound and his wound stinking, but he was not ashamed. He might die like a dog, but he had struck a blow for his country. At home, in León, he would be remembered as a hero.

'At first we thought it was madness,' he told the stranger, his words grunted between knotted jaws. 'To sink an enemy ship? Surely it could not be done. But in the end it was easy. You want to know how we did it?'

Jepson let him talk. It had taken him a long time to find his way to St Pierre – time he didn't have and he knew it was only by chance that this one conspirator remained alive. Judging by the state of him, it would not be for long. Even with a surgeon and proper treatment, there was little now that could be done.

'We did it in fishing boats, my friend. Imagine that! Two fishing smacks sinking an American battleship!'

He managed to laugh despite his pain.

'The *Albany*. That's what she was called. The plan was to intercept her as she passed through the straits. The Englishman told us exactly where she'd be. Both boats were packed with explosives, you see, but only one was to be blown up – the first one to see the *Albany*. The crew of that one was to feign distress by dismasting and signalling, begging to be taken alongside. As soon as she was made fast, they were to light the fuse, abandon ship and blow a hole in the *Albany* right on the water line.'

He grimaced as he spoke, and Jepson was impressed. The man's lucidity, given his condition, was remarkable. But he felt no sympathy for him. He had met such men before. Zealots, radicals, fire-eaters. People who thought their own martyrdom more important, more significant, than the innocent lives of others.

'The other boat – my boat as it turned out – was to ignore the *Albany* and sail straight to Haiti. There we'd announce the success of our attack to the European representatives in Port au Prince and watch as news of our achievement spread like fire around the globe. Spain would at last have something of which it could be proud.'

'But something went wrong?' Time was short and Jepson was not there to argue.

The Spaniard nodded, his face ashen.

'We are not sailors. We misjudged the tides or the currents or some such thing, and hit the rocks here, in this little corner of hell. The barbarians arrested us and bound us. I don't know why. Because they are savages, I suppose, and because we are white.'

'The people here are not savages,' Jepson corrected him. 'But they are coarsened by war. And if you tell them you have important information for the government in Port au Prince . . . Well, it was an unfortunate introduction.'

The Spaniard shrugged. 'It is no matter. Our fate is unimportant. News of what we've done will shake the world. It will reawaken the fighting blood of Spain. My comrades on the other boat will see to that.'

'Your comrades on the other boat are dead, my friend.' Jepson was in no mood to spare him. 'And so is every American sailor on the *Albany*.' His voice was hard, without mercy. 'I'm guessing that the first explosion set off the *Albany*'s magazine store. She must have gone up with an enormous bang. Which wasn't quite what your friends expected, was it? No survivors. No witnesses. No one to tell the world how clever you'd been.'

The Spaniard shrugged again, a curious writhing motion given the awkward position in which he lay.

'The Englishman who helped us. He knows. He will speak of it.'

Jepson's voice remained cold. 'I'm afraid, my friend, he is the very last person who will ever admit to knowing you. From the moment you set sail out of Guantanamo in those little boats of yours, you were on your own.'

'It is no matter,' the Spaniard said again. 'We die proud of what we have achieved.'

Jepson considered him thoughtfully, then reached inside his jacket and produced a slim, silver hipflask.

'Brandy,' he said. 'I think it will help a great deal with the pain. But first . . .' He placed the flask on the mud floor, beyond the reach of the injured man's bound hands. 'But first, this Englishman you speak of. I'd like to hear more . . .'

Years later, when Dale found himself moved to revisit the official records, he was still amazed that Jepson had pulled it off. It was as if by sheer force of personality he had managed to shape the writing of history.

The USS *Albany* left the port of Aspinwall on the Panama isthmus with a full crew. She was bound for New York but never reached her destination. After Aspinwall, no further sighting was ever reported. Searches were made but proved fruitless: between Panama and the Greater Antilles there is a broad expanse of open water, and it was recognised by some that the *Albany* was not perhaps the most seaworthy vessel in the US navy. The ship is simply recorded as lost at sea.

A quick glance at a map showed Dale that one route open to the *Albany* would have passed through the narrow strait between Cuba and the republic of Haiti. That this fact was never deemed significant always astonished Dale. But then again, why should it have been? No sightings of the *Albany* were ever reported from those waters.

Of course Dale knew that the absence of reports was entirely down to Jepson. It must have been a superhuman effort. A battleship does not sink quietly.

Some years later a story circulated around New York that a group of Spanish patriots had claimed the sinking of the *Albany* was their work, retaliation for the various American invasion attempts on Cuba. But there was nothing to substantiate such a story, and by then the Civil War was raging across the southern states. The people of America had more pressing things to worry about. When Dale heard the rumours he simply smiled.

There was more than a month between Jepson's dramatic departure and his return to Havana. To Dale that period seemed like an age, but in retrospect, considering what his compatriot achieved, he realised it was a very short time indeed.

To his surprise, Jepson came to him directly upon his return, finding his way from the docks straight to the small villa Dale kept on the outer edge of the Havana suburbs, a place with a view of the sea in one direction and a faint blue smudge of hills in the other. On weekdays, Dale mostly remained in the centre of Havana, in his city apartments, but at weekends he liked to put the dust and the dirt behind him. With no wife to supervise arrangements, his household was run for him by a housekeeper, a rather younger woman than was usual for such a post. He rarely entertained.

It was into this suburban idyll that Jepson was dropped late one afternoon, deposited by a hired carriage. He was very visibly dirty, his hair was unkempt, and he appeared to have no belongings with him but the clothes he stood up in. Yet his manner, although subdued, did convey an element of quiet satisfaction.

'No war,' he declared when Dale greeted him on the front veranda. 'At least, not yet. Not until I've had a bath and a drink at any rate.'

And he refused to say very much more until he was seated in Dale's drawing room, looking out at the mountains, with a large drink cradled in his hand. His clothes had been sent for laundering, so he was wrapped in one of Dale's dressing gowns, apparently completely at ease, although the garment was stretched almost to bursting across his shoulders and the sleeves were four or five inches too short. He was tired certainly, and melancholy too, but nevertheless in the mood to let the tensions of the previous month ebb gradually from him.

Dale waited while the big man admired the view, praised his brandy and complimented him on his housekeeper. Even when a silence fell, Dale did not interrupt it.

'It was mostly luck,' Jepson began at last, shaking his head. 'More luck than you'd believe. If the cards had fallen any differently, news of the sinking of the *Albany* would be racing around the world by now. The Spanish government would be denying any involvement, of course, but the bunch of idiots responsible had managed to persuade a minor regional governor from some godforsaken corner of Spain to write them a letter urging them to act for the glory of their mother country. They were going to use it to implicate Madrid in their plan. Though that probably wouldn't have been necessary. I think war would have been inevitable regardless.'

He shook his head again, as if weary of the human predilection for conflict.

'The plot was ambitious, Mr Dale – remarkably ambitious – but it was not particularly complicated. It was the work of former army officers – no more than a dozen of them – who called themselves a secret society and honestly believed it was Spain's destiny to reclaim its New World empire. Such imbeciles can be found in every corner of the earth if you look hard enough. Stupid men with stupid causes. It's the easiest thing in the world to encourage them, then to disown them should anything go wrong.'

Dale nodded. Some would have argued that the recent attempts to invade Cuba from America were a similar case.

Once he'd begun, Jepson seemed keen to tell his tale. As he spoke, the dusk began to hurry the day to its close. Below them, between the villa and the sea, the lights of Havana were appearing, slowly at first, as individual specks; then with a rush, smearing into little knots of lamplight, then threads, then ropes, until a tangled net of light and darkness lay over the landscape. It was the time of day that Dale loved the most.

'And so, you see, simple enough. Our navy has something of a reputation for gallantry in these waters. Persuading the *Albany* to come to their rescue was not as unlikely as it sounds.'

Dale nodded, but he was thinking just how ambitious the plot had been. It isn't easy to stop a battleship, especially with only two small boats at your disposal. The chance of intercepting the *Albany* at all wasn't that high. When he said as much, Jepson smiled.

'I know. Impressive, isn't it? They had to be in exactly the right place at the right time, bang on the *Albany*'s course. If they'd been working alone, there was no chance of that bunch of blunderers pulling it off. But with British help . . . The British knew just where those boats needed to be. And of course there's a lot of small shipping in that strait, so the *Albany* would have been taking it steady and would have been keeping a particularly careful watch.'

'So what went wrong?'

'She just sank far too quickly.' Jepson spoke lightly, but Dale could tell he was feeling the loss of all those lives. 'I've spoken to some of the fishermen at sea that day. A lot of them headed straight towards the plume of smoke to look for survivors. But nothing. Not even very much wreckage, apparently.'

'So there *were* witnesses then? Those fishermen?'

Jepson nodded. 'Decent men. Honest too. I told them frankly that if the American public knew their ship had exploded in Cuban waters there would be a war. They could work out for themselves what that would mean for their livelihoods. And I promised them very large sums of money if the news did not come out. Luck was with me all the way: surprisingly few boats in the immediate vicinity, and a captain of police in Guantanamo who had been a friend of Alvarez. He was the one who alerted me to the whole thing, and he made sure he submitted no report on the subject before I got there. So as far as the administration in Havana is concerned, the *Albany* never reached Cuban waters.'

'And the Englishman who helped them plan all this? Did you get his name?'

'Not his real one. He called himself John Bull. I think they thought that really *was* his name. They met him in Havana. He told them he supported their cause and that many of his country-men wanted to see imperial Spain restored to its former glory. At first, he only gave them money and encouragement, then he came up with the idea of attacking the *Albany*. So no name ...' He paused teasingly. 'But the description of him was excellent.'

'You recognised it?'

Jepson pursed his lips as if with distaste.

'It pains me to say this, but the person they described was undoubtedly our friend Lavender. And they weren't aware of anyone else involved.'

Dale chuckled. 'So you think your rat might be Lavender after all?'

'In my heart of hearts, no. I want someone better than Lavender for my rat. But my head is beginning to accept that a lot of fingers are pointing at him.'

There was an awkward pause. Dale thought he already knew the answer to the next question and wasn't sure he wanted to ask it.

'And the Spaniard you spoke to in Haiti ...?'

Jepson shrugged wearily.

'Haiti's a dangerous place, Mr Dale. If you fall into the wrong hands, unpleasant things happen. Let's just say that our patri-otic friend won't live to see the rebirth of the Spanish empire. And he won't be saying very much about the fate of the *Albany* either.' He shrugged a second time. 'To be honest, I'm not weep-ing for him. Because of him, a lot of innocent young men are dead. No, Mr Dale, I don't think I shall have any problem sleep-ing tonight.'

And he was as good as his word. Jepson accepted the offer of a bed for the night and retired early, then slept for fourteen hours. When he finally woke, he ate the largest breakfast Dale had ever seen. Then he smiled the sort of energetic, irrepressible smile Dale remembered from before.

'Well, Mr Dale, I think it's time to put a bit of pressure on our friend Lavender. I need to know for certain whether or not he's my rat. So the next step is to track him down and make him very uncomfortable indeed.' He checked his pocket watch. 'At this time of day, I should find him in his office. You know, Mr Dale, this might be one of my last breakfasts in Havana. It's hard to see what can go wrong.'

LV

At Backhouse's suggestion, they met at a café by the water, a quiet spot in early evening when the dusk had brought the boats to anchor and had driven the crowds to brighter, noisier places. At first Jepson thought it a surprising choice. He'd been expecting to make the journey out to El Cerro to see the Englishman. But of course a café had its advantages. Jepson was not altogether surprised to find Backhouse already seated, with a glass of American whiskey placed close to his right hand.

The American took a seat beside him and laid a hand on the Englishman's shoulder.

'Suicide, eh? The news was a shock to me, too, Mr Backhouse. But not your fault, if that's what you're thinking.'

Instinctively Backhouse moved away from Jepson's hand.

'I don't know what I'm thinking, to be honest. I just wish I'd had nothing to do with it, nothing to do with the whole squalid business.'

Jepson nodded and was silent for a few seconds.

'You need to remember that Lavender was involved in some very dirty work, Mr Backhouse.' He didn't feel able to tell the Englishman about the *Albany*, but he wanted to make the point anyway.

'I know it. And I'm not trying to forgive him for any of it. But I find a little part of me also feels sorry for him, now that it's too late.'

'Pah! Save your sympathy, Mr Backhouse. Lavender was playing a brutal game. He knew it, yet he persisted. He decided the rewards outweighed the risks. I suppose the same was true of his private pleasures.'

Backhouse looked across at him. There was a lot to like about Jepson, but a lot to dislike too.

'A game. That's how you always refer to your occupation, Mr Jepson. And now a man is dead.'

The American waved his hand dismissively. 'Many people are dead. The truth is that people die all the time, whether I like it or not. It's the business of being human. I couldn't help but wonder . . .' He hesitated, not sure how to bring up the subject. 'Did Lavender say anything about his involvement in all those incidents over in America? Anything that would interest me?'

Backhouse smiled drily. 'He told me he took his orders from London. He swore it was someone in London who organised everything.'

Jepson said nothing but looked out across the water.

'Was this someone called Jerusalems by any chance?'

The Englishman turned to him sharply. 'You know him?'

'Oh, barely. But I know he's a clever man. You would probably consider him a scoundrel; he would call himself a patriot. And he'd claim that he works for his country, not for any particular government.'

Backhouse tried to remember London as it had been when he left it. Respectable, civilised, straightforward. Sometimes even slightly dreary. Already it seemed impossibly far away.

While Lavender was the subject of their conversation Jepson had ignored the many waiters who fluttered up to him, as if out of respect for the dead. Now he raised his arm and called for service. His order placed, he settled more comfortably into his chair and turned to Backhouse.

'On a different subject, Mr Backhouse, do you remember telling me about that break-in at the British consulate? Well, I've learned a little more since then.'

As succinctly as he could he summarised Crawford's explanation of the missing jewels and a little of what he had learned on his trip to Santa Maria. Backhouse toyed with his drink while he listened, but he didn't really want to know. He'd vowed to be a braver man, and in Havana a truly brave man rose above all the plotting and the scheming and the corruption. He had made a promise to his son, and he would keep it. The truth was that he longed to be back in London, back in Hans Square, where there was no scandal and nothing sordid, and no one played games with other people's lives. Havana, with its secrets and its dirt, its long nights and its dark-skinned sirens, was a dangerous city. If he had his chance in London again, he would make a good deal more of it. He was a different person now. A wiser one. And a good deal more resolute.

However when Jepson finished speaking he felt obliged to respond.

'So you think the night-watchman who died that night was in the pay of that man O'Driscoll?'

'That's right. He was the fellow who took in those incriminating papers.' Jepson chuckled. 'For what it's worth, O'Driscoll also believes Lavender was working alone. Says he was taking direction only from London.' He sighed. 'It pains me to think the man I came here to catch was Lavender. I suppose I'd hoped for a more substantial adversary. I don't think I'll really believe it until I've seen something that links him for certain to all those incidents back home.'

'I suppose it must be possible to take a look around his office,' Backhouse speculated. 'His landlord would have the key.'

'Oh, I've been to his offices already, my friend. That was the first thing I did today. But there's nothing. Nothing of any interest to me, at any rate. Any idea where else I might look?'

But Backhouse was shaking his head.

'I'm taking your advice, Mr Jepson,' he explained, 'and trying not to interest myself in anything but the work of the Mixed Commission.'

The American laughed, but Backhouse was deadly serious.

'You said something to me once about the dangers of being an impoverished official in Havana. At the time I thought it was an insult. I thought you meant that I'd be tempted to take bribes. But there was something Lavender said too. He said he always felt he was working for his country, so taking the money never felt wrong.'

'And who's to say it was?' There was a kind of sadness in Jepson's smile. 'I've known lots of people like that. Not bad people at heart, but not heroes either. Just people making their way, taking decisions they don't fully understand, until one day they find they have blood on their hands. Are you in debt, Mr Backhouse?'

The question was outrageous. No Englishman would have asked it. No self-respecting Englishman would dream of answering it.

'Yes,' he replied quietly. 'Yes, I am.'

'Badly?'

Backhouse wasn't even sure. Badly enough. Worse than he had told Grace, probably worse than he had admitted to himself.

'If we economise a little . . .' he began, then shook his head. 'It's the living expenses here. For a family, they're ruinous. Grace and I have even spoken about her going home with the children for a year or two. I could live much more cheaply here that way. And I think Grace would be happier at home. She never complains, but I know life here is difficult for her in a way it never was at home. She has her mother there, and she wouldn't have to worry about the perpetual threat of fever.'

Jepson considered this, nodding slowly.

'And if your friend in London . . . What's he called? Staveley? If he were to write to you thanking you for your help in uncovering Lavender's unpleasant activities, and telling you that a grateful government has granted you an extra payment as a token of its thanks, you would accept it with gratitude?'

Backhouse shook his head. 'I suppose I would have done, once. Now . . .' He shrugged. 'But Thomas Staveley, whatever his faults, is not trying to lure me into any traps. I've known him for years. I count him as a friend.'

The American frowned and put down his brandy.

'If you take my advice, Mr Backhouse, you'll talk to your wife tonight and get her on the earliest boat back to England. When she's gone you'll work every hour of the day until your debts are paid off. If there isn't enough work to keep you out of trouble for sixteen hours a day, invent some. Write a book. Think up some poems. Learn Greek. Keep busy, and find an excuse to follow her home as quickly as you can.'

'Run away, you mean?' Backhouse grimaced. 'I'm not sure I can do that.'

Jepson shrugged. 'Your choice, Mr Backhouse. Your choice. But if you've got any friends here, people you trust, stay close to them. You may need them.'

With that Jepson changed the subject and began to talk to Backhouse about England. They shared two further drinks in a companionable enough way, and when the American finally departed, Backhouse realised he felt better. It had been soothing to talk.

Even so, it was time to go home and discuss things with Grace. He had been too cowardly for too long. Living alone in Havana was not an appealing prospect, but if the debts were to be repaid it was one he must embrace. After that, another posting, closer to home, might perhaps be found for him. Staveley would surely speak up on his behalf.

At that hour of the evening, although still early by Havana's standards, the quickest way for him to return to the villa in El Cerro was to cross the old city to the place by the Puerta de Montserrate where there would be cabs waiting. That took him very close to his office, where there were certain papers relating to official expenses that hitherto he had chosen to ignore. But he would do so no longer. However petty it might appear to insist upon reimbursement of such small sums, he would claim them anyway, and damn the eyebrows raised back home. He would no longer borrow from his wife's relatives to subsidise the work of the Mixed Commission.

However, on approaching the building where his office was situated, he saw a light burning in the window and began to regret his decision to return. More than once he had come across

Dalrymple there late in the evening, though never, of course, engaged in any official duties. His clerk seemed to be in the habit of using the place as his own private retiring room in the old city, somewhere he could retreat to when a little the worse for wear. On at least three occasions Backhouse had found him drunk at his desk; once he had found him passed out and snoring, his head resting on an official ledger.

The porter at the front door told him the other gentleman had gone up only a few minutes before, and it occurred to Backhouse that he could simply withdraw and continue on his way. But he was no longer the man to tiptoe around Dalrymple. Dalrymple could go to the devil for all he cared, and he mounted the stairs two at a time to tell him so.

On reaching the room where the light was burning, his first thought was that his clerk had been seized by some sort of frenzy. Cupboards and drawers stood open, and piles of papers had been stacked – mostly in neat rows – all over the floor. His second thought, as he sensed a movement behind him, was to wonder why on earth Dalrymple had concealed himself behind the door.

He had already begun to turn when the blow fell, catching him with great force on the temple before he could raise a hand in his own defence.

When he came to, the lamp on his desk was still burning; so brightly, he found, that it caused him real pain to open his eyes. Oddly, his head didn't hurt him at all at first, not until he moved it and tried to stand up. Then a great shudder of nausea convulsed him, and to his horror and shame he vomited all over his own hand and down his shirt front.

Still only half upright, he reached for his handkerchief to dab at his mouth, and then felt hastily for his wallet. But it was still where it should have been. He had not, at any rate, been robbed.

It must have been a full minute before he next attempted to stand, this time much more cautiously and with more success. Looking around, still slightly dizzy, it occurred to him that the papers he'd seen on the floor had all now been put away, and the cupboards and drawers were shut. When he was able to reach out and open the nearest cupboard, its contents appeared as neat and organised as they had always been.

Downstairs, the porter had disappeared, although whether he had fled or was simply running some errand for another user of the building Backhouse had no way of knowing. He would have to raise the alarm himself. But he had a horror of appearing in the street in such a state: unsteady on his feet and covered in his own vomit. The road outside was not particularly busy but he couldn't hope to avoid the notice of the crowds for very long. And in his confusion, he was uncertain where he should go to report the assault. Was the nearest police post left or right? He wasn't even sure they would believe him. There was no evidence of any burglary, and he had been drinking that evening. Another Englishman unable to stomach his rum.

Still undecided, he saw a vacant cab rumbling in his direction. Without any plan at all, he hailed it.

LVI

Rosa was away, so Leonarda went to the door herself. She had been lying on her day-bed reading when she heard the knock. It was still only mid-evening so she had not yet begun to undress, but her feet were bare and her hair tumbled freely over her shoulders. She was not expecting callers and evidently the porter downstairs had been caught away from his post. As she stretched up to peer through the peephole she was not expecting to open the door.

At first she thought he was drunk. He was leaning, slightly stooped, with one arm against the door jamb, and everything about him that was usually so correct seemed crumpled or soiled or skewed. She could hear his breathing, loud and unsteady, as though ascending the stairs had been a very great effort.

She knew immediately that his coming was a mistake. Whatever his difficulties, the wisest solution did not lie in the Calle Chacón. She would be doing him a favour, she thought, were she to go back to her chair and leave him in the hallway until he decided to find his own way home.

Then he looked up, directly at the little shuttered viewing slot through which she was watching him, and what she saw in his eyes shocked her. There was confusion and pain, and a raw, naked helplessness. Of the well-starched Englishman who had snubbed her on their first meeting, there was nothing.

She wished he had not come. She wished he was less trusting, more like Crawford and all those other haughty English merchants. Havana was no place for the innocent or the honourable.

But she opened the door and helped him inside.

★   ★   ★

He let her remove his stained jacket without demur as he stood unsteadily in the hallway. And when she seated him on the stiff-backed chair next to her front door, she allowed her to kneel beside him and dab at his shirt front with a cloth until the worst of the crust that had formed there was gone and the wet fabric began to adhere to his chest.

'I'm so sorry,' he said, repeating the words over and over. 'I was going home,' he added once. 'Somebody hit me. I felt better before. Now I'm a little dizzy.'

'Where were you hit?' she asked, and not understanding he replied, 'In my own office.' But his hand had gone to the side of his head and when she investigated, her fingers found the place, under his hairline, a little above his ear. No blood, but the swelling was already evident.

She knew she needed to move him somewhere less precarious in case he should faint, but just as she was wondering if he was strong enough to stand, the remaining colour drained from his face. Still kneeling, she had to catch him as he slumped forward, one arm around his chest holding him to the chair, the other stroking his hair as he vomited again and again, over her arm and down his already soiled shirt.

She held him that way until he was finished, until she felt a little of his strength returning.

'I need to move you to the other room, to the armchair,' she told him. 'Can you help me?'

He nodded.

'But first this needs to come off.' She tugged at his soiled shirt. 'Can you sit up?'

He offered no resistance as she removed his tie and collar. He seemed barely aware of what she was doing.

'I'm sorry,' he said again. 'Someone hit me. Didn't want to go home like this. Grace would worry.'

Removing his shirt was not easy. She had to tug hard to free the shirt tails from beneath him and a sudden lurch of his weight as she grappled with one shirt stud was countered by a pull that tore the fabric. When finally she held the garment in her hands, she examined it for a maker's mark but found only the name and address of a London tailor.

'Where do you get your shirts made?' she asked gently, kneeling again so that she was close to him.

'Jermyn Street,' he replied faintly but decidedly, as though the answer was obvious.

'Here, in Havana?'

'Oh.' The question didn't seem to strike him as an odd one. 'That man with the funny moustache. Can't remember his name. By the Golden Cross.'

She nodded. 'I know him. Now, if I support you, can you stand?'

He made the journey to the armchair in her drawing room largely through his own efforts, using her only as a prop to help him balance. He seemed stronger after his fainting fit, but even so, when the chair was reached, he slumped down heavily. In that dark, exotic room, his thin white torso looked dangerously pale. She covered him quietly with a blanket.

'You need to rest,' she told him. 'There's no bleeding anywhere, but you've had a bad knock.'

He nodded, touched his temple, then leaned his head back and shut his eyes obediently.

'I'm sorry for coming here,' he told her. 'Wasn't thinking straight. Didn't want to be seen in such a state.'

'Of course not.' She waited for a few moments, and when he remained still, she stepped out into the hallway and pulled at the bell-rope that hung by her front door. A minute or two later, when her summons was answered by a small boy, she gave him detailed instructions and a silver coin, then returned to her patient. She found him sleeping.

She had already thought about calling for a doctor but felt certain Backhouse would not thank her for it. Doctors in Havana were not necessarily discreet, and to attend a half-naked English official at an apartment on the Calle Chacón would give any physician a tempting opportunity for gossip. Instead she returned to the jacket lying in her hallway. It was not as filthy as she had feared. After a few minutes scrubbing with soap and a stiff brush she felt confident it would pass muster.

When he opened his eyes, he was for a few moments utterly confused. His head ached with a blunt, persistent pain, and he could recall clearly enough the moment of entering his office and knowing that a blow was about to fall. But after that . . . He could remember clambering into a cab. He hadn't wanted to go home, hadn't wanted to make a scene . . .

Suddenly the dark, unfamiliar surroundings made sense to him, and filled him with a sort of horror. Had he really chosen, of all places in Havana, the boudoir of Leonarda Leigh? Yet perhaps it was not so surprising. It had not been so very far away, after all. And in Havana his choices were few.

He shut his eyes again, in shame this time. She had helped him out of his jacket, he remembered it now. She had rubbed at his clothes. And at one point he'd swooned and she had held him. And after that . . . Was it possible? He was certain he could recall her fingers opening his shirt. No, he hadn't imagined it. Beneath the blanket that covered him, he was naked from the waist upwards.

Opening his eyes for a second time, he realised he was not alone. Curled on the day-bed, her feet tucked up beneath her, Leonarda was reading. The room, with its tiny candles and low lamps, was mostly lost in darkness, but she had pulled a lamp close to where she was sitting. It touched her face with soft light, and he was aware of the smoothness of her skin, the line of her jaw, those brown eyes looking down. Her lips were pursed slightly in concentration. Her hair was loose and shocking in its freedom; an errant strand lay across her cheek as she read.

Backhouse had grown into adulthood knowing that the fairness of one's skin was a token of God's favour; that his dark-skinned brethren were less fortunate than he, less generously favoured by divine grace. Yet her face made a mockery of all that. It shone with intelligence and with compassion. And in it there was a serenity and a composure and, yes, a perfection of form, that might have inspired the painters of angels.

Unaware he was watching her, she continued to read.

What to do now? He could not deny that it was good to sit there in that calm twilight, letting the pain come and go. It felt safe. Secret and hidden, a sort of refuge. But he knew he must leave at once, for the sake of her reputation as well as for his own. When he sat forward in the chair, he groaned despite himself.

She looked up then and stirred herself, swinging her bare feet to the floor.

'Don't get up,' she told him firmly. 'You're probably still a little weak.'

And it was true. The sudden movement had made him dizzy. Yet as soon as he could stand he must leave. For Grace's sake, he must get home, must try to avoid a scandal. Or was it too late?

'What time is it?' he asked abruptly and rather ungraciously.

'It has not yet struck ten.' She placed her book beside the lamp, carefully marking her page before she put it down. 'You haven't slept for long. What time are you expected home?'

He searched his memory.

'I was meeting a man down by the harbour and I warned my wife not to sit up. But she never sleeps until I'm home.'

'So if you return by midnight, that will not occasion any remark?'

'I should return a good deal sooner.' He made to rise, but with only a blanket covering his chest did not know how to do so with any dignity. 'Señora, I'm so sorry to have intruded . . .'

'Oh, please!' She was shaking her head. 'Not that word again. Even when barely conscious you were always apologising. Enough of it.'

The rebuke surprised him and foolishly his instinct was to apologise again. Biting the words back, he found he had none to take their place.

'Señor, forgive me.' She was laughing now. 'But you are very ridiculous. You have no shirt. I have undressed you in my hallway.

I have wiped your chest clean. There is no one here but the two of us. Yet still you are so formal.'

Backhouse blushed, the first colour she had seen in his cheeks since his arrival. Formality, he felt sure, was more important than ever in such circumstances, but to pursue the argument just then was beyond him. Another wave of pain was pressing at his skull.

'Perhaps you are right. But I know I shouldn't have come here. I was confused and not sure what I was doing.'

She clicked her tongue.

'I cannot think, señor, that any situation is ever made better by constantly rehearsing one's regrets.'

There was enough brisk truth in that to stop him short, and again he was lost for a reply.

'Besides, you have nothing to apologise for. You were assaulted and left dazed in a dangerous city. Your instinct was to find help. You worried for your wife's peace of mind if you returned injured. In your befuddled state, this was the address you thought of. None of that is surprising. And if I thought it wrong, I should not have admitted you. Besides . . .' Here she laughed again. 'You cannot leave now even if you wish to as you have no shirt to wear. Your own is ruined, and its replacement will not be here for another hour or more.'

'Its replacement, señora?'

'Your tailor will furnish you with another. It will cost you five times the usual amount, but it will be here before midnight. If you return home in a shirt made by your customary Havana tailor, your servants will surely not notice the substitution. Not unless they are more attentive than I suppose.'

He shut his eyes and leaned back in his chair.

'I see there is no end to the gratitude I owe you.' He paused. 'But I shall not attempt to express it for fear of being laughed at.'

Leonarda smiled. 'That's right. Besides, gratitude is not the intolerable burden you imagine. Accepting help is not a sin.'

'Yet coming here, allowing you to help me . . .'

His eyes remained shut. Talking felt easier that way.

'I have a wife. These things feel like a betrayal. Coming here was wrong. But I was brought up to believe it a gentleman's duty to shield his wife from unpleasantness, so going home tonight, in the state I was in, seemed out of the question.' He paused for a moment. 'Yet I suspect Grace would prefer me to return home bleeding than to turn for help to a stranger.'

'And that stranger a woman? The sort who keeps rooms on the Calle Chacón?'

He opened his eyes then and met her gaze evenly and frankly.

'I know nothing about you, señora, only that you have been generous with your kindness in a city that is not a kind one. I judge you only by that.'

'But your wife may judge differently.' It was not a question, simply a quiet statement of fact.

He lowered his head. 'Yes, that's true. But perhaps what shames me most is that I have absolutely no right to ask for your help. I have imposed myself upon you, and more than once.'

She made no reply but rose and retrieved his jacket from the foot of her day-bed.

'I understand your need to be gone. It will not be too long now.' Holding the garment to the light, she checked the lapels once more. 'I didn't want to send this out for cleaning. I thought that might be indiscreet. So I did it myself. I think it will pass.'

She said it quietly, almost to herself, but the words moved him. In all his previous dealings with her, he had thought only of himself, of his own difficulties and anxieties. Very little of her.

'But *why*?' He asked the question almost with wonder. 'Your kindness humbles me, but I don't understand it. You have no reason to help me as you have done.'

She looked down then. He was, ostensibly, a slightly ridiculous figure, with his English whiskers and his very pale shoulders peeping above the blanket. But there was nothing funny or ridiculous in the way he spoke. The pain she had sensed in him sounded in every word.

She crossed the room then and sat close to him, curling herself on to a cushion near his feet the better to see his face. Such an action would once have embarrassed him acutely, but he did not pull away.

'I was alone in this city once,' she told him. 'Someone helped me, gave me a home. Not for any reason at all, just out of kindness. Because he saw a child who needed help, that's all.'

She had not intended to tell him the story. She hadn't told it to her first lover, nor to the dying Englishman she'd married. Even Rosa, who had been at her side for so long, knew only parts of it. She had kept her history hidden so she could be free to invent her own. But this bare Englishman was, in his own, brittle way, as lonely and helpless as she had been.

So she told him how she had been rescued by Hector from an angry crowd, how he had nurtured her and taught her to read. How she had fought him for so long, and made his life so difficult, defying him almost for the sake of defiance, running free at night, begging, stealing. Then leaving him without a word, taking up with a Spaniard whose soft fingertips had turned her head. And most of all, worst of all, never once giving him a word of thanks.

'I thought he would always be there,' she said quietly. 'He always had been, all my life. A few years ago I left the island. I went with the man whose name I bear. I hardly knew him really, and I never told Hector I was going. There would be time enough for that when I returned. I wrote to him once or twice from Jamaica but had no reply. Post does not always reach St Simeon. And then, when I returned . . .'

She tailed off, swallowing her grief as she had always done.

Whether it was the heat or the half-light or the blow to the head, Backhouse could not have said, but he listened to the story almost as a child listens, lost in the tale, forgetting his own discomfort and his own anxieties, his shirtlessness, even the ache in his head.

She was no longer looking at him but staring at the window, her eyes lost somewhere in the candlelight.

'I never even told him . . .' She paused. She hadn't said the words aloud before. 'Never told him that I loved him. That even when I was away, running free, I always loved him. If I had just once said those words . . .'

She shook her head.

'Perhaps if I had, I could find a better sort of peace. But it's too late now.'

'He died?'

She turned then, and looked up at him so that their eyes met.

'He was the night-watchman at the English consul's office. The one who was murdered.'

'I'm so sorry.' He said it softly, almost tenderly, but something uncomfortable was stirring in his memory.

'I'd been away more than three years, much longer than I expected. When I came back I was told there'd been a burglary. Just another ordinary crime, it seemed. So I went to see the place he died. I thought that would help me to say goodbye. But it didn't.'

Her gaze had slipped away again but she had rested one of her hands on the edge of the armchair, so close to his that their fingers almost touched.

'When I saw the place, none of it made sense. And the more questions I asked, the less simple it all seemed. I don't want to be always asking questions. I'm not interested in mysteries. But I have to know why he died. To know that someone struck him down so deliberately, and not to ask any questions . . . It would feel like a betrayal, as though I were walking away from him all over again.'

She was thoughtful for a moment, looking down.

'But all I really want to do is say goodbye. Just a quiet goodbye, without all those other, horrible things in the way.'

Backhouse watched her, unsure of himself.

'I was talking to an American tonight, a man called Jepson. He confirmed that the jewels were fakes. He says the consul carried them off himself, when he discovered the burglary. To protect a lady's honour, apparently.'

Leonarda nodded as though the idea were not new to her. Backhouse went on.

'Jepson also mentioned some papers delivered to the night-watchman there. Jepson thought the night-watchman was in someone else's pay.'

She looked up sharply then.

'What do you mean?'

'He thinks someone was paying him to spy.'

'No.' She said it very firmly, her body suddenly tense. 'He must have made a mistake.'

'Those papers contained someone's name. Men had already died for them. They . . .'

Backhouse tailed off, thinking it better to leave the subject there; but clearly his words had wounded. Leonarda lingered over them.

'Hector would have been the very last man to take bribes. It was something he took pride in. Your friend is mistaken. Will you tell him so?'

'Of course. Yes, I will.' Backhouse wished he had remained silent.

'It's horrible that anyone should think such a thing. His honesty was all he had.'

Prompted by the pain in her voice, Backhouse leaned forward and placed his hand upon her shoulder. It was an unthinking, instinctive movement, done without awkwardness.

'Please . . . Don't trouble yourself. I will tell him. I'll make sure he understands.'

He felt her hand move over his and rest upon it, but she did not speak. Outside he could hear the street, still busy, the crowds hurrying by, but in Leonarda's dark room neither of them moved. Then, abruptly, a footstep creaked on the stairs near her front door. He straightened quickly and removed his hand.

'Your shirt,' she said, and rose to her feet, but no knock followed. She listened for a moment and then relaxed. 'No. Only a visitor to the floor below. How does your head feel?'

'Horrible,' he replied, 'but I'm sure it will survive.'

'I would offer you brandy to revive you,' she said lightly, 'but I think you'd be better off without.'

Backhouse was grateful. The thought of it made him feel sick again.

'So all your kindness to me . . . It is because you think me alone, as you were, and in need of help?'

There was no outrage in the question, though once he would have found such condescension unbearable.

She looked at him.

'Is that not the case?'

To his surprise, she was settling herself back on to the cushion by his chair. It was done quite naturally, as though the idea of sitting anywhere else had not occurred to her.

'Yes, I suppose it is.' As soon as he had said it, he felt relieved. *Alone and in need of help.* Why not admit it? The way she looked at him, it did not seem such a terrible thing, not a moral failing, not a personal humiliation, just a regrettable truth. 'It's funny,' he told her, 'those are two things I was brought up never to admit. Perhaps, when I was very young, I thought a husband and his wife might share such things, but with Grace . . .'

He searched for words to explain what all his life he had taken for granted.

'In our circles, a man shields his wife from life's hardships. Only a weakling or a blackguard would burden her with problems he was unable to sort out for himself.' He laughed, a dry, slightly scornful sound. 'The irony is, I don't think she'd mind very much. She's very brave and capable. But *I* would feel wretched and worthless.'

He paused again, considering his words.

'Does that sound very selfish?'

'Yes. And very sad.'

'It's only since I came here. I think in London I told her everything. But Havana seems to breed subterfuge and secrets. Those letters I showed you . . . The man who wrote them has killed himself. I denounced him. I cannot, I simply *cannot*, tell Grace that. I am too ashamed of it.'

She could hear the disgust in his voice and it puzzled her.

332

'But if he had done all those things he wrote of . . . None of that is your fault. And surely his was the English way, to take his own life rather than face the consequences?'

He looked at her then, and she could see genuine anguish in his eyes.

'Don't you see? It's as you said. Those letters didn't come to me by chance. Someone sent them to me very deliberately. They knew I'd work out who had sent them. They *wanted* me to denounce him. I wasn't doing anything brave or honourable. I was simply being used to do someone else's bidding. And I hate that. I can't bear that I've been manipulated into doing things I don't understand, and which have such terrible consequences.'

Leonarda's hand moved closer to his.

'And you have no idea who sent those letters to you?'

Backhouse shook his head. 'None. Someone with a grudge against Lavender, perhaps. I don't know who. Lavender would have had me believe that everything here is part of some enormous conspiracy.'

'And you really have no one in Havana to advise you?' It was still hard for her to grasp.

'No.' This time he said it without embarrassment. 'I suppose that's why I'm here.'

Again a moment of silence, this time their eyes meeting. Three seconds, no more, but more intimate than anything that had gone before. And then another smile and she was getting to her feet.

'This time it *is* your shirt.' He'd heard nothing, but the bell rang before she'd reached the door. 'I'll leave you here to dress, shall I?'

He wanted to thank her again but understood it was unnecessary. The shirt, made to his measurements, fitted perfectly. It was accompanied by a clean collar and necktie, and when he looked in the mirror his jacket appeared no better or worse than after any other dusty day in Havana. The clocks had not yet struck eleven.

It was not until much later in the evening that Leonarda allowed herself to cry. However determinedly she refused to believe it, the

thought that Hector – her honest, honourable Hector – had somehow become entangled in something so tawdry was more than she
could bear. She should have done nothing, asked no questions, and
allowed him to lie with honour in his grave.

But now she had no choice. If someone had trapped him,
ensnared him in something he didn't understand, she would find
out who. She would find out why. Or she would never rest again.

And she would start with Moses, Moses Le Castre, who knew
more about Hector's work than anyone. Moses who was so reluctant to meet her. It was time for Moses to sit down and talk.

But the next day, when Leonarda tried to find him, Moses had
gone to ground. No one at Mother Alençon's had seen him for
some days, nor had he been seen at any of his other drinking
places. It took her two days to follow his trail as far as his lodgings,
and there she discovered he'd left earlier that same week, in haste,
grabbing only a few of his things and leaving his bills unpaid. His
disappearance, it seemed, was deliberate. He did not want to be
found. But if he was still in Havana, she would find him. She knew
the city as well as he did. And she was a great deal more
determined.

LVII

From the moment his hansom pulled up outside the house in Lowther Street, Thomas Staveley knew something was different. It was past four o'clock on a February afternoon but the shutters at the front of the house stood open, the rooms behind them dark. At first he hesitated on the steps, unsure whether to knock. But when he did, a familiar footman showed him into the library as though nothing was untoward, then very shortly afterwards returned and ushered him into John Jerusalems' chaotic drawing room.

The contrast with his previous visits could not have been more marked. The lamps were not yet lit and the fire had burned very low, to little more than glowing embers. Through the tall windows, the tired grey light was enough to show him the piles of books and the clutter on the tables, but at first he thought he was alone in the room. Only on a second glance did he make out the form of his host, reclining motionless in an armchair pulled close to one of the windows. His face was turned to the darkening sky.

'John?' Staveley asked quietly.

'Come in, Thomas.' Jerusalems did not stir. 'Pull up a seat.'

It was with some difficulty that Staveley complied, eventually manoeuvring a straight-backed chair past the piles and clearing a space for it opposite his host. As he seated himself, he saw that his host was cradling a tiny liqueur glass in his hands.

'Benedictine?' Jerusalems asked, as though sensing the object of Staveley's gaze. 'There's a bottle around somewhere. I seldom indulge, but, as you can see, you catch me at a low moment.'

Unsure where he would find a glass to drink from, Staveley declined the offer with a shake of his head.

'I came as soon as I heard about Lavender. A grim business.'

Jerusalems nodded, still studying the sky, then turned to face his guest.

'Yes. Yes, indeed.' He straightened himself a little in his chair. 'A very sorry outcome. But I comfort myself that ultimately Lavender was the architect of his own downfall. We tried to move him on, you and I, did we not? Sadly the less salubrious side of Havana life had him in thrall. Once he'd told me the Spanish were trying to blackmail him, I knew his time there was up.'

'Blackmail?' Staveley was surprised. 'Oh, I see. Those letters to Colonel Aguero. They weren't for personal gain then? I wondered what he was up to.'

Jerusalems didn't reply, but turned to face the window again. When he spoke, he seemed to be changing the subject.

'There is an American in Cuba at the moment, Thomas, a man called Jepson. A surprisingly resourceful individual. He doesn't like the fact that someone in Havana has been sending us such excellent information. Nor the fact that someone has been arranging some very significant bits of business on our behalf, business that has not been to America's advantage. But when I heard that he was heading for Cuba, I didn't think we had too much to worry about.' Jerusalems passed a hand over his eyes, as if extremely weary. 'But I was wrong, Thomas. I hate to be bested, but on this occasion I have to accept Jepson has got the better of me.'

'Over Lavender?' Staveley was struggling to understand the connection.

'Over various things.' Jerusalems turned to look at his guest, his eyes suddenly amused. 'So talk to me about ships, Thomas. You said you would come and see me if you heard any rumours of attacks on an American vessel. Have you really heard nothing?'

'No, not at all, John, or I would have let you know. I've been keeping an eye on all the shipping news for you, but there's nothing to report. An American pilot managed to ram a small rock off Newfoundland a couple of months ago, and an American battleship was lost at sea in bad weather off the coast of Panama. But no dastardly Spanish attacks or acts of sabotage.'

To Staveley's surprise, Jerusalems chuckled.

'Jepson, you see! I told you he was resourceful. My word, though, Thomas, I've no idea how he did it.'

'I'm sorry?' Staveley was finding his host, in this strange mood, difficult to follow.

'The sinking of the *Albany*. It wasn't a storm off Panama, Thomas. The *Albany* went down off the coast of Cuba, in crowded waters. And she must have gone down with a bang.'

'The *Albany* . . . Then you knew she was missing? So in that case . . .' Staveley leaned forward, his fingers laced in front of him, and examined his fingertips as though they puzzled him. 'So wait a minute, John. Are you telling me you knew about this? You knew about the *Albany* and you believe she was sunk deliberately? My word, you were always *so* convinced there was going to be an attack, weren't you?'

He looked up at Jerusalems, and there was, in his face, a look almost of awe.

'Good God, John, you knew all along, didn't you? Long before I did. And that must mean . . .'

Again Staveley looked down, his brow deeply furrowed.

'Those rumours about a Spanish attack on American shipping . . . They seemed ridiculous to everyone but you. But you were adamant they were true. You had definite information. No, wait, it's worse than that . . .' The awe was rapidly turning to horror. 'You had a hand in it, didn't you? You *wanted* to see the Spanish and the Americans at each others' throats. God in heaven, you've been sitting here in Lowther Street trying to start a war!'

Jerusalems had put down his glass, and now he leaned forward, closer to his visitor.

'And if I have, Thomas? Would that really be so bad?'

'A *war*, John!' Staveley exploded. 'How can you say that after all the miseries of the Crimea? Please tell me I'm misunderstanding this.'

'Oh, really, Thomas!' Suddenly Jerusalems was back on his feet as if his customary energy had returned. 'What was it you said during your last visit? Sometimes our best interests and our moral purposes do not always align?'

Staveley rose too. 'So you do not deny it? You have been plotting to attack an American ship?' Staveley was aghast, but also a little overawed. The scale of Jerusalems' ambition was far beyond anything he had imagined.

'Most certainly I have.' Jerusalems sounded utterly unabashed. He had begun to prowl around the room from point to point in his usual way, as if energised by Staveley's disapproval. 'Think about it. If the Spanish and Americans went to war tomorrow over Cuba, who would be the winner?'

Staveley was reluctant to answer, but felt he had no choice.

'The Americans, undoubtedly.'

'Wrong, Thomas. Completely wrong. *We* would be the winners. That's the beauty of it.'

It was as if the sluggish man of two minutes earlier had never existed. Jerusalems was now pacing and turning, pacing and turning, pausing only to gesticulate in the direction of his guest.

'Just think it through, Thomas. An official American invasion of Cuba would be the end for the Spanish in the Caribbean. They simply aren't equipped to survive such a conflict. But it would be at a terrible cost to the Americans too, because the Spanish are still strong enough to make a fight of it, and because we would hit the Americans very, very hard at sea.'

He favoured Staveley with a brilliant smile.

'By treaty we'd have to support the Spanish, wouldn't we?' He clearly relished the prospect. 'So we'd have *carte blanche* to play havoc with American shipping and supplies, and our naval friends are dying to establish a decent base on Cuba. And we wouldn't even think of fighting on the island itself. We'd simply send in a lot of guns and start raising slave militias to oppose the invaders. That should shake things up nicely! A free slave army on America's doorstep, Thomas!'

He held his palms upwards, at the level of his shoulders, like a market-place preacher at the climax of a sermon.

'But the Americans would still win, wouldn't they?' Staveley reasoned calmly. 'On the island itself, I mean?'

'Tchah! You're asking the wrong question, Thomas.' Jerusalems relaxed, and resumed his prowling. 'On land, in purely military terms, that may be so. But not at sea. Not if it happens *now*. Their navy is not currently primed for a confrontation with the Royal Navy. If it came upon them quickly – if they blundered into war in anger – we'd be confident of controlling the sea, even with so many ships tied up in the Crimea. But if we wait, if we let America grow stronger and Spain weaker, the balance changes.'

Staveley shook his head, still bewildered by the outrageous breadth of Jerusalems' vision.

'But, John, apart from wreaking destruction on American shipping, what would we get out of any of this?'

Jerusalems made a tutting noise, as if taken aback that Staveley was still so many moves behind.

'Think about it, Thomas! Once it was clear to our American friends there was going to be no simple victory, no unchallenged occupation of Cuba, just a long, costly, messy struggle, we'd have a number of very agreeable options. For instance, we could let the French broker a tripartite agreement for an independent Cuba. They'd love that. The Spanish would complain, obviously, but no one would be listening to them.'

'Would that work?' Staveley sounded doubtful, but he began to see the direction in which Jerusalems' logic was taking him.

'Most certainly!' The little man's eyes were bright with excitement. 'To help the Americans swallow it, we'd package it as an American victory, a triumph for freedom and democracy over imperialism, and then we'd let the plantation owners keep all their slaves. And we'd agree that the French and Americans could establish naval bases on the island as well as ourselves, with rights in perpetuity. That would sugar the pill nicely. Yes, I think we could be sure of an agreement. And an independent Cuba, guaranteed by all three powers, would draw a very neat line under any American plans for further expansion in the Caribbean.'

Jerusalems sighed, as if almost overcome by the beauty of his plan.

'What an outcome, eh, Thomas? Instead of a volatile, disruptive island where we have no foothold, an island constantly threatening to drop into American hands, we'd have a pleasantly weak republic, grateful to Britain for saving it from the Yankee yoke, as well as a naval strongpoint just where we need it. And our American friends would have to turn back to the Pacific for their dreams of expansion. And to achieve all this, this perfect, beautiful equilibrium, all we had to do was sink a ship. We *did* sink a ship.' He shook his head, bemused. 'But somehow no one noticed.'

But while he'd been talking, Staveley had been thinking, remembering other things John Jerusalems had said.

'Lavender and those letters . . . John, you said just now that Lavender was being blackmailed. But if you *knew* that, you must have known he was writing those letters to Colonel Aguero. None of the correspondence Backhouse sent us was a surprise to you, was it?'

Jerusalems began to answer, but Staveley held up his hand to silence him.

'I see it now. Lavender told you he was being blackmailed, and you told him to cooperate. My God, yes. Of course. You probably told him what to write! And by tempting Colonel Aguero into that correspondence, into sanctioning sabotage on the American mainland, you were actually *creating* the evidence you needed to start a war. That's why you were so desperate to get hold of the originals!'

To his surprise, Jerusalems did not demur. The little man simply paused in his pacing and nodded.

'It is a very simple technique,' he said quietly. 'If one doesn't have the tools needed to achieve some favourable outcome, it may be necessary to manufacture them.'

'Which is what happened to that spy who was shot. What was his name? Alvarez? He was spying for the Americans but was keeping himself well hidden, so you made it look as though he was spying for you.'

Jerusalems acknowledged the suggestion with an almost imperceptible shrug.

'I regret the necessity. But Alvarez was a problem.'

'And Lavender . . .' Staveley's mind was racing. 'Lavender was becoming an embarrassment because he was growing so indiscreet in his personal conduct. But you can't just sack people in his line of work because of what they might say. So you have to persuade them it's in their interest to retire. That's why you wanted Backhouse appointed, isn't it? You needed someone honest in Havana to stumble across Lavender's secrets. Was it you who arranged for Backhouse to get those papers?'

But Jerusalems didn't answer. He had returned to the seat by the window, and when Staveley finished he was once again looking up at the sky. Dusk was already well advanced.

'Lavender did a great deal for me, Thomas. And when things in Havana were getting too dangerous for him, I did what I could to persuade him to go. No one was sorrier than me to hear what befell him.' In fact, the sadness was audible in his voice. 'For a long time, everything in Cuba was simple. But now, well, a chapter is over. Lavender's dead, and a lot of threads will unravel from there. My friend Jepson will make sure they do. And the *Albany* is simply missing off Panama. So Jepson can go back to America knowing his job is done. I hope he enjoys his triumph.'

It was said with sorrow, but also with finality, as though Jerusalems felt there was nothing else to be said.

And Staveley made no reply. He felt certain this visit to Lowther Street would be his last.

That night, he did not shake hands with Jerusalems, or even say a proper goodbye. He left his host, motionless and silent, in the exact position in which he'd found him.

LVIII

The days that followed the assault on Backhouse at his offices were, it seemed to him, strangely uneventful. On returning to the scene the next day, he found everything as he remembered it, with no sign of any disruption to his files nor, so far as he could tell, anything missing. Of course Backhouse had inherited a great deal of paperwork from his predecessor, and he had no way of knowing for certain whether or not any of that had been removed; but such was the state of order that prevailed, he might have begun to doubt his own recollection of events had the lump on his head not provided him with a persistent reminder.

As to the identity of his assailant, the young porter at the door was of little help. An extremely timid young man and new to the post, he was able to say only that the other gentleman had claimed to be the assistant of Señor Backhouse, and spoke Spanish like a local. Backhouse guessed the young man's shyness was such that he had barely even looked the caller in the face.

One thing, however, was certain: Dalrymple could be acquitted of the crime. It soon emerged that he had spent that evening getting rather drunk at a café near the old wall, as numerous disapproving Europeans were all too willing to testify. This did not come as a particular surprise to Backhouse, as instances of his clerk's unseemly behaviour were becoming more and more frequent. It was increasingly common, too, for Dalrymple to appear at the office rather the worse for wear, and his attendance was more erratic than ever. However, Backhouse's remonstrations were invariably met with a mewling self-pity, or with the complaint

343

that a clerk's salary was simply not great enough to sustain respectable living in Havana.

Typical of the annoyances Backhouse encountered was his discovery one day, a few weeks after Lavender's death, of an envelope marked 'George Backhouse Only' among Dalrymple's papers. When challenged about it, the clerk appeared completely unconcerned. It had arrived a few days earlier, he thought, although he couldn't remember precisely when. An official had dropped it off, he seemed to remember. Apparently it had been among the things found on Lavender's person at the time of his death. Dalrymple had been rushing out when it arrived, so had plopped it down on his desk, intending to pass it on when he returned. Since then, it had simply slipped his mind.

When Backhouse finally had a private moment in which to open the envelope – a moment free from his assistant's undisguised prying – he found it contained the address of a building near the southern docks and a single iron key.

It says something about Backhouse's mental state that for three days the key remained untouched in a secure compartment of his desk. His dearest wish was to follow Jepson's advice: to keep his head down, to settle his debts, and to get back to London at the earliest opportunity.

But an unexplained key whispers mysteries, and to Backhouse it felt like a challenge. Lavender had considered him a pretty poor specimen: naïve, over-honest, spineless even. Well, he was spineless no more, and certainly a good deal less naïve. And not ashamed to be honest, even here in Havana.

Four days after receiving the envelope, Backhouse left his office at noon and called for a carriage to take him to the southern end of the city. The address in the envelope proved to belong to a tall, rather run-down building on the cheaper, south-facing side of the Calle Paula, one that had evidently been divided up into apartments so that every window was dressed differently, without any regard to its neighbour. On its front steps, smoking a cigar as he waited, was Washington's special envoy to Havana.

'You're very prompt, my friend.' Jepson grinned cordially. 'Now tell me what I'm doing here.'

Ever since Lavender's death, Jepson had been seeking some sort of proof; something to satisfy him that his rat had, all along, been lurking beneath Lavender's disappointing façade of ordinariness. It didn't matter to him greatly what anyone else told him. If Lavender was his man, then somewhere there would be evidence. If not, then he would go to his grave unconvinced.

His contacts in Havana had come up with one or two suggestions, but these had yielded no results. Yet all the time word was reaching him of petty officials and small-time informers – the sort of people his rat had once nourished – who were betraying unmistakable signs of hardship, as though Lavender's death had brought to a halt a long-standing source of income.

Then, when Jepson had all but called off the search, a note from George Backhouse of all people. And a George Backhouse rather different from the stiff, anxious official he'd first encountered in Havana.

'As I said in my note, Mr Jepson, you have to agree to my terms first.' He gestured vaguely at the row of buildings in front of them. 'You see, somewhere along here is something Lavender wanted me to see. I may be wrong, but I have a feeling it might be exactly what you're looking for. Either way, I will decide what happens next. You are here to argue your case, but I decide. Do you agree?'

'The cards are all in your hand, Mr Backhouse.' The American did not seem displeased by this display of forcefulness. 'So, yes, I agree. Now, I'm guessing it's this block . . .'

He looked down at the key that lay in Backhouse's palm and grimaced.

'Top floor. In this heat. I really should have guessed.'

The staircase lacked windows and the climb left both men perspiring and uncomfortable, but the key turned easily in the lock. As the door swung open it revealed a simple, single-roomed apartment with a polished wooden floor, empty but for a desk and

345

a number of small chests of drawers. Not all the drawers were properly shut, and it was clear even from the doorway that they were full of papers.

When Backhouse made to step past him, into the room, Jepson held him back.

'One moment.'

Backhouse watched his companion kneel down on the threshold and peer across the room at ground level.

'Dust,' he explained. 'Not the thickest, but no marks on it. How long has Lavender been dead? It might be thicker, I suppose, but no one's been here for at least a few days. Go on, Mr Backhouse, lead the way.'

To Backhouse it was quickly obvious that his suspicions had been correct. Everything Jepson was looking for seemed to be there, all of it neatly filed and alphabetised. A confession of sorts – Lavender's last, dramatic gesture, made when he still expected to make a clean escape to Mexico. Or, if not a confession, perhaps a warning.

After a few minutes Backhouse stood aside and watched Jepson at work. He had never seen the American so transported. At first he approached each file cautiously, as if expecting a trap, but as the contents revealed themselves, he began to dig in at random, all method abandoned, his excitement growing with every document.

'Let's see . . . What's here? Kansas . . . Topeka . . . Missouri . . . We've got payments, names . . . By Jupiter, Mr Backhouse, it's all here, all in the neatest copperplate! Everything I ever said about my rat was true. I knew someone was stirring up trouble, and I knew that trouble was coming out of Havana!'

His jubilation was almost endearing.

'You see, my friend, I wasn't mad after all. I could smell a rat, and here are his footprints, exactly as I predicted. In Washington they thought I was crazy but this will change their minds! Lavender, eh? Who'd have thought it? I honestly had him down as a nobody. I thought I'd been doing this long enough to recognise his sort.'

Backhouse cleared his throat.

'So if I were to walk away from here and leave you with the key, Mr Jepson, what would you do with all this?' It was beginning to occur to him that the names on the papers belonged to real people.

Jepson clearly understood the question.

'Oh, don't worry, my friend. America is not imperial Spain. We're not talking about summary executions here. Most of this is structural stuff. There are names, yes, but most of those are honest American citizens. Objectionable ones with extreme views, possibly, but in America it's not illegal to accept money to support a cause you believe in, however misguided that cause may be. No, this stuff is valuable to me because it means I can dismantle the web of supply that Lavender built, which should make it a little harder for the troublemakers to make trouble.'

He continued to rifle through the papers, his delight growing with every bundle he opened. Finally he turned to Backhouse.

'So, my friend, what's your decision? I could use all this to take some heat out of things back home, to damp down the firebrands who want to set Americans against each other. Or you could keep it for yourself and . . . Just what *would* you do with it, Mr Backhouse?'

Backhouse shrugged. 'Crawford is looking after Lavender's affairs. I suppose I should pass the key to him.' He shook his head. 'But to men like Crawford, knowledge is just the means to a profit. I confess I'm not inclined to indulge him.'

Jepson nodded.

'I can have every shred of paper out of here by evening,' he promised.

'And use it in the interests of America?' The question was asked lightly, but it was an important one, and both men knew it.

'In the interests of *peace*, Mr Backhouse. In the interests of moderation. I give you my word.'

And Backhouse believed him. Whether Jepson's commitment to peace was greater than his loyalty to his country, he rather doubted. But, for the time being, both seemed to share the same path.

The two men shook hands. As Backhouse prepared to leave, Jepson detained him with a light touch on his arm.

'You know something, Mr Backhouse? It takes a lot to impress me. You've no real reason to trust me, have you? But you're taking a risk because your instinct tells you it's the decent thing to do. That's not something I come across very often. Oh, I know you despise the games John Jerusalems plays. But he is a countryman of yours all the same, and a lot of people would see no further than that. Right and wrong, good and bad. These things can start to look alike, especially in a city like Havana. Them-and-us is a much easier game to play.'

The American gestured at the room behind him.

'This is years of work for John Jerusalems, you know, and all gone up in smoke. I can't deny that the thought gives me a great deal of pleasure. And I confess I'd have paid hard cash to see the look on his face when the *Albany* was listed as missing off Panama.' Jepson allowed himself the faintest of smiles, then dismissed it with a wave of his hand. 'But it's not about that, is it? The plain truth is that someone was trying to set things ablaze, someone else was determined to keep the peace. You had to choose between us. You've done the right thing, Mr Backhouse.'

But Backhouse had no particular desire for the American's approval, and the reference to the *Albany* meant nothing to him. As he descended the gloomy staircase and stepped into the brightness of the street, he felt no curiosity, no camaraderie, only relief. It was over. All the intrigue and the plotting. Lavender and his friend in London had played their dirty game but now it was done. Lavender was dead and the board was swept clean. That last bit, at least, was something for which he could take some credit.

Early the following month, Grace and the children left for London. Their departure saddened him immeasurably, and in some sense it felt like a defeat. But there was relief in their goodbyes too. The moment they stepped off Cuban soil, Backhouse felt they were safer, that in boarding a British ship they had been welcomed back into a world of order and sense and decency. It was a weight off his shoulders, a weight that had been there since their first night in Havana, growing more burdensome with every day that passed.

He did not, at once, give up the villa in El Cerro. The lease did not permit it, and the rent itself was paid by the Spanish. But once Grace was gone, there was no question of his entertaining as he had done. He had become, in society's eyes, a bachelor, and the economies accrued accordingly. Occasionally he did invite an acquaintance to dine at the villa: Faraday, a newly arrived shipping engineer was one; another was Callaghan, the Irishman who sometimes helped him out as secretary when Dalrymple was absent.

Most often, however, he would return early in the afternoon to spend an hour or two in the garden before dining alone and passing the remainder of the evening with a book.

It was on one such occasion that he returned a little earlier than usual, while the servants were still sleeping through the hour of siesta. The villa was very quiet but for a series of small noises coming from his study. When he investigated, he found himself confronted by an unseen figure who stepped out from behind the door and held a gun to his head.

LIX

The world of the gangmaster, O'Driscoll, had once been full of reassuring certainties. He had established – ruthlessly and over time – a deserved reputation for brutality and efficiency, two qualities that were essential in his line of work. As a result, he was widely feared by his associates, and that fear made many things easy for him. If a rival needed to be removed from the field every now and then, it improved both his profits and his reputation.

But the gangmaster's encounters with Jepson had upset all his comfortable certainties. The American had demonstrated his power in ways O'Driscoll understood, and by contrast Lavender no longer seemed quite such a desirable ally. O'Driscoll was perfectly willing to switch allegiance when it suited him, and Jepson, he felt certain, was not someone to oppose.

So O'Driscoll celebrated the news of Lavender's death as something that made his world a safer place. Now he could side with Jepson with impunity. After all, even Lavender couldn't strike at him from beyond the grave.

But after the Englishman's death, things began to change. People he had worked with for years no longer wanted to deal with him. The respect he commanded was neither so widespread nor so sincere. He felt he had been marked for a fall, and that those around him were standing back for fear of being caught in the crash.

O'Driscoll however was no fool. He had learned to trust his instincts, and it seemed to him it was time to leave Havana. There were plenty of places in the world where a man like him could prosper. To stand and fight was the philosophy of a fool. But if he must run, he would not run in the direction his enemies expected. And he would wait until he knew for certain that he was in danger.

Yet when the axe fell, it took him completely by surprise. He had been out that morning on the docks, trying to raise money against the labour gang he still controlled. He had even managed to attract a very fair offer, and he returned to his rooms on the Calle Picota in unusually upbeat mood.

Perhaps good spirits made him incautious, because he had reached his own landing before he realised that three policemen had followed him up the stairs. And his front door, he saw, was already ajar. Inside his apartment he found another half-dozen policemen waiting for him under the command of a small, moustachioed officer who introduced himself as Major Moreno.

O'Driscoll's instinct was to run, but with his retreat cut off his only refuge was indignation. What was the meaning of this intrusion? It was insulting and outrageous. Clearly there had been a mistake. Would someone please explain what was going on?

The small officer listened with a smile, and when O'Driscoll had finished his reply was curt.

'I am here, señor, to arrest you for the murder of a night-watchman at the offices of the British consul in July 1851. You are to accompany me at once for further questioning.'

As soon as he heard the charge, O'Driscoll knew he was finished. Not because he was guilty. That was irrelevant. But because the forces arrayed against him were too strong. This charge was not something the Spanish police had thought up for themselves. Someone was guiding their hand, someone who'd make sure he didn't leave Havana alive.

'As I said, officer, there must be some mistake. What possible reason could you have for thinking I was involved in such a thing?'

Moreno's eyes signalled to one of his men and two objects were produced from a table near the door: a paperknife and a pocket watch. He recognised both as items he had once removed from the British consul's offices.

'These things are inscribed with the name of Señor Crawford, the British consul,' the officer explained. 'They were reported missing from the scene of the murder and were never seen again until now. You would perhaps like to explain how both objects came to be hidden at the bottom of a drawer near your bed?'

O'Driscoll knew they had been planted there. He'd handed both items to Lavender on the very night they were stolen. But it was not Moreno or his colleagues who had placed them in his room. The police were simply acting upon information they'd received. Someone had kept those objects safely stored away for years for precisely this purpose, and now they had chosen to deploy them. Lavender. But Lavender was dead.

Moreno seemed to take O'Driscoll's silence as a confession and signalled for his man to return the objects to a place of safekeeping. It was a moment that gave O'Driscoll a very slight chance. Eight paces away from him, the window stood open. It was a high first-floor window and to evade the man nearest to it he would have to dive head first. The drop would almost certainly kill him. But if he remained in custody, he was dead anyway.

He bowed politely to Major Moreno, then sprang for the window.

In the end it was the proprietor of the Gull tavern who delivered Moses Le Castre to Leonarda. Word travelled quickly in the dirty alleyways off the Calle Damas, and Moses had too few friends there to protect him. A small reward, discreetly advertised, was all it took.

She timed her visit for early afternoon. At that time of day the alleyways were emptier and less intimidating than after dark, but nevertheless Leonarda took precautions. She dressed very simply and carried a knife, and arranged to be accompanied by the silent African who had been a friend of Tartuffo Martinez.

They found Moses in a small, grubby room near the Gull, and as Leonarda had guessed, he was sleeping. They entered without knocking, but it was enough to wake him and he sat up blinking and cursing, groping under his pillow as if for a weapon. He wore nothing but a pair of loose trousers, and without his clothes he looked even older than before: skinny and hollowed-out. The hair on his chest was white. On recognising Leonarda he reached for a crumpled cotton shirt and pulled it on over his head.

'Who is your friend?' he asked, both suspicious and resentful.

'Only that. A friend.' At Leonarda's signal, Arturo moved to the door and placed his back against it. 'And you, Moses? What are you?'

'What do you mean?' There was a little whine of complaint in his voice. 'Why have you come here?'

'Because I want you to tell me about Hector. Properly, this time. I want to know why he died.'

She spoke firmly, but once again he wasn't meeting her eye. He seemed to be ignoring the question.

'I'm getting out,' he told her. 'To Panama. There's a man I worked for here. He's warned me to go. Havana's a dangerous place. Hector knew that.' He said it with feeling. 'Hector always knew that.'

His eye alighted on a small pocket knife lying on the floor near his bed, but Leonarda had followed his gaze. A gentle flick of her foot sent it sliding into the far corner of the room.

'Did Hector know you were taking money to run errands for English spies?' she asked him. 'Did he know you were receiving deliveries for them when you stood in for him at the consul's offices?'

Moses was still looking down, cradling the fingers of one hand as though it had been his fingers that she'd kicked. But he said nothing, so she carried on.

'Hector was genuinely fond of you, you know, Moses. He thought you were a good man at heart. So tell me. I need to know. Did you kill him?'

'No!' Her question seemed to shock him, and he jerked his head up to look at her. 'No. He was good to me. He was my friend.' And to her astonishment, he burst into tears.

She waited while he sobbed, mopping at his eyes and nose with the hem of his shirt.

'It wasn't me,' he insisted, he voice deep with misery. 'I swear to you, it was the white man who killed him. The gangmaster. He told me he wanted to ask Hector some questions. That was all. I have blamed myself every day ever since . . .'

The story came out slowly. Moses told it as though a thick poison were being coughed from his lungs. In between, there were sobs. Leonarda had been full of anger that morning; she had cornered Moses with every intention of making him cower. But watching him there, on that dirty bed, there could be no denying his pain, nor the suffering that had eaten into his soul.

It had begun innocently, he swore. He ran errands. He had always run errands. The white man with the Irish name had been introduced to him by a friend of a friend, and had always paid him well. Never for anything particularly dangerous: watching, spying, carrying messages, that sort of thing. The rewards were good, and the better he knew the white man, the better they became. Soon he found himself accompanying the gangmaster on certain jobs, began to witness things that were less pleasant. He saw intimidation, sometimes beatings. Afterwards, he was often asked to dispose of items: weapons, usually, but sometimes the papers stolen from an unconscious man.

The more he witnessed, the better the pay, and the more he feared the gangmaster. He never dreamed of telling Hector about the situation he found himself in. It was a year or more before he witnessed his first murder, a young man beaten to death in an alley. Afterwards Moses prayed to God to remove him from the life he led, to find a way to pluck him from danger and return him to the innocent joys of poverty in St Simeon. But no miracle occurred. He took the gold and kept his tongue, and did what he was told because he could think of no other course.

When Hector asked him to cover some nights for him at the British consul's offices, Moses had been pleased to do his friend a favour. Hector was tired, he knew, but even so it was unusual for him to ask for help. And when the gangmaster, knowing where he would be, asked Moses to receive some papers for him, he thought nothing of it. It was a simple task, and nothing to worry him.

But that day the cramps had seized him. Moses was prone to them, crippling pains in the stomach that came with diarrhoea and vomiting. Each bout laid him up for two or three days. So he had sent word to Hector that he could not work that night.

He had forgotten all about the gangmaster's delivery.

'The next night, the gangmaster sent for me. I was still sick, afraid I'd fill my pants with shit right there in front of him. I told him I'd been ill, that my friend would have the papers. We could go at once to collect them.'

Moses paused for breath, his chest still heaving.

'That was all I did,' he insisted, his eyes searching out Leonarda's as though desperate for some evidence of sympathy. 'I just took him there. Hector didn't really want to let us in, I could see that. I could see he was angry with me about the papers. But he still had them, and he handed them over to the gangmaster without any complaint. He refused a tip, I remember that. Just dug out the papers from the little box by his stool and passed them over. They were loose and tied up with a string, but that's all I remember about them. We were only there for three or four minutes, and that was that.'

Moses shook his head, as though still struggling to understand what had passed.

'But the next evening, the gangmaster asked to go back. He said he'd a question he'd forgotten to put to Hector, and he needed me to go with him. Nothing was different the second time, except the gangmaster carried a bag. I thought it was empty.'

'Go on.' Leonarda's voice was hard, but inside something was hurting. It felt like ice falling away from her heart.

'Hector *really* didn't want to let us in that second time, but I begged him as a special favour. So he opened the door and led us through to the study where we couldn't be seen from the street. I remember him putting down his lamp, and before I knew what was happening the white man had hit him from behind. There was a piece of heavy pipe in his hand, and as Hector fell, he hit him again. He was trying to kill, I could see that. There are ways of hurting someone, but this was not that. He was clubbing him to death.'

Moses passed a hand over his face as though the images he described were still there in front of him. Leonarda remained standing, and to Moses it seemed she was listening without emotion. But the African by the door, who watched and said nothing, saw the fingernails of both hands pressed deep into her palms.

'I swear he was dead by the time he hit the floor.' Moses looked up beseechingly. 'He must have known nothing about it. I cried out and ran to him, but he was already gone. Meanwhile the white man was at work filling his bag. I couldn't help Hector. And I was afraid.'

'But why?' Leonarda's voice came as a whisper. 'Why did he have to die?'

Moses shut his eyes.

'Before we left him, I found the courage to ask. The white man just bent down and picked up a book from the floor. It was the book Hector had been reading. *This is why*, he said, but I didn't understand. I asked what book it was, and the white man smiled and said it didn't matter. He said the book was the reason he'd come back.'

Once again Moses looked across at Leonarda.

'Do you see? Those papers. That was why Hector died. The papers had come to him by accident, when they should have come to me. I was a safe person, you see. To me, they meant nothing. But Hector could read.' He shook his head. 'It was the book in his hand that betrayed him. If it hadn't been for the book, he'd still be alive.'

Backhouse felt a hand shove him between the shoulders, forcing him face down on to the floor. As he lay there, the gun was placed against the side of his head.

'Let's be clear,' a voice said, 'there is absolutely no advantage to me in keeping you alive. If you make a noise, or struggle in any way, I shall kill you.'

'O'Driscoll?' Backhouse asked. He had met the gangmaster only once, but his voice was distinctive.

'I need English money, as much of it as you've got.'

Backhouse was aware of the search starting up again, feet shuffling to and fro across the room's smart, vanilla floorboards.

'There's a very small amount in the box by the window,' he announced in the direction of the moving feet. 'That's all though. My wife recently returned to England. Obviously she took all the currency we had.'

He heard the feet move to the window, then the box being emptied of coins.

'Is that what you came here for? To steal money?' The curt, insolent fellow who had deigned to meet him at the Golden Flag had seemed to Backhouse rather above the theft of copper coins.

'I came to sell you something. Information.' O'Driscoll's voice sounded clipped, as though he were in pain. 'But as you weren't here, I thought I'd help myself. I don't have much time.'

Backhouse rearranged his arms so that he was lying more comfortably. By altering the angle of his head, he was able to see O'Driscoll much more clearly. He saw that the man's trousers were torn at the hip and at the knee, and that blood was caked on his forehead. He seemed to be moving with a limp.

'What information?' Backhouse asked.

'You wanted to know about the Royal Navy sailing plans. I was going to tell you. If you made it worth my while. What else do you have?'

'There are a few dollars in my wallet at the back of the desk,' Backhouse offered. 'Or is it only English money you want?'

'I'll be on a boat bound for Liverpool within the hour. I want a letter to your wife.'

'My wife?' Backhouse was genuinely bemused.

'A letter asking her to pay your dear friend the bearer, let's see . . . Ten pounds?'

'That's a lot of money. She's unlikely to have that much in the house. And she would certainly think it odd. You'd do better asking for, say, two or three guineas.'

'Five pounds,' O'Driscoll insisted. He'd moved to the other side of the room, where Backhouse could no longer see him so easily.

'Very well. I'll write that letter. If you let me get up.'

Backhouse was making a rapid calculation. Whatever boat O'Driscoll was catching, it was unlikely to be a particularly quick crossing. Direct shipping from Havana to Liverpool was rarely the fastest, and often would stop at the Canaries anyway. Meanwhile a letter to London, were he to write it that afternoon, and were it to catch the American mail boat to Boston, might just possibly make it on to one of the very fast Cunard boats . . . Yes, there was every chance he could have the authorities waiting for O'Driscoll on the docks.

But of course, O'Driscoll must know that too. With perfect clarity, Backhouse understood. O'Driscoll couldn't afford to leave him alive. The knowledge didn't frighten him, it made him angry. Not the flaming anger that burns as rage, but that cold, blue anger that sharpens the focus and tautens the nerves. Yet another man was lying to him. Yet another man counted him as nothing. An irrelevance. A dupe.

The gangmaster allowed him to get to his feet and seat himself at his bureau, watching all the time from a distance of five or six feet. Backhouse knew very little about guns, but Crawford had once shown him an example of the latest American revolver. The item held by O'Driscoll looked sufficient for its intended task.

'So tell me,' he prompted. 'About the navy's sailing plans, I mean.'

'That was Lavender.' O'Driscoll said the name with something like anger. 'He'd collect them from Jamaica himself, once a month. I don't know who gave them to him, but there never seemed to be any difficulty. When he got to Havana, he used to pass them on to someone else. He wasn't involved in the actual selling. I used to do Lavender's dirty work for him, which is how I know.'

'That's not what you told me before,' Backhouse pointed out. It felt strange to be writing to Grace at such a time, knowing that they might be the last words he ever addressed to her.

'I checked with Lavender before speaking to you. He told me to tell you enough to keep you interested, so long as it pointed away from him.'

'I see.' To Backhouse, the importance of small talk had never seemed so great. He needed time, the right opportunity. 'So can I ask about your sudden eagerness to get to Liverpool, Mr O'Driscoll?'

'The police came for me today. They've got evidence I killed someone. They found some things I once stole from the British consul.'

O'Driscoll paused and Backhouse wondered if he was in pain, but when he turned to look he realised the gangmaster was puzzling over something.

'That shit-tucker Lavender . . . It was him. He's sold me to the Spanish. I took some things that night to make it seem like a burglary. Mostly rubbish, but Lavender chose certain items to keep. Two or three, I think. I'd forgotten all about them until I saw that watch today. The rest of the stuff went to the idiots who were going to take the blame for it all. But they weren't the only ones being set up, were they? Lavender had planned this all along, keeping those things in case he ever wanted to stick a murder charge on me. And today he did.'

'But Lavender's dead.' Although the letter was finished, Backhouse was keeping his pen close to the paper.

O'Driscoll shrugged. 'He must have arranged it before he died,' he said, 'when he was planning to get out. Part of his plan to tidy up. He'll have paid someone to do it, and told them when to tip off the police. Anyway, it doesn't matter. If I make that boat, I'm a free man. I've got the papers of a farmer who was press-ganged on to an American ship. A man called Smith, which will suit me very nicely. From Liverpool, I can ship to Canada and no one will ever find me. Havana's a city that bears grudges. I'll be glad to be gone.'

He held out his hand for the letter and Backhouse passed it to him.

'What in hell is this?' O'Driscoll's eyes were cold. 'You little prick. If you think you can play games with me . . .'

He raised the gun, a gesture the more threatening for being instinctive. But Backhouse was beyond fear.

'There is a problem with the letter?'

'Don't act the fool!' He thrust the paper at Backhouse's face. 'This is in Latin.'

'Of course.' Even as he spoke, Backhouse marvelled at his own serenity. 'My wife and I always correspond in Latin. It is a little habit of ours over many years.'

'And how am I supposed to know what it says? You think I'm going to *trust* you?'

Backhouse shrugged. 'I could write it again for you, in English, if you wish. But were I to do so, my wife would know at once it was written under duress. The choice is yours.'

'I don't believe you. You little piece of scum. If I'm not getting a letter from you . . .'

Backhouse had once punched a man in an alley off Regent Street. The fellow had been a drunkard, and was pawing a weeping flower girl. The blow had taken both men by surprise, and Backhouse had been astonished how easily the other had gone down.

A man like O'Driscoll was, of course, a very different proposition. Under usual circumstances, any physical confrontation between them could have had only one outcome. But O'Driscoll was injured and in pain. And, like the drunkard, was clearly not expecting even the slightest resistance.

So when Backhouse swept at him, hard and fast, with the paperweight from his desk, O'Driscoll barely saw it coming. Even in his debilitated state, however, he was quick enough to raise an arm to ward off the worst of the blow. By chance the arm he raised was the one that held the revolver, and Backhouse heard a shot ring out and a window shatter just as he saw O'Driscoll stagger. Had the man's legs been uninjured, he would surely have ridden the blow, but as he fell Backhouse was upon him, hitting at his head with the nearest chair, repeatedly and without mercy, until its leg splintered and O'Driscoll lay still, moaning softly.

The servants who rushed to the scene thought at first that Backhouse was injured too. They found him slumped on the floor, his face pale, and when they tried to raise him his limbs would barely support him. But there was a look on his face that they had never seen before – authority, confidence, perhaps even pride. They had tended to think of their master as an object of derision, another ignorant foreigner to be flecced. But this time, as one was sent for rope, another dispatched to bring the police, they ran to follow his orders with alacrity.

'No, wait!' Backhouse held up his hand. The clarity he'd felt while the gun was pointing at him was gone, replaced by a vague sense of nausea. 'You, there. You wait here. Stand guard. I shall go for the police myself. I'm in the mood for a little fresh air.'

LX

They met for a second time under the lemon trees on the Cortina de Valdés, where the light broke into fragments on the waters of the bay and the shade offered a forgiving respite from the heat of the city.

The captain of police had suggested the rendezvous some days previously, well before the order came for O'Driscoll's arrest. Events in Spain had been moving quickly too, more quickly than he had anticipated, and he found himself with a great need to confide.

'You see, señora,' he explained as they walked beneath the trees, 'I shall be returning to Spain early next month, and it will be four months before I return to Havana.'

'I see.' Leonarda could sense an announcement of some sort was pending, but was unsure of its nature. 'And is your journey undertaken for professional or personal reasons, Captain?'

'I am to be married.' He said it baldly, and the words still seemed strange to him, as if they must apply to someone else. His almost-engagement to the daughter of his father's oldest friend had been part of his life for as long as he could remember. He had grown accustomed to it and had learned not to think of it, as one might stop noticing a weak knee or a stiff shoulder. Some day, of course, something would come of it, but he seldom wondered when. The negotiations, it seemed, had been conducted entirely without him.

'My congratulations, Captain.' Leonarda's words were suitably polite, although she sensed he had no desire to be

362

congratulated. 'When you return to Havana, will you bring your bride with you?'

'I do not think so.' The idea appalled him. Cuba was no place for such a delicate flower. And he had a vague sense that young officers who appeared exemplars of gallantry in Madrid might not appear to such shining advantage when observed, day in, day out, on duty in Havana.

'Yet separation is not easy,' Leonarda pointed out, 'especially when a marriage is so young.'

'I'm sure my . . . my wife will be more comfortable at home with her family.' He simply could not imagine her exposed to the discomforts and the immoralities of such a strange and lawless city.

They walked a little further without speaking, and the captain of police wondered why he had felt it was so important to share his news with the woman beside him. Did he think she might offer him some alternative, some reckless and passionate proposition? Might she declare herself in love and offer herself to him without conditions, if he would only disappoint the Spanish señorita?

But of course such ideas were nonsense. In the wakeful watches of the night he touched the soft darkness of her cheek, her neck, allowed his fingertips to drift downwards, slipping beneath the lace that covered her breasts. But the daylight reminded him of the sorry truth, that he had never even touched her ungloved hand. They walked a foot or more apart, like genteel acquaintances in a monastery garden.

Yet he felt no bitterness, no resentment, not even a sense of rejection. She had conducted herself throughout with perfect propriety. When he thought of his prolonged absence in Spain, he realised he would miss her company.

'There was something else,' he added, suddenly made awkward by the direction of his own thoughts. Briefly, and rather disjointedly, he told her about the bungled arrest of O'Driscoll earlier that day.

'He cannot get very far,' he assured her. 'He is injured from his fall, and his is a well-known face in this city. He may well have been recaptured already. I tell you this because of the charges he faces. Information was received that it was he who murdered the watchman at the British consul's offices.'

To his surprise, she said nothing, so he went on.

'It seems O'Driscoll was the paid assassin of a British spy, a man who is now dead. Last week the chief of police received a letter about the gangmaster, a letter denouncing him. When his rooms were searched, my colleagues found certain objects that had been stolen from the scene of the murder. I have them here. Come, let us sit.'

He indicated a narrow bench, one of many positioned beneath the lemon trees, facing out across the water. Before Leonarda could sit, he pulled out his handkerchief and brushed the bench for her.

The first object he showed her was the wooden paperknife marked with the consul's initials. She turned it over between her fingers once or twice then silently handed it back. Next was the gold pocket watch, inscribed on the back as a gift to the consul from his wife. It was the old-fashioned sort that had been in vogue twenty years before, the sort with a hidden compartment at the back. Leonarda slid it open idly, then shut it again hastily and passed the watch back, as if suddenly aware that examining such an intimate object was repugnant to her.

'I'm charged with returning these things to the consul,' the captain of police explained. 'But there was a third item in the drawer at O'Driscoll's place. It did not appear on the list of objects reported stolen, so my colleagues have no interest in it. But I thought you might.'

From inside his jacket he produced a thick, rather battered copy of *Don Quixote*, its red calf binding worn and rubbed smooth.

She recognised it immediately, but at first was reluctant to take it. Moses Le Castre's words were still loud in her head. *It was the book that betrayed him. It was the book that betrayed him.* But no, it

364

was not the book, it was Moses who had betrayed Hector. Moses, and the white man who was prepared to kill to preserve his secrets. Moses had convinced himself that if Hector had never learned to read he would still be alive. And it might be true. But he would not have been Hector.

Eventually she took the book from the captain of police and sat with it unopened in her hands.

'Thank you,' she said. 'He loved this more than anything.'

'Anything?' The captain of police looked at her closely. 'Perhaps there were other things more dear to him.'

But she shook her head.

'This never let him down. Never changed or disappointed him. It was a constant friend. I wish I could say the same.'

The captain of police knew nothing of age, nothing of death, very little about love. But sitting beneath the lemon trees, looking at the book and then at Leonarda, he felt certain she was wrong.

'Even so,' she continued, 'I am glad to have it. It was part of him. And I suppose it is also part of me.'

'We will catch the man who killed him,' the captain promised. 'He will pay for his crime.'

But Leonarda looked away, out to the point where the bay opened into ocean. The gangmaster was now an injured fugitive. She found his fate no longer mattered to her as she'd thought it would. She had tried to convince herself that she wanted vengeance, but she didn't. She just wanted Hector. And the guilt at leaving him, at never having said the things she should have said, was still in the way.

'Thank you for this, Captain. For everything.' She looked down and he realised her eyes were blinking, as if dazzled by the brightness of the sea. 'I think this book will help.' Her grip on it tightened. 'It was a place where we could always meet,' she said. 'Here, in these pages.'

The captain of police had reserved a table at a little restaurant just below the Cortina. He'd imagined Leonarda accompanying him there, joining him in a last drink or a last ice before his journey. But he had learned enough in Havana to relinquish his plan without complaint. He left her in the deep shade, sitting quietly, the book still unopened in her lap.

She did not open it until that night, very late, as she lay in bed. She knew difficult things awaited her between those covers: great pain and great love and memories of unbelievable tenderness. More significant to her than the text itself were the marks and stains that punctuated it. Each one was familiar. Her childhood was all there, remembered in the spills and the grubby fingerprints, the smeared reminders of life with Hector.

By contrast, deliberate marks on the pages were few. Hector had taught her that to sully a page with ink was a great sin unless to highlight for serious reasons a significant or special piece. As a result, Leonarda had very rarely marked the pages deliberately. But Hector's markings were all still there, all as she remembered them, his favourite passages neatly edged in faded black ink. She knew each one by heart, and reading them again she found her eyes filling with tears. She could hear his voice in every line, and see his smile, and remember his joy in every word.

It was not until a little before dawn that she came across a passage she herself had marked. She barely remembered doing it. It had been on one of her last evenings in St Simeon, when she was already transferring her life to the rooms of her Spanish lover. Hector had not been there. He had been working, and she had been avoiding him, embarrassed by her own behaviour. They had not seen each other for many days.

She had made the mark on impulse, and had hardly thought of it again.

'There were no embraces, because where there is great love there is often little display of it . . .'

By the lamplight in her room the thin line she'd drawn next to those words looked faded and indistinct. But next to it, much clearer, in Hector's black ink, was a second line. It had not been there when Leonarda made her mark. Hector must have made it later. He must have added his own line next to hers.

When she finally closed her eyes, she slept heavily, peacefully, and did not wake until the sun was high in the sky.

LXI

Jepson left Havana on the day of the candle festival. He was not inclined to linger, although at dusk, with a candle in every window and with tiny lights lining every street of the old town, Havana was said to be at its most beautiful. At noon, however, when he said his farewells to Dale at the latter's suburban villa, the day was as breathless and uncomfortable as any other, and the city as dirty and malodorous as always.

Dale was sorry to see him go. Jepson, however, was in high spirits and plainly delighted to be moving on to other things. He had declined to pay a final visit to the American consul on the grounds that it was quite unnecessary, and when Dale offered to pass on his compliments, the big man simply laughed.

'By all means, although he's probably forgotten my existence by now. If not, tell him I have utterly failed to prevent the Spanish reading our mails and have returned to Washington in disgrace. That should cheer him up.'

'And what does the future hold for you now?' Dale wondered.

Jepson shrugged. 'Colombia? Central America? There are some nasty little wars brewing, and the British are always sniffing about the Caribbean coast. Someone needs to keep an eye on our interests. But before that, before I kiss this godforsaken island farewell, I have one more call to make.'

Dale stood at the front of his villa and watched his visitor go, rumbling down the uneven street in a smart hired carriage. After a few moments he was joined on the veranda by his young housekeeper, who slipped her hand into his. For a minute more they watched together, until the rising dust closed around the vehicle and hid it from view. Then they turned and went inside, the peace of the place re-forming around them as the dust settled on the road.

Jepson had arranged to meet Backhouse at a café near the Plaza de Armas, not far from where his ship was due to sail. He had no reason to see the Englishman again, no significant news to impart or vital information to glean. But when he was making the arrangements for his departure, something had moved him to drop Backhouse a line suggesting a final meeting.

The Englishman did not keep him waiting very long. He found Jepson installed in a shady corner, the inevitable brandy already at his elbow and a smile of deep contentment on his face.

'So this is how it ends, my friend,' he declared cheerfully as Backhouse took a seat and ordered lime and water. 'Another hot day, another cold drink. Everything pretty much as I found it. I came to stop a war, and look – peace prevails. You and I have a good deal to be proud of. Yet within a week this place will have forgotten me, forgotten I was ever here.'

'You sound pleased at the prospect.' Backhouse envied the American his departure.

'Oh, I am. And I don't suppose I'll be back. Not until my countrymen next decide to invade the place, at any rate. Which *will* happen. At some point it will happen, you can be sure of it. America will never be completely at ease until it has Cuba in its palm. In the meantime, did you hear about O'Driscoll?'

'O'Driscoll?' Backhouse suppressed a smile.

'The gangmaster. He's been arrested for that murder at the British consulate. Nothing to do with me, though I confess I'm eager to see him hang. It would seem that even in Havana the sword of justice sometimes finds its man.'

'I dare say.' If there was a note of amusement in Backhouse's voice, Jepson didn't seem to notice it.

'The night-watchman he killed had been given a glimpse of some papers that compromised Lavender, so he and O'Driscoll decided to keep him quiet. O'Driscoll was that sort of person. A willing servant to the right man, and without a conscience of any sort. It's good to know they've got him safely in the Tacón gaol. Now, what about you, Mr Backhouse? What's your plan?'

So Backhouse explained about Grace's departure, about his determination to live frugally and to avoid trouble. He hoped, with Staveley's support, to be back in London within four years.

'Well, Mr Backhouse' – Jepson stretched his arms behind his head – 'I'm going to do a very unusual thing. I'm going to leave you an address where messages will reach me. If I can ever be of any assistance in the future . . .'

The American passed him a card on which had been scribbled a few lines in blue ink. Then he stretched again and prepared to rise.

'I like you, my friend. I like the fact you're not quite the pen-pusher we all expected.' He held out his hand. 'Tread carefully, Mr Backhouse. And next time someone sends you a package of uninvited papers, burn them.'

Before the first candles of the day were lit, Jepson had left Havana.

Backhouse did not go at once to the rooms on the Calle Chacón. Jepson was not the only person of his acquaintance leaving Havana, and he had no particular desire to remind himself of the fact. He had always *felt* alone in the city. Now it seemed he was to be left alone indeed.

So instead of going directly to find Leonarda, he returned to his office and applied himself, diligently and without interruptions, to the futile and frustrating business of the Mixed Commission. It was not until the light was fading that he tidied away his papers and made his way back down to the street below.

He had forgotten all about the festival of candles, and he stepped out of his darkening offices into a world transformed. Where there had once been dusty avenues and dirty streets, now there stretched before him broad causeways of light, the edges of every road picked out by tiny candles as though a galaxy of stars, roped together, had been draped across the old town. In every window a light burned, and the interiors of shops and cafés shimmered like jewelled caves. As well as the lights, there was music and laughter, and the smell of food roasting over hot embers. But it was the lights that moved Backhouse. He'd never seen the like of it.

He had intended to hail a cab for his journey, but instead he made his way through the streets on foot, his face full of wonder.

Yet this was not his first year in Havana. The festival had come and gone before. Where had he been? Why had he and Grace not embraced such a spectacle? But they would have been at home in the suburbs, safe in an English house, sharing with their compatriots the Anglo-Saxon suspicion of the island's unruly and unregulated traditions.

In the Calle Chacón, the lights seemed more numerous and more magical than anywhere, and looking up he saw that Leonarda's windows were unshuttered. Even from the street he could make out the pinpricks of coloured lights in the room behind them.

When Rosa opened the door of the apartment to him, he found empty packing cases assembled in the narrow hallway. But when he was shown into Leonarda's living room, nothing had changed. All the drapes were still in place, the velvet hangings, the dark-patterned rugs. The only difference was the lights. Instead of lamps, the room had been scattered with dozens of tiny glass lanterns, each one a different colour, each with a tiny candle burning within. Leonarda stood by the window, her back to the room, a perfect silhouette against the not quite dark sky.

She turned when he entered and smiled as though she were expecting him.

'My favourite Havana festival,' she said.

'Remarkable,' he acknowledged, and then, as though he'd heard the formality in his own voice, added hastily: 'Amazing. Astonishing. Like a picture in a book from my childhood. I don't even remember the story, only the picture. And how it made me feel.'

'Happy?' she asked.

'Transported.' And it was true. How had that little boy so full of wonder become a Foreign Office copyist, someone with no aspiration greater than to win the favour of men like Addington and Staveley?

'I used to think,' she told him, 'that somewhere there must be a place where every night was like this. I used to promise myself that some day I'd find it.'

'And is that what you intend? I passed this way yesterday and saw Rosa outside with the packing cases. Are you decided then? Are you really leaving Havana?'

She turned her back on the night and looked at him. The coloured lights shone in her eyes.

'Yes. I'm leaving Havana. It's time to start afresh.'

'But why? I thought . . . You *have* heard of the murder charges against O'Driscoll?'

Leonarda nodded. 'Yes. The truth has come out. But not through my efforts. Not because right has prevailed. Only because someone has decided that finally the truth suits them. That is the Havana way.'

'So you are leaving?'

He was still standing by the door. The whole room was between them.

'Not only because of that. Because of this.'

She moved into the darkness at the corner of the room and held up something. He could make out only that it was a book.

'The gift Hector gave me.'

He didn't understand so said nothing and waited while she returned to the window. When she spoke again she was turned away from him, looking out over the city.

'When the man I married died, I inherited his money. His estate. There's a steward there running it. A good man, I believe. And there is a school. A very small one, teaching children to read. I thought I could live comfortably here in Havana while he did good on my behalf. I suppose I imagined myself living the life of a lady, taking coffee in the new boulevards, going to the opera, enjoying all the things I've seen other people enjoy.'

The book was still in her hand and now she raised it to her chest.

'But there is nothing for me here. I know that now. Hector is gone, and I find I cannot after all spend the rest of my life living on a dead man's money.'

She laughed and turned to him again.

'The truth is, I don't know. I don't know what I'll do, or even where I'll go. Everything is confused. But Hector wouldn't want me living here, in the Calle Chacón, hoarding his books for my own pleasure. The wealth the Englishman intended for me is not a gift, I see that now. Only a burden. I have no true claim to it, and without it . . . Well, without it I will have to find my own way, as Hector always knew I would. In Jamaica there is a school. If the estate did not have to support me, there could be another.'

Her eyes wandered back to the window.

'So, yes, it is time for me to leave Havana. No matter how dearly I love the festival of candles.'

There was such sadness in her voice that he stepped forward into the centre of the room.

'So, that book . . . It is the one you spoke of, the one you were looking for?'

She nodded, the faintest movement of her head against the night sky.

'It was found at the gangmaster's house, along with Señor Crawford's watch. It was one of the things taken that night Hector was murdered. I was lucky. Someone found it for me. Otherwise it would have gone back to Crawford along with his horrible, tawdry watch.'

He couldn't make out her expression, but her voice was suddenly full of contempt.

'That man . . . The watch was a present from his wife, one of those with a special compartment. You're meant to put a picture of a loved one there, or perhaps a lock of her hair. But the hair Crawford kept there wasn't his wife's. It was his mistress's hair. Black hair. And not hair from the head, either. What kind of man enjoys that sort of joke? I hate to think that Hector died in the service of such a man.'

At a loss for words, Backhouse approached the window and placed his hand upon her shoulder.

'I'm sorry,' he said.

The two of them stood like that for a minute or more, looking down on the spectacle of lights below them. He was so close to her he could breathe in the scent of her hair.

'I love this island,' she said at last. 'I love it with every part of me. But I hate its lies and its jealousies and its petty, sordid cheating. Crawford and Lavender and O'Driscoll, and the plantation owners who go to church on a Sunday morning then pick out one of their slaves for an afternoon's pleasure. That's why I'm leaving. It will always be like this here. Always corrupted by the people who want something from it. Never allowed to be happy.'

His hand was still on her shoulder and he tightened his grip very slightly before moving it away.

'Coming from England,' he told her, 'I despised everything I found here. Now I think a part of me could love this city too. But it's too late. That's not the person I'm supposed to be. I should go home.'

'Yes,' she said softly, 'you should go home.'

She turned then, so swiftly that he was taken by surprise, and put her arms around him, her cheek against his chest. For the briefest moment only. Then, before he could speak, before he could respond in any way, she was gone from the window, gone from the room, the door closing softly behind her. He waited a minute or more, gazing stupidly into the night. Then he followed her into the hallway. But there was no sign of her there, only Rosa waiting with his cane.

He didn't want to leave. He wanted to wait till she reappeared, wanted to speak to her again. But in the end he took the cane and said nothing, only a polite goodnight, then stepped out on to the dark staircase, and from there descended into the flickering wonderland of Havana by candlelight.

LXII

Thomas Staveley met John Jerusalems once more in the months immediately following the sinking of the *Albany*. He had been out of London for more than a week, paying certain visits both social and professional in the north of England, and the final leg of his journey had taken him to Liverpool. There, his business complete, he had booked into the Adelphi Hotel for a night, with the intention of catching an early train the following morning.

Liverpool was not a city where he had many acquaintances, and tired by his days of travelling he had been looking forward to a quiet dinner and an early night. It was over a cigar in the smoking room that he recognised the voice of his friend from Lowther Street, animated and full of humour, apparently trying to explain to a waiter that it was not an apple brandy he had ordered but a simple apple: a request that was clearly not a common one in the smoking room of the Adelphi.

It crossed Staveley's mind to ignore the coincidence, to trust to the high sides of his armchair to hide him. But evasion is rarely a sound policy in social situations, and although he rather resented the upheaval, he put down his newspaper and hoisted himself to his feet.

Jerusalems seemed delighted to see him. If there had been any sourness between them at their last meeting, the little man appeared to have forgotten it. He insisted on Staveley joining him by the fire, for it was a chilly spring evening, then interrogated him about his tour of the north with real interest and enthusiasm.

'And what about you, John?' Staveley asked at last. 'What brings you here?'

'Oh, meeting a boat.' Jerusalems waved the question away as though it could not possibly be of interest. 'Or arranging for a boat to be met, which is the same thing. It's a long time since I was up here, so I thought I'd come and have a little look for myself. Have you been down to the docks?'

Staveley hadn't. His visit had been a brief one.

'Perhaps you are wise. I'm told they can be a dangerous place. A lawless place at certain hours. A man who did not know the city, who blundered into the wrong area in his ignorance, could find himself beaten and robbed within minutes of disembarking.'

'Which presumably is why you feel the need to meet that boat. Who is your visitor? Anyone significant?'

'Potentially.' The little man nodded. 'One who could cause difficulties were he not given the right sort of welcome.' Jerusalems rose from his chair and began to pace the hearthrug. 'Now what about you, Thomas? Are you still angry?'

'Angry?' Staveley knew what Jerusalems was referring to but pretended that he did not.

'About my plans for Cuba. You cannot deny that my little bit of policy-making there shocked you. But if you are honest, you will also agree that the current situation is too volatile to be healthy. My scheme would have given us peace for a hundred years.'

'I suppose,' Staveley confessed, 'I was hurt you'd not confided in me. You were telling me many things that were true, but you never told me the truth.'

Jerusalems looked at him curiously.

'And would you have wanted to know, Thomas? The sinking of a battleship. Would you really want that on your conscience?'

'No,' Staveley agreed. 'I suppose not.'

Jerusalems returned to his seat and stretched out his legs.

'Which, of course, is why our betters encourage me in my activities. If no one knows, no one is responsible. Everything can be denied. It is a convenient arrangement.'

'And what about *your* conscience, John?'

Jerusalems smiled.

'I do not deny a sleepless night from time to time. But not so very many.'

After Jerusalems' reversals in Havana, Staveley had expected to find the man rather less buoyant, and he said as much.

In reply, his companion raised his teacup by way of a toast.

'Reversals? Yes, I cannot deny them. But not all was lost in Havana, you know. Not by any means. The storm passed but the tree did not fall. I'm happy with the situation there. People say it is a city of secrets, but I'm confident we shall continue to know more of those secrets than anyone else.'

Staveley wasn't so sure. It seemed to him quite possible that Jerusalems was allowing his optimism to vanquish reality. Lavender's demise must have been a heavy blow.

'And of course,' Jerusalems continued, 'we are always going to need someone solid in Cuba. Things are constantly stirring around the edges of the Caribbean. The Americans will not go away. Someone needs to be looking after our interests.'

As Jerusalems sat and talked, and toasted his feet by the fire, Staveley allowed himself to be drawn away to worlds he could barely imagine, where everything was lush and exotic and dangerous. It was all a very long way from Liverpool and a cold spring evening, and the grey fog descending on the Mersey.

LXIII

The truth did not come to Backhouse in one blinding flash. It crept up on him over days, persisting stubbornly even as he tried to push it away.

Night was the worst time, sleeping alone in the empty villa in El Cerro. Try as he might, he could not prevent his mind from turning it over, recalling past conversations, chance remarks, digging up scraps of information he had previously discarded without a thought.

It had begun while the candles were still burning on the night of the festival, still touching the city with their magic. Rattling homewards that night, Backhouse's thoughts had all been with Leonarda: that darkened room, the tiny lights, her sadness; that hurried, unlikely embrace. It was as if her life in Havana had drawn to a natural close. She had her book and her memories, and now her life was to begin again, even if she had no idea where. But he did not worry for her. She would find her way. Strength and confidence came from her like a slow, comforting heat. When he compared her strength with his own, he felt ashamed.

Yet that night, even before he'd reached El Cerro, the thought had already occurred to him. However hard he tried to dismiss it, it remained. In the days that followed, it grew awkwardly and uncomfortably into a conviction. Despite himself, he began to ask questions: about a ship called the *Albany*, about the staff and the geography of Colonel Aguero's offices, about the early careers of Havana's richest merchants. There were things Jepson had told him, that O'Driscoll had told him, even things Leonarda had told him herself . . .

Once he would have dismissed his own theories as nonsense. And even now he could turn his back upon them if he wished, could pretend ignorance even to himself. It would be simple to follow Jepson's advice to avoid everything that was not ordinary and unthinking and mundane.

But he found he could not. To ignore was to condone. It would be to slip back into the murky waters from which he'd dragged himself.

One evening, he passed Francisco Marty in the street. The Cuban merchant touched his hat and moved on, but there had been something in his bearing – a confidence, a contentment, a serenity almost – that Backhouse could not stomach. A week later, towards the end of the day, he presented himself at Marty's apartments above the fish market and demanded an audience.

He was rebuffed, of course. The manservant at the door informed him firmly but politely that Señor Marty was not receiving visitors. So Backhouse scribbled a note on to the back of an old receipt he found in his pocket. It was only a few words.

'I'll wait,' he said.

Nothing happened for a full five minutes. When the servant returned, he seemed surprised to be ushering Backhouse up a flight of stairs and directly into Marty's study.

It was an enormous room, light and airy, and cooler by some degrees than the staircase that led to it. The furnishings added to the sense of space: light floorboards, pale furniture and plenty of space between the framed maps on the walls. A large globe stood on a pedestal in the centre of the room, and when Backhouse was shown in, Marty was standing next to it, spinning it idly.

'Señor Backhouse? Please, will you sit?' Marty's English was as good as Backhouse remembered. 'Are you quite well, sir,' he continued when Backhouse remained standing, 'or can I ring for something? Your note is . . . extraordinary. I don't know quite what to make of it.'

'On the contrary, señor . . .' Backhouse had never felt so confident, so sure of himself. 'You know exactly what to make of it. We are not children. We do not need to play games. And it would seem that, in a manner of speaking, we are on the same side. As my note pointed out, you are a spy for the British. More specifically, you are a spy for a man named John Jerusalems.'

Marty laughed out loud, but Backhouse continued regardless.

'By my estimate, you have been working for him for more than twenty years. All that unexplained capital when you first started out in Havana ... Jerusalems evidently made a very shrewd investment.'

Marty laughed again, and brought the spinning globe to an abrupt halt.

'Do you know what, Mr Backhouse? When you were first appointed to your post here, they told me they were sending someone who would cause no trouble. Someone very straightforward who liked to do things by the book. It was an underestimation. May I ask what in particular led you here today?'

'The consul's watch.'

Backhouse decided to take a seat after all. If Marty was willing to talk, he might as well make himself comfortable. Without waiting to be asked a second time, he selected an armchair near the window. Meanwhile Marty was looking a little mystified, so Backhouse explained.

'When we first met, you said something rather sneering about Crawford. I didn't think much about it at the time. If anything, I agreed with you. You said he was the sort of person who keeps his mistress's hair in a watch given to him by his wife.'

Marty nodded slowly, as though enlightenment were dawning.

'And of course that is exactly what he *did* do,' Backhouse continued. 'But how could you possibly have known? It was too precise an observation to be a guess, and Crawford certainly hadn't shared his sordid little joke with you.'

From his armchair, he could see Marty was nodding. Not a confession, he knew, merely an acceptance of Backhouse's logic.

'That watch was stolen from Crawford four years ago by a man called O'Driscoll, who passed it directly to Lavender. I have all that from O'Driscoll himself. When O'Driscoll found the same watch planted in his rooms, he assumed Lavender had retained it for precisely that purpose – to use against him when required. But Lavender took orders from London. I don't think he did keep that watch. I think he was told to pass it on with the other items, to someone here in Havana. Someone else who liked to have that sort of power. Lavender would never even have known who.'

Backhouse paused. He didn't feel elated or triumphant, he felt *clean*, as though finally able to scrape away the last vestiges of Havana dirt still clinging to him.

'And that's how you knew about the consul's watch, señor. Because Lavender passed it to you. For years it has been in your possession. You understood its value as evidence, which is why you wanted it. And you used it against O'Driscoll when you wanted him out of the way. He'd been talking to Jepson. It was safer to get rid of him.'

Marty smiled and gave the globe another spin.

'And that's it, Mr Backhouse? A frivolous remark over a glass of champagne, and you decide I'm a traitor to my country?'

Backhouse met his eye and didn't look away.

'What's really clever, señor, is the way Jerusalems paid for it all. Jepson once told me he couldn't understand where your money was coming from. Jepson's good at following money, or at least that's what he claims. He reasoned that if the British were paying huge sums to fund someone's activities over here, he should be able to find some trace of the money. But there were no big payments from London, were there? That's what was so cunning – it was all self-financing. Jerusalems arranged for Lavender to get hold of the Royal Navy's sailing plans in Jamaica, and you made a fortune selling them to the slave traders. Lavender never knew who he was passing them to, and Jerusalems didn't mind that the navy never caught anyone because he knew the Mixed Commission never convicted anyone anyway.'

Marty finally turned away from the globe and moved closer to where Backhouse was sitting, nodding as he did so.

'There's something in what you say, señor. My friend John Jerusalems is a genius in that way. Come, let us have a drink together. As you say, we are adults. Whisky? Rum?'

Backhouse accepted a small whisky. Marty's attitude was suddenly different, almost companionable, as though the sharing of his secret created a bond between them.

'I met John Jerusalems in Jamaica many, many years ago,' he explained. 'I liked him from the first. We were both young then, and very similar in many ways. Both of us were daring, both adventurers of sorts. The main difference between us at the time was that I was about to be hanged for piracy. Jerusalems arranged for all the charges to be dropped. Then we sat down and talked. I told him what I needed to build an empire of my own. He found money for me. That's how it started.'

'A happy ending. We should both raise a glass.' But there was no humour in Backhouse's voice. 'Not so happy, however, if you happen to be Lavender. Or Jepson's friend Alvarez. Or a sailor on the *Albany*. Or any of the people Lavender and O'Driscoll murdered in order to keep your secrets.'

'To keep *their* secrets,' Marty replied sharply. 'They were very diligent in saving their own skins.' He chose a seat near Backhouse, but instead of sitting on it he perched lightly on its arm.

'And were you any less diligent, Marty?' Backhouse asked. 'When Señora Leigh tracked down one of the men accused of the murder at the British consulate, she told you all about it. She travelled there in your carriage, so you knew the precise location. And a few weeks later he was ambushed there.'

Marty looked utterly unconcerned.

'I passed word on to Lavender, it's true. Anonymously, of course. It was up to him and O'Driscoll to decide what they wanted to do about it.'

'Anonymously.' Backhouse nodded. 'That was the other clever thing, wasn't it? *You* knew all about Lavender, but Lavender knew nothing about you. Jerusalems managed to convince him he was the most important spy on the island. He thought he was receiving information from dozens of anonymous informers. But I'm guessing all that information was really from you, wasn't it? You and Jerusalems controlled Lavender between you. And by then he was in so deep, he was prepared to do anything to protect himself.'

His host sighed theatrically, as if greatly pained.

'You make it all sound so *complicated*, my friend.' Marty drained his glass and rose to refill it. 'In truth, these things happened almost without planning. If Lavender had been slightly less keen to play the master spy, very few of these things would have happened.'

It was the mildest of defences, and Backhouse ignored it.

'The thing that puzzled me at first,' he said, 'was those papers you sent me. Lavender's letters to Colonel Aguero. I assume you bribed someone in Aguero's office to give you the originals?'

'Of course.' Marty held up the decanter. 'More whisky? No? Talking so much must be thirsty work.'

Backhouse ignored that too.

'It took me a while to realise that you and Jerusalems needed someone honest here in Havana who could stumble across the truth about Lavender. That's why those papers came to me. Jerusalems had designed them to be so incendiary that they would probably start a war all by themselves. And poor old Lavender never realised they could be used to destroy him too.'

Marty sighed again. 'Lavender was quite happy to get his hands dirty. But he was at heart a trusting soul.'

'I was supposed to send the originals to London by the first post, wasn't I? And then to make so much noise about them in my official correspondence that the truth would have to come out.' Backhouse shook his head. 'But I didn't make a noise. I went to Jepson instead and averted a war. And I didn't send the originals to Jerusalems either, which was something he'd relied upon. That's why you had my offices searched. But you were too late. I'd already destroyed them.'

The Cuban raised an eyebrow at that.

'You had? My word, that was very bold of you. Those letters were evidence of actual crimes. They were documents of international significance. And you have taken it upon yourself to suppress them altogether? Frankly, Mr Backhouse, you're not the man we thought you.'

Marty strolled across to the window and peered out.

'It should have all worked so well. Lavender was becoming unreliable and the Spanish were on to him. He needed to be prodded into retirement. But before he went, we got him to write those letters, which implicated Aguero and the Spanish government in genuine attacks on America. All you had to do to make war inevitable was to send them on through the conventional channels.'

He took another sip of whisky.

'It never occurred to us that you would start thinking for yourself. And apart from you, our plan was perfect. That American friend of yours, Jepson, had come over here to cause trouble for me. People like Jepson are difficult. They don't just go away. But with Lavender on his way out anyway, we had the chance to tie up everything together. It was Jerusalems' idea to let Jepson have our Kansas contacts, the whole book of them, to convince him that he'd flushed out his spy. And it worked, Mr Backhouse. Jepson's gone. I'm still here.'

Backhouse could detect no discomfort in Marty's voice, not a trace of regret. The neatness of the plan was its own justification.

'And all along,' Backhouse pointed out, 'you and Jerusalems were planning to attack the *Albany*. By then Lavender had probably convinced himself that a battleship was a fair target. And that bit about the *Pilgrim* in his letters was deliberately intended to throw Jepson off the scent, wasn't it?'

'Of course.' Marty chuckled. 'And it worked.'

'But you can't possibly have known I was going to show Jepson those papers.'

'Certainly not. It never occurred to me. But once something like that is out there, it has a life of its own. I'd have made sure Jepson got hold of the information in time to find his way to the *John Bunyan*. You must admit, it was an elegant feint. I'm extremely proud of it.'

Again, not an iota of remorse. Backhouse rose and faced his host across the room.

'But *why*, Marty? Why would you want to start a war? Why would you want to help the British in the first place?'

'Ah, my friend . . .' Marty smiled sadly. 'You don't understand, do you? I'm not helping the British. I don't particularly like the British. On the whole I find you a joyless race. No, I'm helping John Jerusalems. We have a bond, he and I. We both love the game, you see. All the trickery and the bluffs and the subterfuge. The landowners here despise me, and the idiots in Spain, well, frankly they don't deserve this island. It gives me infinite pleasure to lead them this way and that. I love the battle of wits, and I love the fact that I always win. And besides . . .'

His tone grew more serious.

'Besides, I am a businessman, and a businessman likes certainty. And there's no certainty here. Spanish rule is over. You know that as well as I do. We are simply watching the twitching of its corpse. And when the last rites have been performed, who runs Cuba then? The Americans, with their law and order and their tedious self-righteousness? Or a so-called republic in which the big families run the island for themselves? Neither option suits me. But a war! Ah, yes! A messy, brutal war . . .'

He raised his glass but did not drink.

'With your devious countrymen pitching in, sinking American merchant ships, freeing slaves, preaching abolition . . . Well, that *would* be a revolution, Mr Backhouse! A real change to everything. And quite apart from the pleasure I'd get from seeing the plantation houses burn, wars bring opportunities. Guns, slaves, there'll always be something. And afterwards, imagine Cuba not as an American state, nor as the plaything of a rancid aristocracy, but a chaos of freed slaves and mulattos, desperate for the merchant and the man with capital to bring some order. Who would rise to the top then, Mr Backhouse? Who would own the island then?'

He laughed.

'And anyway, what have I to lose? Whatever the outcome, people will still want fish, and opera. Now tell me, Mr Backhouse . . .' He returned to the globe and appeared to study it. 'What do you propose to do with all the information you have? I can hardly see you taking it to the Spanish authorities. As you say, we are nominally on the same side.'

Backhouse was aware again of that unfamiliar surge of confidence.

'Well, señor, it seems to me I have two options. I could content myself with the knowledge that your plan to start a war has failed, and could wash my hands of the rest. Or in three months' time, I could return to London on leave. When there I could insist on a personal audience with Lord Clarendon himself. I think he would see me because if not I should send an open letter to every peer in the House informing Clarendon of what is happening here under the pretence of British interests. Oh, I know that would ruin me. I've almost no proof. But I would have told the truth. So tell me, señor, which option do you think I will choose?'

Marty turned and studied him closely.

'A wise man would choose the former.'

'No doubt.' Backhouse rose. 'Of course, were you to leave Havana, were you to pack up your goods and disappear to Mexico, then I should have no decision to make.'

Marty looked at him with astonishment. 'You come in here, you lay all this before me, and now you expect me simply to walk away? To give up a lifetime's work? Come, Mr Backhouse, you are being fanciful.'

'In that case you will not discover which option I have chosen until I arrive in London.' He indicated the door. 'Shall I find my own way?'

But Marty didn't move.

'And that's all, Mr Backhouse? No negotiations? No favours to ask? No attempt to turn all this knowledge to your advantage?'

'No. None of that.' Again, a sense of cleanliness.

'What if I reminded you that there's still work to do here in Havana, Mr Backhouse? Work you could be proud of. Jerusalems wants to stop America's power growing any further. He talks about ways of turning the different states against one another. And he thinks the way to achieve that is an all-out assault on slavery. You and I could work together for that.'

'Not me.' Backhouse placed his hand on the door handle. 'But no doubt there will be someone else. Assuming there's no scandal, of course. Assuming the Spanish authorities don't get wind of any rumours coming out of London. If they did, I imagine things might be rather difficult for you here. Much more pleasant in Mexico, don't you think?'

'I dislike Mexico.' Marty joined him by the door. 'The climate doesn't suit me. I shall await your decision with interest, Mr Backhouse.'

'And I yours, señor.'

'You know, my friend . . .' Marty paused on the threshold. 'I've always said Havana is the wrong place for honest men. I hope you find your way home soon.'

Marty accompanied Backhouse down the stairs in silence, but as they stepped out into the sunlight, he turned back to him.

'Come and see me again, Mr Backhouse,' he urged. 'Come and see me whatever you decide.'

Backhouse smiled, pleased to have avoided a handshake. Then he turned his back on the fish market feeling lighter and happier than ever before in Havana. The city had taught him something, and for that he was grateful. Meanwhile, his path was clear. His plans were made. He would be gone from Havana far sooner than he'd led Marty to believe.

Backhouse was engaged to dine that night with Callaghan, the Irishman, a pleasant enough fellow, affable company and a good storyteller. But now Backhouse rather regretted his invitation. Since Grace had left, he had grown accustomed to his own company, and that night in particular he would have liked to be alone, to reflect on his interview with Marty and to ponder the world as he now knew it. Most of all, he wanted to write to Grace.

But the invitation had been extended, and to cancel at such short notice would be poor form. Besides, Callaghan would not stay long. There would surely be time at the end of the evening for his letter.

Backhouse was still dressing when a note arrived for him, brought not by the usual scruffy messenger boy but by a young uniformed police officer. A note, he saw with surprise, from the chief of police in person, and written in the florid style to which he was now accustomed. But for all its embellishments, the information it contained was clear.

His Excellency apologised for troubling Señor Backhouse, but recognising Señor Backhouse's great valour in personally apprehending such a dangerous criminal, His Excellency wished to communicate to Señor Backhouse directly news of an unfortunate incident. That very morning, as a result of negligence that would be severely punished, the criminal O'Driscoll had again escaped from custody. Searches were being undertaken across the city but it was believed the felon might already have taken ship for England. He was known to be carrying the papers of an American called Smith, and British officials had duly been notified. His prompt rearrest, whether in Havana or in Great Britain, was therefore in little doubt. His Excellency could only apologise to Señor Backhouse, and assure him that the profuse regrets of the Spanish government were exceeded only by the esteem in which Señor Backhouse was held . . .

It was a letter that left Backhouse feeling slightly uncomfortable. O'Driscoll was no longer his concern, but it had been satisfying to think of him held safely in the Tacón gaol. The man's persistent refusal to accept his fate was unsettling. Yet the news should surely not prevent Backhouse from enjoying a good dinner.

And it *was* a good dinner. With perversity typical of life in Havana, the performance of Backhouse's cook appeared to have improved considerably now that there were no longer large parties of his compatriots to impress. His single guest ate with evident enjoyment, and made up for Backhouse's taciturn mood with plenty of conversation of his own.

Dinner had been cleared away and only the brandy remained on the table when the door of the dining room burst open. Backhouse, at the far end of the room, rose at once, and he saw Callaghan rise too, an exclamation of surprise dying upon his lips.

The intruders were large men, roughly dressed, only their eyes visible above kerchiefs that had been tied to hide their faces. Both carried knives.

For a fraction of a moment all four men stood still. Then Callaghan began to lift his open palms. His voice when he spoke was urgent.

'Robbery, Backhouse. For God's sake, raise your hands.'

And instinctively Backhouse started to comply. But even as he moved his arms, the taller of the two men stepped towards him and Backhouse understood. The length of the room lay between them but there was no chance of escape. Backhouse found he barely cared. He would not run. He would not even back away. Never again, not another step. An image of Grace rose before him, of Grace on the British ship with Alice by her side, fair and smiling; then an image of his son by moonlight, thin and helpless in his arms; but both were gone in an instant, leaving in him only a sense of unbearable sadness.

Then the intruder took another step closer and Backhouse stepped forward to meet him.

Rosa brings me the news. She has heard it by chance, from a cousin working in El Cerro. She is flustered, upset, as though such things are new to her.

I do not go at once. I pause and ponder your wishes. It is already very late. The streets are growing quiet. You are alone.

A junior policeman lets me into the room where you lie. He pulls back the sheet, exposing not just your face but your chest as well. I remember how once, when you were barely conscious, I felt your heart beating beneath my palm.

Your face is pale, but not yet with that waxy whiteness of those confirmed in death. You are sleeping death's first, soft release. I am struck by the neat handsomeness of your features. All the awkwardness is gone from them. You look, not peaceful, although there is peace in your face, but strong. Calm and certain and serene.

The policeman says it was a simple burglary, but I see how your hands and arms were slashed in the struggle. How you must have fought! He tells me your companion was bound, but nothing was stolen. After you fell, both assassins fled.

They arrested a man nearby, of course. A well-known rogue, a mulatto, his guilt self-evident. It is always the way. There are many such robberies in Havana. Many rogues with knives. In the weeks to come, rich habaneros *will visit the place where you fell and will shake their heads and fan themselves against the heat.*

You died yearning for home. The last time we spoke I could feel the yearning so strong inside you that part of me feared for you. Because Havana is not an easy place to leave. It touches you without you knowing and leaves a mark that never quite fades. Some say it creeps into your blood. I worried that your safe, smiling country with its meadows and its churches might no longer hold you so comfortably as before. It is hard to forget the way the drums at night in the Plaza de Armas beat deeper than your own heart.

I kiss you before I leave. Chastely, on the cheek, because someone should. I wish you had not come.

They will try the mulatto. They may even find the evidence they need. But I will be gone before his trial. I will not ask questions about your last moments, about how the villains entered, or what they wanted, or why they stole nothing. I will not gnaw and worry at the truth, unsure why I want it, or what to do with it when I find it. I will try to find a better way to remember you.

A second kiss. Then I replace the sheet and step outside into the darkness. As I drive back with Rosa towards the old town, I am struck by the city's rare silence. It is a few minutes after four o'clock. Havana is sleeping.

NOTES AND ACKNOWLEDGEMENTS

In compiling these notes, and in so many other aspects of writing this novel, I am greatly indebted to Professor Luis Martínez-Fernández, whose marvellous book *Fighting Slavery in the Caribbean* (ME Sharpe, 1998) first introduced me to George Backhouse and his story. For a factual account of Backhouse's years in Cuba and for an introduction to the wider context of his time there, I cannot recommend it too highly.

George Backhouse

In December 1852, in the very last hours of Lord Derby's minority government, the Secretary of State for Foreign Affairs authorised the appointment of George Backhouse, a minor Foreign Office clerk, to the post of Judge in the Havana Mixed Commission for the Suppression of the Slave Trade.

Backhouse was thirty-four at the time, the son of a more successful father. His Foreign Office career was far from stellar, and all his applications for consular posts abroad had been unsuccessful. His wife, Grace, was twenty-nine, and their daughter Alice was only six months old. The unexpected appointment promised a salary far higher than his existing post, along with a tempting pension and expenses allowances that appeared extremely generous. The post was offered to him by Henry Addington, the Permanent Under-Secretary at the Foreign Office, in the presence of Backhouse's superior, Thomas Staveley. After consulting Grace, George accepted the very same day.

The Backhouses arrived in Havana in March 1853. The theft of jewellery from the offices of the British consul – and the murder of the watchman – had taken place before their arrival, and the second theft described in these pages, for which Backhouse's assistant James Dalrymple was arrested but not charged, took place only a couple of months after Backhouse had taken up his post. No one was ever convicted of either crime.

Neither Grace nor George found life in Cuba easy: Havana was expensive, and integrating into the small British community was not straightforward. There were mosquitoes and fevers, and John, their new-born son, very nearly died.

In April 1855, in response to their severe financial difficulties, Grace returned to London with Alice and John. In August the same year George was dining with the Irishman, Callaghan, when their evening was interrupted by intruders. Callaghan was bound; George fought. Nothing was stolen and again no one was ever convicted of his murder.

The Mixed Commission and the Slave Trade

Great Britain had pressured Spain into abolition of the slave trade in 1817, and abolished all slavery in its own West Indian territories in 1834. But long after that slavery remained crucial to the economy of Cuba, as well as to many parts of the United States, and the transatlantic slave trade continued to flourish despite British efforts.

On an island where the most influential individuals had a financial interest in the trade continuing, the Havana Mixed Commission proved a totally ineffective tool against the slave traders.

Diplomatic Tensions

When the Backhouse family arrived in Havana in 1853, a large private army was gathering in the United States with the aim of invading Cuba. Such 'filibustering' raids were nothing new: there had been privately led invasions of Cuba in both 1850 and 1851. To pro-slavery interests in the United States, the annexation of Cuba, with its powerful slaving interests, appealed as a possible way of strengthening their political position at home.

The invasions of 1850 and, particularly, 1851, were disastrous failures, and it is very hard not to be reminded of the Bay of Pigs invasion over a hundred years later. In addition, they heightened diplomatic tensions. Britain and France responded by increasing their naval presence in the region. There was a danger that a Spanish–American war over Cuba in the 1850s might have escalated into a much broader and bloodier conflict.

Despite all the various machinations against it, Spain retained its hold on the island until 1898, when war with America finally came. In February of that year, the American battleship *Maine* was destroyed by an explosion while anchored in Havana Bay. The cause of the explosion was unclear: the Americans blamed the Spanish, the Spanish blamed the ship's design. War between Spain and America followed in March.

The USS *Albany*
The USS *Albany* left the port then known to Americans as Aspinwall on the Panama isthmus in late 1854 bound for New York. The ship was never seen again and her disappearance was never properly explained. The vessel is simply recorded as lost at sea with all hands.

The US Mails
The tendency of the Spanish administration to read the US diplomatic mail during this period was a symptom of the diplomatic tensions between the two countries. The letter of complaint quoted in this novel is part of a real letter to the Captain-General of Cuba from the US consul of the time.

Havana Society in the 1850s
Cuban society in the 1850s was dominated by white men. Nearly 50 per cent of the population of the island was white, around 41 per cent was black. Of the black population, over 80 per cent were

slaves. In Havana itself, the proportion of white and mixed race people was greater than elsewhere on the island, and there were proportionally fewer slaves. Ninety per cent of Cubans of mixed race were free.

Men greatly outnumbered women: around three men for every two women in Havana. Among the population of European descent, the disparity was even greater, with a ratio of around 1.8. Perhaps as a result of this imbalance, white women in Havana were so jealously guarded as to be almost invisible. For instance, it was considered improper for them to walk in the streets at any time, even if accompanied. By contrast, free black and mixed race women in Havana enjoyed much greater freedom of movement.

Joseph Crawford

When the Backhouses arrived in Havana, Crawford had been the British consul there for more than ten years. Backhouse found him a difficult character and the pair clashed unpleasantly, although I should note that Crawford's involvement in the thefts from the consular offices is entirely speculation on the part of the author.

After Backhouse's death, Crawford succeeded in obtaining the vacant post on the Mixed Commission for himself. And when Dalrymple left Havana, Crawford secured the post of clerk to the Mixed Commission for his own son.

James Dalrymple

Dalrymple is one of those real-life characters a novelist would delight in making up. Disreputable, scheming, whining, perennially short of money, he undoubtedly caused George Backhouse all sorts of problems. On one occasion, for instance, he is reported to have lured an English governess to Havana to fill a post that did not exist – for motives that can only be guessed at.

Dalrymple left Havana – and Maria Guadalupe – after Backhouse's death. He never returned to Cuba.

Francisco Marty y Torrens

Marty is another historical figure who, from a fiction-writer's point of view, is almost too good to be true. Stories of his rise from obscure origins to tremendous wealth in Cuba suggest he had very few scruples. In his 1855 memoir *Crotchets and Quavers* the opera manager Max Maretzek gives a good flavour of Marty's influence in Cuba and beyond:

> *The Captain-general Concha had at one time determined upon depriving Marty of the privilege of exclusively dealing in fish. He had therefore obtained the revocation of the grant from the Spanish Ministry. The worthy Senor Francisco had, however, been informed of the proceedings with this view, by his agents, and had acted in accordance with the intelligence.*
>
> *When summoned by General Concha to the palace, and notified by him that his privilege had ceased, by command of the Queen, he very coolly asked the Captain-general the date of this order. The document was handed to him. Marty looked at it and drew another from his pocket, which was dated exactly one day later. It revoked the former one and reinstated Don Francisco Marty y Torrens in all his former rights and privileges.*
>
> *The General was for the moment thunderstruck, as Marty said to him 'Your Excellency not appearing to have received the communication, believe me, I shall feel most happy in providing you with this copy of it.'*

The Death of Daniel O'Driscoll

Not all freed slaves in Cuba were really free. Many were forced to work out long contracts for little or no reward, and exploitation of these *emancipados* was systematic and profitable. Men such as the gangmaster O'Driscoll could make good money from their misery. O'Driscoll himself is my own creation, but something of his character – and of his flight from Havana – was suggested to me by an entry in the notebooks of the author Nathaniel Hawthorne, then the US consul in Liverpool, who recorded a visit by a badly injured man claiming to be an American farmer called Daniel Smith. Smith said he had been press-ganged on to a US ship and then, being no sailor, had been beaten mercilessly for his incompetence, before being abandoned on the docks in Liverpool. Hawthorne next heard of Smith when he was summoned to his death bed. The man was unconscious and died shortly after, but not before Hawthorne had noted the nautical tattoos on his arms; tatoos which, according to other inmates of the hospital, showed beyond doubt that hc was 'a seaman of some years' service'.

Fanny Runge

Fanny Runge is not named in *Havana Sleeping*, and is referred to only as an acquaintance of Mrs Crawford. I mention her here because her simple but remarkable act of kindness deserves mention. The generosity and impulsiveness of the note that she sent to Grace Backhouse at the crisis of her little son's illness remains touching more than 150 years after it was written. It saved a life and rescued a family from despair.